BLACK SKY BURNING

Rob Birks

PRAISE FOR
THE VANISHING GIRL

"More cosmic than *The Hunger Games*, but more relatable than *Dune*, this novel is bursting with space pirates, plasma rifles and robotic aliens, but still manages to keep one foot on planet Earth. Exciting and fun."

"I can't remember the last time I read a novel with such a fast-paced, wide-ranging, action-packed storyline!"

"I was immediately engaged with both the storyline and the characters and couldn't put it down."

"There's a message of hope in the story which is often missing from contemporary sci-fi. If you want to read something fresh and exciting, give it a go!"

"The action was fast paced from the start and I was hooked by the evolution of the main protagonist."

5 STAR READER REVIEWS

BY ROB BIRKS

THE PARADISE MOON DUOLOGY

BOOK 1: THE VANISHING GIRL
BOOK 2: BLACK SKY BURNING

For Becca.

Stars will always be above us.

CHAPTER ONE

For now, Isabella's private beach was perfect. No—better than perfect. Isabella didn't have to touch any of it. She could enjoy her sun-soaked slice of Barbados just fine from her hammock, just fine behind designer shades. Lazy waves lapped at the gazebo's stilts. Thatching shielded her from the scorching sun. As long as her postcard of tranquillity remained untouched, it was enough to make anyone happy.

For as long as it lasted.

Isabella turned the page of her graphic novel. Sand was coarse, sunstroke stung and the sea was as cold as a mothertrucker, but her favourite graphic novels never failed to disappoint. Neither did her Cuddles on the Beach mocktail. Without her eyes leaving the page, her glowing purple hand lifted an umbrella-crammed coconut until its straw found her lips. Sweet, peachy perfection.

A miserable refrain from the sadder end of the indie rock spectrum blasted out of her phone, indicating a surge in private messages on her socials. Well, that figured. Like a grave knew the cold, Isabella knew happiness never lasted.

Peeling her eyes off a gorgeously inked panel promising more gratuitous violence, Isabella scooped up her phone from the wicker table. Although not bulky, her phone wore stronger armour than most PROXUS Rangers. NASA's frighteningly clever busybodies had designed its protective casing especially for her, which was handy given her lifestyle. She thumbed off the alert with her human hand and checked her messages. Her socials were exploding, which was not unusual, but this time they were exploding with streetside footage of something else that was exploding in a more literal sense.

Flying.

Falling.

Crashing.

Exploding.

Her glowing purple hand fed the straw back into her mouth without her asking.

One more for the road.

Thanks, Isabella replied to the alien inside her. *So much for a holiday.* Ever since Sau Darans had kidnapped her from Earth three years ago, life had been an endless routine of brief happiness interrupted. She gulped down another peachy mouthful while her human thumb worked her phone for more information.

We got a few days away.

Tucking her phone into black linen trousers, she drifted to the polished wooden railing and gazed out over the beach's untouched beauty.

Feels like we only just arrived.

Then stay.

Yeah, right.

Anyone could have too much of a good time—unless they were Isabella. Instead, too much of a bad time felt normal, so she had learned to love that instead.

We're heroes. That means hero shit, baby!

Isabella pushed her sunglasses tighter up the bridge of her nose, took a final sip of her mocktail and disappeared from the gazebo in a swirl of purple smoke.

She reappeared on the pavement where London's Parliament Square met Bridge Street, in the heart of a surging crowd of evening commuters and tourists. Everyone was garbed in thick coats and other winterwear—including the occasional Santa hat. Those who noticed her brandished phones to snap a photo or film, but most eyes remained on the sky. This was only the second London crowd Isabella had met that moved with anything less than an impatient rush. The first had been on Westminster Bridge three years ago, when she had taken down a squadron of PROXUS starfighters intent on reducing London to rubble. Like then, this crowd was spilling all over what should have been busy central London streets. As always, everyone was more interested in gawking than moving out of her way.

A scything winter wind cut through her thin black tee, sending a river of goosebumps up her back. Barbados to London was a shock at this time of year, especially when you travelled as quickly as Isabella. She loved the skull emblazoned on her tee, grinning and top-hatted, but she wished the fabric was ten times thicker and stretched longer down her left arm. Her human arm. Unlike her glowing right arm, her left still felt the cold. Defiantly, Isabella lifted her chin exactly the way her body language coach had taught her and slid through the crowd towards the crash site.

The alien spaceship was easy to spot. That tended to happen when something from another world, probably another galaxy, crashed into Big Ben's clockface. Steadying her mocktail against the crush of strangers, Isabella scrutinised the flaming carnage. All she needed was a glimpse of somewhere on the crashed spaceship stable enough to support her weight, then she could leave the crowd behind.

You know, most people wouldn't see a burning spaceship and immediately think 'oh, I know, let's go up there and see if we die'.

Are you complaining? Isabella asked the alien.

Paradise Moon laughed inside Isabella's head.

Gods no! I want to know who's up there.

Whoever they are, we'll save them.

Yeah, that too. I'm just saying. You know.

What?

We're weird.

Choking coils of black smoke escaped the wreckage, drawing filthy wrinkles on a pale sky laden with the promise of snow. It was hard to make out anything else. Isabella dug a freezing hand into her trousers and pulled out her phone. Shutting out sirens, flashing blue lights and the thunder of a helicopter, she zoomed in on the spaceship with her phone's camera. At least, she was aiming for the spaceship. Her left hand, shaking in the cold, could barely find Big Ben. Her right hand, glowing and purple, steadied the phone and adjusted her aim.

Thanks, she told Paradise Moon.

Don't mind me, arsehat. You look good for the cameras and I'll save the day. As per.

You're insufferable.

I love you too.

Through a pixelated screen of shivering flames and inky smoke, Isabella's phone found a suitable stretch of the spaceship's sleek metal wing to vanish onto.

That looks large enough to stand on.

The wing fell off.

Hurtling down Big Ben, metal struck tarmac with a shuddering, twisting crash that echoed through the crowd. Although the impact was well within the section of Bridge Street cordoned off by police cars, fire engines and long stretches of blue and white tape, the crowd still gasped theatrically and pressed against each other in an ineffective penguin shuffle to get closer to the action. Isabella, who had seen much worse on a slow Sunday of hero shit, didn't flinch.

Erm, we're running out of spaceship to land on.

"Here, hold my drink," said Isabella, thrusting her coconut into the hands of a bemused elderly gentleman huddled under a trench coat and trilby. Without waiting for a response, she left in another swirl of purple smoke.

The same purple smoke kissed Isabella's body as she reappeared on what remained of the last silver wing attached to the spaceship. The purple smoke left her in an instant, bleeding into churning fumes that darkened the clocktower's austere Victorian face. Isabella gagged on heavy mouthfuls of ash. Close enough to feel the aftermath of the explosion warming her cheeks, she crept up the wing. It rocked and groaned beneath the timid tread of her combat boots. Her first impression was of a sleek, angular and very much *on fire* spaceship. She didn't have time for a second impression because the wing was melting her boots.

Purple smoke stole her. She reappeared even higher, crouched on Big Ben's minute arm as it aimed at a quarter to six. Had it been fifteen minutes earlier or later, she would have been hanging from a vertical shaft. For once, time was on her side. The melted sole of one boot dribbled down the clock arm. Flames below ate it with a hiss. Okay, time was partly on her side.

I've never been so glad you don't wear flipflops.

What's good with fire? Water, right? We put out that house fire by taking the house to the middle of the ocean.

That house sank.

Okay, space then. It's a spaceship. The vacuum will—

Kill whoever's inside. There are more holes in that spaceship than in any of our plans.

Sand then. We take it to the desert.

Have you ever been to the Sahara?

Not yet, Isabella admitted. As powerful as the alien inside her was, she couldn't vanish anywhere. Only to somewhere, something or someone she'd visited before—or that she could see close enough to count as visited. *Fine. Sand and water. We've got this.*

But Isabella had to wait for Paradise Moon. Unbidden, a glowing hand folded Isabella's shades into her trouser pocket and smoothed windswept hair from her eyes.

Do you want to get this done or put on a show?

What do you think?

Leaping from the clockface with all the poise and athleticism of someone who knows the world is watching and has trained for it, Isabella fell towards the burning spaceship. As she passed it, her glowing arm reached out and tapped the wing with a purple palm.

Hero shit, baby!

Woohoo!

Purple smoke engulfed Isabella, along with the spaceship as she took it with her.

Cold, salty water sprang up to meet her at the other end of her journey. Smothering her face underwater. Drenching her hair. Stinging her flesh like a coffin of ice. Spluttering and gasping, she hauled her head above the ocean's surface. Her arms floundered and splashed desperately until she realised her knees had already found the sandy floor of the shallows. She was kneeling. Grudgingly, Isabella stopped drowning for long enough to acknowledge the sea's icy grip barely reached her chest.

She stood, straightening her back. Tinkling water cascaded off her. She smeared the sea from her eyes to find a gentle tide lapping at her thighs with all the menace of a puppy's tongue. Although Barbados wasted no time unleashing its searing sun on her skin, for once Isabella was grateful for its warmth. She was more worried about the clouds of steam hissing from the spaceship's doused flames, not to mention the fate of anyone inside.

We should probably remove the pilot, or at least turn them over so they're cooked evenly.

Dragging herself through the shallows with a human leg tingling at the sea's rapidly rising temperature and a fleshless purple leg that couldn't care less about such base problems as burning, Isabella waded around the spaceship's flank. Now it wasn't skewering Big Ben or on fire, Isabella got her first proper look.

This spaceship was unlike anything she had seen before. PROXUS starfighters were conspicuous for their worn, dull exteriors and precise military markings, not to mention their pilots were usually trying to kill her. That was hard to miss. Space pirates went weak at the knees for a wacky paintjob and a custom retrofit. Meanwhile, Sau Daran ships were alive—which was very hard to miss—and having been formed from living metal, their hulls looked unmistakably as though they had been grown, not built. But this spaceship wasn't PROXUS, nor was it space pirate or Sau Daran. If whatever the far future looked like could have been distilled into a single craft, Isabella was staring at it.

The hull was a sparkling mirror shaped like a once sleek arrow, punctured with a haphazard mess of charred holes and impact craters. The wing on this side had been completely torn off. She had seen it fall. No doubt that wing was making its social media debut where it landed on the streets of London. The gaping hole where the absent wing should have met the fuselage was wreathed in shredded cables and twisted rods of smoking metal.

She tugged off her partially melted left boot and kitten-infested sock. A purple glow shimmering up through the water from her foot. With a glowing hand, she grabbed a thorny shard of broken spaceship and pulled herself out of the water. She was careful to land only her glowing purple foot on the floor of the spaceship's damaged hull. Sizzling and unharmed, it was as impervious to the hull's heat as Paradise Moon was to common sense. Her human foot hovered unneeded.

"Hello?" Isabella tried. Sometimes, you had to open with the classics.

After hearing no answer, she leaned inside the torn opening. Enough spears of sunlight punched through the cheese-gratered hull to illuminate its interior. There was no cockpit, no navigation station. As far as Isabella could tell, there were no controls of any kind. Instead, the spaceship seemed to have two main sections. At one end, thick smoke hung over the blackened remains of what looked like a bed surrounded by ruined crates. At the other end, every millimetre of space was lined with what would have been wall-to-wall dashboards—had all the hull still been there. Some dials and displays gasped spasmodically for life, their readouts blinking and flashing with symbols that meant less than nothing to Isabella. Most screens, however, had been cooked to death. Lying at the far end of the spaceship, near what must have been the root of the craft's pointed nose, was a body. What filed him under body and not person was his lack of movement coupled with the bloody Jackson Pollock surrounding him.

Purple smoke brought Isabella to the body without risking a single step of her right boot on the roasting floor. Tenderly, she laid her human hand on a head of long, dark hair sodden with hot sweat and ash.

Purple smoke cradled him all the way to the beach faster than a single heartbeat within Isabella's chest. Kneeling in coarse, unpleasant sand, she rolled him over.

He was definitely human. Around her age, maybe a few years older. No more than early twenties. Broken and burned, his face was a litany of weeping wounds with no promise he would see tomorrow. The only part of his face not concealed by baking blood was his long, singed hair. She caught no glimpse of the rest of his body, which was buried beneath a shell of chipped blue armour crammed with dense wiring and circuitry.

She held her cheek over his mouth and was relieved to feel his fragile breath on it. The pulse in his neck was weak and irregular, but it was there. Extending his arm, she lifted his knee, cupped her human hand around his, pressed it to his cheek and rolled him onto his side.

Purple smoke accompanied them to the usual place. A monstrous skyscraper in New York full of suited agents and lab-coated employees whose doctorates spanned everything from medicine to space travel. Wet and stinking of smoke, Isabella lay the pilot on a familiar hospital bed and felt grateful that for once it wasn't for her, its crisp sheets flanked by banks of monitors ready to announce the life or death of their patient. Staring at the stranger's eyes—too bruised, still closed—Isabella wondered which it would be this time. Life? Death? At eighteen years, she had seen too much of both. And yet, no asteroid travelled through space remaining perfectly smooth. Asteroids were rugged splinters of rock—scarred with memories of past collisions, always landing fresh blows, crashing into satellites and planets and yet more rocks, always knocking lumps out of each other. Never still. Never calm. Never safe. And better for it, with every collision moulding them. Like her, they were tougher to break after every hard knock.

With an expression hardened by the cold pragmatism of countless collisions, Isabella left the pilot's body behind and returned to Barbados. Purple smoke bled off her, dissolving into hot, stifling air unkissed by any hint of a breeze. The beach was as she had left it—a postcard of tranquillity tarnished by a smouldering space ship.

Happiness never lasts.

Isabella's phone chimed more gently than last time. A single message from a saved contact, rather than a dramatic alert. NASA, perhaps. Maybe a prime minister or president. Or probably Nato. They usually messaged around this point.

With a groan, the ruined spaceship collapsed into two lumps of space-age debris beached in the shallows. Isabella dragged her dripping phone from her trousers and glanced at the screen. It was her therapist.

Yeah, that figures.

But before Isabella went anywhere else, she had one last job. She knew how the world worked and how she paid her bills. Enough hard knocks had taught her it wasn't enough to be a hero for the whole planet. Such tranquillity around her, tarnished though it was, demanded to be put on the map if she were to benefit from such luxurious—and free—hospitality again.

Her dripping phone captured the scene perfectly. She tapped in a few words to accompany her short film. A thumb-twitching instant later, she and the crashed spaceship had landed on her socials and begun racking up the likes.

Ample parking on the beach. #Barbados #BestHoliday #BookNow

CHAPTER TWO

Dull grey buildings clung like ulcers to the asteroid's underbelly. As their stolen shuttle crept closer, Beauregard caught his first glimpse of Tiberius Omega Mining Colony through the shuttle's viewscreen. Below them, the neon glow of precious ores leaked through cracks in the asteroid's surface. Clusters of identikit PROXUS buildings had been built over the largest neon fissures, where mining prospects would be richest. Deep in those mines, Beauregard expected to find prisoners in their hundreds of thousands, but he and Braga were only here to rescue one. Lady Fleur Fontaine.

The shuttle's airlock fastened around one of Tiberius Omega Mining Colony's many docking stations with an ungodly rumble of heavy mechanisms.

"You sure they ain't gonna check this ship?" he asked.

Braga wrinkled her nose and rolled her eyes with all the patience of a moonweed addict. "Would you relax? We're pirates. This is what we do."

"I ain't gonna relax until Fleur's back with us. And I ain't no phyxin' pirate, that's all you." He punched the door release and stepped inside the airlock.

"You tell yourself whatever you want, old man," Braga called after him. "But you're not one of them anymore."

Beauregard turned in time to spy Braga throwing a thumb over her shoulder at the groaning, untidy pile of PROXUS Rangers they were leaving inside the shuttle. Six pairs of wrists, all bound in restraints. Four of the subdued Rangers were still encased in dark combat armour—except for their foul expressions, which had been left naked by their confiscated helmets. Without the comms in their helmets, none of them would be alerting local security any time soon. Which was just as well. Beauregard and Braga had no friends at this end of the Known Galaxies. Or, indeed, most ends of the Known Galaxies and most places in between. Meanwhile, the final two Rangers shivered in their underwear.

"You're one of us now," Braga reminded Beauregard in that annoyingly superior tone she liked so much. "You keep forgetting that."

With a grimace, Beauregard caught the helmet Braga tossed him and levered it on. She followed suit with her own borrowed helmet, cramming her vivid blue mane behind a dark, faceless visor. As well as her flamboyant hairstyle, the helmet also hid the tattoo on her cheek. A bird in flight, inked in blue. Everyone in the Known Galaxies knew this marked Braga as a space pirate—an occupation they weren't inclined to advertise at Tiberius Omega Mining Colony. If caught, they might be offered a much longer stay.

The airlock had barely hissed open when Beauregard marched his aching joints out of it and into a grey corridor, its shadows lined with countless grates and grilles. He had survived enough firefights to appreciate the lifesaving benefits of his stolen armour's stiff shell. Yet he longed to tear it off. The helmet in particular felt interminable. He stomped down the corridor, his peripheral vision shot, his senses dulled. Too quickly for comfort, vacant docking stations and derelict consoles disappeared into the shadows on either side of him. His weary scowl was hidden too. There was no escaping how much he missed the reassuring feel of his plasma pistols hanging against his thighs. Sadly, a gunslinger's brace of pistols was far from PROXUS standard issue and would have ruined his disguise. He kept his borrowed plasma rifle ready, its grip held calmly in his right hand. Two fully functioning hands would have been better than one and given him a firmer grip on the long-barrelled weapon. However, since stepping between Isabella and the wrath of Sau Daran god Midnight Twice three cycles ago, two working hands were a luxury he didn't have. Not that it would affect the outcome of any firefight. His rifle would kill just as swiftly with its barrel braced under his crippled left arm.

Once they found a star lift, Braga's helmet peered back down the deserted corridor of docking stations. "No one's going to find our shuttle down there," she assured him. Behind his own visor, Beauregard's lip curled into a snarl. She had the arrogance of a flaming comet and was full of just as much hot air.

They slipped inside the star lift's cylindrical pod. Beauregard didn't bother paying attention as Braga punched instructions into its interface. Inside the privacy of the small windowless capsule, he tuned out the universe and let whichever deadly part of Tiberius Omega Mining Colony they were hurtling through flash past uncontemplated.

When the star lift's doors hissed open, Beauregard started paying attention. He began with the PROXUS Ranger carrying the biggest gun and worked his way down from there. Stray blasts from Braga's plasma rifle were lost in the precise torrents of red plasma that Beauregard hurled into the security control centre. Once he had run out of targets, he scanned the smoke-filled room through his helmet's visor and grudgingly found its smoke filters and vision enhancers more effective than he wanted to admit.

Beauregard stared at the bodies scattered across the control room. He had lived too many cycles to feel remorse. Not for them. Not when he knew what they did here. Once PROXUS had won the war against the Sau Darans a generation ago, all PROXUS Rangers had been given two options. Serve with the fleet or guard labour camps like Tiberius Omega Mining Colony. He had forged a long career in soldiering after taking the first option, having never considered the alternative. Many of the prisoners here would be innocents who had objected too passionately to the Empress invading their world and bringing them forcibly into the People's Republic of Xarr and United Systems. Into PROXUS. Worlds that, in a past life, Beauregard was ashamed to admit he had invaded in the Empress' name. But Rangers who took a posting in places like Tiberius Omega Mining Colony were worse even than him—and that was saying something. He had only killed soldiers. Keen to escape the frontlines, however, the guards here preferred enemies who couldn't fight back. Enemies who had done nothing wrong and would spend the rest of their lives mining ores that would become new PROXUS ships primed to conquer yet more worlds. If Beauregard felt anything at killing these guards, it was galaxies from remorse.

They tossed aside their helmets and got to work. Being a control room, everything here that wasn't a person was a display or an input device. It was a hacker's wet dream and Beauregard's worst nightmare. He didn't understand how any of the buttons, dials, switches, touchscreens, holopads, projections or keypads could be manipulated to get what they wanted, but he understood this was the place to stage a rescue. Braga settled at the largest console, took off her heavy Ranger gloves and began conducting the console's controls to her tune. Meanwhile, Beauregard checked everyone was dead.

"How many alarms did we set off?" he asked as he dropped another limp body back onto the workstation it had been draped over.

"None." Braga flashed him a grin. "I'm too good."

All the warmth drained from Beauregard's expression. "Ain't no one that good," he said with the cold, grim certainty of experience. "Just lucky or wrong."

Braga seemed too engrossed in her work to notice, her tattooed, painted fingers dancing over the console. "Almost found her."

As well as the door through which they had entered, numerous star lift pods waited along every wall in the control room. Casting aside the last corpse, Beauregard watched the doors warily. If Braga was speaking, he wasn't listening.

When she retreated from the console and retrieved her helmet and gloves, he took his cue and slipped on his own helmet with another snarl, then followed her into a different star lift.

This was a longer journey with a host of unintended stops and unexpected arrivals in the star lift that prompted enough scrutiny to derail their rescue mission. Questions of orders, callsigns and duty rosters were negotiated by Beauregard's helmeted silences and Braga's frantic button pushing to take the star lift elsewhere. In fact, Beauregard barely killed anyone in the time it took them to reach the dormitory level where Fleur had been imprisoned.

Their task grew more difficult the moment their boots finally stomped out of the star lift. On this dormitory level, security was at its tightest. So tight they almost marched into a squad of PROXUS Rangers in the entrance chamber. Had security not been focused on the threat from prisoners inside the facility, they might have been in trouble. As it was, their unexpected arrival barely prompted a glance from the uniformed, pale-faced clerk who was too busy logging records on a vibrant touch screen that filled one wall. Rows of Rangers standing to attention filled the rest of the chamber, helmets angled steadfastly at the closed blast doors that led into the cells.

Loitering on Braga's shoulder with his plasma rifle ready, Beauregard waited for her to talk them out of whatever trouble they were in. "Straight through," Braga announced, pointing at the blast doors without slowing.

The clerk raised an eyebrow. "Just the two of you?"

"Are all the cells locked down?"

The clerk raised his other eyebrow. "Of course."

"Then just the two of us," Braga replied confidently. Beauregard could almost feel her winking beneath her helmet in that annoying way she always did. He fought to keep his trigger finger from tensing. "Open up," she urged, "we're on the clock."

The clerk scrutinised her as though sucking on the sourest of weeji berries, but there was nothing for him to examine other than their faceless PROXUS armour. Nodding, he tapped the display behind him. The blast doors yawned open with a hydraulic moan.

As the pair squeezed through the thick ranks of Rangers, Beauregard kept watch on their vast array of plasma weapons—brandished in such a tight space with absolutely no cover to hide behind if things turned ugly. He was relieved when the blast doors closed behind them with a heavy clunk of finality. From there,

Beauregard consigned himself to following whatever route Braga's screen-tapping in the control room had revealed to her.

Every cell they passed was closed off from the passage by a wall of blue energy. Inside were groups of malnourished prisoners clothed in rags and shadows, but nothing else. There was nothing Beauregard could do to help them. He only had the means to skin one forcefield. Unless a prisoner happened to be in the same cell as Beauregard's comrade in arms and Braga's comrade in cuddles, the denizens of Tiberius Omega Mining Colony would find this rotation just as vented as the rest.

"Sometimes I wonder how you did this to people," mused Braga, the tilt of her helmet lingering on an elderly man infested with lesions.

"Only sometimes?"

"Good people ground down in the mines until there's nothing left except bones and gristle."

"We ain't here to be heroes." Beauregard reminded her. "We get Fleur out or we die tryin'. Nothin' else."

Braga stopped. "And that isn't being a hero?"

"It phyxin' ain't. It's bein' a friend."

Sighing through the filters in her helmet, she picked up her pace. "You're impossible."

Beauregard imagined shooting Braga in the back and found a rare smile behind his own helmet, but if he did that things might be awkward with Fleur after he rescued her. Instead, he allowed Fleur's terrible choice of wife to lead him towards another wall of shimmering blue energy. Behind it, Fleur would be waiting for them. Or at least she should have been. Clearly no one had told Fleur, because the cell was empty.

Braga tore off her helmet and hurled it at the wall of blue energy. It bounced off and clattered further down the passage. "It said she was here! Why isn't she here? It's phyxing empty!"

Patiently, Beauregard cast off his stolen helmet. More faces were emerging in the shadowy cells that lined this section of passageway, all of them leaning closer to the blue energy of their forcefields. Braga's tantrum was attracting a crowd.

She thrust a gloved finger under his nose. "I'm not leaving her," she insisted, her voice threatening to break.

"Ain't no one leavin' her." Beauregard took a closer look through the wall of blue energy separating them from Fleur's empty cell, but the shadows inside were too thick. "Open it," he suggested.

"I never should have trusted you," continued Braga. "I knew I should have just come on my own. If we don't get her out of this place…"

Beauregard was confident from her moving lips that Braga hadn't stopped speaking, but he had definitely stopped listening. His cold blue eyes calmly checked both ends of the passage before it disappeared around distant corners, his plasma rifle ready to deal with any trouble that came their way. When he noticed Braga's lips had stopped moving, he indicated the wall of blue energy in front of her cell. "Can you still get that thing down?"

Braga drew a metallic marble from one of the pouches on her armour. It was carved with intricate tributaries of black runes. Beauregard didn't even slightly understand how it worked, but he knew it cost her half a cycle's worth of loot. "We could save a whole cell of people with this," she warned. "That cell's empty."

"We ain't here for them. We're here for Fleur. Without lookin', we ain't gonna know where she went."

Cursing, Braga threw the metal marble at the blue wall of energy shielding Fleur's cell. As it struck, the ball's black ley lines lit up with a radiant explosion of white light. The forcefield sparked, spluttered and died. Braga retrieved her helmet. Poking her gloved hand inside its cavity, she toggled on the torch affixed to one side and aimed it in front of her. A pale beam of probing light dispelled shadows from the centre of the cell.

Together, they edged inside.

Beauregard's eyes scoured shadows unused to light or examination, but he found no convenient air duct or dubious trash shoot that might have enabled an escape. Nothing to reveal the whereabouts of Fleur and her cellmates. The walls, floor and ceiling were equally evasive under interrogation from the beam of light shining out of Braga's helmet. No blood. No bodies. No way out. This cell wasn't only empty of prisoners. There were no clues here, either.

"Well, this is most unexpected," said a reedy voice behind them.

Beauregard was pleased to see his plasma rifle ready to fire a fraction before Braga's as they spun and aimed at the passage outside Fleur's cell. Watching them was a small rat-like man in an expensive waistcoat that didn't tally with all the dirt covering him. Both his plasma pistol and his confused expression were aimed at Braga. Beauregard could sympathise with the confused expression, but he felt it would have been more prudent to aim the pistol at him instead of Braga. Clearly, the stranger was a dpresh.

"Who in the Empress' name are you?" Beauregard demanded.

"Who am I?" the stranger echoed in his irritating, reedy voice. Everything about him had edges, from his thinning spiky hair down to his tiny metal-toed boots. He tore off his spectacles with his free hand and brandished them accusingly at Beauregard. "Who in the Empress' name are you and what in the Known Galaxies have you done with Lady Fontaine?"

"She ain't here," snarled Beauregard.

"And she's not a lady," added Braga proudly. "She's my wife."

"We ain't got time for this. Whose side are you on?"

The stranger tutted. "Well, you're clearly not proper Rangers." Holstering his plasma pistol and putting his spectacles back on, he wiped enough sweat and dirt from his face to reveal a white tattoo of a half-eclipsed sun beside one eye. Although different to Braga's tattoo, it was identical to Fleur's.

"Oh phyx," muttered Braga.

Beauregard scrunched up his face in confusion. "Pirate?" The stranger nodded. "Same clan Fleur ran with?" The stranger nodded again. "Same clan betrayed her to PROXUS?" Another nod. "So you work for—"

"Her father," finished Braga, her expression more menacing than Beauregard had ever seen before.

Tired of nodding, the stranger pierced them with a glare. "Do you have any answers, or just questions?"

"Well, she ain't here."

"Thank goodness you came," the stranger remarked with slick sarcasm as warm as a long walk in space. "I can't imagine what I would have done without you."

"She's not gone that way," said Braga, pointing in the direction of the passage they had walked down. "And she was supposed to be in this cell."

"Oh how wonderful, yet more things you don't know." The stranger peered curiously at the incarcerated spectators lining up to watch this unexpected theatre from behind their shields of blue energy. "Might any of you know where the inhabitants of this cell went?"

"Never came up from the mines," someone muttered from a shadowed cell. "Still down there."

"Phyx," cursed Beauregard.

"Phyx," cursed Braga.

"You didn't ask anyone at all?" the stranger demanded incredulously. "Lady Fontaine is missing and you didn't ask any of these lovely prisoners if they had seen her return to her cell?"

"Well, how did you get here?" asked Braga.

The stranger's tone sharpened to a lethal point as he carved out his frustration one word at a time. "I. Came. Up. Through. The. Mines."

The passage chose that moment to rock with the force of an explosion. Beauregard caught the wall to steady himself, his rifle no longer aimed at the stranger. He understood the level of firepower it took to make a facility like this move, and it wasn't good news.

"Your lot?" Braga asked the stranger.

"I am my lot," said the stranger. "I work better when untethered from the interference of others." He glared at them. "Your lot?"

Braga shrugged. "This is all of our lot too. What you see is what you get."

"That little?"

The passage shook again.

"We ain't leavin' without Fleur. If she's in the mines, get us down there."

"I'm uncomfortable with this sudden presumption there is any 'us', but a professional of my unimpeachable skill and endeavour certainly could get us down there. If I wanted to."

"Good. Because we're gonna be melted into slag if we don't get out of here. Those explosions ain't localised. This whole prison's under attack."

The shockwave of the next explosion sent every forcefield flashing then dying in a shower of sparks.

Braga smiled in a way that made Beauregard want to strangle her. "Time to haul arse, old man."

After that, everything got messy.

CHAPTER THREE

Y ou're on fire," chided Isabella's mum. "And you're all wet."

Annoyingly, she was right twice. Isabella brushed out the embers of her sleeve but pretended not to see the droplets of ocean puddling on the parquet flooring.

"Better?"

Snorting with despair, her mum tossed her tablet onto the sofa and pinned Isabella with the warmest hug. "You're safe, despite all that jumping around on Big Ben."

"Yeah, Mum," moaned Isabella, pulling away from the comforting smell of her mum's cardigan. "I'm fine."

Far from satisfied, her mum retreated out of their living room and disappeared deeper into their apartment. "Was anyone inside the ship?" she called after herself.

"Mum, we were literally in the same room. Don't leave if you're going to ask me a question."

"Pardon?" her mum called from another room.

How come I'm eighteen years old and I'm still living with my mum?

Because you're a loving daughter?

Try again.

Because your sponsorships pay the rent?

Bingo. And remind me why we haven't murdered each other yet?

How would I know? I'm just a god.

Given their Hyde Park apartment spanned over four thousand square feet of luxury, it was hard not to get lost inside, let alone track down a moving target. Sighing with more stress than she had felt when leaping off a burning spaceship hundreds of metres above the ground, Isabella chased after her mum and found her in the kitchen.

"What, Mother?"

Smiling innocently enough to start a riot, her mum began emptying the floor-to-ceiling fridge of every vegetable they owned. "I wasn't expecting you home tonight, I thought you were still on holiday."

Isabella settled on a stool and let her face collapse onto their brunch table with an exaggerated sigh of exhaustion. "Yeah, it sort of lost its appeal."

"Your post about the beach got a lot of likes."

Instead of answering, Isabella plucked an apple from the fruit bowl and tossed it in her hand distractedly.

"You could have used the hashtags we agreed with the tourist board. You didn't even tag them. I know you don't pay attention to the contracts you sign, but I do."

Isabella tossed the apple again, its lush red coat shining as it spun. Paradise Moon took control of Isabella's glowing purple arm for long enough to catch it with an unnecessary flourish.

"Don't forget you're booked in for a round of morning TV tomorrow before you-know-what happens."

"Mum, you can just say it."

Her mum dropped a clutch of carrots in the path of a rogue cauliflower rolling across their vast expanse of marbled kitchen counter. "It's your body and what you choose to do with it is entirely up to you. It doesn't bother me at all. It's your funeral if she does something stupid again and puts you in danger. I've warned you. That's all I can do."

The apple spun back and forth from glowing purple hand to human fingers, each catch punctuated with the sigh and blank stare combo Isabella had perfected as early as the onset of puberty.

"Your dad called again." Isabella's human hand snatched the apple out of the air and held onto it while she waited for her mum to continue. "It's okay, love. I told him no. If he wants to get re-elected, he can do it without your endorsement."

Relaxing, Isabella took a large bite out of the apple. Her stress slid off her like her sweat had in the flames of that burning spaceship and she found calmer breaths. It was easier to hate her father when all he cared about was himself. Never her mum. Never her. Only what was in it for him and his career.

Her mum brandished a courgette at her. "It's late, what do you want? Your nutritionist says you need to eat more vegetables. Was there someone in that ship?"

Vegetables? Killjoy.

"Yeah, he's stable." Isabella had checked in on him after leaving Barbados, but he had been dosed up on drugs and fast asleep. "The doctors are looking after him. Vegetables? Really, Mum? It's Thursday night."

"So?"

Isabella glared. "So tomorrow's Friday. Come on, I need a treat. While this body's still mine."

I always give it back.

Yeah, but you never tell me what you've done with it.

"I know what kind of treats you like." Now it was her mum's turn to cross her arms. "Not under my roof. Under no circumstances are you eating pizza tonight unless I've cooked you something healthy first."

Isabella smiled and hugged her mum. "Lucky it's my roof, then, isn't it?"

By the time they were settled on the sofa with a takeout pizza and bottle of red wine, Isabella had enjoyed a scalding shower and was wrapped in fluffy pyjamas complete with a hood pulled up so its warm cocoon cuddled her ears.

What are you gonna do tomorrow?

I could do your TV rounds for you. Hit them with all my godly charm, show them a bit of fun.

Never again. I'll make sure I'm done early, though. I promise. You'll get your day.

Thanks, arsehat.

So what are you gonna do?

Oh I dunno... I don't have any plans. Maybe I'll see where the mood takes me.

Lies!

The alien inside Isabella laughed.

Seriously, aren't you gonna tell me?

Tell you what?

Yeah, right. Nice one. What you get up to. Where you go. And who you do it with.

You know me. I'm a free spirit.

Isabella laughed out loud, prompting a murmur from her mum on the sofa beside her. *A free spirit with too many secrets and my body all to yourself.*

A girl's gotta have some fun, am I right?

A motherly arm wrapped itself around Isabella and caressed her shoulder, telling Isabella more than she'd said all night.

"Mum, I'm fine." That provoked a probing look. "It always looks worse than it is after something like that."

"Are you seeing your therapist tonight?"

Isabella crammed the last slice of pizza into her mouth. "No, Mum, it's late," she mumbled through a mouthful of cheese and pepperoni. "And I've been drinking. I'll see her on Saturday. I promise."

"You've only had one glass."

"And I'm in my pyjamas."

Her mum peered over her glasses with a stern look fuelled by love. "You're supposed to see her whenever something like today happens. No matter what."

Isabella glanced sourly at her phone. Its protective case had kept out the seawater, but it smelled awfully salty. Unread and unanswered, a string of messages from her therapist lingered on the screen.

"But it's so late," Isabella moaned at the universe.

"Aren't you still on Barbados time?"

CHAPTER FOUR

The Empress of the Known Galaxies watched Isabella with what she hoped was a kindly expression. Of all the ways to arrange a face, she found kindness the hardest. She had been practising this expression in the mirror for the better part of a cycle, even since landing on Earth, but she suspected it still wasn't quite right.

"I'm fine, you don't need to worry," insisted Isabella. She was slurring her words ever so slightly, or at least elongating them, as though she wasn't entirely sober.

"You were on fire," the Empress pointed out, her words precise and crisp. "I watched it. Are you okay?"

Isabella leaned back in the deep armchair she always chose during their sessions. A trained therapist might have known what Isabella's choice of seat meant on a deep psychological level. The Empress didn't care.

"What can I say?" asked Isabella. "Some bits of me just don't burn." With the subtlety of a PROXUS battle station arriving in orbit, Isabella emphasised her point by waving a leg whose glow was concealed by her jeans, and a hand whose exposed purple glow travelled all the way from her fingertips up into the sleeve of a clean t-shirt. The coven of vampiric elves on its front looked no less ridiculous than the rest of Isabella's wardrobe.

"Your fresh trim survived too." It felt like Isabella restyled her hair every time they saw each other. Which was often, given the lifestyle Isabella led. Whether it was the colour, the parting, the fringe or simply how outrageous Isabella wanted it, her hair never looked the same two therapy sessions in a row. This rotation's style was shorter and spikier than last time, with no colouring bar her natural darkness.

"Thank you for noticing."

The Empress pretended to ignore the dissent in Isabella's tone. "Some people would describe what you did as dangerous. Do you think it was dangerous?"

"Maybe, but it was the right thing to do. And it worked out, didn't it?"

The Empress hid her disapproval. Throughout all their therapy sessions, she couldn't recall a single time when Isabella had shown even a shred of responsibility or good judgement. The girl who had been kidnapped from Earth three cycles ago was truly dead. After being hunted across deep space by PROXUS, Sau Darans, space pirates and bounty hunters, that Isabella had finally died on the same rotation she stood up to defend her home planet from Striker's unsanctioned PROXUS invasion. In her place, a monster born of celebrity and hero worship sat before the Empress, eighteen cycles old and as brazen as the Sau Daran parasite lurking inside her.

The sooner she tore Paradise Moon from this young woman's lifeless body, the better. Perhaps she would do it now. In the next few rotations, certainly. That would be smarter. By then, she would have the codes for the nuclear weapons stashed in her bedroom wall. That would give her enough leverage to make Isabella do whatever the Empress wanted, such as returning with her to her home planet of Xarr and harvesting the parasite inside Isabella for clean energy. That would power Xarr and all the ships in the PROXUS fleet for many cycles to come, and should be enough to help the Empress regain her throne.

And yet… killing Isabella now would feel sweeter.

"How is Paradise Moon?" the Empress asked evenly, keeping her counsel when it came to murderous intent.

Isabella laughed so hard she had to cover her mouth. "She says it's lovely to see you again," Isabella lied, after a long pause. Some people were better at lying than others, and Isabella was the worst.

The Empress attempted a smile. "I'm sure."

Familiar silence followed.

Oh! How badly the Empress wanted to close the gap between them and rip out Isabella's throat. Instead, waiting in silence for Isabella to finish her private conversation with Paradise Moon, the Empress took a slow sip of cool water and leaned back in her armchair.

Everything she needed to know came back to that ship. The Empress understood how challenging it was to land a spacecraft undetected on Earth, conceal it from the planet's primitive inhabitants and insert oneself into society. She had thought there could be nothing more challenging—until she had attempted using London's transport system to reach a destination on time. Had she been the Empress of London's tiny empire, so many heads would have rolled.

"And the pilot you rescued?" the Empress continued, probing for useful information. "How are they?"

Isabella smiled vacantly. "You know you shouldn't ask me those sorts of questions. Agent Glass gets agitated."

"Of course," the Empress replied in her most cordial tone, which admittedly was a low bar. She paused, thinking. It felt like a while since she had asked Isabella how she felt. The Empress didn't understand much about being a therapist, but she had the impression that was something therapists asked. "I imagine it's traumatic dealing with a casualty. It can't be easy knowing their life is in your hands. How did you feel about that?"

"You don't need to worry about me," Isabella assured her. "I know what I'm doing."

The Empress stifled an improper, potentially relationship damaging cackle at the idea Isabella knew what she was doing. She had stamped on scuttling grublins with better judgement. Instead, she searched her barren toolkit for kindness and unleashed what she hoped was another encouraging expression. "My dear Isabella, isn't it my job to worry?"

"You tell me. You're the therapist."

"Well then yes, I do worry about you." Every lie, practised so carefully, slid easily from her lips. "It's one traumatic event after another. Just one of these ordeals in a whole lifetime would be enough for most mortals. It must take its toll. Emotionally. Mentally. Physically. You pay me an embarrassingly large sum of money to worry about you, and I'm not ashamed to admit that of course I do. How could I not, after all this time together?"

Isabella paused, a familiar smirk on her face. The Empress had come to understand this meant she was speaking to the Sau Daran god inside her. "Thank you for caring, it means a lot." Isabella's smirk left her face for a heartbeat. "Even if I don't show it. You've always been here for me, and you've always listened. Thank you."

"You're welcome. And you'll have to excuse my natural curiosity about that ship."

Isabella didn't make eye contact with the Empress. "Like you say, it's natural."

"That ship just looked so… strange. Don't you think?"

Strange was an understatement. That ship was unlike anything the Empress had seen in the Known Galaxies, and she thought she'd seen everything. Plus, its hull looked like it was crafted from mythium, which was as rare and strong as metals got. No one could afford to make ships out of mythium, not even her. Did it even have a star drive? Or was it powered by something else?

A swell of pride rose inside her, far too strong to stifle. Star drives. Her gift to PROXUS. When she had led the Known Galaxies to victory against the Sau Darans, she had transformed space travel. Harvesting defeated Sau Daran gods into star energy had been a masterstroke that powered her PROXUS fleet faster and further than anyone who opposed her, while keeping the lights on at home without relying on the dirty energy that had destroyed Xarr's atmosphere long ago. Her mastery of this new, clean energy harvested from Sau Daran gods had literally fuelled her dominion.

But without her reserve of star energy on Xarr, no ships flew anywhere and the lights went out. It was Isabella's bad luck that the Empress' clean energy was extracted from the same species of Sau Daran god trapped inside Isabella. A prize the Empress was so desperate to tear from Isabella's flesh that she could feel the impulse almost consuming her again. But first she needed information about tonight's crashed pilot and his mysterious ship's technology.

"Well, there isn't going to be much of that ship to look at anymore," admitted Isabella.

"What a pity. That must be so disappointing for your friends at NASA."

Isabella smiled her vacant smile and said nothing.

The Empress held up her hands. "You can't tell me. Don't worry, I understand." She changed topic with the swift economy of a flashing blade. "How about your nightmares? You can tell me about those without breaking the Official Secrets Act."

Isabella's eyes roamed around the Empress' sitting room. As always, her gaze eventually departed out of the full-length windows. They stretched the length of one wall and boasted horizon-flooding views of London's pathetic attempt at skyscrapers. Tonight, those buildings were a mere cluster of lights on a dark horizon. The Empress fought to keep the contempt from her face. Although uninhabitable outside airtight structures, Xarr's surface was filled with mountainous skyscrapers that skimmed the soft underbelly of space. London boasted small pockets of these pathetic things they claimed were skyscrapers, but such thimbles of primitive industry scraped nothing but the fringes of failure and delusion.

"It's Friday tomorrow," the Empress reminded Isabella. "How do you feel about that?"

"The same as I do every Thursday night." Isabella's eyes never left the window. "Absolutely fine."

"Because if you didn't, that would be okay." The Empress tried to catch her eye, but it was impossible. Conversations were such hard work. She had to be so... pleasant. She missed being able to brandish the threat of imprisonment on a mining asteroid whenever she wasn't getting her way. "I understand it's difficult to talk freely when you're never truly alone," she tried, soothingly.

Isabella dragged her eyes away from the window long enough to smile. It was an infuriating smile. "Everything is peaches. I trust her, it's fine."

Sensing weakness, the Empress smiled disarmingly and lunged with her next question. "Even though she won't tell you what she does with her Fridays?"

"What's the worst that can happen? Until I die, we're stuck in this body together. Whatever happens to me, happens to her too."

During their earliest sessions, the Empress would have probed more deeply for no reason other than to undermine Isabella's confidence. A relationship with a therapist is sacred, and the Empress enjoyed exploiting it to the very limits. However, she had learned a great deal about Isabella since those initial sessions. When presented with a fight, Isabella started swinging and thanked you for the opportunity before her brain arrived. For reasons a real therapist might have been able to fathom, she enjoyed the battle no matter how bloody it got. No, the Empress understood she could only plant the seeds of doubt and leave them to fester unattended, if she wanted to cause lasting pain. "You're right, of course. If you trust her, there's nothing to worry about."

Isabella's phone launched into an unwelcome dirge of greasy, ear-splitting music. "Oh what a shame," Isabella said with pantomime sincerity. "Sorry, I have to take this. It's Agent Glass."

CHAPTER FIVE

Whenever Agent Glass summoned Isabella, she ended up surrounded by suits. This time was no different. They were waiting for her beside the pilot's bed, which was unexpectedly empty. They hurried in her wake along guarded corridors of polished marble as she searched for anyone in a lab coat. They watched her quiz the missing pilot's doctors, who gave nothing away.

When her unanswered questions were spent, the suits insisted on encircling her while she waited in another gleaming lobby. Even though the blinking lights were taking forever to count down the lift's descent from an impossibly high number, the suits showed no signs of impatience. No emotions whatsoever. Their expressions were as exciting as worn tarmac. Like the missing pilot's doctors, they would have made excellent poker players.

Regretting the glass of wine she'd had earlier, not to mention the sleep she hadn't, Isabella tapped her foot. Huffed. Leaned against a lusciously panelled wall. Sighed long and hard to the heavens. "Screw this, I'll meet you at the top."

Before the suits could object, Isabella left the lobby in a swirl of purple smoke and reappeared next to a startled Agent Glass inside his office on the top floor. As he jumped in shock, only some of the steaming coffee leaping from his mug found his crotch. Most of it went everywhere else. Inelegantly, he tried to dodge all of it and ended up catching more wet, scalding patches of coffee with the rest of his suit than if he had stood still.

He looked down at her as though she were a puppy who had chewed the sofa yet again. "I thought we agreed you would at least use the elevator, especially after what happened last time."

Isabella crossed her arms. "You agreed. I didn't. Time's wasting. And it's a lift, not an elevator. Where's my pilot?"

Agent Glass pointed her to a seat. She obliged. Everything about him was middle-aged and slightly past its best. His once blonde hair was on the turn, his eyes badgered by sleep deprivation. Even though his suit was a looser cut than when Isabella had first met him, its taut lining bulged in more places than it used to. Sighing with the resignation of someone whose life was passing by faster than he liked, Agent Glass stowed his World's Best Dad mug on a tower of binders that would have given Pisa a run for its money. His desk had always been overgrown with paperwork. In the three years they had known each other, Isabella still had no idea what colour it was underneath.

Agent Glass did not sit.

He paced.

"The pilot is gone. Every door in the facility was locked down. No one saw anything. The only evidence is an empty bed, the stolen contents of three personnel lockers and missing camera footage from the last hour."

"How much missing footage?"

"All of it. No trace of him anywhere. He's not in the facility and he's not leaving a trail." Wearily, he ticked points off on his fingers. "Nothing on facial scans. Nothing on number plate recognition. Given our resources that is frankly impossible, unless he turned invisible." He pinned her under a scrutinising look. "Can he do that?"

"He's been gone for an hour and you're only telling me this now?"

You're only saying that because you wanted to get out of therapy.

Agent Glass stopped pacing, his face twitching with unconcealable irritation. "Sometimes I get the impression you think we work for you."

Finally! The chumps in suits get it!

Isabella smiled all the way from her eyes to the corners of her lips. "Well, you did call me here to save your arse. Right?"

Agent Glass silently attempted more than one response before he replied, and even then he still didn't look happy about his choice of words. "Right, well, okay," he agreed uncomfortably. "I don't suppose you could..."

His keenness to trail off and let Isabella fill in the gaps was undone when the silence he teed up was interrupted by Isabella's herd of suits from the lobby. Apologetically, they failed to bundle into his office discretely.

Isabella winked at Agent Glass, knowing it would infuriate him. "Always happy to help."

Purple smoke took her from Agent Glass' office to the seat of a train. Thankfully, an empty seat. Paradise Moon was clever like that. The carriage rattled along with cold afternoon sunlight streaming through its frost-rimed windows. It was a tired, worn carriage with stained seats encased in battered beige panelling. Outside the window, a claustrophobic diorama of mirrored glass, smog and concrete loomed beyond the tracks. Unmistakeably, she was still in New York.

A handful of passengers yelped at her sudden arrival. They must have all lived under the same rock, where no one had ever heard of the vanishing girl and the alien trapped inside her. However, these yelping passengers were an overwhelmed minority. A barrage of excitement lit up the rest of the carriage. Eagerly, phones were aimed at Isabella, many with their owners in the foreground, arms outstretched, filters undoubtedly on. Some narrated over each other, while others waited for Isabella to deliver a performance. She smiled as though they weren't all insane, just like she'd been taught.

But she wasn't here for them.

The pilot's expression was lost in the dead space between bewilderment and delight. Both, perhaps, a response to the seat next to him suddenly gaining a new occupant. His face had used the time since she had last seen him to decide how it felt about the crash. It had reached grave conclusions. His black bruises were ripening, his scars—although expertly glued—were inescapably raw, and he held his body as though it might fall apart at any moment. Gone was his extravagantly wired shell of armour. In its place, an unbuttoned overcoat hung open to reveal a woman's flowery blouse and chinos. Nothing, however, could top his cosy fur-lined slippers.

And yet...

Without his armour spoiling the view, she could see so much more of him. Sleek muscle down his arms. The broad, tall frame of a body used to hard work and long hours doing... Isabella didn't know what. Lifting things? HIIT workouts? Getting all sweaty? Even his bizarre ensemble of stolen clothes couldn't distract her from how pleasing he was on the eye.

And yet...

Despite its burnt and tousled state, his long hair refused to look anything other than luxurious, gliding over his ears and past his face before defiantly brushing the shoulders of his overcoat. Quite possibly, it was the finest head of hair she had ever seen on a man.

And yet...

He was a stone-cold space hottie.

"Hey," Isabella told him, holding out her human hand. "I'm the girl who saved your life."

The pilot studied her proffered hand as though it were weaponised, looked at her other hand—which Isabella was willing to concede *was* weaponised—and did the most unexpected thing. He laughed. It might have been excitement, might have been relief. Or something else entirely, Isabella wondered. Keen not to be left hanging, she withdrew her hand.

Closing his eyes, the pilot calmly raised his own scarred hands as though conducting a séance. Isabella was about to ask if he was okay in that overly polite tone reserved for people who clearly aren't, when every phone in the carriage began playing Royal Blood's *Out of the Black*. Isabella knew it well. In longer than she could remember, she hadn't listened to any song more.

Why's everyone playing our song?

She dragged her phone out of her jeans in time for the first bass riff to announce itself. Her phone was making as much noise as everyone else's, playing the same sweet, sweet song.

"Never liked their earlier stuff," muttered a moron further down the carriage. Isabella might have considered teleporting whoever it was up a deserted mountain if she didn't have more pressing matters to attend to—like the escaped pilot who had made every phone in the carriage play her favourite song.

The pilot opened his eyes. Unlike the rest of his beaten-up face, those eyes sparkled. Unblemished. Intense. Flecks of electric blue glowed inside them where previously they hadn't and where typically they shouldn't. Not unless there was a Sau Daran god inside him. It was a familiar sight Isabella had seen in the mirror all her life—whenever Paradise Moon took control or made her presence felt. Only these were blue, not the purple flecks that invaded Isabella's eyes.

Well, this is unexpected.

Cautious understanding crept over Isabella's face with the reluctance of someone who couldn't afford to be wrong. All the while, *Out of the Black* soaked her soul and rattled her heart with every rumbling expedition up and down Mike Kerr's fretboard.

"You know what I am, don't you?" asked the pilot.

Isabella nodded, praying to the gods of indie rock'n'roll that she did.

Oh, we know. We absolutely know.

"You too?" he asked.

Does a Sau Daran god shit in the woods?

Isabella nodded again. Spellbound in an inky ocean of heavy beats and rib-pounding riffs, all Isabella wanted to do was keep nodding and staring into his eyes.

"Can we go somewhere quiet?" he asked.

Reluctantly, Isabella stopped admiring his eyes. He had a point. The carriage was watching. The world was watching. Social feeds would be live. And Isabella had become accustomed to playing the role expected of her. Imagining her body coach whispering in her ear, she straightened up and made sure as many spectators as possible had the best view of her face.

"Let's go for a ride," she told him. After waving casually at her audience, she gently touched the arm of his overcoat. Her fingers found the unyielding curve of his bicep—accidentally, of course. Still, there was no harm in appreciating it. A gorgeous mound of moulded metal that felt even better than it looked.

Purple smoke escaped with them from the carriage, landing them on a mountaintop flooded with lush conifers. The rumble of the city died instantly, but it took Isabella a little longer to grudgingly let go.

"You wanted somewhere quiet?" Isabella spread her arms out wide. "Welcome to the Azores!"

The broad crescent of trees around them swept down to a faraway tranquil lake bluer than the sparks in the pilot's eyes. Isabella never swam in that lake, but countless times she had stared down from the mountains and lost herself in its blue intensity. Something else it shared with the pilot's eyes. On the other side of the lake rose another crescent of rampant evergreens. Beyond them, spilling over the ocean's horizon, smudged embers of sunset bled into the evening gloom.

Swaying, the pilot swallowed hard and steadied himself. He looked like he was struggling to adjust after being teleported from New York to an island in the North Atlantic Ocean. He said something, either "That was excessive" or "That was impressive".

As much as she hated to interrupt such a good tune, Isabella took out her phone and paused the song. A riotous bass riff died mid-rebellion, but at least they would be able to hear each other better. "Not nearly as impressive as the fact you haven't been sick yet," Isabella said encouragingly. "That's usually what happens on someone's first time."

Would you quit playing around and just ask him? Please!

"Just so we're all on the same page," Isabella continued, with no idea how she was going to say this, "there's an alien inside you too, isn't there?"

God! I'm a god, not an alien. Seriously, where's the respect?

"I mean," stumbled Isabella, her mouth leaving her brain behind as she stared once more into the blue specks of otherworldly lightning in his eyes, "obviously you're an alien. You crashed on Earth. So whatever's inside you is, like, an alien in an alien, right?"

Smooth, you just called your space hottie the babushka stacking doll of aliens.

The pilot held out his hand in a poor imitation of when Isabella had offered hers on the train. "I am Talyn. The god inside me is Nova Sky."

He said god. I like him.

Trembling, Isabella took his cold hand in hers. Her warmth bled into him. "Isabella. The irritant inside me is Paradise Moon."

Wow. Thank you very much.

Talyn chose that moment to collapse. A blanket of thin grass did little to soften his fall. Grimacing, Isabella knelt beside him. "You okay?"

That's his second crash today. What a pilot.

Talyn held up his hand. "I'm fine." Trying to sit up, he promptly vomited over his fur-lined slippers. Isabella muttered what she hoped were reassuring noises, her hand instinctively reaching out to rub his back. Her palm found yet more pleasing slabs of firm muscle. They shifted beneath her touch, and she chose to focus her attention there instead of on the puddle of vomit on the grass.

Talyn spat the last of the sick from his lips and wiped them on the sleeve of his overcoat. Sighing, he dragged off the overcoat and abandoned it on the grass.

"You can just do that?" he asked.

"What, vomit?" asked Isabella, her mind still absorbed by how the muscles in his back felt beneath her touch as she rubbed them.

"Sorry, I haven't done that before."

"It's fine, really. It happens to everyone."

Talyn waved at the mountain's canopy of evergreens and the horizon's red glow. "I meant," he clarified, "you can just bring us here?"

"Not quite, it has to be somewhere, something or someone I know."

Talyn laughed. It was the second time he had done so, and Isabella liked how it sounded. "Is that all? How limiting!" He glanced up and smiled. "Isabella, that is astounding and you are remarkable."

Blushing, Isabella settled on the grass next to Talyn and stared at the horizon so she didn't have to make eye contact. "Well, what about you and your little phone trick?" she asked. "Your alien does something too, right?"

"Oh, I just talk to machines. I asked your phone what song you play the most, then I asked everyone's phone to find the same song and play it."

"You can actually talk to machines?"

"Yeah, but it's nothing like what you do." Talyn stared out at a curtain of mist creeping up from the lake below and snaking through the evergreens. "Where are we?"

"São Miguel Island. It's just this place I go whenever I need to escape all the, well, all the everything."

"That happen a lot, does it?"

"It's been known to."

Talyn smiled warmly. "You have an incredible gift."

There were so many questions she wanted to ask him that she found it difficult to say anything. Words tumbled and jostled in her throat. "I can't believe you talk to machines. Literally any machine?"

"Anything that runs on electricity. I talk to them, they listen. That's how I got out of that place, how I found the train and how I knew where to go."

"My phone told you my favourite song. That's ridiculous."

Smiling, Talyn nodded.

I hope the god inside him isn't as smug as he is.

"Doyouthinkthey'dliketo—" Isabella caught her tongue and slowed down enough to wrap it around her words. "Would Nova Sky like to speak to my alien? To Paradise Moon?"

What?

"That would be pretty special. There aren't many gods left to speak to. Since the war ended, Nova's only spoken to one other god that I know of."

I'm not ready for that.

Yes, you are.

What if I say something dumb?

Then at least they'll have met the real you.

I did not agree to this.

"It would mean a lot," admitted Talyn. As he stared at the ocean, Isabella found more life clinging to the dying sunset than his fading smile. "But it won't be possible."

"Oh, okay."

Shit.

Sorry.

"Is your alien… alright?"

Sighing, Talyn shook his head. "Not even slightly."

"The crash?"

"No, he's just a prick."

Isabella couldn't help herself. She was sure her laugh carried far enough across the ocean to reach the Portuguese coastline.

That sounds familiar.

Wow. Thanks.

Talyn's face remained grim. "You don't understand."

"No, really, I do," Isabella assured him. But he looked so sad—she couldn't believe she had laughed. "I wasn't laughing at you," she clarified. "Paradise Moon and I have our challenges too."

You mean all those times I saved your life?

Or tried to kill me.

Are you still hung up on that?

Talyn sank onto the grass, avoiding her gaze.

"Trust me," Isabella tried, "I know all about aliens who are pricks. Most of them tried to kill me, if that makes you feel any better."

"It doesn't." Talyn spread his palms on the grass behind him, straightened his arms and leant backwards with his face tilting up to catch the breeze. The flowery blouse tugged upwards with him as he stretched, revealing enough bare flesh to draw Isabella's attention away from the increasingly grumpy, increasingly unattractive expression on his bruised face.

"When you're done laughing at me, are you going to tell me what you want?" he demanded. "What is this? What are you trying to get from me?"

Instead of answering, Isabella drifted away from Talyn and kicked a stone down the hillside. It disappeared into long evergreen shadows, yet somehow this conversation was heading downhill even faster than the stone.

I'm messing this up.

He's just being weird.

"I asked you a question. What's this all about?"

Smoothing a hand through her hair, Isabella rubbed at the stiffness in her neck. "That's what I asked you."

"You came to me," Talyn reminded her. Annoyingly, he was right. "You came to that train without knowing what I am or anything about the alien inside me. You hunted me down for a different reason."

"You crashed on our planet," Isabella pointed out, keen to line up facts in her favour too. "People had questions after you ran away. *And* I saved your life. You forgot that bit."

Finally, Talyn's eyes found hers. "People had questions? Who? The people who locked me up?" He studied her every movement, every expression.

They glared at each other, then broke off embarrassed. As each escaped the other's gaze, Talyn feigned indifference by studying the grass while Isabella hid her frustration by examining the suddenly fascinating trunk of a tree.

Are you having a fight with the first person we've ever met with another Sau Daran god inside them?

Looks like.

Impressive.

Thanks.

Isabella's mind fought to catch up with reality. Everything had been going perfectly... until it hadn't. It wasn't supposed to go this way. "Let's start again?"

Sighing, Talyn held out his hand in an improved Earthly gesture of friendship. "Talyn."

She took his hand. "Isabella."

"Thank you for saving my life, Isabella and Paradise Moon. I would like to know you better."

"I'd like that."

That makes two of us, arsehat.

Talyn inhaled a lungful of the crisp evening. "The air here is clearer than in your city. It's good, reminds me a little of home. Just a little, though. It's a lot warmer here than back home."

"Oh, that was *not* my city," Isabella explained hurriedly. "But wait until you see, erm... Reading. You were in New York, which was where I took you after the crash. To fix you up."

"Fix me?"

"Well yeah, all those people you ran away from last night. They wanted to help you. You really should go back to them. You can trust them... I think."

Well that sounded convincing.

"The people who wanted answers I didn't owe them?" Talyn rubbed his eyes with a grimace. "I don't think any of you can help me."

"Why? What were you even doing on that train?"

"I was going to the Natural History Museum."

"Right… You came all the way to Earth for that?"

He looked at her solemnly. "I'm on a mission from a god. We need answers."

"Okay, how can I help?"

"Really?"

"Really. What's your mission?"

Talyn's expression escalated from solemn to grave. "I'm here to save every Sau Daran who ever lived and ever died."

CHAPTER SIX

Fleur Fontaine's companion punched another passcode into the floating holo of symbols being projected from yet another set of door controls. Code accepted, the latest blast door blocking their escape flew open.

Fleur ushered their entourage of prisoners into a deserted canteen. The décor inside was coated in dull greys that were no more appealing than the dour tunics Fleur and the other prisoners were wearing. Manual labour, meagre rations and the constant threat of death had been a challenge for Fleur, but her grey tunic was utterly intolerable. For starters, it did nothing for her skin tone or her afro. Making her wear such an embarrassment of fabric was nothing short of barbaric, and another crime the Empress of the Known Galaxies would pay for. Once the last prisoner from their cell had hurried through the doorway, both women dashed deeper into the canteen, passing long bolted-down tables and running under empty walkways overhead.

"Where did you get all these passcodes?" Fleur asked as they ran.

Her companion delivered a stern look, which caused the old plasma burns that had eviscerated her face to twist and stretch cruelly. "I pay attention."

That was certainly true. Her surgical recollection of the Rangers' patrol patterns in the mines had stopped them getting spotted ever since they had hidden down there at the end of their shift. It had been a long wait for the Ranger bribed by Fleur's companion to manually log them into the dormitory system and upload the pre-recorded footage of them in their cell. Once the waiting was over, everything had moved fast. So far, so not dead. However, Fleur had never travelled this deep into Tiberius Omega Mining Colony. Everything here was unknown and untested. For her, at least. Her companion acted as though she knew the whole facility.

Gliding with more athleticism and grace than the other prisoners, whose withered bodies had endured too many cycles here, Fleur and her companion hurried to the front of the rushing group. Along with a few of the strongest prisoners from their cell, they were armed with whatever basic tools they had been able to steal from the mines. Largely, this meant an arsenal of blunt instruments from the inner workings of larger mechanisms that, like them, were never intended to leave. Fleur gripped a giant metal pin thicker than her forearms and as tall as Isabella when they had first met. She carried it in both hands like an ungainly spear. Her companion held the shaft of a lever shorn from a drill the size of a spaceship. Neither of their makeshift weapons would be as effective as Fleur's plasma pistol, but they were certainly big enough to make an impression.

Fleur's companion hurdled another long table, leading them towards one of the many doors on the far side of the canteen. Nothing slowed her down. Although old, her companion's body was sinewy and strong, able to effortlessly forge more powerful strides across the canteen than Fleur expected. Especially in bare feet. Inexplicably, throughout the handful of rotations they had known each other, Fleur's companion had kept her feet bare whenever she wasn't working in the mines. Even during an escape effort, now was no exception as her bare soles floated over the canteen floor.

"Honey, you look like someone who knows where she is going," Fleur observed, without needing to catch her breath.

"Like I said, I pay attention."

That sounded odd to Fleur, given they were somewhere only security personnel were supposed to be, but she was too busy running for her life to let it bother her. Another keypad was met with another passcode from her companion. They flooded through a pair of heavy blast doors and into a large star lift that sped off at her companion's command.

"Control centre?" asked Fleur.

"Next stop."

Fleur organised the prisoners with improvised weapons so they were closest to the pod's exit. "As soon as the star lift stops, run as fast as you can and take everyone down before they get off a shot. Everyone else, stay in here until we call you in."

Soberly, the other prisoners nodded their understanding. Nervous glances and itchy anticipation spread between everyone except Fleur and her companion. Fleur was at home with such danger so close at hand, which said more about her life than she liked to admit. She glanced at her companion and found her feeling much the same. Until the star lift began shaking violently—and didn't stop shaking. Fleur hid her concern as the prisoners rattled into each other. The only time Fleur had been in a star lift that started behaving this erratically was when the PROXUS battle station she had been on was being pulverised by a bombardment of plasma fire. A complication they could do without.

Still rocking all over the place, the star lift finally slowed. Fleur focussed on the door and made sure everyone else did the same. The group's jaws were set as tight with tension as the strangled grip on their meagre weapons. Exuding calm, Fleur and her companion stepped to the edge of the exit, first out the door. Fleur hefted her giant pin. Her companion lowered her rod, ready to skewer the first Ranger she saw.

At the hiss of the door opening, they tore out of the star lift. Everyone apart from Fleur and her coolheaded companion was pumped up on adrenaline, screaming for freedom and murder. They needn't have bothered. Someone with the same idea had got to the control room first. Fleur nudged the nearest armoured body. Limply, they dribbled off a console and onto the floor.

Navigating an unconcerned path through the carnage, Fleur's companion made herself at home at the largest workstation. Her fingers blurred, working the console. "Someone used this workstation to find our cell."

"Another mystery for another rotation, honey. Do we have a way out?"

Without her eyes leaving the workstation, Fleur's companion pointed at another star lift. It was much smaller than the one they had ridden here.

"We go in fours," Fleur told them. "It won't hold any more." The control room shook and the distant echo of an explosion rumbled on the periphery of Fleur's hearing.

"Fours!" snapped Fleur's companion, as though she was used to giving orders. "Go!"

As the small star lift's door sealed the first foursome inside its pod, the control centre shook again. The lights died. Patiently, Fleur waited in darkness. A handful of heartbeats later, a red glow blinked awake and painted consoles, prisoners and corpses alike in muted crimson.

Up and down the star lift ran. Fleur and her companion were among the last group of four to step inside the cramped star lift. At the end of their ride, a poorly maintained and shadowy passage was waiting for them. All grates and grilles. Their fellow escaping prisoners were spaced all the way down, peering into every vacant docking station. At the far end, one prisoner shouted in delight at the discovery of a docked shuttle.

When Fleur reached it, she was greeted with one last keypad, which guarded the docking station's airlock. She gestured invitingly. "Yours, I presume."

Without returning Fleur's smile, her companion punched in a code and the airlock hissed open. Once inside the shuttle, Fleur stared at the pile of six bound Rangers, whose expressions first rose in excitement at the prospect of rescue and then plummeted into even darker concern.

"Kill them," suggested Fleur's companion.

Fleur shook her head. "That might help our escape, but not my conscience. We are not murderers." Her companion pulled a face that suggested this was a mistake, but she held her tongue. Fleur gave every prisoner a hard, uncompromising look. "Listen carefully. They are already restrained. Leave them outside the airlock. Unharmed."

Most prisoners avoided her gaze, but none challenged her. She would have asked them to gather the Rangers weapons too, a pile of plasma pistols and rifles in one corner of the shuttle, but there was no need. The other prisoners had wasted no time in retrieving these.

Dodging past the bound Rangers as they were bundled out of the shuttle, Fleur slid into the pilot's seat. Instantly, she felt at home. Her fingers glided over the flight controls without thinking, before she glanced up at the viewscreen and for the first time saw what sweet Hell was unfolding outside the shuttle.

"Well, that complicates things," said Fleur.

As complications went, a PROXUS battle station was a major one. Three black rings floated around its central black spine, which was as big as a city. This was no different to the battle stations Fleur and Beauregard had served on as PROXUS Rangers under the Empress. However, Tiberius Omega Mining Colony was a PROXUS facility. The battle station should have been hanging watchfully in the shimmering darkness of space as sentry, not invader. Instead, it was looming over them, casting savage blasts of green plasma from thousands of assault cannons bristling along all three of its rings. A melee of glowing green shards spat back and forth across space between the PROXUS battle station and Tiberius Omega Mining Colony. While the shuttle rocked with every heavy impact the prison took, only half-hearted flurries of green plasma flashed from the prison to strike back at the obdurate blue glow of the battle station's shields. It had been over a cycle since the PROXUS civil war had started. Fleur was no closer to understanding it, but she would settle for surviving it.

By the time she flicked the last switch to trigger the shuttle's power-up sequence and pre-flight checks, the bound Rangers had been discarded outside with only a few extra bruises. In their place, the shuttle was crammed with more prisoners than Fleur had imagined possible. Reaching around stray limbs and accidentally elbowing another prisoner in the face, she released the docking clamp and engaged the shuttle's thrusters.

"Are they going to fire at us?" asked an old man whose cheek was being smeared against Fleur's shoulder by the crush of bodies.

"Us? They have every reason to think we are on their side," Fleur reassured him. She was lying, of course. Who in the Empress' name could tell what to shoot at in a civil war when everyone flew the same colours?

She lit up the star drive and hurtled away from the asteroid as fast as the shuttle could go.

CHAPTER SEVEN

Inside the stolen shuttle, Fleur was struggling with the ripe odour of sweat clinging to tired miners who hadn't washed in forever. Not that she let it show. Tolerating the cramped press of freed prisoners with impeccable grace, she calmly announced herself to *Haven*'s duty officer over the comm. A delighted whoop greeted her in response. More importantly, no one shot her down as she flew the shuttle closer to *Haven*.

The first time Fleur had seen *Haven*, she had been terrified. That had been three cycles ago. Before the Sau Daran ship had taken the name *Haven*. Back when they were only a Husk. A dead ship. Now, thanks to Isabella and Paradise Moon, *Haven* was a living ship once more.

The shuttle hurtled towards *Haven*'s glistening sphere of obsidian and silver, which was growing ever more distinct. An outstretched shard here, a grown bubble there. Myriad extensions and additions to their hull. All living metal. Any prisoners who could see the shuttle's viewscreen gasped when they noticed their destination was a Sau Daran ship. Given all the Known Galaxies knew about Sau Darans was that they'd fought a war against them, it was hardly surprising. Even Fleur's companion raised an eyebrow. But *Haven* was more than a living Sau Daran ship. They were Fleur's home. And her friend.

Once Fleur had landed in her usual hangar bay on *Haven*, an eager semi-circle of friendly faces gathered around the shuttle. Squeezing through the escaped prisoners, some spilling out with her through the force of sheer physics, Fleur bounded down the shuttle's ramp and into the arms of the friendliest face who had ever worked for—and then betrayed—PROXUS.

"Find these poor wretches as much food and water as they want, will you?" she asked Dash, after she had managed to peel him off her. "It was a long flight."

Grinning through his long curtain of blonde hair, he chose not to get Fleur's hint and hugged her again with unquenched enthusiasm. She was too exhausted to fight him off. "What happened?" he asked, finally releasing her.

"There are a lot of miners back there."

"Minors?!" Dash's earnest expression ruptured with horror. "Oh, how terrible! Not even children are safe from those PROXUS dpreshes!"

"Miners. As in working in a mine."

"Oh, thank the Empress!" said Dash, cheering up easily. If space wasn't a vacuum, his mood would have changed with the breeze. More prisoners edged down the shuttle's ramp, their joints clicking and tunics hanging off meagre skeletons. His expression soured as he watched. "They still look vented. We'll sort them out."

A smattering of concerned faces stared at Fleur from the rest of her greeting party. "I am fine," she insisted. Gratefully, she accepted a gauntlet from one of them. She tugged it on and with a few taps of its holographic display was logged back into *Haven*'s local comm feed.

Lending an escaped prisoner his shoulder to lean on, Dash invited all the prisoners deeper into *Haven* and towards whatever sanctuary the Sau Daran ship could offer them. The rest of Fleur's crew rushed to help.

As the hangar bay cleared, Fleur noticed her scarred cellmate had remained. She was scrutinising every detail of the living ship with eyes sharpened to a point. Every ridge of the arched ceiling, every jagged rack that grew up the walls for hanging tools and ship parts, every transparent bulge in the walls and ceiling that glowed with ample light to flood the hangar bay.

"First time?" asked Fleur. It was a safe bet. Barely anyone in the Known Galaxies had seen a living Sau Daran ship since the war, let alone stepped aboard. The other escaped prisoners hadn't let their awe or fear hold them back from the promise of a solid meal and hopefully a wash, but Fleur's cellmate was taking her time to absorb everything. Nothing went unprocessed or unlogged, except perhaps Fleur's question.

As soon as Fleur had shown her new companion to a private room and told her how everything on *Haven* worked, she excused herself. Swiftly, she waved at the console on the wall to shut her companion's door. Finally alone, she collapsed against the corridor, closed her eyes with an exhausted sigh, then keyed the comm on her borrowed gauntlet. With it, she set up an open channel with Ezra, Beauregard and Braga. "I will be in my quarters. Quit hiding and come say hello."

"Oh it's so good to have you back!" Ezra cried over the comm. Every syllable swelled with relief. "I'll be along now. Thank the Empress you're home."

Gently, Fleur stroked the corridor's curved, corrugated wall. "It is good to be home," she whispered to the ship.

In response, the wall warmed to her touch. Then the corridor creaked and groaned into motion. It needn't have moved at all—Fleur's personal quarters would already be creaking and groaning towards her—but if *Haven* was anything, they were kind. Moving corridor and quarters until both were united would return her with optimal speed, minimal wait. Typical *Haven*. Fleur gave the corridor's wall another caress to signal her gratitude.

If one perk of calling a living ship home was the lack of commuting, another perk was that a living ship grew. Not just outwards like the shard-shaped shield arrays and comms relays she had seen on her approach in the shuttle, but everything inside *Haven* as well. It helped that *Haven* was a generous ship. After Fleur, Ezra and Beauregard had helped Isabella bring *Haven* back to life, one of the first non-critical growths the ship initiated had been personal quarters for her core crew. *Haven* must have observed them first to learn how humans needed private spaces of their own, as well as methods of cleaning, resting, eating and socialising. Having gathered data about their crew, *Haven* had grown them—and eventually everyone else—exactly what they needed. The ship's systems grew moisture and waste recycling systems to remove whatever the humans produced that wasn't wanted, breaking it down with a cocktail of chemicals no PROXUS scientist would ever get their head around before developing a migraine, then returning it as basic raw materials for humans to live on *Haven*. Fleur tried not to think about it too much at dinner time, but it kept their merry band of fugitives safe to roam deep space without hunger driving them into unnecessary supply runs and raids.

Zombie-shuffling from the relocated corridor into her relocated quarters, Fleur let her usually composed face collapse into a stupid grin. Her body hit the bedsheet with all the force of *Haven*'s artificial gravity behind it. Nothing had ever felt better. The fabric was a coarse military fibre from a PROXUS supply ship they had borrowed from—at gunpoint—a couple of cycles ago.

Some necessities *Haven* couldn't grow. But it was ultimately better than a PROXUS mining prison and, even better, it smelled of home. And Braga.

Fleur keyed her comm. "Your wife is home and about to take a shower. In case this is unclear, that was a hint."

Braga's signal evaded her gauntlet's transmitter for now. Too tired to investigate, Fleur tapped a short sequence on her gauntlet's holographic symbols to preserve her message on Braga's comm. The message would be waiting for her, although if she waited too long her wife wouldn't be.

Finally able to enjoy the shower she had promised herself and her absent wife, Fleur took her time washing all traces of captivity from her body. They disappeared down the refresher unit's waste reclaimer and began their journey through *Haven*'s recycling system, as eager for cleansing and renewal as Fleur.

Content in the embrace of her own clothes, if not her wife, Fleur lay back on their bed. Above her, a holo of her and Braga riding moonwhales on Eigis Ryval played on a loop. The day of their wedding—Braga's blue hair wet and salty and slicked back against her scalp, Fleur's afro enjoying its own joyride. Laughter danced easily from their lips amid exuberant explosions of ocean spray.

A weighty knock with plenty of fist behind it echoed through the oval door to Fleur's quarters. Without giving Fleur time to accept or decline, the door rolled away to reveal Ezra staring up at her. *Haven* was generous, and she was most generous to her favourites. Above all, Ezra.

As always, he wore an earnest expression and loose-fitting tunic. The tunic covered him down to his thighs—below that, there was none of him left to cover. His legs ended too soon, stumps beneath the draped fabric. The cost of bad luck, Fleur had told him. The cost of heroism, Beauregard had claimed. Or, as Ezra unerringly preached every few rotations to anyone who would listen, the cost of being young and self-righteous with a plasma pistol in his hand and everything to prove raging in his heart.

Ezra lingered inside the doorway to Fleur's quarters. Behind him, the corridor was gone. Instead, he had emerged from a deep chamber lit by a huge glowing crystal at its heart. This was either *Haven*'s battery (if you were Braga or Beauregard) or soul (if you were Ezra or Fleur). Either way, it was what kept *Haven* alive, and how Isabella and Paradise Moon had given the Husk renewed life. Ezra rarely left this chamber. Fleur often found him with his palms pressed against the crystal, words and images passing between him and *Haven* in a conversation that had spanned three cycles already. They could have spoken using the neural implant *Haven* had grown for Ezra and inserted into his inner ear. Sometimes they did, but he preferred the crystal. Fleur wondered what a Sau Daran ship and an ex-PROXUS Apprentice Ranger had to talk about, but whatever it was had had a profound effect on the young man. In all that time, he hadn't lifted a plasma pistol once.

Fleur bent to embrace him. His smile was wan and wonky, his dark hair dishevelled, his skin pallid, but his hug was as warm as it had ever been. Once she pulled away, Fleur noticed how Ezra's dewy eyes couldn't help but dwell—more than once—on the impressions the prison had made on her skin. Scars and bruises best left ignored. Shuffling beneath his straining forearms as they took his weight one push at a time, he hauled his body back into the crystal chamber.

His slow, grunting progress brought him to a low-lying rack of living metal. On it, an array of prosthetics waited for him. Most were legs that came with a boot pre-fitted, while others were a curved L-shape made from low-grade synthetic material on Earth. Blades, Isabella called them. That Ezra had all these prosthetics was thanks to her. Being outlaws, points were tight for *Haven*'s crew. Meanwhile, Isabella could get anything they needed, provided Earth had the technology. Such were the benefits of being a planet-saving celebrity. Although Fleur would have preferred a more high-tech prosthetic from a PROXUS hub world, outlaws couldn't be choosers.

Distractedly, Ezra's fingers fell upon the most comfortable of his prosthetics, but he didn't lift it off the rack yet. "We were so worried," he tried to tell her. Only he didn't say it that easily. It took him many more words—gushing, self-interrupting.

"No need to worry," Fleur assured him. She followed him inside, her hand tenderly finding his shoulder as he paused for breath. "Now, time is wasting. Where is that old lump of meat who calls himself a gunslinger and where is my wife?"

Ezra looked stunned. "They came back with you."

"No, why would they be with me?"

"Why wouldn't they be with you? They left here on the shuttle you just came in on."

"What?!"

By the time they were done talking, Fleur was doing everything she could to hide her panic. Luckily, her face was used to it. No doubt her expression was as serene as ever, while she struggled to make sense of the latest mess they were in—and how in the Empress' name they were going to climb out of it.

"Whatever you're thinking, don't," Ezra insisted. "It'll be fine. We'll get them back." Okay, so maybe she wasn't hiding her panic as well as she thought.

Both their comms pinged. Fleur answered first. She was still wearing her gauntlet, whereas Ezra's lay discarded beside the crystal and that was a long way for him to collect it.

Dash was at the other end of the comm. A small cargo hauler was approaching *Haven* and hailing them.

"What do they want?" Fleur asked over the comm. She didn't have the time or patience for this—whatever this was.

Dash didn't know much, but what he did know he told her fast. The ship was small and no match for *Haven*. It couldn't store nearly enough soldiers or firepower to make a dent, let alone knock their rotation off its axis.

"Did you scan it for explosive devices?" she asked.

"*Haven* already has," Ezra interjected. So while she'd been speaking to Dash, he'd been speaking to *Haven* on his neural implant. "They said it came up clean. Maybe it's Beauregard or Braga?"

Fleur shook her head. If it was either of those two troublemakers, she would have been overjoyed. But it couldn't be. If they had been taken hostage, the approaching ship would have at least named them. Or there would have been some telltale indications those two were involved. Like explosions.

"Well, ignoring them is not an option," Fleur decided. "They are here now and they clearly want something."

"Could be they have work for us?" Dash suggested.

Fleur smiled at his blind optimism. "Well, any work would be welcome." Operating in the grey areas outside the law of PROXUS had become even harder once the civil war began. The Known Galaxies were too volatile. Any work that came their way seemed liable to get them killed, but they took whatever they could get. Offers were scarce, points scarcer. "Okay, give them somewhere to land. Anywhere they can do the least amount of damage."

Fleur used *Haven*'s room rearranging trick to gather reliable members of her crew. She wished Dash could join them. He was good in a fight, but she needed him in the cockpit of his Scimitar, ready to blast their unexpected guests into stardust and slag if they tried anything. But even without Dash, she had plenty of gun arms to rely on. Trusted crewmates gathered on either side of her as the cargo hauler drifted inside the hangar bay's anti-vac shield. It was a tired, battered ship. Small enough to be run by a tiny crew—ten at most—but with a captain who likely filled every molecule of space on board with goods to sell and trade.

Fleur's previous cellmate was beside her. She looked as sharp as ever and keen to assist, despite her stint in a PROXUS prison. She carried a borrowed plasma pistol and Fleur couldn't ignore how easily she held it. Without tension, but with plenty of familiarity.

Ezra stood ready on Fleur's other flank, although she wasn't entirely sure what he was ready for. She noted the blades he had donned, but those were only good for running. His hands were empty—and she knew better than to offer him a spare plasma pistol. She didn't doubt Ezra could still shoot straight, but nothing had yet persuaded him there was another gunbattle left inside him. He had sworn off violence ever since the events three cycles ago, which had begun with his massacre of Sau Daran engineers in the Outer Rim and ended with far more dead PROXUS soldiers than in their darkest nightmares. Defending himself against PROXUS Rangers and the Empress' murderous Silver Fists was one thing, but killing a defenceless outpost of Sau Daran engineers was something else entirely. Indoctrinated from birth by the Empress' lies, Ezra had done everything he had been trained to do when he found that outpost. He would likely spend the rest of his life recovering.

The cargo hauler's rear end split open like a blossoming flower, separating from its centre into three opening doors—one rising, the other two yawning open to either side. A man emerged, young enough to be

Fleur's junior and sporting a vibrant explosion of beard, but old enough to carry more than a few scars and one fewer eye than was traditional. He stood in the shadow of his ship and gave his welcoming party an ugly grin.

Fleur didn't even blink at his appearance—living was tough in deep space, and some of the hardest spacers in the Outer Rim were among the softest souls she had done business with. Still, she kept one eye on the plasma pistol stowed across his chest in a cross-draw holster.

"Name and cargo?" asked Fleur, respecting protocol.

Their visitor spat on the deck, which wasn't exactly against protocol but was a black mark against anyone's name on a living ship. "Captain Daedalus Thorn," he announced with an unmistakably posh Xarrish accent. "We have slaves," he added as an afterthought.

The atmosphere dialled up from wary to hostile. Safeties on plasma weapons clicked off. Teeth ground. The welcome party became an increasingly unwelcome party, glaring hotter than a plasma blast.

"Leave," Fleur told him. "We do not trade for slaves."

"But we can't just leave them," Ezra insisted.

There was a lot Fleur wanted to say to Ezra in that moment. About how much she agreed. About how she couldn't attack a trader—even a filthy slave trader—after she had granted him safe passage to land. But mainly about how Ezra was the only person in the hangar bay without a weapon, which was the only persuasive means scum like Thorn respected.

Instead, Fleur held up a hand to forestall any further protests from her crew. "Let me rephrase," she suggested to Thorn, who hadn't moved. "Leave quickly."

Raising his hands in surrender, Thorn grinned something ugly again. "Now hold on, you haven't seen our cargo."

"We do not need to. Trust me on this," Fleur led him with her eyes to the arsenal of plasma weapons poised on either side of her. "You do not want us to see your cargo. You came in peace and if you want to leave in peace, now is your only chance."

Thorn's hands settled on his hips, leaving one far closer to his plasma pistol than Fleur was comfortable with. "Well that's a real shame, because she asked for you especially. Led us right here."

"Asked for us?" said Ezra.

"Led you here?" said Fleur.

Thorn tapped a glowing icon above his gauntlet and more of his crew sauntered out of the cargo hauler. Their plasma weapons were very much holstered but still very much there. Among the newcomers—Fleur counted eight—was a lone woman being watched warily by their visitors as they spread into the hangar bay. Her head was concealed within a black synthetic bag. Fleur's heart melted in disappointment, then hardened to ice. This woman was not Braga. Her arms and legs were too thin, her build too slight. But whether Fleur knew her or not, she was still a slave and Thorn was still a slaver. They had seen the slave now. She was real and she was here. And that was... complicated.

The visitors stopped the woman in the middle of their own impromptu circle by pulling on a leash fastened around her neck. She jerked to a halt, but resisted any urge to raise her restrained hands to her gasping throat—if anyone could preserve their dignity with a bag thrown over their head, she was managing it.

"How did you know where to find us?" Fleur asked the bound slave. There was enough authority in her voice to remind Thorn she was still in charge, but enough tenderness to hopefully show the bound and blindfolded slave that Fleur was on her side.

Thorn shook his head. "Points first, then you talk."

Ezra, who these rotations was usually the placid one, was practically snarling. "We don't buy slaves," he warned Thorn. "We free them."

There was Thorn's ugly grin again. "You're welcome to try. Can't imagine that would make you too popular with my clan." He pulled aside his sleeve to reveal a red tattoo of a vitraxi's snarling jaw on his forearm. Fleur had heard of pirates becoming involved in slaving, but as an ex-pirate she hadn't wanted to believe it. She knew the clan sigil—it was from one of the bigger pirate clans. Oh what shame she would have felt if that had been her clan. Her sigil. Even her father would have been ashamed, and that was saying something.

Fleur signalled for her crew to lower their weapons. Reluctantly, muzzles nudged towards the floor and fingers eased off triggers, but only slightly.

"We respect you arrived under a truce. If this woman directed you here believing we would pay you to set her free, she must have a reason. I will hear it, and if I agree with her then the points will be yours."

"But they're slavers!" Ezra's fist was balled up tight. He might not be willing to take another life, but the fight inside him still burned hot.

Thorn ripped off the black hood with a flourish and tossed it aside. Only Fleur hid her shock and stifled the same gasp as those echoing around her.

They were staring at the most recognisable face in the Known Galaxies. Her ashen hair was burned by a streak of crimson locks down one side. Her face was old, but not as old as it should have been given her reported age. Her eyes were colder than the desolate edges of space. Fleur had to give it to her, despite being surrounded by slavers who wanted to sell her and fugitives who wanted to kill her, the Empress of the Known Galaxies was demonstrating glacial calm.

"How did you know we were here?" asked Ezra.

The Empress' stiff, disinterested expression didn't thaw. "Pay the man."

Inwardly, Fleur fought every temptation to shoot a defenceless woman. Outwardly, she carefully wrapped her mouth around the first ever words she had spoken to the Empress of the Known Galaxies. "Get. Locked."

"Along with my intel?" Her eyes were as calculating as her face was impassive.

Fleur holstered her plasma pistol and addressed Thorn. "You have nothing I want. Slavery is too good for her. Take her back."

"You said—" Thorn began, but the Empress silenced him with a glare more deadly than any plasma pistol.

"Pay these wretches," the Empress ordered Fleur. "Afterwards, when I am relaxing in the comfort of your delightful Sau Daran lair, I shall not only tell you how I found you, but how to defeat PROXUS and save your miserable lives."

"We are not freedom fighters," said Fleur. "Get the Resistance on the comm if you want to defeat PROXUS."

The Empress clicked her tongue in irritation. "Any freedom fighters I knew the location of died the moment I found out. Now hurry up and pay the man."

A single plasma shot echoed through the hangar bay.

Fleur had sensed the plasma pistol moving to her right as it was raised and, instinctively, her palm had arrived in time to parry the barrel high enough for the blast to only singe the Empress' hair instead of melting her face.

Before Fleur could draw her next breath, it suddenly became fashionable to be aiming a weapon. Everyone, apart from Ezra, was doing it. Her crew. The slavers. Even the Empress' icy glare looked weaponised. Twitching nervously, plasma pistols and rifles jerked unfired from target to target, figuring out who to shoot first. No one seemed to find an answer, but everyone looked close to taking a guess.

A great deal closer to picking her target than anyone else, Fleur pressed her pistol into her former cellmate's gut. "Don't make me fire this."

Her former cellmate didn't struggle against Fleur's other hand, which still held the barrel of the plasma pistol she had fired at the slave. Her livid face swung round, and finally Fleur saw it. Behind the plasma burns that had destroyed her face and burned off her hair. The same posture. The same physique. The same frigid glare when she didn't instantly get her own way.

A second Empress.

CHAPTER EIGHT

Isabella was exhausted, but sleep was for other people. She needed answers from Talyn. And she needed to banish the dying light of the Azores. With the conifered hillside now smeared the colour of charcoal, she was more likely to trip on a tree root than find the answers she needed.

Returning to her fourth country in as many hours, Isabella leant on the convenience of a purple smoked retreat and hoped Talyn wouldn't vomit again.

The New York diner hit them with vibrant, post-work energy. Jukebox music from another time. Steaming jugs of coffee and trays of tall beers. Warmth cocooned against pale, frosty windows. The far-off sizzle of grease a high note against the clink of plates and cutlery. The dull muddle of conversation from every table, every booth, along the counter.

Their arrival caught a handful of new customers off-guard, but what were a few broken glasses and spilt beers between fans? Isabella waved a greeting to the young and spritely Sallyann, who always took her order straight away and guarded Isabella's booth with her life. Sallyann rushed over to Isabella, the bobble on her Santa hat dancing with every eager step.

Three coffees and half a plateful of fries and hamburger later, Talyn still hadn't been sick. He had an impressive appetite, and Earth food seemed to agree with him. It must have been better than whatever he ate on his ship, anyway.

"How long has Nova Sky been inside you?" Isabella asked as Talyn took another bite of his burger. She was still building up to the big question. The showstopper. The answer to how they were going to save every Sau Daran who had ever lived. And ever died.

"Not long," he said through a mouthful of bread and patty. "You?"

Where do I start?

With how awesome I am. Obviously.

Isabella grinned stupidly from behind the half-eaten hamburger clutched in her hybrid human and purple-glowing grip. She was still overwhelmed with unfamiliar delight at meeting someone else with an alien trapped inside them. Absolutely wired on coffee and lack of sleep, she launched easily into a highlights reel of memories she never finished telling. Almost immediately, she was scratching the itch to ask her own questions and interrupted herself. "What do you mean not long? Mine's been with me all my life. Do you get on? We're pretty up and down. What's he like? Is he a he? Mine's a she."

Talyn rushed to swallow too much burger without chewing. "I've never met anyone like me either, so I don't know what's normal." He paused to actually chew, then even longer to pick his words. "Nova Sky is a he, but I can't tell you much about him. He needed a volunteer for this mission, so here I am."

"You volunteered?" She grinned. Again. Like she was some kind of grin factory and he kept pulling her lever. Whatever that meant. "You're cool."

Talyn put the back of his hand against his cheek and shrugged. "I don't feel cold."

Isabella could literally feel Paradise Moon rolling her eyes. "I mean you're awesome! Some alien—"

—God—

"—tells you he can save a whole species you've never met and you just volunteer. We call that hero shit."

"Hero… shit?"

"No, like this." Pumped up on too many coffees, if that was even a real number, Isabella spread out her arms and crowed with glee. "Hero shit, baby!"

As numerous eyes in the diner turned towards them, Talyn's eyes smouldered with a self-righteous pride that Isabella recognised far too well. "It was the right thing to do, that's all."

The universe was a big place, but despite her abilities Isabella had struggled to find many people with the power and will to do the right thing. Often, it felt like doing the right thing was always left for someone else. For the last three years, she had tried to be that someone else. And now she found herself staring at another someone else, who also happened to have the dreamiest eyes and a physique that usually required a slab of marble and the greatest sculptors armed with the finest chisels.

"One sec." Isabella swept her phone from her pocket and pinged Agent Glass a quick text to let him know Talyn was safe. The phone disappeared back into her pocket, then came back out again as she sent another text saying she'd never help him again if he tried to abduct Talyn. "So you're telling me Nova Sky's never taken control of you?" asked Isabella.

Talyn's face grew cagey. "Why would he do that? We want the same thing."

I don't know, why would he do that?

How about so I could save your life?

"Well, it keeps things interesting," Isabella admitted with another smile. They paused for Isabella to take selfies with a cluster of teens in signed VANISHING GIRL tees that Sallyann sold behind the counter. They clustered around her booth, excitedly gushing and preening. It felt amazing to show off her followers in front of Talyn. "Fans," Isabella explained casually.

Talyn watched them totter off accompanied by the sort of giggling only a group of teenage girls could conjure. "They love you, don't they? You're so confident with them. I'd be too embarrassed."

Showing zero decorum, Isabella smugly screwed up her face in a way that would have made her body language coach need a lie down. "They're just fans. When you can do what we can, everyone wants a bit of you."

"Really?" Talyn asked with genuine concern. "Which bit of me do they want?"

Isabella laughed. "It's just a saying." Although now she came to think of it, she had a few suggestions.

The diner's strung-up Christmas lights flickered nervously above them. "I can keep all my bits?" he asked.

Isabella leaned across the table to take his hand and reassure him that, yes, he could keep all his bits, but she chickened out before her hand was even halfway across the table. Diverting, she downed her coffee instead. "I didn't mean it literally. It's fine. Your bits are all yours. No ritual sacrifices, I promise."

Then she realised she had been a heartbeat from holding his hand and was talking about his bits. With slow shyness, her hand crept into her lap. Learning to survive the centre of attention was one thing, but relationships were a whole other worry. Craftily, her glowing purple hand crept unbidden towards Talyn's.

Don't you dare! If you hold his hand, you're not getting a whole day in control.

The purple hand made its own sudden detour and stole one of Talyn's surviving chips instead. Beside her, Sallyann topped up her juice. Isabella shook her head at the offer of a fourth coffee.

"Do you talk to each other?" asked Isabella, her human hand creeping up her neck and tangling through her short hair.

Again, Talyn looked cagey. "Why?"

She explained her situation with Paradise Moon, embellishing on the highlights she had already shared and focussing on their most heroic moments. Talyn listened. The corners of his lips creased. His eyes shone. Blue eyes, sparkling like an unblemished ocean. Echoes of lightning in a radiant fragment of cloud. A perfect glacier floating serenely over—

—Isabella realised she had finished talking, and Talyn had taken over, his lips still moving. But she hadn't been listening. She wondered how long her head had been elsewhere. Too long. As she wondered, she missed the end of his reply too. Ignorant of whatever he had said, she nodded with a confidence she didn't feel.

"I'm glad you agree," said Talyn. "That's why I had to come here, although I'd planned a better landing."

You didn't listen to a word of that, did you?

Do a girl a solid. What did he say?

And you wonder why I take control? While you were fantasising about your stone-cold space hottie, he admitted he's too good to be true.

Why, what did I miss?

You're unbelievable.

Please?

Everyone on his planet lives with Nova Sky. They worship him. When Nova Sky found a way to save the Sau Darans, he needed someone like

Talyn to help. So, you know, it's not like you missed anything important.

Someone like Talyn?

Someone with a body to donate.

How does that work? You can't leave my body until I die.

Exactly. They take worshipping their Sau Daran god very seriously.

But that's suicide!

Only after they save every Sau Daran.

So when he said he volunteered…

He gave up his body. Sounds like an idiot.

Worry was spreading over Talyn's face. "Are you okay? You've gone quiet."

"Sorry, alien issues." She pointed at her head and rolled her eyes.

He smiled back. Despite the cuts and bruises surrounding it, he had a cute smile and she liked how it made her feel. "Did I say something wrong?"

"No, it's just an internal debate." Isabella brushed his concerns aside with a casual wave of her hand that sent her glass of juice flying across the table. Three years ago, she would have blushed with embarrassment. Instead, she laughed it off without forgetting to tilt her head to present Talyn with her best profile—just like her body language coach had taught her. Hidden behind her convincing smile was a familiar shadow of dread. A terror she kept at bay by never looking back, never doubting herself, never slowing down to think. Her eyes staring forever only ahead.

Shifting uncomfortably in his seat, Talyn watched Sallyann wipe down the table. "It must be so strange having another voice inside your head."

Isabella shrugged. "It's normal when it's all you've ever known." She didn't add how gutting it was that Talyn didn't know what it was like. Couldn't talk to his alien anymore. Finally, she thought she had found someone who understood. Trust her to be stuck with the only delinquent, overly talkative alien in the universe. "What happened next?"

"After I let Nova inside me? He shared images of a device he calls the Spark. I need to find it."

You ever heard of this Spark thing?

Not a clue, but I did have half of me ripped out of you that one time. I've been foggy on a lot of details since then.

"Okay," said Isabella, "I'm listening." And she meant it. "Tell me everything."

Talyn's answer was long enough for Isabella to finish her burger. However, it only grew colder as she listened in rapt silence. She was listening so carefully she even ignored the girl who sidled over for an autograph. Paradise Moon picked up the spare, using a glowing purple hand to produce a flamboyant scribble on her VANISHING GIRL baseball cap along with a conspiratorial wink of purple-flecked chestnut. Isabella barely noticed. If Talyn was to be believed, Nova Sky really could save the whole Sau Daran species. Not only the scattered survivors in hiding. Everyone. Every single Sau Daran who had died in the war. Every Husk. Every dead engineer. Every dead soldier. Every dead scout. Every dead envoy. All Nova Sky needed was for Talyn to find a device that had been left on Earth.

The Spark.

"So?" asked Talyn. "Can you help?"

"Tell me what you need. I'm all yours."

"Seriously?"

"Seriously. Why was the Spark even here?"

"It's supposed to give life," said Talyn.

"How? And seriously, why is it here? Earth's as far away from the Known Galaxies as it's possible to be."

"Doesn't Moon know?"

Can I tell him what happened? Why you know jack shit?
Sure, go ahead.
"We met some Sau Darans once. They meant well, but they sort of tried to kill us. They tore Paradise Moon apart, taking most of her memories."

Talyn shook his head. "Sau Darans would never do that to anyone, especially a god."
See! He said god! He gets it.
"How do you know?"

"Back home, Nova told us stories," he replied defensively. "Sau Darans are just innocent explorers."

"Don't get me wrong—I don't blame them. Violence and war do things to you," she admitted soberly. Another shadow crept behind her expression, but she didn't let it show. Feeling its darkness settle unseen, she pushed it deeper until she told herself she couldn't feel it anymore. "Being a survivor means enduring loss. Being broken comes with the territory."

Innocence shone in Talyn's eyes, unblemished and endearing. "That's a very negative view of the universe."

Isabella's expression grew colder. "It's a view." Talyn opened his mouth to reply, no doubt with something charmingly naïve, but Isabella jumped in first. "Now, weren't you about to explain why the Spark is on Earth, as the alien—"
—God—
"—inside me doesn't remember?" Isabella leaned across the table. "We want to help."

Sitting up straighter, Talyn's eyes drifted around the diner. "Okay. There are obviously these gods inside you and me, from this other universe."

Isabella nodded. "Been there."

Talyn blinked back his shock. "You've *been* there?"

"This was, like, just before that universe died."

"Seriously? How is that even possible?"

Would you quit interrupting? I'd really like to hear what he's got to say.

"Long story," said Isabella, "I'll tell you all about it. But it's not important right now. How do we save everyone?"

Talyn's face rearranged itself as he clawed back all the thoughts he had lost with her revelation. "So, in the beginning these gods gave the Sau Darans life using this thing called the Spark."

"And that's what you're searching for?"

Talyn shook his head. "No, that was what they used in their universe to create the Sau Darans."

No more interruptions! Seriously, you're even pissing him off and this kid's basically Gandhi.

"Before that," said Talyn, pushing on, "their ancestors made another Spark. A prototype. Some of them left their universe with the Spark to create life in this one as a test. They never returned."

"And *that's* the Spark you're searching for?"

Talyn nodded.

"A different Spark to the one that created the Sau Darans? One that created life in this universe?"

Talyn nodded again.

Isabella's face wrinkled uncomfortably as she wrapped her mouth around words she'd rather not say. "So, I hate to keep asking this, but… Why would it be on Earth?"

"There are humans all over this universe, so the Spark clearly worked."

"Wait, Sau Daran gods created humans?"

Haha! In your face!

"Nova reckons the gods who brought the Spark to this universe would have used it on each suitable planet they found. Nova said the Spark didn't actually create humans. It just started them off and gave evolution the nudges and support it needed so humans always ended up how the gods wanted."

Sounds convincing. I'm not only a Sau Daran god—I'm a human god!

Oh god.

Exactly! Behold, for it is me!

Isabella's lips stumbled over an avalanche of false starts. *Oh shut up.*

That's 'oh shut up, God'.

You're going to be more insufferable than ever, aren't you?

Talyn ploughed on. "Once humans were far enough along in their evolution on one planet, the gods were supposed to move the Spark on to the next planet, and then the next... Nova said they would have finished on the least advanced planet in the universe, the planet that had had the least time for humans to evolve. Well they didn't get all the way to the other side of the universe, but the planet with humans on that's farthest out—"

"—is Earth," Isabella finished for him.

Talyn stared at her intently, divine purpose burning behind his eyes. "Nova said we'll save them all if the Spark's still here. We just need to find it."

"And you trust Nova Sky?"

"Why shouldn't I?"

Because, as gods go, we're a bunch of untrustworthy egoists who when things got tough abandoned at least one species we created. Two, if he's telling the truth...

...was not what Isabella said. "Okay. How do you want to do this?"

"I asked the phones on the train, but your planet has never heard of the Spark."

"Okay, so we work the problem. Where do you need to go to get the information you need?"

"Well, the Spark would have been left here at the start of this planet's evolution of humans. So we need to find somewhere very, very old."

Impulsively, Isabella grabbed Talyn's hand before she could convince herself this was a bad idea. His skin felt smooth. Gentle. Cool against her skin.

Purple smoke.

Gone.

Ornate stone arches glowed under cold spotlights, stretching over Isabella and Talyn towards a mesmerising ceiling of glass, stone and iron. A skeletal head hung above them, while nearby a jigsaw of black bones belonging to a grand, prehistoric creature had been carefully arranged on a wooden plinth. Isabella's second sunset of the day bled through the glass ceiling, dousing them and the dinosaur.

"How is this for old?" she asked, her voice echoing back at her in the museum's deserted entrance. She peered at the sign next to the dinosaur. "This big chap's late Jurassic, apparently. And a Barosaurus. Is 155 to 145 million years old enough for you and your mission?"

"It's not quite what I expected," Talyn admitted. He wandered across the entrance, peering at a smaller dinosaur beside the Barosaurus. "I asked you to take me to the oldest place on your planet and you took me where, exactly?"

"New York's Natural History Museum. This *is* where you were headed on the train, right?"

"Which is how old?"

"Well, actually some of the exhibits—"

Talyn's eyes flared with flecks of electric blue, in much the same fashion as Isabella's did when they burned purple and Paradise Moon took control. He cut her off with a raised hand, as though silencing a child. "This isn't a game, dpresh. I came to this planet to save an entire species. Don't waste my time."

Did he just shush you?

I think he did.

With his hand?

Yep.

"You were already going here when I picked you up," Isabella pointed out. "And I've been here before, so I know it has some great exhibits *and* a fantastic gift shop."

You really need to work on your boasts to visitors from other planets.

"I was only going here because it was next to where they locked me up. I can't just teleport anywhere—unlike some people." Snarling, Talyn crossed his thick arms over his chest. "I thought you were going to take me somewhere more sensible."

"Only places, things or people I've visited before," Isabella insisted. "That's all. And you're welcome."

Talyn rubbed his head. He was swaying. "Sorry, I don't know why I said those things. It's not... that's not me. I'm not usually like that, I'm sorry."

"Are you okay?"

"Fine, really. What am I here to do again?"

"Read," Isabella told him firmly.

But Talyn didn't read. Instead, he collapsed.

With a flash of purple smoke, Isabella deleted the distance between them. She caught him before his head cracked against the marble floor. Gently, she helped him down and rolled him into the recovery position. Once again, she was holding him in her arms. Fresh blood crept from old wounds, staining her fingers.

"Shit."

CHAPTER NINE

Amazingly, no one was dead. Not yet, anyway. Fleur wasn't sure how long that would last. As always, she fell back on the calm embrace of logic to dispel her next catastrophic panic attack before anyone else guessed it was incoming. She sorted through each problem, ranking them in order of most likely to kill her and her crew.

Problem one: Slavers were aiming plasma pistols at them. Their captive had just been shot at and they looked angry enough to start firing back.

Problem two: Her crew were just as nervous as the slavers and just as ready to start shooting.

Problem three: The woman beside her was the Empress of the Known Galaxies. She had been imprisoned on a PROXUS mining facility, a fate no one was meant to return from, and she had gone to great lengths to hide her identity. Not insignificantly, Fleur had given her a plasma pistol.

Problem four: The slavers' captive was *also* the Empress of the Known Galaxies. And the Empress next to her had tried to murder the slavers' Empress.

Problem five: Seeing two Empresses was giving Fleur a headache.

She swiftly resolved problem five by designating the captive as the Slave Empress and the woman beside her as the Burned Empress. Crude but clear. Her first problem down and no one was dead yet. Problems one and two threatened the same likely outcome—everyone got shot. No matter how important her other problems, they would feel secondary to dying once the plasma started flying. Making problems one and two her priority, Fleur kept her plasma pistol pressed into the Burned Empress' gut.

"Will you stop that!" chided the Burned Empress. "We're on the same side."

Ignoring her, Fleur addressed the slavers. "This woman is not on my side. She is not a member of my crew. We will deal with her."

The slavers' plasma pistols jerked from target to target. Thorn glared at Fleur. "She's on your ship and she attacked us."

Fleur gestured with her free hand at the Slave Empress. "No, she attacked her. And I stopped her, so let us deal with it."

"Stopped her?" Thorn waved his plasma pistol at the new parting of singed hair the Slave Empress had been given. "She was this close to killing our cargo."

"Cargo?" echoed Ezra. "She might be an ice-cold murderous dpresh, but she's still a person." He was the only unarmed person in the hangar bay, but he brandished his self-righteousness like a plasma cannon.

"Person? In the case of the Empress, that is debateable," Fleur said guardedly. "But you are right. Sort of." She glanced at Thorn imploringly. "No one needs to die this rotation."

Thorn jabbed the Slave Empress with his pistol. "Spoiled merchandise. We'll never get as many points for her now."

"She is still the Empress of the Known Galaxies. No one else can make that claim." Somehow, Fleur kept a straight face. "I am sure PROXUS will give you fair points for her."

"Fair points!" Thorn snorted. "Look, you dumb dpresh, we tried selling her to PROXUS already. Had to star leap outta there halfway through negotiations before they atomised us."

Fleur was impressed he even knew the word 'atomised', let alone could use it in a sentence without getting a nosebleed, then she remembered his accent and the fancy upbringing he had likely left behind. Fleur could guess their problem with selling the Slave Empress, but she hoped she was wrong. It didn't stretch Fleur's disbelief to imagine there was a third Empress out there. A third Empress who wanted the rest of her dead.

"She says you're the only person who'll buy her," insisted Thorn, as though this was Fleur's fault.

Fleur eyed the Slave Empress warily. "Why would I pay points for you? I am a fugitive. You want me dead." But she recognised the same contempt in the Slave Empress' expression as she'd seen on the Burned Empress when Fleur dug her plasma pistol into her gut.

"PROXUS wants you dead, I want to survive," the Slave Empress informed her frostily. "Clearly those interests don't currently align. Do keep up."

Fleur smiled disarmingly, although sadly not in any literal sense. "Get her off my ship. We will let you fly out of here if you go now and go quietly."

The Burned Empress' face flushed with anger. "Don't be foolish. You can't let her live, she's too dangerous."

Fleur raised an eyebrow. "She is too dangerous? And that is coming from you?"

"Yes," snapped the Burned Empress. "Trust me."

The slavers hadn't moved, but Fleur could see their appetite for a fight waning. "Safe passage out of here," she reminded Thorn. "No hard feelings."

The Slave Empress clicked her tongue in irritation. "Dpresh, stop being ridiculous and pay the man his points. I knew how to find you, remember. Do I have to spell it out?"

Fleur hadn't remembered. She had been too distracted by the most feared individual in the Known Galaxies being on *Haven* twice at the same time. And both were angry at her. "We know how to hide from PROXUS," Fleur assured the Slave Empress.

"But not from me."

"Kill her!" raged the Burned Empress. "She's bluffing."

For the first time, the Slave Empress graced the Burned Empress with a look so cold it wouldn't have thawed in the heart of a star. "We," said the Slave Empress most deliberately, "never bluff."

"Who else knows how to find *Haven*?" asked Fleur.

The Slave Empress smiled wide enough to send a chill through every cell in Fleur's body. "Only myself and one other. That should be enough to make you pay the points. Go on. Get on with it."

Fleur amended her problem matrix. The dpresh had her. If someone else out there could find them, Fleur had to know who it was—and how. The lives of *Haven* and her crew depended on it.

Thorn held out his gauntlet.

As Fleur tapped hers against it and data transferred between them, her jaw almost tightened in annoyance at the sum—the slave Empress did not come cheap. But life as a fugitive had meant a galaxy of hard choices, which followed hard choices she had made as a PROXUS

Ranger and, before that, as a space pirate. Life had never been easy. She punched a code into her gauntlet, selected an emergency account. What were emergency accounts for if not emergencies? Two Empresses on *Haven* certainly qualified.

As soon as the points transfer was confirmed, the slavers couldn't leave fast enough. Once Thorn had transferred the code for the Slave Empress' restraints, they were no more than another glint in the starscape.

"They're off sensors," Dash reported from his starfighter. "They've made a star leap out of the system."

"Thank you, Dash. Get inside so we can do the same." Firstly, Fleur pointed at the Burned Empress. "Take her weapon and lock her in a cell." Unsurprised, the Burned Empress handed over her plasma pistol and calmly allowed herself to be led away. Secondly, Fleur pointed at the Slave Empress. "Her too. Keep her restraints on."

As the crew filed out, Fleur exchanged an exhausted glance with Ezra. "Well, no one died this time."

"Yeah, but those odds always go up when Beauregard and Braga aren't here."

She gave Ezra a sliver of a smile. As much as she loved them, that pair were regrettably talented at generating a steep body count.

"What now?" asked Ezra.

Fleur took her deepest breath in cycles. She was too afraid to think about her problem matrix. She tried a few sentences, but they never made it as far as her lips. They were too negative, too unhelpful. She needed positivity. "Right," she said, beginning an unvetted sentence that she hoped would come good, "my wonderful wife and the big man are tough enough and ugly enough to take care of themselves. They made it onto Tiberius Omega Mining Colony alive. They can find a way off. We cannot go back to them, but they can come to us. Make sure we have a comms specialist scanning the full range of channels in case they get in range of a relay."

"*Haven* can listen out for them better than any human," Ezra assured her, a little too defensively.

Fleur squeezed his shoulder. "I am sure they can. In the meantime, I need to make sure *Haven* is still here when they return. Which means I need to have a conversation with two Empresses."

"Two?"

CHAPTER TEN

Furiously, Striker marched his latest body down the Empress' freezing corridor of cloning pods on Xarr. More had gone wrong than he had ever believed possible. For starters, he was dead.

Again.

That was embarrassing.

And so were the rest of his clones on *Black Nebula*, thanks to that irritating little boy Lynch who had torn them apart on the Empress' orders. Damn her! All Striker had left, all that was keeping him from the empty oblivion of true death like some peasant in Xarr's undercity, were clones the Empress had grown of him. Like the one he was currently wearing.

However, the Empress of the Known Galaxies was not renowned for her mercy. Worse than dying, that stupid girl Isabella and her elusive Sau Daran parasite Paradise Moon were even further from his grasp. He was stuck here, on Xarr among the hub worlds, while she and her parasite hid on some backwater embarrassment of a planet on the far reaches of the Outer Rim. It would take him considerably longer to catch up with her this time, given he couldn't just shoot himself and arrive in one of his now deceased clones on *Black Nebula* as it hunted Isabella in the Outer Rim. When he finally caught up with that girl, he would bring the full might of PROXUS down on her pathetic little planet and make her watch him blast it to scrap.

Reaching the end of the chilly corridor, he launched through the door and donned whatever robe had been left at the top of his drawer. He mentally adjusted the comm on his implant, but whichever channel he tried and whomever he attempted to reach, he was met with a wall of silence. Even when he tried opening a channel to some of his agents on Xarr, the implant did nothing. That had never happened before.

He rode a familiar shuttle to his latest audience with the Empress, entertaining the different ways in which he might frame his failure. But for the Empress' meddling, he would have apprehended that dpresh of a girl. But it had not been the Empress who allowed this to happen. The blame and failure were his alone, and he would have to wear those as he had to wear this body the Empress had grown for him. Not to worry. He had becalmed her wrath before—he would do so again.

After he disembarked, the shuttle's ramp closed with a clunk. Unable to conceal his anger after a lifetime of impeccable diplomacy, Striker marched away from the shuttle with an expression that would have melted his own PROXUS battle station down to slag.

A giant's roar sent Striker glancing straight up in surprise. The landing pad's roof was levering open, allowing Xarr's noxious atmosphere to enter through an ever-widening breach. Deadly coils of green and black clouds unfurled towards Striker and the landing pad.

Striker sighed. Now everything made sense. It didn't matter whether the Empress knew of his assassination plans for her, or whether she was merely upset with his recent performance. The result would be the same.

As Xarr's toxic atmosphere tore Striker's flesh from his body and began dissolving his insides, with his last thought he wondered how many times the Empress would inflict this fate on him before she forgave him.

Already, he could see one potential issue—besides the inconvenience and agony. He was willing to shoulder the burden of pain no matter how many deaths it took to sate her fury. However, he was more than a little concerned she hadn't grown enough clones. What if she ran out of bodies before she ran out of wrath?

CHAPTER ELEVEN

Striker's eyes hadn't opened yet, but the Empress of the Known Galaxies had no time to waste. Another Empress clone already lay twisted and still at her feet, and there were plenty more cloned Empresses lurking nearby.

She ripped out the last of the tubes embedded in Striker's final surviving clone. His eyes burst open. All his other clones had been melted into fleshy puddles by Xarr's toxic atmosphere a whole cycle ago, with Striker's consciousness inside each of them as they died. She had taken great pleasure in watching him die over and over. A suitable punishment for failing to capture the girl with the Sau Daran parasite—not to mention failing to assassinate his Empress. If he had meant to kill her, or the version of her that existed before the clone she was inside now, he should have done a better job. He hadn't even managed to kill her once.

"Hurry up," ordered the Empress of the Known Galaxies as he struggled awake. Glancing back down the thin corridor, she saw no fresh shadows in the gloom. It was hard to see along these dim walls. Frost-encrusted pipes connected a line of Striker's vacant cloning pods, whose glass doors had been left open for a whole cycle. She saw no threats. The door at the far end of the corridor remained closed. Just in case, she kept her improvised and already bloody glass shiv ready. She had wrapped one end in fabric from her torn-off sleeves, making the jagged, makeshift weapon usable—if she didn't mind a little more agony in her palm.

Striker's huge naked body slumped against the side of the cloning pod. A pale, shaky arm found purchase on the pod's outer rim. Muscles that had been conditioned by electrodes for countless cycles flexed for the first time as Striker pushed himself out of the pod and took his first ponderous steps in his new clone.

His bare feet slid on fresh blood. His hands snatched at the cloning pod but they were still adjusting to being alive and caught only air. He crashed with a meaty landing on top of the dead Empress clone. Like the Empress standing over him, the clone he had fallen over had a thin face free from wrinkles—despite her age. Parts of it were covered by a spray of ashen hair with a streak of crimson burned down one side. Her trim body was wrapped up tight in a white uniform bearing the Empress' unique rank insignia. Unlike the Empress standing over him, the dead clone's uniform still had sleeves and had been spoiled by over twenty stab wounds to her back. It was sodden with dark blood now seeping into the corridor.

The Empress wasn't surprised when Striker didn't ask for a helping hand. He knew better than anyone she had no use for someone who couldn't fix their own problems—as well as hers. He was breathing heavily, as people out of physical shape were prone to do when dragging themselves back to their feet. Using the cold glass door of his cloning pod for support, he climbed up it like a drunken mountaineer. At the top, he caught his breath. His feet and hands were thick with blood from the dead clone, plenty of it smeared on the rest of his naked body.

"Greetings… Empress," Striker managed cordially, in between deep breaths. He glanced at the dead clone, a perfect copy of the perfect copy who had woken his own clone out of hibernation and was waiting impatiently for him to get his bearings. "How may I be of service?" Striker asked without a hint of concern.

The Empress nodded her approval. That was exactly the resolve she would need from him if she was to escape Xarr, and exactly the sort of practical question she valued. "Clothes for you. Transport for us. And an agent who can get us off-world."

"Happily," said Striker. Already, a warmer colour was returning to the robust outline of his cheeks.

Stepping over the dead clone but not seeming to care about the spreading pool of blood on his already drenched feet, he exposed his back to her glass shiv and strode down the line of abandoned pods towards the door at the far end. The Empress' crisp, deliberate strides were armed with sharp glances at every shadow.

They paused outside the door.

"Do you expect more?" Striker whispered, with a nod towards the dead clone behind them.

"Plenty," replied the Empress evenly.

He glanced at her shiv. She nodded. For two people who had fought wars together and conquered galaxies, that was an entire conversation. The Empress eased her diminutive body into the shadows beside the door. In the narrow corridor, there was just enough room for her to cram her body into the corner next to the door without her being visible once it opened.

Striker mouthed a short countdown, then he must have used his neural implant to hack into and open the door because it slid aside without him raising a finger to tap the holo interface beside it.

Any information he learned from looking through the open doorway, he kept secret. Had he attempted to share anything, even mouthing a handful of words to her, he would have revealed he wasn't alone. She waited for him to step inside, then listened for someone trying to kill him.

"Oh dear, what a mess," muttered Striker from inside.

"They killed each other," replied a familiar voice, also inside the room.

"How fortunate," replied Striker. "Would you mind if I put some clothes on?"

"Aren't you worried I'll kill you when your back's turned?" asked the familiar voice.

"Empress, there are two of you dead at my feet. You are going to need all the help you can get to stay alive. Shooting me will not aid your escape from Xarr."

Shooting you? Thank you. It was helpful for the Empress to know the Empress clone inside was armed with a plasma weapon. Particularly when she wasn't. She would have to pick her moment carefully if she was going to get close enough to use her glass shiv. *But he's not armed and you haven't killed him yet. What are you both playing at?*

"Empress, please may I ask what's happening?"

"Some dpresh in the Resistance killed me, which is more than you ever managed despite all your scheming," answered the familiar voice. "Hurry up and get dressed so we can leave."

"Of course, Empress." In between Striker's words, she could hear him huffing and puffing as he threw on fresh robes. "I expect you have a plan."

She did. As she explained it to Striker, it sounded no less familiar to the listening Empress than her own.

"I do wonder, Empress," mused Striker, "just how many of your clones are out there."

"Oh, hundreds."

It was the truth. Whatever terrorist act the Resistance had committed this rotation, it had been more than a mere assassination. Before they killed her, they had hardwired her cloning facilities to release all her clones at once, instead of only waking up one clone and downloading the Empress' ID tag into that clone—and only that clone. For the first time since she had formed PROXUS and her self-styled title of Empress, she had no more clones left as back-up. If she died, she would stay dead. Which made her feel so oppressively... common.

Worse, she was being hunted. They all were. By each other. Even now—mere moments after waking up in these bodies—the Empress clones were already killing each other. It was too dangerous to let the other Empresses live. Only one of them could take the throne and lead PROXUS. But no one was deadlier than the Empress of the Known Galaxies—and didn't they all know it. With so many of her out there, the Known Galaxies were more perilous than they had ever been. Every clone housing the real Empress' memories and the real Empress' authority. All of them biological equals. Every one of them a perfectly matched rival for power.

Even worse, they all knew the unrelenting, calculating way each other thought. The Empress would have to be the first to strike, certain in the knowledge they would all be thinking the same.

"Hundreds?" asked Striker. "Presumably that's not including those two on the floor?"

"As I said, they did that to each other," said the familiar voice. "I arrived afterwards. Did one of them wake you?"

"No, I was woken up by the clone hiding in the corridor out there."

You little dpresh.
"Is she armed?"
"Only with a glass knife."
You big dpresh.

The Empress stilled her breathing, not letting even the faintest hint of a breath escape the corridor and venture within earshot of the familiar voice inside the antechamber. She strained to listen for any telltale signs of movement inside, but it was silent. In all likelihood, she and the other clone were playing the same game.

There was no cover in the corridor. It was narrow enough that even with her short arms, the Empress could have stood in the middle and touched the frozen pipes on both walls. Of course, had she done so she would immediately have been wearing a barrelful of plasma holes in her chest.

Her grip tightened on the fabric handle she had fashioned for her glass shiv. It was enough to stop the shard of glass she had shattered off the door of a cloning pod from slicing her palm too deeply, but this was not a long-term solution for cutting down enemies. Already, the fabric clutched in her palm was frayed and torn where it had rubbed against the glass and her palm was red and sore. She doubted she had more than a few swift thrusts left in the weapon before she was forced to either drop it or let it bite her. Either way, it would be a short fight.

The problem with knowing her enemy as well as the Empress did, was she also knew they knew she knew them as well as she did. If the familiar voice inside the room was smart—and she certainly was—she would have backed away from the door to ensure she didn't surrender the advantage of her plasma weapon. As long as there was space between them, the familiar voice was in control. And control mattered. It mattered to the familiar voice. It mattered to the hundreds of clones like her. It mattered more to them than it did to anyone else in the Known Galaxies. Yet they all knew this. Every clone would have to think forward to each move, each bluff, each gambit the other might make.

There was a grunt from inside the room, followed by the unmistakable whine of a plasma pistol.

"You can come inside, Empress," said Striker.

"Can I though?" asked the Empress. She had heard the shot, but she hadn't seen what it hit. She kept the shiv ready to drive into the central mass of anyone who entered the corridor. "You were quick to sell me out."

"I assure you, I did no such thing, Empress," Striker replied patiently.

"Convince me," ordered the Empress.

A plasma pistol landed in the corridor. It was within her reach, but to collect it would require her exposing herself to the doorway.

"Did you really kill her?" asked the Empress. "Or is she still listening, with another plasma pistol ready to blast me when I pick that thing up?"

The door shut.

Dropping her shiv, the Empress reached down and grabbed the plasma pistol. Quickly, she shrank back into the corner beside the doorway.

The door slid open.

"There is no great plan, Empress," Striker assured her from inside the room. "No ruse, no scheme. Except for how I killed that clone."

She checked the weapon she had picked up. The plasma pistol boasted an almost full charge, and there was cauterised blood stuck to the muzzle.

"Empress, you are the first clone I met after I woke up in this body. If I betray you, the first Empress I swore loyalty to, the other clones will learn of this and none will ever trust me. I will be untrusted by every Empress in the

Known Galaxies. My life will be in greater danger than that of any other human in existence."

"Except perhaps mine."

"You can be sure at least one of you doesn't want you dead," Striker pointed out with irritating logic. "Unless you're feeling uncharacteristically suicidal."

Leading with her new plasma pistol, the Empress swung through the doorway. When she had last been inside the richly carpeted antechamber, on her way to Striker's cloning pod mere moments ago, she had been the only person here. Now, three perfect copies of her were already lying dead on the carpet.

Two of the clones were wrapped together on one side of the antechamber, their white uniforms bloodied beyond belief by the makeshift glass shivs in their hands. The Empress' gaze followed the white wrappings of fabric bound around the shard of glass they each clenched in one fist, then up the bare flesh of their arms to where they had torn their uniforms at the shoulders. For all she knew, they had thought so alike that they had attempted the same manoeuvres in their brief struggle and drawn identical results. The glass shiv buried in each of them was indisputable. She glanced at her own uniform torn at her shoulders, at her own bare arms and at her own glass shiv lying discarded in the corridor. She thought too much like her enemies—enough to get her killed. That was why she needed Striker to give her the edge no other Empress clone had.

The third body's sleeves were intact, as was the rest of her pristine uniform. Her only deviation from the Empress' appearance was the half of her face that was missing, along with the burn marks and cauterised blood coating the smoking bits of her face that remained. From the angle of the burn, it looked as if Striker had forced the plasma pistol under her chin when he pulled the trigger. Easy enough to do if he was behind her.

Having confirmed the clones were all dead, the Empress stepped briskly over them towards the exit. Every wall of the antechamber was covered in mirrored wardrobes crammed with meticulously labelled drawers. She caught her reflection in one of the mirrors as she passed. Silently, she was satisfied to observe her perfectly straight posture looking as imperious as ever.

The drawer with Striker's label was open, pulled out from the wardrobe and empty. The last robe it had contained was now stretched over his huge body, which waited for her beside the grand carved wooden door that led out of the antechamber and into a much larger underground complex. It was a beautiful blue robe, with ornamental patterns of crashing waves and great submarine beasts from the depths of First Duke Striker's overwhelmingly oceanic home planet. The Empress didn't waste any time admiring it.

"Hurry up and tell me how I can trust you after all that," the Empress instructed. "If I need to shoot you, it would be easier to do it here."

She checked his face. He knew she meant it.

"A thousand apologies, Empress. Allow me to clarify." Striker had a manner of speaking where his words and the way he delivered them always matched perfectly. For now, he sounded inescapably deferential and earnest. Yet, if one were to unshackle his words from the honey in which he coated them, the Empress wondered how else she might interpret them. 'Allow me to clarify' could just have easily been 'Let me explain why I'm smarter than you'. Confidently, he clasped his hands behind his back. "I needed the clone's attention on you so I could kill her. The alternative, requiring you to strike the killing blow when she held a plasma pistol, would have put you in the firing line. That was unacceptable."

"Unacceptable?" She gave him a look that would have made most subordinates wither.

Striker didn't flinch. "Someone has stolen a great deal of my access codes and I can't reach any of my assets over the comm. I need you alive because I can't get off Xarr without you."

The cold logic of that last line swung it for her, as no doubt Striker had known it would. "That is acceptable," she told him.

She marched him from the antechamber and indicated for him to lead them deeper into the cloning facility. She didn't share any plans with him. She had plenty, but they would all have to be abandoned. Striker was leading now. Nor did she object to the suboptimal routes he navigated through the facility. Once she had seen the grim mirror held up to her own actions by the pair of dead clones inside the antechamber, with their matching glass shivs and torn sleeves, it had been clear she would have to rely entirely on Striker. The alternative was meeting and killing all the other clones enacting the same exceptional plans as herself.

CHAPTER TWELVE

Half a rotation and only a handful of dead clones later, the Empress and Striker had traded the cloning facility for a grim alleyway deep in a neighbouring undercity.

Like every undercity on Xarr, it was known only by a string of letters and numbers. At the bottom of Xarr's food chain, no one mattered enough for words. At least, not that the Empress was aware of. She wrinkled her nose at the thought of sharing oxygen with these degenerates. Down here, petty criminals and starving vagrants were as rife as impoverished citizens, whose meagre points barely paid for their dreadful homes.

They lived forever at the Empress' mercy, in a dense network of undercities beneath the planet's surface that protected them from Xarr's deadly atmosphere. Those with more points could afford to live closer to the surface. But those with real power and influence, those who had truly made a name for themselves and had the points to prove it, lived above ground. Along with everyone who enlisted in the Empress' military.

Her stolen cloak felt like a thinning rag between her fingers as she pulled it tighter around her cold shoulders, longing for the comfort she used to find above ground inside Xarr's reinforced skyscrapers. Hidden by thick toxic clouds, each skyscraper stretched for an eternity before it reached the limits of Xarr's atmosphere. Within their towering spires stood unrivalled power and privacy for those who could afford it.

Instead, the Empress was down here.

With the trash.

As with every step since leaving the cloning facility's antechamber, this bleak undercity was Striker's idea. Except he was no longer beside her to endure it, having left the Empress alone to scowl at the shadows.

Above her, deafening vehicles swept past at furious speeds along a tightly packed grid of criss-crossing traffic. Every vehicle in the undercities, along with all the PROXUS ships and battle stations in orbit above them, was propelled by star energy. Even the thought of her crowning achievement wasn't enough to bring a smile to her grim face. A generation ago, she had pioneered the harvest of this vital energy resource from all the Sau Daran parasites her forces had captured during the war against the Sau Darans. Parasites like the elusive Paradise Moon. Such technology had revolutionised not only how the Known Galaxies powered everything, but also the speed at which the Empress' PROXUS forces could conquer and coerce everyone else. Clean energy had arrived too late to save Xarr's ruined atmosphere, but the Empress' monopoly on cleaner, more powerful energy had been enough for Xarr to tighten its grip on the rest of the Known Galaxies. Everyone who mattered used star energy, replenished from her secret reserve on Xarr, and they all bowed to her. Except now there were too many of her to bow to.

The architect of the Known Galaxies' clean energy revolution skulked from shadow to shadow below the undercarriages of rushing traffic, too wary of encountering another of herself to risk calling anyone for aid except her dependably treacherous First Duke.

Finally, Striker swept out of the bar he had been inside for far too long. Such drinking establishments long predated the Empress, but she had found them an essential tool for dampening sparks of rebellious vigour by warming spirits and dulling minds. They also offered plenty of dark corners for the quiet meetings on which Striker had built his career as her spy master.

Even without the hooded cloak concealing Striker's expensive robe and recognisable face, she would have known him. He strode towards her with that infuriatingly calm, patient gait that took him everywhere. He slid into a shadow beside her. "Everything is arranged."

Unblinking, her face froze in a grim concession of his temporary authority. She couldn't even look at him. "Get on with it, then." He hadn't told her the plan, which meant she wouldn't like it. She didn't have to wait long to find out why.

Riding rickety star lifts that stank of urine, they climbed a fraction above the undercity's lowest level. A passenger transport was waiting at the nearest transit pad. A standard two-tiered transport, its lower tier was a long, windowless passenger area below the pilot's small bubble cockpit.

The Empress stepped up to the transport's closed door, fearing an inevitable rubbing of shoulders with the citizens who lived down here. However, she couldn't have been more wrong. Although the transport was large enough to ferry a small crowd of Empress clones out of the undercity, when the door opened it revealed an empty transport. A neon glow flickered inside, shedding fractured light on its filthy, graffitied interior. The moment the door hissed shut behind them, she had to grab the wall as the transport lurched off the pad.

The Empress perched on the edge of the seat nearest the door, careful to keep her stolen cloak between her and the stains on her seat. "Do we really need something so big? Who are you expecting will join us?"

Striker settled down next to her. "No one. This is privately chartered."

She gestured at the empty seats surrounding them. "Is this really necessary then?"

Striker shrugged. "Anyone searching for us is searching for two people. This is a transport for forty."

After that, they rode in a long, torturous silence all the way to their destination. Once the transport bumped down with less precision than the Empress was accustomed to, Striker led them out onto another transit pad. This one was suspended high above the undercity. It was the first structure the Empress had seen here that was hanging from above rather than held up from below.

However, she and Striker were in the wrong place. The Empress' brow furrowed. "We're nowhere near any transport hub. I told you we need to get a ship off Xarr before any of them take control of my military."

Striker pointed up. "Everything we need is up there."

The Empress glanced up again, this time more carefully. In the gloom, the tube of a narrow star lift extended from their pad all the way up into a synthetic structure clinging to an underbelly of rock that signalled they were at the surface. A spark of furious realisation ignited inside her as she understood his plan.

"Absolutely not."

"It's the safest path, Empress."

"The atmosphere will kill us."

"I have taken precautions."

"Precautions? The best precaution is not to go outside in the first place."

Crossing his arms, Striker stared down at the undercity's blur of flying traffic, decaying shadows and sprawling buildings. "Hundreds of copies of the deadliest woman in the Known Galaxies are on a seek and destroy mission down there and along every exalted corridor on the surface. Almost all of them will die. Those who escape or end up sitting on a throne will do so only through sheer luck. I offer a more secure promise than mere chance."

The Empress could conjure plenty of alternative solutions. Unfortunately, so could all the clones she needed to avoid.

At the summit of the star lift, they stepped out into a small room lined with lockers and heavy industrial tools. Its centre housed a railed platform directly below a thick hatch in the ceiling. Waiting for them on the platform were two pairs of folded environment suits. The one-piece suits were a thin synthetic fabric, dyed the same dull brown as every other PROXUS engineering outfit, complete with heavy boots and scuffed worker's gloves.

Seeing her foul expression, Striker quickly busied himself by undressing and pulling on the larger of the two environment suits.

Reluctantly, the Empress forced herself to pick up her suit. "At least tell me you've killed whoever is helping us."

With one leg inside his suit, Striker turned and attempted to smile disarmingly. "Respectfully, I have not. Bodies attract more attention than pilots unaware of their cargo and workers ordered to abandon their environment suits and take a full rotation off work."

The Empress ignored his smile. Her mood was too hot even for him to disarm. "I can't imagine you have many workers who are exactly our size."

Striker probed the suit's second trouser leg with his foot. "Mine was certainly easier. You have a young trainee to thank for yours."

Moving with crisp precision, the Empress placed her suit and pistol aside, then dropped her cloak next to them. She undressed, choosing to ignore the repulsive way Striker's eyes lingered on her bare feet when he thought she wasn't looking. "A telling combination of sizes for anyone searching for us."

"Data that will be found," Striker admitted. "But not data anyone will be looking for until it's too late."

The Empress folded her uniform neatly before pulling on her environment suit and retrieving her plasma pistol. "What if these suits are faulty?"

"Suits fail all the time, but these won't. The overseer checked them personally." The Empress wasn't so sure. Striker's suit bulged everywhere, looking like it might split at any moment. He fastened his oxygen recycler to his chest strap and made sure it was cycling by checking the readings on its holo display. Then he strapped on his tool belt and attached its shield pack.

"You trust him?" she asked, once he was done.

"The overseer? I trust the points he was paid."

The Empress raised an eyebrow. "Points you no longer have, after that boy stole them along with everything else."

Striker waved this away. "Points can be squeezed out of anywhere—if you know where to squeeze."

"That easily?"

"As I started from nothing, so I shall rise again." Striker tossed his robe on top of the Empress' belongings, then picked up the whole bundle under one arm. When he thumbed on the shield, a thin film of translucent green energy washed over his suit and the bundle he was holding. Clinging to the outline of his body, the energy shield was so close it almost touched him. A single blast from a plasma pistol would be enough to short-circuit the shield, but as long as they kept out of trouble the shield would hold back Xarr's poisonous atmosphere. At least, until it ran out of power and Xarr's atmosphere melted him alive, or his oxygen recycler failed and he asphyxiated.

The Empress mirrored his actions until a film of translucent green energy descended over her vision. Instantly, the world was reborn behind a green tint. Striker unravelled a cord from his tool belt and hooked it onto the Empress' belt. He didn't need to explain that they wouldn't be able to see a thing on the surface, and without tethering their suits together they might as well wave goodbye to each other now.

She gave him a stern look. "How will you know where to go? You can't see either."

"There's a beacon transmitting from the airlock we're heading to. My implant will relay its signal and direct me."

Once they were both positioned on the platform, Striker summoned the holo controls for the hatch. A projected sphere of blue light emerged from the railing. The sphere was formed of symbols and dials, which Striker studied and tapped until he was satisfied. With one more tap of a symbol, the hatch above them groaned open and their platform rose creaking and shuddering into a small cylindrical airlock.

The hatch shut below.

Another waited above.

For now, it was closed too.

Striker stared at the spherical projection, but made no move to tap the final command to open the hatch and launch their platform up into Xarr's hostile atmosphere.

"What's wrong?" asked the Empress.

For once, Striker didn't reply with something smart or calculated. He didn't reply at all. He stared into the middle distance, seeming not to have heard her question.

Their shields sizzled and flickered against each other as she grabbed his arm. "What is it?" she demanded. If they were about to die, she'd like enough warning to do something about it.

Still there was no response beneath the mask of green energy painted over his vacant expression. Unless something more sinister was happening. While the Empress had disconnected her clone's neural implant the moment she realised there were other Empress clones sharing the same network, Striker did not have that problem. His neural implant was his alone to command, along with whoever he wished to communicate with in private. She had no way of knowing what he was doing, or who he was speaking to.

"First Duke," she prompted. "What are you up to?"

"Empress?" he asked, as though he hadn't heard a word she had said.

She attempted to jog his memory by thumbing off her plasma pistol's safety. "What was that?"

"Nothing, Empress," Striker assured her with his typically untrustworthy assuredness. "Opening the hatch now. My sincerest apologies, I must still be adjusting to my new clone."

"Cease." The Empress pressed her plasma pistol under his chin. "You don't do anything until you've told me what just happened."

Striker's hands shook. "It was nothing, Empress."

She had never witnessed any loss of composure from her First Duke before. Certainly, she had never seen his hands shake. She pushed the plasma pistol harder into the fleshy underside of his jowls, his energy shield bending inwards as the weapon forced aside anything softer than gunmetal. "Reconsider how little I trust you and adjust your answer accordingly."

Striker's neck craned back beneath the pressure of the plasma pistol. Wherever his mind had been, or whoever he had been listening to via his neural implant, his attention was now entirely where it belonged. On his Empress. "I am afraid that would be unwise. You don't know where we are heading on the surface, Empress. Everything is arranged. Without me, you would be unable to complete the plan."

"I can find other ways."

Striker's gaze met hers. "Then you will have other clones for company. Other clones with the same idea."

The Empress shook her head. "Not once I'm out there. That's the last place I'd want to go." Striker winced as she rammed the plasma pistol deeper into his flesh. "I don't have time for your lies," she warned him.

"Very well, I had a panic attack," he admitted haughtily. It was probably the first genuine emotion she had ever seen his lips elicit.

"A panic attack? You barely moved."

"I know, it's embarrassing. Please forgive me."

The Empress kept her plasma pistol ready to blow his head off. "What's going on, First Duke?"

"Don't you remember?" he asked. "You watched them all."

"All of what?" snapped the Empress.

"My deaths."

Well, that explained a lot. It had slipped her mind but, yes, she had watched in glorious colour and all three dimensions as Xarr's atmosphere dissolved every cloned body Striker had except for the one he was wearing now. It was the most downtime she had given herself since becoming Empress.

"I didn't realise it would be this difficult going back out there," he admitted. "Rest assured, it will not be a problem."

She checked his hands.

They had finally stopped shaking.

"See that it isn't." Ensuring the safety was on, she sealed her plasma pistol inside a deep pocket running down the outside of the suit's leg.

"Yes, Empress," intoned Striker. "I live to serve."

With his firm tap of a final symbol on the projection, the hatch above them opened and once more the platform rose. This time, into an impenetrable ocean of roiling blacks and greens. Toxic clouds smothered her in a wall of gaseous malachite swirls. She felt the changes in pressure and relentless drag on her body as ferocious winds tore at her without scoring a hit, grasping nothing but the shimmering barrier of her shield.

The Empress felt a tug on her tether.

Grinding her teeth, she allowed the cord to dictate her route and trudged after Striker. Every so often, the tension in the cord pulled her left or right, and she grudgingly reoriented herself. It was bad enough being led, but this time Striker quite literally had her on a leash.

Their progress was hampered not only by the abysmal visibility, but by the gargantuan foundations of every skyscraper between them and their destination. Even though she followed in whichever direction Striker pulled her, staggering half bent when the winds dictated, it didn't stop the foundations of yet another skyscraper punching her in the face as it loomed out of nowhere.

After that, she learned to keep her gloved hands out in front for protection from the agony of unexpectedly hitting her face into the energy shield when it came up against anything solid on the other side. Like a wall. However, this did nothing to ward off the surprise factor.

Every time she landed her palm or cheek against bruising hard matter, an insistent tug on the cord reminded her to keep moving. Far off, the only glimmer in the darkness came when her shroud sparkled and crackled, the hot promise of lightning always too close for comfort.

The cord slackened, and she felt her palm close around what felt like Striker's shoulder. At least, she hoped it was Striker's. Whatever was out there in the darkness was anyone's guess—she had never felt more vulnerable.

Striker pulled her into a doorway. She grasped its rim and steadied herself against the wind. Pulling herself inside, she wasted no time in unclipping the tether from her belt. The airlock was already filling with the greenish glow of toxic clouds that had chased her inside, barely giving her long enough to process more than its basic cylindrical shape, akin to the airlock through which they had left, before her vision was obscured again.

The hatch clanged shut behind her.

Turbines roared as the airlock cycled. Beneath the dissipating clouds, a familiar platform grew more visible at their feet. Once the clouds had completely cleared, she saw a small metal cone with flashing green lights. Striker flicked off the beacon's power and its flashing lights died.

Waving to confirm the atmospheric reading on his neural implant was clean, Striker deactivated his shield and recycler. The Empress waited for him to start melting. While she couldn't see anything physiologically wrong with him, she couldn't help but notice how his strained expression was struggling to compose itself. It was like watching a fish battling to breathe underwater. If there was anything Striker always did well, it was maintaining his mask of composure. The sooner he regained that mask, the sooner the Known Galaxies would feel right again.

"Problem?" asked the Empress frostily.

Striker drew his body upright with a heavy breath. "No problem, Empress."

Satisfied Striker wasn't going to die because the airlock hadn't cycled properly, although far from assured of his mental state, the Empress deactivated her gear.

She readied her plasma pistol at where she expected the platform to descend into the floor. However, when Striker brought up another holo console and started the platform moving, it went sideways instead of down. The wall behind them slid aside, admitting their floating platform into another changing area. Inside, two folded pairs of drab citizen outfits waited.

"Where are we?" asked the Empress. "If this is another phyxing undercity, I will shoot both of us."

"Nothing of the sort. On the other side of that wall is a private bay in our busiest space port."

"You booked us passage?"

"Of course not." Striker smiled, but his smile wasn't as reassuring as he usually made it. He was too pale and rattled after their trek across Xarr's surface and whatever demons the experience had invoked.

"Bookings make us predictable?" asked the Empress.

Striker nodded. "Why risk booking a ship..."

He left the sentence hanging, ready for her to finish.

Glancing at the plasma pistol she was still holding, the Empress smiled. "When you can take it."

CHAPTER THIRTEEN

Hands on hips, Fleur examined the Slave Empress through her cell door. Like all doors on *Haven*, this one was oval. However, instead of the usual living metal from which *Haven* grew their hull, the cell door offered Fleur a clear view of its interior through a faint tint of blue. Inside the cell looking out, the Slave Empress' view would reveal only a solid blue screen without even Fleur's silhouette visible.

The Slave Empress' words echoed unspoken once she had finished recounting how Striker helped her escape Xarr. A terrifying tale, now industriously building a permanent residence of terror inside Fleur's head. *More than two Empresses. Far more. The Known Galaxies are well and truly vented.*

"That is quite some story," admitted Fleur.

"It's true," insisted the Slave Empress from her cross-legged position on the cell floor. The stolen PROXUS flight suit they had found for her smelled much better than the dirty clothes she had arrived in, and even though it would have ripped tight on most people it still hung loose and baggy off the Slave Empress' absurdly trim, skeletal figure. Despite the restraints pinning her wrists together and the dark, cramped cell, she appeared perfectly calm. "The moment I lie, my worth as a source of intel ends and there's every chance you'll kill me. As long as I'm honest, I'm your most precious resource."

"Fine. Be honest then. Why are you here?"

"You are the most famous fugitives who ever escaped my grasp. I can think of no better shield to place between myself and the clones hunting me."

Fleur examined the old woman on the floor in front of her. Athletic to the point of zero body fat. A slender house of bone and muscle for a cold, twisted mind. Not to mention a glare that could knock a PROXUS battle station out of orbit.

"How did you get a tracker on here?" asked Fleur.

The Empress smiled at the blank blue wall blocking the exit to her cell. "Ask the First Duke."

Fleur's expression hardened. "All I care about is keeping my crew safe. How do I contact Striker so I can stop him tracking *Haven*?"

"*Haven*?" asked the Empress. "Oh, you gave this ship a name. How quaint. No, Lady Fontaine, you will not contact the First Duke. He is my leverage. He will remain out there. Unseen. Treat me kindly, and he won't sell you out to PROXUS."

Fleur laughed darkly. "Striker is the least trustworthy bucket of vitraxi dung this side of Xarr."

"Reliably so," countered the Empress. "However little you trust me, consider that the other Empress you have locked up is even more dangerous. Don't trust her. She would have known much of what I told you about the other clones. How forthcoming was she?"

Fleur didn't know what to do with that, so she hit one of the spherical buttons *Haven* had grown into the curved wall next to the cell. An audio dampening field settled over the cell's entrance, cutting off any further wisdom or threats the Slave Empress might be tempted to impart.

Keeping herself calm with practised, gentle breathing, Fleur tried Beauregard and Braga yet again on the comm. No response.

On another level, down another corridor, in another cell, the Burned Empress was waiting for her.

"I can only presume you've been speaking to that other one," said the Burned Empress.

Oh phyx. I have them in stereo.

Fleur stared through the cell's blue boundary. The Burned Empress was standing, hands clasped in the small of her back, eyes staring dead ahead at the cell door. Fleur tapped a spherical button and the door's blue tint dissolved so the Burned Empress could see her.

"It must have taken a lot of surgery to hide the most infamous face in the Known Galaxies."

"Less than you would think." She pointed to the heavy plasma burns on her face. "Self-administered insurance."

Fleur stifled her reaction, not wanting to reveal anything. She knew the Empress of the Known Galaxies was ruthless, but shooting yourself in the face with a plasma pistol was brutal even by her standards.

"You hid who you are."

The Burned Empress drew her hands out from behind her back and indicated her cell. "You can imagine my reluctance towards honesty."

"Your intel would have made us all safer. And it would have been helpful to know Striker is tracking *Haven*."

The Burned Empress sighed with boredom. "Clearly, I didn't know that. I can only presume the First Duke told that other one how to do it after she brought him back. We did always have a soft spot for him."

"You kept things from us. When we were escaping, you knew exactly where to go."

"And here you are, alive and liberated because I used that knowledge to help you."

"She warned me not to trust you."

"Of course she did. And you would be wise not to trust her."

Fleur rubbed the back of her neck and tried to loosen her shoulders. "I should vent both of you and save myself the headache."

"She likes to manipulate people. Don't let her."

Fleur managed to keep her face free from frustration. "You are genetically identical."

"Of course," added the Burned Empress, "she's also highly intelligent and exactly the type of dangerous ally you're going to need if you want to survive this civil war. Every breakaway PROXUS force you encounter will be led by one of us. We know how each other think. We have access codes and overrides. Intimate knowledge of how PROXUS operates."

"I wondered what you would offer me."

"Does my help sound so unattractive?"

"No," said Fleur thoughtfully, "just desperate." She reactivated the cell door's blue tint.

"What did the other one offer you that I didn't?"

Fleur turned away. "Threats. Nothing you would not offer me if you could, because you are after all the same person. And that, honey, is how I know just how desperate you are." With another tap of the holo beside the cell door, any response the Burned Empress offered was cut short by the sound dampening field activating.

Fleur leaned back against the corridor's curved wall, letting her shoulders roll forward and arching her back. She stretched out her arms until they were taut. Then she slumped onto the deck. She missed Braga's irritatingly brazen swagger in every movement, every word, every touch. She missed Beauregard's calm, dumb, deadly demeanour. At least she didn't miss their constant bickering. But she did need a hug.

Her gauntlet chirruped. She tapped open a channel. "Hey Ez, I was just thinking I would come and find you."

"Fleur," said Ezra, "it's Beauregard…"

Already, she was sprinting down the corridor. *Haven* was way ahead of her, opening every exit panel before she got there. All around, heavy clunking and rumbling told her *Haven* was shuffling rooms to give her the fastest possible route to Ezra. Over the comm, his words shuddered and bloomed through her head and heart, a double-edged blade of sharp terror and growing hope.

"…he needs you," finished Ezra.

CHAPTER FOURTEEN

Darth Vader's theme dragged Isabella from the dreamless sleep of the dog-tired and bone-weary. She had been too tired even for night terrors, which was rare respite. Pale, fragile morning light crept through the gap in her curtains, needling her retinas and forcing her to squint. Rolling to the edge of her ridiculously huge bed, she sent her human hand fumbling over her bedside table to silence her ringing phone. Unseen bedside paraphernalia clattered onto the carpet. Half awake and aching all over, she didn't care.

Usually, Isabella could think of nothing worse than waking up to Agent Glass' special ringtone. Bad news always followed the thrum of Vader's imposing theme. But for once she had been praying Agent Glass would call. If she was lucky, he might break the habit of a lifetime and bring her the good news she was waiting for.

With drowsy clumsiness, Isabella disconnected the charging cable and dragged her phone with her as she collapsed back onto her bed. "Is he okay?"

Both last night and this morning, if she accounted for the time zones of all the countries she had been in, she had returned Talyn to Agent Glass and his army of doctors in New York. They had whisked him away without telling her anything. After waiting long enough to realise there wouldn't be any news for a while, she had returned home to sneak in a few hours of sleep.

"What do you think?" complained Agent Glass. "His injuries weren't helped by you taking him halfway around the world then back to New York for dinner. His ship crash-landed out of space, or had you forgotten?"

Isabella scrunched her eyes shut and pretended she didn't have a headache. "Is he okay or not?"

"He's stable. Somehow," added Agent Glass, his tone laced with judgement. "And he won't stop calling your name. He's saying a lot of other things too, but until your space-age friends finally agree to inject us with their translator thingy I won't have a clue what he's saying."

"But he's okay?"

"Yes," sighed Agent Glass, as though she deserved worse news and he was sad to be the bearer of such positive tidings. "He suffered an intracranial haemorrhage, but he's responding well to treatment. Exactly the sort of injury we would have picked up had he stayed here under observation. May I suggest—"

After hanging up, Isabella hauled on the nearest clean clothes she could find.

I guess you're not giving me your body today.

Isabella hopped into the other leg of her jeans. *You'll get your usual Friday. I promised, didn't I?*

That was the deal.

Then don't sweat it. You gonna follow up on this Spark thing while you're driving me around?

Meh, I'd like to... but I doubt we're gonna find out much anytime soon.

Really? I thought you'd want to be all over this.

Yeah, when I can actually do something about it. I've been on this planet for eighteen years and I've never even heard of the Spark. Have you?

Fair. Well, let me sort this thing out with Talyn and check he's okay, then you can do whatever you want.

Whatever I want?

I take it back. Absolutely not whatever you want.

Purple smoke brought Isabella to Talyn's bedside. It took her a few moments to process the dimly lit room with nothing but night—or at least very early morning darkness—outside the window blinds. As her eyes adjusted, she recognised the same medical room she had left him in—twice, now.

"So, I hear you can't stop talking about me," she said softly, settling into the chair next to his bed.

Wincing, Talyn levered himself upright and leaned back on his pillow. His face was as pale as the strip lighting overhead, his stolen overcoat and blouse replaced by a more modest blue gown. Isabella figured it would have been inappropriate to look under the bedsheets, but she presumed they had confiscated his chinos and vomity slippers too.

"They don't want me to leave again."

Isabella gave him a stern look. "Well, they're worried you'll die."

"They barely know me. Why do they care?"

"Yeah," said Isabella, "but you did almost die quite a bit. And your ship is way ahead of our technology. And you're another person with abilities like me. They probably want to learn more about you and how your ship works and stuff. While you don't die."

Talyn pursed his lips. "I'm not here to help you build spaceships. I'm here to save a whole species."

"I know, I know. The Spark. As soon as you work out what you need, we'll help you. But we've been on this planet a lot longer than you and we've never even heard anything about it." She looked away guiltily. "It might take a while to figure this out."

Grabbing her human wrist, Talyn wrenched her gaze back to his. "I have to do this." Despite the injuries he had endured, his grip was strong.

She stared at this space hottie who had allowed an alien to invade his body on the promise he might save an entire species. His jaw set hard with conviction. His eyes burned with enough of a smoulder to prompt her to bite her lip. His grip tightened even harder around her wrist—hard enough for her to know about it, perhaps even like it. "Help me understand what you're looking for," she suggested. "Exactly how long before humans is the Spark you're looking for from?"

"Hundreds of millions of cycles. We're talking about how multicell life started on this planet."

"Okay, that's something to work with. You could have told me that earlier."

Talyn stared hotly. "I did!"

Yeah, I think that was around the time you were staring into blue and dreamy's eyes. In the New York diner.

Shitballs! He already told me? That's why he got so mad?
Maybe.

Why didn't you say something?

He shushed you. With his hand. I'll always have your back, you know that.

Urgh, that is so sweet and so unhelpful.

Keen not to repeat her mistakes—at least, not this one—Isabella gave Talyn her full attention. "You talk to machines, right? I'll ask the suits to give you a phone. Talk to it, ask it more questions than you asked those phones on the subway, see what you can find out. You'll have the whole sum of human experience at your fingertips."

There's no internet access in this building. It's a high security black zone. Don't you remember that time when we—

Gah! Okay, we'll keep working the problem.

Talyn opened his mouth to reply, but the conversation had moved on without him.

"If you leave here, will you nearly die again?" Isabella asked as sternly as she dared. Usually when she tried to be stern, someone laughed and Paradise Moon said something unhelpful or undermining.

Talyn shook his head. "No, I promise."

Well, that's reassuring. He's going to try not to die this time.

But it was enough for Isabella as she stared back into Talyn's wild eyes and let his softening grip linger around her wrist. She could feel his desperation. His hope. His beautiful, unrelenting strength.

"I'll be fine," Talyn assured her. "Nova's power keeps me together, makes me tougher than I'd usually be."

Isabella knew that feeling well enough. After she'd lost an arm and a leg under one of Ezra's grenades and a roomful of burning, collapsing metal, Paradise Moon had pumped all manner of alien juices through her body to dampen the trauma and keep her upright, if a bit lopsided on one leg.

"I'll need my armour, though."

Isabella grinned. "Sure, no problem!"

This time, Agent Glass only spilled cold coffee on his lap when Isabella arrived with a swirl of purple smoke in his office. Regaining his composure, Agent Glass glared at her. Then he turned his back and busied himself reheating what was left of his coffee in a shiny microwave.

Calmly and firmly from the other side of his laden desk, Isabella made her case for taking Talyn away again. Even from the growing hunch of his shoulders, she could tell Agent Glass hated the idea, but she was only too keen to point out how little he could do to stop her.

"You know I'll do it anyway," she added with casual craftiness and a smothered grin, "but he'll be much safer with his armour."

Muttering something about lack of sleep, Agent Glass burnt his tongue on his reheated coffee and with a grimace set it down on top of the microwave. It was either that or balance it on one of the skyscrapers of manilla folders surrounding him.

Patiently, Isabella waited for the inevitable.

Once Agent Glass had reluctantly conceded with a defeated shrug and a shake of his head, she vanished back to Talyn's bedside. It wasn't long before Talyn's weird, wired armour arrived courtesy of a pair of sullen suits with chiselled jawlines and bodybuilder physiques.

Talyn climbed out of bed and tugged on the tied bow at his shoulder to open his gown. Reluctantly, Isabella turned away from the beautiful contours of his toned body. "You're very pale," she said, watching the wall.

"It's cold where I come from—everyone's pale." Behind her, Isabella could hear the whirring of motors, the clicking of metal plates slotting into place, the suck of pressure as Talyn's skin was sealed inside his armour. "You can turn around now."

She turned in time to catch Talyn laying a hand on the suit's chestplate. He smiled as though greeting an old friend, and for a moment she thought she saw burning specks of blue lightning spark inside his eyes. "I feel better already," he told her. And he looked it. Still badly beaten, but with a little extra vitality behind his pale complexion.

"Okay then." Isabella held out her hand. "Let's go."

Talyn took her hand. Even though his touch was calloused and bruised, it felt good.

Purple smoke.

Gone.

It was three years since Isabella had visited Reading Library. The last time she had borrowed a graphic novel instead of buying one. Everything inside looked comfortingly familiar, except there were fewer people than last time. Mainly parents with children in tow, plus a few wrinkled faces peering curiously at her between bookcases. But whether they were leaning on a pushchair or a walking stick, clutching the latest hardback or queuing patiently to make returns, nothing could slow the avalanche of phones suddenly aimed at Isabella and Talyn. Ignoring Paradise Moon's insistence that she bow and make a welcoming address, Isabella smiled graciously and waved. Even the kind-faced, bespectacled and becardiganed librarian, stoic guardian of these hushed halls, snuck a sly photo on her phone.

Isabella introduced the librarian to Talyn and offered generous promotion of the library on her social feeds if they gave him PC access for the day. It wasn't ideal, but the alternative was bringing him home and she wasn't ready for him to meet her mum yet. Who knew what she'd say to him? And the sad truth was, their home aside, she had nowhere else to bring him. And no one else. Not on Earth, anyway. Everyone on this planet knew her, but the reverse couldn't be further from the truth.

She knew no one.

Although the librarian was fastidious about signing up Talyn—an alien—for his library card first, she was willing to trade unlimited access to their facilities and her kindly supervision in exchange for anything Isabella could do to remind the world that libraries still existed and were wonderful places—especially this one.

"Got everything you need?" Isabella asked Talyn.

"Not even slightly."

"It'll be fine. This is a public place, nothing's gonna happen. When you find what you need or if you want me for anything, ask anyone here to IM me on my socials."

"I have no idea what any of that means. Can't you stay here with me? We'll research together."

You sure you don't want to?

Nope!

Don't you want to see what he finds?

Let's skip to the end when he's ready for our help. I'm no use with all this studying and you're the one who fancies this space hottie, not me.

"Well?" Talyn pushed. "Won't you stay?"

Maybe we should stay with him.

He'll be fine.

He looks like a lost puppy.

I am not spending my Friday babysitting.

But he'll be okay, right?

Yeah!

It's okay to leave him?

Sure!

Isabella raised her hands in the universal sign language for everything being out of her control. "Sorry, I made a promise. I'm sure you'll find what you need. Good luck!"

Standing next to the library PC's login screen, Talyn watched purple smoke wrap around Isabella's body. Her human hand waved as she vanished.

She arrived outside the door to Paradise Moon's private bedroom, which was stowed among the lavender walls of her London home's uppermost floor. When she had been gifted this house by one of her sponsors, she had insisted its pristine white walls be repainted. Any colour was fine, as long as they weren't the same pristine white she associated with PROXUS corridors. The only exception was inside Paradise Moon's bedroom, which was off limits to Isabella and decorators alike. Isabella had no idea what was inside.

Isabella felt her thumb tap, tap, tap against the side of her forefinger. Memories of *Black Nebula* and everything she had been subjected to inside its pristine white walls threatened to seep from the vanquished corners of her mind. She held them back. With enough focussed breathing, she was back in the corridor again and it was lavender. Not anything else. Lavender. Finally, her thumb stopped tapping.

Thanks for waiting.

I still get my twenty-four hours, right?

That's what we agreed.

It's good to check.

Just don't break anything. Don't break me.

Below, Isabella could hear her mum calling for her.

Don't worry, I won't keep you any longer. Whatever she wants can wait until I'm back in control tomorrow.

Isabella stared at the locked door to Paradise Moon's bedroom, wondering what might be on the other side.

If you're meeting a boy—

—I know, I know. Glowing limbs only. Nothing above the knee or the elbow.

Thanks. Have fun.

I always do!

Flecks of purple exploded among the chestnut in Isabella's eyes.

CHAPTER FIFTEEN

Paradise Moon only needed a moment to slip into her bedroom so she could use its en-suite to have the shower Isabella hadn't. She only needed another moment to get changed into clothes that were… less Isabella. And she only needed one more moment to slip into Isabella's bedroom and collect the gauntlet Fleur had left for her on Earth. Sometimes, Paradise Moon was even willing to be a good little god and check Isabella's messages on the gauntlet.

But Paradise Moon didn't get a single moment to do any of those tasks. Still wearing Isabella's clothes in the hallway outside her private bedroom, she was ambushed.

"What *were* you doing with that boy on the train?" demanded Isabella's mum, her face flushed from racing upstairs. "He was the pilot who crashed, wasn't he? I saw it *all* on social media! He played you a song on the train and disappeared with him, and then you were with him in an American diner of all places. If he's making you eat junk food, I will not be held responsible. Then you broke into a museum. You know you've missed your TV spots this morning, don't you? After all that hard work we've done on your public image, I can't understand—"

"We didn't break in," interrupted Paradise Moon, unable to resist correcting Isabella's mum. She said it in an exaggerated, singsong tone guaranteed to annoy. "We didn't know it had already closed."

"Oh. It's you." Isabella's mum went on a facial expedition beginning with shock and ending with an impression of someone sucking a lemon. "She's still letting you clown around in her body, then?"

"It *is* Friday." Paradise Moon forced Isabella's lips into a devilish smile. "And we trust each other."

"Don't you dare make my beautiful girl's face smile at me like that. I know the difference. Whatever she tells you, whatever she lets you do, you have no right."

Paradise Moon held up both hands placatingly in a gesture she hoped might calm things down.

"Don't taunt me with that thing!" snapped Isabella's mum, pointing an accusing finger at Paradise Moon's glowing purple hand. "Everything's a joke to you."

Crossing her arms, Paradise Moon hid the offending hand under Isabella's armpit. "I wasn't… I didn't…"

The face opposite her set as hard as concrete. Isabella's mum lifted her daughter's chin with cupped fingers. "No good you do now will ever make up for what you've already done to my daughter. She had barely taken her first breath when you trapped yourself inside her. Hid in there and made her lie to me all those years. You destroyed her life before she had a chance to live it."

"What I did was wrong," admitted Paradise Moon through lips she had stolen so many times over the years. "But she pulled me back in here instead of letting me die. When she had the chance to get rid of me, she chose this instead. She saved me."

"I know how special my daughter is," Isabella's mum assured her. She glared into her daughter's eyes, at Paradise Moon, no doubt staring at purple flecks among chestnut. "I wish she'd let you die."

"Let go," said Paradise Moon, glancing down at the hand gripping Isabella's chin. "Please."

Sure, she let go. But she didn't stop glaring. In all their encounters, she never stopped glaring.

Paradise Moon fled into her private bedroom and slammed the door. Leaning against it, she tried to force back the tears shaking down Isabella's cheeks. She didn't care about Isabella's gauntlet. Not now. Even a shower and fresh clothes would have to wait. She needed him. Now more than ever, she needed him.

With an urgent whisper of purple smoke, Paradise Moon vanished from her bedroom and arrived deep in an explosion of frosty foliage. Frigid plants surrounded her. White ferns laced with electric blue veins. Glowing trunks thick with snowy bark. She dried her eyes and pushed through a frozen canopy of spray winter petals. This wasn't where she had expected to appear, but if it was where she had arrived then she was in the right place. Wherever she was, there was only one person she wanted to see. And she'd vanished straight to him.

"Thought you weren't coming," Lynch grumbled. He was leaning against a snow-drenched tree. His lazily stubbled jaw rearranged itself into an uneven grin. "You bored of me already?"

Every time Paradise Moon saw him, Lynch was wearing even more space tat than before. Sure, he had enough points to burn after stealing Striker's fortune three years ago, but did he have to spend so many points on fashion? Bad space fashion. He looked like a cyberpunk store in Camden had thrown up on him. He was wearing more fastenings, catches, clasps, magically resealing pockets, buckles and zips than an escapologist would know what to do with. His clothing shimmered as he moved to embrace her, even though everything he was wearing had been dyed a thousand shades of black.

Piloting Isabella's consensually borrowed meat sack, Paradise Moon presented Lynch with a glowing purple hand—outstretched, expectant and hastily wiped dry of tears. More tenderly than anyone but Paradise Moon would have expected, Lynch took her hand and kissed it. He pulled her close. Cradling her forearm in one hand and her elbow in the other, he wrapped himself around her. But he never touched anything that wasn't glowing and purple.

"You smell like shit," he told her.

Paradise Moon brushed one leg, which glowed purple beneath her jeans, against Lynch's leg. "No time to wash. Everything's been crazy back home." Relaxing into the comfort of Lynch's arms, Paradise Moon stared out into the arctic jungle. Pale light twinkled through the canopy above them. Isabella's human body shivered. "I thought you were moving your team somewhere warmer."

Lynch sighed, his breath rippling over Isabella's neck. "PROXUS turned up. We left in a hurry."

"You get everyone out?"

"Yeah, but not our supplies. We're setting up a new Resistance base here. You like it?"

Silvery light sparkled over the blanket of crystals frosted over nearby trunks and boughs. Even though she was freezing Isabella's tits off, Paradise Moon had to admit it was beautiful.

"I'm glad all your little freedom fighter friends are okay. If you want those supplies back from your last base, I could just pop over to the caves and—"

Lynch dragged her around to face his warning glare.

"Fine." She rolled Isabella's eyes and grinned impishly. "I was just offering."

Unamused, Lynch shook his head at no one and nothing. After too many close calls with PROXUS and too many fun, plasma-charged scrapes, Lynch had made Paradise Moon promise they would never put Isabella's body in harm's way again.

He caught her off-guard with a gentle peck on her glowing forearm. "You took your time. Everything okay?"

Paradise Moon laughed. "Is everything okay? I don't know, probably not. But important things needed doing so we did them."

"Anything you want to talk about?"

It was caring questions like this that helped Paradise Moon see there was more to Lynch than an irritating boy she had kicked in the nuts three years ago. "Probably. Not yet."

"Not yet?"

Paradise Moon flung Isabella's body out of reach via an inelegant pirouette, before planting both hands on her hips. "First, you owe me a date."

Lynch scratched his stubble and grimaced. "Yeah, so about that…"

Paradise Moon looked down Isabella's nose at him. "What *about that*, exactly?"

Lynch groaned in an exaggerated fashion that almost turned into a snarl. Before he got any further, Paradise Moon was already laughing at him. "What?!" He looked convincingly annoyed, but Paradise Moon knew better.

She grinned—more devilish than impish. "Oh, just you." She ensnared his hand in her glowing grasp.

"We'll get to the date," Lynch promised. "First…" Kissing her purple hand, he led her away into icy undergrowth that crunched beneath their boots. She ducked under vines as well-endowed as ropes you could hang anchors from, their veins luminous with the same blue tributaries as the ferns at their feet.

Lynch pulled aside a final curtain of frosty vines. Beyond, an untouched vista of thriving arctic jungle swept and teemed as far as the limits of Isabella's eyesight.

"It's beautiful," whispered Paradise Moon. Three blue suns, each a paler shade than the last, were blushing low on a horizon that was crawling with outlandish wildlife. "Is that a dinosaur?"

"Sort of." Lynch shrugged. "You like it?"

"It's perfect." Tenderly, Paradise Moon's glowing fingers stroked the human hand in her grasp. "Can we blow shit up now?"

"Don't look at me, you're the god."

Purple smoke stole them away.

Their arrival was met with molten, fiery bursts of hot puddles and amber rain that lit up a crooked landscape of slate and obsidian. Immediately, Paradise Moon recognised the crater where Lynch had crashed his first stolen spaceship three years ago. That had been shortly after Lynch escaped from Xarr with Striker's ID chip, shortly after Paradise Moon—admittedly with help from Isabella—had saved Earth from Striker's invasion.

This secluded spot in the Known Galaxies had been where they reunited. Isabella had wanted to take him and his stolen ship elsewhere, but he had refused her help. Happily, she had subbed Paradise Moon into the driving seat, and the god had watched Lynch struggle to repair his ship while keeping his spirits up by telling him the best stories she knew, which were all about herself. Using the stolen knowledge in Striker's ID chip, Lynch had figured out the repair. Eventually. Besides, she had been happy to remind him how amazing she was with her wildest stories, and he hadn't forbidden her from topping up their mojitos from a bar in Soho while he worked. Apparently, that didn't count as accepting help. And everyone knew there was nothing like a mojito to take the edge off crashing on a planet of raging volcanoes.

This crater was the only surviving evidence of his crash. Within it, a new collection of stolen PROXUS cargo crates waited for them. Lynch popped the lid of the nearest crate. A swarm of flying saucers, each the size of his hand, zipped up into the ashen sky. Buzzing eagerly, the borrowed PROXUS target drones lit up and hovered in anticipation.

"Date time?" asked Lynch.

Paradise Moon popped the lid of another crate and pulled out a plasma pistol. Lynch was already drawing the pistol he kept holstered against his thigh. Paradise Moon flicked off her weapon's safety and grinned big. "Thanks babe, I really need to shoot something."

CHAPTER SIXTEEN

From the comms chatter Beauregard was picking up, the power to every cell block on Tiberius Omega Mining Colony had failed. Panicked prisoners surged in every direction, free from the confinement of their cells but quickly discovering navigation was not a mob's greatest strength.

Beauregard and Braga dispensed helping hands and harsh words wherever they were needed along Fleur's cell block, but all were batted away. Adding any sense of order to the chaos was impossible. Their definitely-not-a-friend space pirate didn't even bother to help. Besides, all the prisoners were moving in the other direction to them. The prisoners were understandably keen to escape the mines and force their way onto a borrowed shuttle. Between their strength in numbers and the chaos of a prison under attack, some might even make it. Beauregard hoped they did—providing no one stole *his* borrowed shuttle. But their unlikely threesome hadn't come here to escape emptyhanded. If Fleur was in the mines, they would have to go down to find her, which meant pushing against the tide of rioting prisoners.

Deep in the mines' barren darkness and industrial shadows, prisoners who had been working during the attack were overwhelming frail pockets of PROXUS personnel, who had been left bereft of the prison's drained security systems. Keeping everyone at the business end of their plasma pistols, the three of them pushed down an endless warren of rockface and machines built for soul-sapping labour, past grim faces and broken bodies whose lifeforce had been drained and pummelled into fragile inconsequence.

Beauregard's shame weighed heavy but silent. The deeper they delved into the mines, the worse he felt. Throughout his career, he had filled labour camps just like this one. Prisoners destined never to return. As PROXUS' longest serving Ranger—at least before he had gone rogue to rescue Isabella from First Duke Striker— he had obeyed a lifetime of bad orders. Wherever the Empress sent him, he landed with guns blazing. Whoever survived the experience of meeting him ended up somewhere like this. Or worse. With PROXUS, there was always somewhere worse.

Braga was the first to acknowledge the futility of their mission to find Fleur, expressing her opinion colourfully and with such drama that Beauregard felt every muscle in his body clench. He forced his gun arm to relax. Nothing surpassed his need to be ready to pull a trigger.

Yet his shame sank deeper. It was worse than failing the Known Galaxies. He had failed Fleur. Searching the mines had been foolish and desperate. Why had he expected anything else? Cramped mining tunnels and vast excavated caverns, searching the whole complex for one person who hadn't even been in the cell she was supposed to be in—all in the middle of an unexpected and unwanted assault. Beauregard didn't do anger, but he did do shame. He served it cold and lonely. Let it sit inside him. Always and forever. He bore its weight without complaint, ready to witness how much it could still grow.

Aside from gunning down the PROXUS soldiers who challenged them, Beauregard left everything else to his companions. Effortlessly, Braga talked them into as much trouble as she talked them out of. Frantic prisoners. PROXUS guards looking for target practice. Echoes of rebellion faded to a distant rumble amid the thump of explosions from outside, as their definitely-not-a-friend space pirate took the lead.

These were quieter, disused passages. No prisoners. No guards. Passing relics of machinery long retired and dull veins of ore long depleted, they snuck through giant pipes intended for extracting… something. It could have been a waste extraction system for unwanted rocks, unwanted prisoners or pure shit for all Beauregard knew. Or cared. He stopped listening to the space pirate long before he heard any indication of the type of waste these pipes were designed to extract. More pressing was the knowledge of the waste it was currently extracting—them—and listening for sounds of pursuit.

Ignoring the stale stench seeping through each joint where the pipes narrowed, Beauregard forced himself onto all fours again and along another claustrophobic crawlspace. This waste extraction system was modular, which meant too many connections and tight squeezes. His hands and knees were slick with fluids he never wanted identified, his old back complaining like a rusty hinge, but he was too proud to show his discomfort.

Beauregard stopped when he felt the sudden arrival of thinner atmospheric pressure. A colonist or someone like Isabella from a backwater nothing of a planet like Earth might have missed the change, but to someone who had spent his military career travelling through space and jumping from ship to planet and back again, it was impossible to miss a shift in pressure. Beauregard wasn't worried about thinner atmosphere, but they would all be phyxed if the oxygen ran out because they took a wrong turn. That would be his fault, Beauregard decided. His fault for failing Fleur and trusting Braga.

As Beauregard paid increasing attention to the pipe he was crammed inside, wondering what had caused the shift in atmospheric pressure, he found the jagged hole cut crudely from the chute's flank.

"Clever," muttered Braga.

Being a tiny dpresh, their definitely-not-a-friend space pirate slipped effortlessly through the jagged hole. With increasing difficulty, Braga then Beauregard clambered out through the hole and into…

Space.

Well, not quite.

They were in space. Or to be more precise, they were closer to space than Beauregard ever wanted to be. Between them and it, a temporary bubble of atmosphere surrounded them and kept the vacuum at bay. The bubble was grounded on—and there was no getting away from this—the *exterior* surface of the asteroid into which Tiberius Omega Mining Colony had been built.

They were outside.

Beauregard had seen similar temporary atmosphere bubbles before. Refugees and space pirates had installed some on the Husk, before the ship was brought back to life as *Haven* and used their renewed consciousness to grow their hull airtight and master the art of pressurisation. This bubble was formed from a weak membrane of energy. It wouldn't be robust enough to withstand a blast from a plasma pistol, and it would definitely ruin your rotation if you were inside the bubble when it burst. However, these bubbles could inflate in a mere moment and sustain a pressurised atmosphere as long as the air remained breathable. This bubble had been sealed around the asteroid's surface and the side of the waste extraction pipe they had escaped along. Oxygen had been escaping with them down the pipe and through the hole cut into it.

Also sealed within the bubble's perimeter, but on its far side, was the door to an airlock. This made no sense. Beauregard saw no ship on the other side of the door. Just a lone door to nowhere sticking out of the bubble. What he did see, however, in flashes of green plasma and hot explosions above them, was a fleet of PROXUS ships tangling with a PROXUS battle station and swarms of small PROXUS snubfighters. The space battle looked evenly matched, which probably meant everyone was going to die. And there was nothing like a civil war to make everyone wonder what they were dying for.

The space pirate extended a hand. "Your weapons."

But the expectation in his tone was misjudged. Faster than a blast of plasma, Beauregard drew his pistol and aimed it from the hip. An ugly expression crawled over his face. "Ain't neither of us givin' up our weapons, pal."

Hands on hips, Braga sighed. "He's a pirate. If he's making demands, he has leverage."

"I don't see no leverage. Just an airlock that leads nowhere." Beauregard waved his plasma pistol. "I ain't got no need for more leverage. Now get vented." Beauregard couldn't understand why the space pirate looked so unimpressed by his plasma pistol.

"If you kill me, we'll all die," he pointed out. "Only I have the code to that airlock. Give me your weapons so you can't double-cross me, and I'll call my ship to get us out of here."

"You're double-crossin' us so we can't double-cross you?" Beauregard asked with a snarl. "Phyxin' pirates!"

This particular space pirate was growing irritated. "Do you want a ride out of here or not?"

"You played us," accused Beauregard. "You couldn't take us out earlier, not on your own."

"He played us and won," clarified Braga. She tossed her plasma pistol and gauntlet onto the asteroid's rocky surface. "Read the room and let's get out of here."

Sometimes, Beauregard couldn't believe her stupidity. "He ain't even asked for our gauntlets."

The space pirate pinched the bridge of his nose as though he had a migraine, then pushed his glasses on tighter. "Gauntlets too. And please hurry, before one of those blasts hits us."

Illuminated by flashes of green plasma from the space battle raging all around their bubble, Beauregard tossed away his weapons and gauntlet. "Ain't you gonna call your ship now?"

"Not yet." He collected their weapons and gauntlets and trudged over to the door to nowhere. Then he allowed himself to smile for the first time. He tapped a button on the airlock—without even entering a code. It was just as well Beauregard had handed over his plasma pistol, or else that alone might have driven him to shoot someone. The door split apart, retracting sideways in both directions from its centre. On the other side of the airlock, there was nothing but space outside the bubble.

Beauregard frowned. "Why ain't this bubble depressurisin'? Why ain't we dead?"

The space pirate walked through the airlock and disappeared. Literally disappeared. One moment he was inside the bubble, the next he was gone.

Braga started running. "Stealth ship!" she yelled.

Beauregard caught on a moment later and dove after her. "Phyxin' pirates!"

They hauled arse over the asteroid's surface fast enough to hurl themselves at the airlock. It slammed shut in front of them, nearly taking Beauregard's face off.

He hammered on the door, hurling his crudest curses at the space pirate on the other side. With the heel of his fist, he punched the same button again and again that the space pirate had pressed.

Breathlessly, Braga leant against the door. "It won't open. Not while it's cycling."

"I know how a phyxin' airlock works," Beauregard growled. "I ain't a complete dpresh."

"Really, which bit of you is missing?"

"Get locked."

"Or maybe you should calm down and stop pressing that button before you break it. When he flies off, this bubble's going to have a big old hole in it."

Beauregard's fist hovered over the button he had been pounding. He glanced at Braga. "I ain't hittin' it because I'm angry, I'm hittin' it so as soon as he's cycled through, this door opens."

Braga shook her head irritably. "He'll engage the deadlock. It won't open."

"He can't deadlock it if the outer door's already open. Safety protocols, ain't it?"

Instantly, Braga gestured at the door with outstretched hands. "Then keep hitting it!"

Beauregard hammered the button with all the focus of someone who knew once the space pirate hit the deadlock on the other side, this outer door wouldn't be opening again before he flew away.

The airlock shot open.

They didn't waste a heartbeat.

Beauregard leaped inside with the grace of a vitraxi giving birth to triplets. He landed in an incredibly small airlock that had been invisible from outside the stealth ship, his face verifying the solidity of the floor by volunteering to be the first part of his body to land on it. He peered up at Braga, who had entered just as quickly but by virtue of a single swift step.

The door flashed shut behind them. Beauregard felt the floor rock. "We're takin' off."

As soon as the airlock had cycled them through to match ship pressure, Braga punched the inner door release. Nothing happened.

"What is it with phyxin' doors?" Beauregard demanded. "I ain't got nothin' against them."

A bored voice droned over the airlock's comm. "It will be safer if you remain here for our flight."

"Safer?" Beauregard snarled at the disembodied voice. "We ain't gonna kill you."

Braga gave him a sideways look. "Do you want to try that again, but maybe a little more convincingly?"

"It isn't for my safety, believe me. It's to stop me shooting *you* before we reach our destination. I'm turning the comms off now."

"Aww phyx, would you just—"

"Goodbye."

The comm disconnected.

Braga smiled. "Well, you really showed him."

"Ain't no reasonin' with you phyxin' pirates."

Braga sank onto the airlock's deck. "Fleur needed us."

He sank down beside her. "Yeah."

They contemplated their shared failure for the longest silence the pair had ever endured, except for all those times when one had knocked the other out cold.

"She's tough," Braga muttered. "She'll still be alive."

"Tougher than all of us, though she don't make no big deal of it," agreed Beauregard.

"You'd know better than anyone."

Beauregard couldn't look at her, kept staring at the airlock door. "I ain't her wife."

Braga snorted. "You've known her longer."

Beauregard answered with silence.

It was eventually broken when, growling at the effort, he began to peel off his stolen armour. It might be a long flight, and comfort aside he doubted they would be visiting anywhere that took kindly to PROXUS Rangers, even if it was only a disguise.

"We'll find her," whispered Braga. "She deserves it."

"Sure. She deserves it. But it ain't no secret how cruel these galaxies are neither. It ain't right what folk lose out here, but the injustice of it ain't gonna save no one."

"This is Fleur we're talking about."

There was a lot Beauregard could have told Braga in that moment. How everything he was feeling was because of his need to be Fleur's hero. How an unpayable debt had been accrued through her endless cycles of friendship to a dpresh like him. How his inability to accept leaving Fleur in danger was because she had far more right to survive than he ever would. How, as much as he hated to admit it, none of this was Braga's fault.

Soberly, Beauregard lit a cigarette. "If you need to piss before we land, hold it in. This airlock's tiny."

CHAPTER SEVENTEEN

Beauregard felt the stealth ship land with a bump. He hadn't seen any point in getting ready for this moment. He and Braga had nothing going for them—and he wasn't thinking about their frayed relationship, but more about their cramping limbs and lack of weapons.

The outer airlock door parted silently to admit the barrel of a plasma pistol. The absence of any hiss from the door made him wonder if this was a special feature of all stealth ships, or whether the hiss had been added to all the other airlocks, ramps and doors he had used previously. Or had he been using doors wrong all this time? Beauregard's bored mind was circling this conundrum when the plasma pistol and the sour-faced stranger gripping it indicated Beauregard should stand. Unmoving, Beauregard gave him the stink eye.

Having already sprung to her feet, Braga glared down at Beauregard—as though somehow he was making her look bad. As if she couldn't do that all on her own.

Languidly, Beauregard rolled his neck, stretched out his arms and levered his body off the deck. The space pirate's face wrinkled even dourer. *Good.* Beauregard needed to get away from wherever they were as fast as the nearest star drive could propel them, and the more off-balance everyone else was, the more likely he would get the drop on them. That was his best hope of hunting down Fleur.

The plasma pistol marched them out of the airlock and into a huge hangar bay. It was loud with shouting and synth music, chaotic with activity and a complete mess thanks to all the discarded engineering apparatus lying everywhere. Snubfighters and cargo haulers were scattered across the vast hangar. Every ship was unique in its style, design and paint scheme. In all, Beauregard was overwhelmingly unsurprised by the whole place. It was exactly how he had imagined a band of space pirates would organise themselves. Which was to say—terribly.

Like the many PROXUS battle stations and larger ships Beauregard had served on, one entire wall of the hangar looked open to space—exposed to a veil of stars stitched into melting obsidian. Atmospheric pressure was regulated by an anti-vac seal, which admitted ships in and out through the seemingly open wall, while keeping all the air—and everyone breathing it—safely inside. The sleek outlines of more ships drifted past among the stars. These were gargantuan warships—in greater numbers than Beauregard had ever seen outside a PROXUS fleet.

More space pirates gathered to escort them out of the hangar, but thankfully not out of the open wall and into space. Plasma pistols prodded them down a dirty, bustling corridor. Their entourage all wore the same tattoo on their faces—a half-eclipsed sun, just like Fleur and the double-crossing pirate they had met on Tiberius Omega Mining Colony. Their escort wore cobbled together military and spacer outfits so different that, walking together in a cluster around Beauregard and Braga, such a gathering of unique outfits served almost as its own distinctive uniform.

They rode a star lift in silence, followed by a march down a cleaner, quieter corridor. At least, their escort kept trying to make it a march. They were slowed by Beauregard's unhurried strides. While they cursed him, snarled at him, eyeballed him, Beauregard counted every weapon and evaluated the attention span of every pirate. From the two-handed axes slung over their backs to the rapid-fire plasma carbines slung at port across their waists, he measured them all with cold eyes that had iced over many, many cycles ago.

Another sigil of a half-eclipsed sun, this one gold instead of white, was elegantly engraved on the door at the end of the corridor. Pleasingly, it opened with a hiss.

"Your prisoners," announced a voice from beside the door. He was a thin reed of a man, and the first unarmed space pirate Beauregard had ever met. Despite his silken finery, he appeared the least likely person to find on a pirate ship. He looked incredibly flimsy and—Beauregard decided—probably chose not to wear a plasma pistol on the grounds its recoil might topple him.

Beyond the door, a great deal greeted Beauregard's tired eyes. None of it excited him, although much surprised him. Yet it was Braga, not Beauregard, who swore. Tensed like a hunter encroaching into the lair of an elusive beast, she balled her fists and stormed towards the man at the far end of the chamber. For someone whose bolts were rarely rattled and who packed an irritating smile for every occasion, Braga looked furious. Even the back of her head looked angry.

Beauregard could have reached out a calm hand to hold her back or give her pause for thought before she did anything foolish.

Obviously, he didn't.

Given they were on a ship and not a planet, the vast chamber consumed a surprisingly great deal of real estate. Its ceiling was extraordinarily high, with ornate banners adorned with far more colours than Beauregard could name draped down every wall. Each tall banner displayed a different clan sigil. Among the banners at the far end of the chamber, next to the man Braga was storming towards, was the sigil of a white half-eclipsed sun set on black. Fleur's sigil. And that was usually where he would have stopped paying attention. He often left details like that to someone else while he focussed on more important stuff—like who to shoot first. Pirate emblems hadn't mattered when he was a Ranger—if they weren't PROXUS, they were all enemies. If his orders were to start shooting, checking who he was firing at merely delayed the inevitable while giving them a chance to shoot back. Besides, whoever they were, it had never mattered—soon enough, they would be dead. It gave Beauregard zero comfort that his darkest self was in his past. His grim face was practised at concealing his shame, a wrinkled pall of apathy and scars stretched tight over his aching bones. As cold and lonely as ever.

However, he no longer had the luxury of presuming everyone was his enemy. Now, very occasionally, people didn't want to kill him. Paying more attention than he would have in the past, Beauregard spotted a banner with a blue bird in flight cast on gold. Braga's sigil. Next to it were the red jaws of a vitraxi inked on white, beside that a black skull emblazoned on green. Neither registered in his memory. Nor did anything else. He did notice how many of the banners' emblems matched the diverse range of tattoos adorning the chamber's audience. They sat in a vast semi-circle of hover chairs and cushioned recliners around the chamber's arena. The chamber stretched far behind this inner semi-circle, housing a much larger secondary audience crammed into stalls that extended in less luxurious, tiered seating all the way up to the banners lining the perimeter.

The chamber felt like an amphitheatre melded with a throne room. Beauregard had the latter comparison in mind largely thanks to the man standing at the other end of the chamber. In the mere moments since their arrival had been announced, Braga had closed much of the gap between them. The man's steepling height was in part due to the afro that spun upwards into a swirling spire from his scalp. He wore an elegant purple robe with armoured plates and elaborate decoration. A stylishly basketed rapier was sheathed at his belt. Dual plasma pistols hung from his thighs in much the same way that Beauregard's had, before one of Beauregard's arms had been rendered arthritic and useless by the mightily pissed off Sau Daran god Midnight Twice.

The man raised a hand, his fingers drowning in a dazzling rainbow of golden rings set with vibrant jewels. Beauregard suspected his jewellery was too garish, too large, too numerous even for Braga's tastes. At the raising of his hand, every pirate in the chamber who had been tracking Braga's progress with a pistol or rifle lowered their weapons. They didn't look happy about it. In the silent anticipation holding the chamber by its throat, he heard more than one pirate grumble. But it gave Braga time to reach the man in the purple robe.

Her first strike was a fist to his gut. The breath escaped him all at once, his surprised gasp of pain riding the chamber's crisp acoustics all the way to the back row. As he creased over, her other hand slapped his temple so hard with an open palm that it floored him. Among their audience, outrage sparked from the mouths of various pirates—but there was also amusement rippling through the throng.

"Dpresh!" Braga screamed. It was the last thing she did before a press of rough hands seized her. Kicking her legs out from under her, the guards carried her away furious and wriggling. "You can get locked for what you did to her," she screamed at the man picking himself off the deck. "I'll kill you!"

Bemused, Beauregard watched them haul her out of the chamber. By the time she was gone, he had a good idea of where he was and—more importantly—the identity of their host. These weren't just members of Fleur's old pirate clan. This was the clan's flagship—and their leader. As the man wiped blood from his lips, Beauregard could see Fleur's resemblance in his high cheekbones, in his intense eyes, in the way he raised a single eyebrow, in the elegant pose he was attempting to reassemble.

"Charming," the man purred in the deepest bass that had ever escaped a man's lips. He grimaced and spat crimson from his blood-stained teeth. "Name and ship?"

Moving so slowly that there could be no confusion over how unthreatening he was behaving, Beauregard strolled to the centre of the chamber. "I ain't no pirate. Kyle Beauregard, freelancer. I ain't got no ship that's mine neither, but let's say I call *Haven* my home. They're a livin' Sau Daran ship." It was the first time Beauregard had ever used his home as a threat, but he saw on the closest of faces watching that it hit home. "And I ain't in no doubt you're Garrick Fontaine."

The man who had been dabbing his mouth with a quilted handkerchief, the likes of which Beauregard had only seen in old holo shows, paused mid-dab. "Count Fontaine, if you please. From your friend's outburst, I can only presume you both consort with my daughter."

"Count? Well ain't that fancy." Beauregard ran his cold blue eyes over the man's curious expression in a manner he hoped was more threatening—and more subtle—than the brief beating Braga had dished out. "You let her strike you. Twice."

Stowing his antiquated handkerchief in one of the robe's outer pockets, Fontaine spared Beauregard a pitying look. "Perhaps I deserved it."

"Oh, you deserve more than a little tickle," Beauregard assured him darkly.

Fontaine held out his open palms invitingly.

Beauregard did what he was good at, keeping his body still and his face impassive. "Not here. Not like that. When you get what's comin' to you, you ain't gonna be gettin' up afterwards."

Once more, Fontaine had to wave away his guards with a flash of his gaudily bejewelled hands as they processed another blatant threat to their leader's safety and rushed to do their job. "Speaking before the delegates of the Free Pirate Conclave, I concede the fault is mine. The slight was done long ago and by me."

Beauregard had heard of the Free Pirate Conclave. They claimed to put the 'organised' in organised crime—pirates working together towards shared goals and shared loot. "You abandoned her," he said. His expression felt as hard and unwelcoming as a reinforced bulkhead. He doubted it looked any less subtle. "You gave her to PROXUS to save your own skin."

Fontaine bowed his head. "A black mark against my name. A mark that shall never be wiped clean, nor forgotten." He raised his chin regally, addressing the whole chamber. "In an attempt to right my wrong, I sent my best agent to free Lady Fontaine from Tiberius Omega Mining Colony."

"She wasn't there," growled Beauregard.

"Alas, we were too late. Such a loss."

"Or maybe she didn't need no one savin' her in the first place. Maybe she got herself out."

"Perhaps." Fontaine's voice grew in volume and stature, filling the chamber with its rich timbre as he addressed the assembled pirates, not Beauregard. "I would tear down the very stars to see her safe."

"Ten cycles too late," said Beauregard, practically spitting his words. "Where were you all those cycles she was workin' for PROXUS? Flyin' for PROXUS? Killin' for PROXUS?" He glanced at the crowd of tattooed faces watching him intently. "Where were you when they captured her? When they spaced her crew? When they gave her no way out but service to the Empress?"

"We are here now. Together, for the first time. Me, Lady Fontaine's father. You, her ally. I implore you, if you care about her half as much as I do then signal her. Find out if she escaped. Put all our hearts at rest."

"I ain't sendin' no signal you can track, pal. And your heart ain't my concern unless you're in the market for someone to stop it beatin'."

Desperation crept into the corners of Fontaine's expression. "Don't you fear for her safety?"

"Don't you fear for yours?" Beauregard bit back.

"Oh, desist!" snapped Fontaine. "I wish to make amends. I have made my intentions perfectly clear before the Conclave."

"Get locked."

Clicking his fingers irritably, Fontaine sank back into his robustly cushioned throne. After a tense wait, an entourage of scowls and plasma pistols pushed Braga back into the chamber. Restraints bound her wrists and a dark bruise shone over one eye. Beauregard was pleased to see a few shiners on two of the pirates escorting her. They shoved her next to him.

"You worked out what's going on yet?" she asked.

"Enough to appreciate those blows you landed."

"Thanks."

"We ain't helpin' none of you," Beauregard announced to the whole chamber.

"Does the insolent one have a name and a ship?" asked Fontaine, strangling the arms of his throne. "We rather skipped the formalities earlier."

Beauregard didn't expect Braga to reply, but he quickly realised how little he understood pirate etiquette.

"Captain Braga, formerly of *Liliana's Revenge*, now serving under Lady Fontaine aboard *Haven*." Beauregard was surprised by her uncharacteristic restraint. "It's a Sau Daran ship with enough firepower and attitude to blow your whole fleet out of the stars," she added.

Ah, there she is.

"Thank you," replied Fontaine. He released his white-knuckled grip on the throne. "I have informed the Conclave I wish to make amends."

Good luck with that.

"Give us your terms," Braga demanded.

Wait, what?

"No harm to either party. Shared resources and intel. A meeting between my daughter and I."

"A meeting brokered by us?" scoffed Braga.

"You appear to be in the most suitable position to arrange it. You clearly care for her." Fontaine's fingers strayed to his swollen lip and came away bloody. "If she escaped, convince her I mean no harm. Vouchsafe our meeting. If you can't reach her, if she's still in PROXUS custody, I'll send our whole fleet to get her back."

A ripple of dissent spread through their audience.

"And if we don't agree?" asked Braga.

Fontaine's face grew stormy, although his regal posture held firm. "Agree to my terms, or you shall both sit in a cell for the rest of your lives. You'll never discover whether my daughter is safe, captured or dead."

Grimly, Beauregard fastened his gaze on Fontaine. "Can't imagine why Fleur don't want to talk to you."

CHAPTER EIGHTEEN

Lynch was the only human who had been inside Paradise Moon's bedroom. At the time, he had grunted something about how strange it looked. Although, being Lynch, he had said it like that was a compliment. Honestly? Paradise Moon didn't see what all the fuss was about.

Sure, it didn't have a bed. That was admittedly unusual for a bedroom. But Paradise Moon didn't need a bed. Isabella always woke up in her own bed, which required Paradise Moon to sleep there too. It was an essential part of their body-sharing routine and, conveniently, how Paradise Moon preserved her privacy. Sure, the walls were bare. No fresh paint, no wallpaper. Just scabbed, smudged, once-white paint as old as the flat. But there was still a carpet—she wasn't an animal. She tore off Isabella's boots and socks, then curled Isabella's liberated human toes into the thick, rich pile. She loved that feeling of soft carpet beneath Isabella's human foot—yet another exaggerated sensation human bodies took for granted.

And sure, there was the crate. The only item in the room. The crate was large enough to hide a body in, but that wasn't the only reason she had stolen it. Now it was on the other side of the universe from the high security PROXUS storage facility where she had found it, sitting innocently in the middle of her bedroom and waiting for her next offering.

Carefully, she drew handfuls of creased ivory flowers from her jeans and scattered them on the crate's lid, making sure to go either side of the hole covered with gaffer tape in its centre. The crate had originally been locked up tight with a secure PROXUS encryption and expensive DNA scan embedded in the mechanism. But Paradise Moon could punch very hard with her glowing purple fist. Now there was no mechanism, no DNA scan, no encryption. Just a hole and some gaffer tape.

Most of the flowers were past their best. Sifting through petals weeping with trickles of melted snow, her fingers gently separated a single perfect flower. Brushing aside the discarded flowers for her future self to tidy up next Friday, she pinched her perfect flower by its stem and held it up to her purple-flecked eyes.

Coyly at first, the memory of her date with Lynch tingled in her fingertips. She rotated the stem between glowing purple finger and thumb, playing back the memory while it was fresh. It washed through Isabella's body in a surge of adrenaline, a physical sensation unlike anything Paradise Moon could dream of experiencing without her own flesh and bone, muscles and tendons, neurons and blood. She felt Isabella's body transforming all her joy and excitement into something she could feel on a sensory level. The memory glowed inside veins and arteries. Blood rushed hot. Isabella's heart quickened. Goosepimples rippled up this human leg, that human arm. Closing Isabella's eyes, Paradise Moon let the sensation sit inside her for as long as she could feel it and hold it and know it.

When the sensation died to a distant ache, she opened the crate. Pushing aside her clothes, she retrieved a small felt box. With the flower tucked safely inside, she stared at it a moment longer before slipping it back into the crate alongside her other keepsakes. She soaked up the last of that feeling, held it, knew it.

She closed the lid and was alone. Safe inside her bare walls. As secure as her boxed-up memories. In a rare moment of weakness, Paradise Moon decided to do the right thing. With what she would have described as heroic devotion to someone else's problems, she pulled out Isabella's phone. She deliberately set a low bar when it came to attempting boring tasks, lest she actually be expected to do them. Therefore, whether left on a phone or a gauntlet, most messages were fated to be ignored until Isabella woke up. If anything was that important, Isabella could do her own freaking admin. She didn't need a god to be her secretary.

But as Paradise Moon—heroically—checked Isabella's inbox and feeds, she had to admit there were some messages even her low bar couldn't ignore. Isabella's socials were flooded with messages. All thoughts of Lynch evaporated as Paradise Moon tried to calculate how much shit she was going to be in when Isabella woke up. Scrolling through the messages while her glowing hand absently smeared ash and melted snow from Isabella's hair, all Paradise Moon saw on Isabella's feed was post after post of her space hottie.

And he was pissed.

In every recording, he kept gesturing at the PC inside the library. These videos had been appearing for hours. Hours. He kept demanding to speak to Isabella, but—as was becoming increasingly apparent to Paradise Moon from all the comments on the posts—Talyn was the only person in the library who had been injected with translation nanites.

Shit.

Isabella had been injected with translation nanites when Striker captured her on his battle station three years ago, so she hadn't had any trouble understanding Talyn. He was, however, experiencing significant difficulty being understood by everyone else. Paradise Moon thumbed down to yet another video and watched Talyn making his case with incandescent frustration to a semi-circle of bemused book borrowers.

Shit.

There was no time to lose. Pausing only to watch a video of a charming gorilla in a tutu, which had crept onto Isabella's feed, Paradise Moon reluctantly acknowledged her responsibilities as custodian of Isabella's body. Chief among them: don't let Isabella find out. She rolled her shoulders, stretched her neck and got her game face ready, just the way she had seen Rocky do in all the films. Retrieving Isabella's sunglasses from her jeans, she thrust them onto her face.

Purple smoke took Paradise Moon to Talyn's side. Her sudden appearance in Reading Library prompted him to freeze mid-rant and glare at her.

The humans gathered around him were in two minds about how to react to Paradise Moon's sudden appearance. The smaller of the two groups reacted with shock, while the larger group rushed to snap the moment on their phones. One fuzzy haired toddler did his best impression of having an electric shock as he jumped almost his full height in surprise but was cheering before he landed. It would be fair to say he had a foot in both camps, as well as another foot on the bent spine of the picture book he was stomping into the carpet.

With their hands too busy taking photos and videos to applaud, many humans burst into the sort of gleeful whoops Isabella handled with such grace. In her absence, Paradise Moon bowed theatrically and pulled silly faces.

"I am so sorry!" she announced cheerfully at Talyn, her arms held aloft like a champion wrestler after winning a bout. "Thank you for looking after my friend!" she shouted at the library's watching humans. "We love you Reading!" She held up both hands, making the peace sign.

The humans stared at her in a cocktail of confusion and anticipation. From the centre of the crowd, the librarian sneezed. She was still wearing her cardigan and spectacles, but was weighed down with a new weariness. "We close at three," she said politely, wiping her nose with a tissue. Taking no chances, she made a small, introverted gesture at the clock on the wall, whose hands were inescapably pointing to the cusp of three o'clock. "Please," she gave the crowd a sideways glance, "we're not a zoo. Today has been the worst day of my life."

"Isabella, where were you?" cried Talyn. Encased in his armour, what little of his body she could see was tense with frustration. Highly unnecessary frustration.

Ignoring the poor librarian, who was being jostled by the sheer weight of the crowd and still waving her tissue, Paradise Moon gave Talyn her full attention. This was clearly a stressful situation for him and she needed to handle it delicately. Or at least as delicately as she knew how. She curled the edge of her grin into something smug and tipped her sunglasses down Isabella's nose to give him a flash of something purple and otherworldly behind her eyes. "Isabella? Not even close, flyboy."

Talyn's face hardened. "Are you going to kill me?" Misplaced suspicion crept over his expression.

Shit shit shittity shit shit shit.

His question was ridiculous. Clearly a joke. Wasn't it? Paradise Moon laughed. Apparently, this was not the correct response.

First, the PC's tower and screen exploded with a fanfare of sparks and cascading components. Gasping and ducking, humans scattered like the little lemmings they were. Then the fluorescent strips of lighting above them flashed and shattered. A storm of hot glass rained down on what was quickly becoming the loudest library Paradise Moon had ever been inside. But as long as Isabella didn't find out, everything would be fine. She could still fix this.

Most of the humans were hotfooting it outside faster than Isabella bearing down on a vintage guitar sale. Those who hadn't moved fast enough, Paradise Moon vanished behind a shelf of hardbacks. She made time to roll her eyes. "Chill out, flyboy," she called from behind the bookcase. "There's people in here!"

When she got no response, Paradise Moon poked her head around the bookshelf. Smoke drifted up from the PC and down from the crippled lights. Through the trail of acrid fumes, she caught the library's front door shuddering closed behind Talyn.

Paradise Moon swore colourfully and inventively. Glancing back to check on the humans she had vanished to safety, she was greeted by a boy thrusting his phone in her face. "Maybe edit that bit out?" she asked hopefully.

"We're live…" the boy whispered. He had as many pimples on his face as there were badges on his jacket.

Whipping out her finger guns, Paradise Moon unleashed her finest shit-eating grin. "Great!" She pushed her sunglasses all the way up the bridge of her nose. "Stay in school, kid."

Crawling out from beneath a table, the librarian wafted at the smoke as she staggered towards Paradise

Moon. With her tissue still clenched in one hand, it looked like she was waving a flag of surrender.

"I am so sorry about all this," said Paradise Moon. "I, Isabella, apologise for everything." She was aiming for sincere and contrite, but she didn't hang around to find out how badly she missed.

Purple smoke.

Gone.

Paradise Moon vanished into the middle of the street, frigid winter air catching in Isabella's throat, and stared straight into the path of a purple bus. It roared towards her, spinning a trail of black fumes. Talyn was beside her in the street, already running away from the library and now away from her. Towards the bus—like the idiot she was beginning to suspect he was.

"Out of the way!" Talyn screamed at the bus.

Anyone dumb enough to stand in front of a bus got a clear view of everything inside. Through its flat window of a face, Paradise Moon saw the panicked driver's hands fly off the steering wheel as it *spun itself* with inhuman ferocity the moment Talyn screamed. Swerving out of the road and up the pavement, the bus buried its face into the glass frontage of an estate agents. Alarms blared. More humans screamed and ran.

Isabella is going to kill me.

Talyn was shouting at Paradise Moon rather than the bus now. "Get away from me! I've warned you!"

But Paradise Moon didn't bend to his will as swiftly as the bus had. Sighing, Paradise Moon set her hands on her hips and pinned him with her best glare, before realising he wouldn't be able to see shit past Isabella's sunglasses.

Ignoring her, Talyn sprinted further up the street. Coated, hatted, gloved lemmings dashed around him, fleeing from they didn't know what. Sparks burst from every security camera he passed, along with a bus stop's explosive digital signage and the quickly igniting, quickly tossed aside phone of a businesswoman who backed as far into the brickwork behind her as physics allowed.

"Stop breaking things!" shouted Paradise Moon.

Another driver's hands flew off her steering wheel as a sleek hatchback swung violently at Paradise Moon. She vanished out of the car's path, leaving it to negotiate a broad Grundon while she reappeared with a flurry of purple smoke next to Talyn at Jackson's Corner. Panicked sweat drizzled down his face as he backed away from her and dove around the green-fronted corner of Jackson's, or Jacks n's if the falling apart, boarded up storefront was to be believed.

"You're being a real prick!" she called after him.

Panting, he tore off the main road and uphill alongside tired concrete pillars towards Market Place. He cast an oncoming taxi aside with a frantic sweep of his arm, giving it the full bollard treatment.

There's no reasoning with some people.

In a stark reminder that if Agent Glass had a superpower, it was terrible timing, Darth Vader's theme thrummed ominously from Isabella's pocket. Paradise Moon thumbed open the call as she watched Talyn sprint up Market Place. "What is it, dickweed?" she shouted into the phone. "I'm in the middle of something."

"Isabella?" classic Agent Glass monotone droned at her with all the joys of spring. "I'm watching some disturbing live videos on social media."

"Then get back to your day job and stop dicking around on your socials."

"Can you control this or not?" Even though it wasn't a video call, she could feel the despairing look Agent Glass was giving her.

"Relax, Glass man. I'm working the problem."

"Glass man?" Agent Glass sighed the hopeless sigh of the defeated. "That's not Isabella, is it?"

"Why does that matter?" Paradise Moon replied testily. She glanced back at the trashed estate agents, the scattering humans, the smoking bus, the bent out of shape hatchback rolling away from a Grundon. "I'm perfectly capable of handling this."

"Oh God, I'm actually talking to the alien. Right. Stand down. I'm sending my own people in."

Erm, no thank you. That's the last thing Isabella would want.

Paradise Moon moved Isabella's lips closer to the phone. "You really don't need to do that. I've got this."

"This is not a negotiation."

"Yes, it is!"

"No, it's not."

"Yes, it is!" Desperation leaked through the rising treble in Paradise Moon's voice. "We're negotiating right now. Can't you hear us disagreeing?"

Being in the driving seat was great and all, but the wildcard was how a meat sack's blood, neurons and adrenaline surged every which way whenever Paradise Moon felt anything. If the news was good, it was exhilarating. But right now, Paradise Moon wasn't a fan of how the phone felt harder to grip in Isabella's sweaty palms and how Isabella's chest felt tighter even though there was no visible weight pressing down on it. "No, no, no, no, no, no, no!" she pleaded, sensing a galaxy of perfectly articulated sass tumbling away from her and becoming lost forever.

"Can I talk to Isabella?"

"Absolutely not!" Paradise Moon felt Isabella's arms do a frantic 'why doesn't anyone understand me?' dance. "I'm handling this. Isabella doesn't need to know anything—it's all going to be fine."

"Stand. Down."

The line disconnected.

"But it's Friday!" Paradise Moon shouted into the silent handset. Shoving the phone into her pocket with a heavy dose of feeling, she surveyed the carnage. Talyn had made an absolute casserole out of Reading's town centre. A zigzag of discarded vehicles smoked from their crumpled bonnets, stunned and furious drivers staggering onto the pavement amid the din of livid car alarms. Ahead, up the High Street towards Market Place, the view was no better.

Isabella really is going to kill me.

Talyn surged up the crest of the hill, sprinting under the shadow of St Lawrence's church at the top, with its flint-lined wall and yellowed stones. As he did so, a conspicuous troop of nobodies were keeping pace with him. Paradise Moon would have known Agent Glass' operatives anywhere. She watched them dodge a one-two punch of bus and taxi from around the blind bend in front of the church. The bus hurtled into the steadfast row of bollards that separated Market Place's cobbled island from the High Street. The taxi careered towards a café. Empty streetside tables and chairs pinged off its bonnet until the café's shattering glass and steadfast brickwork hammered the taxi to a sudden, smoking stop.

Belying their tedious attire, the operatives swept into the road in a ring around Talyn.

"Get back!" Talyn warned them.

A gathering tide of outstretched phones swarmed closer from the pedestrianised street at the top of the hill. Among the chaos and destruction that inexplicably seemed to follow Paradise Moon everywhere, blue lights were flashing and sirens were screeching.

Vanishing to the crest of Market Place and inside the ring of Agent Glass' operatives, Paradise Moon grabbed Talyn's shoulder and withdrew him from all this madness with a swirl of purple smoke.

Even though Talyn's startled expression disagreed vehemently, São Miguel Island in the Azores felt like a perfectly sensible place to bring him. However, Paradise Moon hadn't factored in the woman, one of Agent Glass' lackeys, who insisted on clinging to Isabella's arm as they vanished. Small and squat, she wouldn't have been out of place near a rugby scrum.

And gods, she was fast.

Given she couldn't have expected to be vanished to a sun-drenched hillside in the Azores, Agent Glass' operative still managed to be an instant pain in Paradise Moon's ass. Her leg swept Isabella's body to the dirt. A bed of sun-hardened earth struck her back, punching the air from Isabella's lungs. Then the woman was on top, pinning her down.

"Don't make me hurt you," she warned.

Paradise Moon giggled at the stoic, stone-carved expression looming over her. "Idiot."

Purple smoke.

Gone.

Paradise Moon and the operative tumbled into deep Alaskan snow. On either side of Isabella's flanks, the operative's knees sunk into the white stuff. Her weight was firmly, crushingly on top of Paradise Moon. She landed one palm on Isabella's throat, her grip claustrophobically tight, and settled her other hand into the snow for stability. Over her shoulder, the distant outline of rising, craggy mountains and clear blue skies would have looked picturesque, had it not been fading and blurring as Isabella's lungs were deprived of oxygen.

"Take us back, or we can stay like this forever."

"Why..."—Paradise Moon gasped—"...are..."—the pressure on Isabella's throat increased—"humans... total... idiots?"

Her glowing purple hand knocked the operative's supporting arm out of the snow with a puff of white powder. She grabbed the woman's flailing arm as it searched for fresh purchase in the snow—and HURLED.

Alien strength infused with irritation at the inconvenience of all this crap were more than enough to post this annoying parcel of professional arsehole high into the air. Signed, sealed and delivered, the operative flew over the snow plain and landed in an even deeper snow drift. Out of reach.

Paradise Moon sat up and took a breath as she watched the operative untangle her limbs and scramble upright. Her depressingly boring clothes were depressingly drenched. Her face was red and furious, her outstretched hands pale and wet.

"If you're angry now, you're gonna hate what happens next," Paradise Moon called across the plain.

Purple Smoke.

Gone.

Warmer sun and drier earth greeted Paradise Moon as she vanished back to Talyn and the lush green tranquillity she had stranded him in. This time, he hadn't tried to run away.

Finally, he's learning.

Talyn raised his fists. "Come on then, I'm ready."

Okay, he's a slow learner.

Paradise Moon knew there were lots of sensible and reassuring things to say to Talyn, she just couldn't think of any. "You can trust me, you idiot!" she scolded. She didn't bother to acknowledge his bared fists as she sat down on a patch of wilting grass on the ridge. "I've done nothing but help you."

"That was Isabella who helped me!" His body was still tensed, his fists still raised. "What if you're lying?"

Paradise Moon waved at his fists irritably. "Oh put those things down, you're embarrassing yourself."

Warily, he lowered his fists, then pointed a finger at his head. "What if you're like him?"

"Like the alien inside you?"

Grimly, he nodded.

"I'm not like anyone, flyboy."

"But you took her body, like Nova took mine. I don't trust you."

Paradise Moon felt her face scrunch up in confusion. That was another thing she hated about driving the meat sack—it gave away everything she tried to keep hidden. "But Nova Sky wants to save my people. You gave up your body to help him, didn't you?"

"Well," Talyn swallowed, "that's what I said. I also said he's a prick."

"So? On this planet, pricks and dicks are as common as bread in a bakery. That doesn't mean you have to look at me like I'm going to tear you apart."

"Will you?" he asked, his expression as grim as a clown's funeral and twice as pale as the headline act.

"Why would I hurt you?"

Talyn's eyes flitted around the grassy ridge, checking for exits. All led down into thick conifers or over a high drop into deep blue sea and rocks below. None would help him escape this conversation. He seemed to bite back a fistful of replies before settling on one. "Nova wants to save your children. But when I said I gave him my body, I lied." Sensing the conversation was drifting as close to unfamiliar territory as it was to an actual point, Paradise Moon shifted Isabella's expression into neutral and waited for Talyn to finish. "He took it."

Shit.

"Now you've taken Isabella's body…."

Removing her sunglasses, Paradise Moon ran glowing purple fingers through the short spikes of Isabella's hair in frustration. "It's not like that."

"Yeah, right."

"No, really. It's not. We have a deal—"

"Sure."

"—every Friday, I get to drive. I never take her body without permission." Paradise Moon left off the word 'anymore' from her explanation.

"Let me talk to her."

"I can't!"

Talyn crossed his arms over wired plates of chipped blue armour. "I can't trust you. If you've hurt Isabella…"

Paradise Moon stared up at him from her patch of grass. "Isabella's fine. But if she finds out what happened today, I won't be. She won't trust me with her body again. I can't bring her back right now. Not if I want to enjoy days like today."

Talyn looked surprised. "Because today's been so phyxing great?"

Paradise Moon laughed, then sighed. "If Nova Sky's that bad, I'm nothing like him. Isabella told you about me, didn't she?"

"Yeah."

"And you remember what she said?"

"Yeah, you sounded like a pain in the ass."

Paradise Moon raised a critical finger. "But I'm a pain in the arse she loves." Her finger retreated. "Actually, never tell her I said that. Ever." Her eyes found his, glowing purple floating in chestnut staring back at the icy cool blues Isabella had become so tragically lost in. "She trusts me. She told you that too."

"Yeah," admitted Talyn.

"So maybe stop being so dumb?"

"You don't seem that dangerous," Talyn conceded. "When I thought you'd taken over…"

Paradise Moon took issue with not seeming dangerous, but this wasn't the time to pick another fight. Instead, she forced a smile. "See, that was easy, wasn't it?" She hesitated. "If Nova Sky's so dangerous, am I going to have to help you deal with him?"

Talyn shook his head. "He's a prick, but he's a locked-up prick. He hasn't had control of me since we were halfway to Earth. But I still have his powers, so I came here to find the artifact and finish the job."

Isabella's face reddened as Paradise Moon contemplated her own reaction to the dire fate of the Sau Daran species her ancestors had created. At the first sign of trouble, she had run to the furthest inhabited planet in the universe. To Earth. Here, she had found Isabella and plenty of time to pretend the rest of the universe didn't exist. Yet here was Talyn, claiming he'd tamed the alien god inside him already and was still trying to save the Sau Darans.

Some people are too saintly for their own good. Why can't he be a useless dumbass like the rest of us?

Paradise Moon looked away, gazed over the sea below. Flashes of burnt gold shimmered across its surface. "Want to tell me why you've been harassing everyone in the library so you can speak to Isabella?"

"I found the Spark. I can save them all."

Unexpected, unbidden emotions clutched Isabella's heart as once again her body became a conduit of betrayal that intensified Paradise Moon's feelings. Afraid she had misheard or the universe was teasing her, Paradise Moon studied Talyn's face. "Say that again."

Talyn's face warmed, and not because of the hot afternoon sun. "We can do it. We can save them."

It was one thing hearing that her Sau Daran people might be saved sometime maybe. This was different. For a start, this time she was driving Isabella's body when he said it. Every part of Isabella's body that could mess up a perfectly good conversation exploded with every chemical reaction her meat sack was incapable of suppressing. Dry lips. Dancing stomach. Sweaty palms. Breaths that could barely finish before the next began.

Pretending Isabella's body wasn't doing all the things she couldn't stop it doing, Paradise Moon studied him for any sign of a lie. "And you still want to save them? Even though he… took your body?"

"I'm here, aren't I? This is all me, not him, and I still want to help. That's why I came."

Forgetting all rules about physical contact with bits of Isabella that weren't glowing and purple, Paradise Moon flung herself at Talyn. She held him tight. Isabella's eyes were leaking, giving away yet more secrets that were supposed to stay safely inside. That was on her—Isabella would never cry in public. She eased her hand up Talyn's back and smeared her tears away while his face was still jammed over her shoulder. Like every other dumb boy on this planet, he would be oblivious to what was really happening, what she was really feeling.

"This is nice," Talyn admitted, his breath on Isabella's neck.

Paradise Moon pulled away fast enough to give Isabella whiplash. "Don't get used to it."

Talyn's expression resembled a scolded puppy. Her face softened. "We can actually do it?" she pressed him. "We can save them?"

"Yeah." Smiling, Talyn nodded to emphasise his point. "And you're really not like Nova at all."

Paradise Moon's witty retort died on the bonfire of hope inside her. For once, she didn't care about landing the last—or better—word. "Just tell me where."

"There's one place that fits the pattern. It's billions of years old and probably where life started on this planet. That's exactly the sort of place I'm looking for— somewhere so old the Spark could have nudged along multicell life on this planet. It's a place called Pilbara."

"Where?"

"Somewhere called Australia," said Talyn. "It's to the south," he added helpfully.

"Yeah, I think I'd better do the navigating. Erm, which bit of Australia?"

"There's a few places worth looking into." He glanced around at the island. "You can get us there, can't you?"

"Damn straight. We're gonna save them all."

Because I left them to die the first time.

Paradise Moon held out a hand.

Talyn took it.

Purple smoke.

Gone.

CHAPTER NINETEEN

Fleur had watched countless viewscreens dissolve into star-pricked space before, but this time felt different. She hid her apprehension as *Haven* dropped them into the star system Beauregard's message had directed them to.

Her father's flagship was waiting. Drifting among a shoal of vessels powered by stolen star drives, the aging behemoth bristled with plasma cannons, its flanks barely blushing with worn purple paint dimmed by time and battle. Unlike anything that had come off a PROXUS production line, no two pirate ships were the same. Every ship in the pirate fleet sported a unique paint job, along with its clan's sigil and extensive technical modifications. The engineer's oil in Fleur's veins burned with pride at seeing the fleet again after all this time, before turning to ice as fast as a pilot going evac in space. Her father would be on that flagship.

No, not my father. He'll never be that again.

The operations room *Haven* had grown three cycles ago gave them everything they needed to run a mission. In particular, the viewscreen was a holo. This allowed

Ezra—now wearing a more comfortable pair of prosthetics than his blades—and the gathered members of her crew to clearly see the projection of ships waiting to greet them.

It had been such a relief to hear Beauregard's voice over the comm. And Braga's. It hadn't sounded like they expected her to respond or even be alive. Hearing their voices had brought her such joy. Then Beauregard had revealed whose company they were keeping. Company she never wanted to keep again. How did Beauregard and Braga go to a PROXUS mining prison to rescue her and end up captured by her fa—by that man? Her wife and the big man were so good at achieving the impossible, but sometimes she wished they would set their sights on a more desirable brand of impossible.

She reached for her gauntlet and tried pinging Isabella's comm again. Earth was too far away for a conversation, but a distress call should reach her with *Haven*'s relays boosting the signal. It had before. But not this rotation. Wherever Isabella was, she wasn't picking up her messages. No quick, purple-smoked rescue for Beauregard and Braga this time, which meant only one thing—Fleur would have to face the man she swore she'd kill if she ever saw him again.

She caught a fragmented reflection of her face in the holo and looked away. She had spent too much—and not enough—of their journey examining, prodding, smoothing, rubbing, grooming, combing, scratching and painstakingly softening every particle of her face and hair. She had enough on her mind already without noticing in this final moment how bad a job she had done.

Ezra's hand found hers. She clasped it. Without letting go, she waited for *Haven* to manoeuvre the operations room until it was next door to the hangar where Fleur's ship lay. She could have already been sat in her shuttle, ready to hurtle out of the hangar bay and get this over with. But she needed one last chance to back away from this madness.

Once the clunking and mechanical groaning died, the operations room's oval door rolled open and Fleur abandoned the safety of Ezra's kind touch for another type of comfort—the familiar sight of her sleek, heavily customised Falchion-class fighter. Every contour of its broad, curved starboard flank settled her heart rate as she ran her fingers down the hull. Like the much smaller Scimitar-class fighter that Dash flew, her fighter was asymmetrical, with the cockpit and crew area on one side, while the other side housed its cargo, engines, weapons and the single scything wing that gave this class of ship its name.

When Ezra offered to go with her, Fleur shook her head. "There is no point risking anyone else. And you do not carry a weapon anymore… I am not entirely sure a pacifist is going to give me the support I need out there."

Ezra grasped her hand again. "This type of support, not the other kind."

Fleur smiled. "Thanks Ez, but I need to do this alone."

From the moment Fleur pulled her fighter away from the safety she always felt inside *Haven*, every pirate ship she flew past was either a dream or a nightmare woven from the past and resurrected. They haunted her all the way to the hangar bay the pirates had prepared for her. After that, familiar faces haunted her all the way to the ornate door leading into the flagship's audience chamber, Clan Fontaine's golden sigil still engraved on its surface.

The door remained closed long enough for her to run her fingers through the sigil's grooves, as she had done when she was a child. That had been a different time, when hope and joy ruled her heart. The door hissed open and the spell was broken. Wearing her boldest mask, Fleur strode down the centre of the chamber. It was lined with representatives from all the major pirate clans, who lazed on their seats with feet up, heads back, munching exotic fruits and throwing down cards. She saw no Braga. No Beauregard. No man who was no longer her father. Recognisable tattooed faces tracked her progress towards the throne. Behind it was a smaller, less ostentatious door. A pair of guards drew her towards it with respectful nods. Reaching the door's holo pad, and doubting this was going to work, Fleur tapped in her old family code. After her mother had passed away, only two people remained who knew this code. The door hissed open. Either Count Fontaine couldn't be bothered to change it, or he reinstated it for her return. She couldn't believe he kept it all this time for sentimentality, given the riches he guarded inside. He had never been sentimental when pointed were concerned.

Within were more familiar sights. Ignoring everything else, her eyes skipped to Beauregard and Braga. She rushed to them, embraced them. Braga flinched as Fleur brushed against the bruises set into her face, but the look in Braga's eyes told Fleur she was fine and any concern was for Fleur. Beauregard accepted his hug without any fuss or discernible response. *Big, dumb, lovable lump.*

Fleur rounded on Count Fontaine. He stood a few paces back among the trove of display cases that filled his private chambers. Each glass case held a rare treasure or trophy with a wild story or boast behind it. Like him, they were all for show. Fleur's hand dropped to her plasma pistol, but it stayed holstered for now. Her companions still needed to make it out of here alive.

"Okay. I am here. Braga vouchsafed you. What now?"

Count Fontaine held himself gun barrel straight with galaxies more dignity than he deserved. "Thank you." Despite his dignified pose, words did not come to him as easily as Fleur expected. He gazed at her in silence.

"You are not phyxing welcome. What do you want?"

Count Fontaine extended his arms towards her and launched into what sounded like an over-rehearsed apology. It was long, fawning and would never be enough.

"Anything else?" Fleur asked once he was done. "Or can we leave?"

Another apology came, this one laced with excuses. Fleur could feel her gun arm itching. "You left us to die," she reminded him.

Yet another apology. More excuses. Pain, too, as his voice cracked between syllables. "You missed your mother's funeral," he added. It seemed he was done apologising, then.

Fleur nearly shot him. "You are going to regret letting me keep my plasma pistol."

"You are Lady Fontaine. No pirate will ever have authority over you."

"Your crew might not see it that way if you fail to survive this conversation."

If her threats were bothering him, he didn't let it show. Idly, he played his hands over the nearest display case—an ancient plasma cannon, a relic from a different age. "But still, your mother's funeral. I was sad—"

"You were sad?" Fleur felt a lifetime of composure abandon ship. "How do you think I felt? I was a PROXUS Ranger. They would never let me go without a fight. It would have been treason for me to leave my post."

"Ah, I suppose—"

Fleur wasn't done. Like a whip cracking with years of hurt, her tongue lashed a flurry of blows as she listed everything else he hadn't considered.

"We could wait outside," Beauregard suggested uncomfortably.

"Stay," ordered Fleur. Then, softer, "Please."

Count Fontaine shook his head, unable to hide a smile.

"What the phyx is so funny?"

"Nothing," he said, banishing the smile. "I felt uncomfortable. I smile when I am uncomfortable."

Fleur didn't believe him. She knew when she was being sneered at. She tried to wrap her mouth around words she couldn't find, but just ended up swearing.

"This is not how I wanted this to go," he admitted. "When I heard you had been captured, I wanted to rescue you. I sent my best people. I was worried. I wanted to start making amends."

"I did not need anyone to rescue me." Fleur pointed at Braga and Beauregard. "But at least they came themselves."

"I sent my finest agent in a stealth ship. Do you know how expensive those ships are?"

"No." Now it was Fleur's turn to smile. "Go on. Tell me exactly how many points you valued my life at."

He sighed. "We are not handling this well."

"We?"

"And you are not making this easy."

"Are we done yet?" she asked.

"Let me prove myself."

"You already have."

"I can help you. Please, listen."

"You have nothing I want and everything I want to leave behind."

"Well, that is not entirely true. I have a job. I may not know much, but I know you need those desperately."

Fleur's hand returned to her holstered plasma pistol. "Not from you."

"Then prove me wrong." He waved his hand and a holo of a planet flashed awake. Saphire swirls of ocean and ice wreathed in alabaster mist were painted across the planet's surface. "Take this job and prove I am everything you say I am. Make a profit, put me in my place. And what a profit you would make!" The holo zoomed out from the planet, revealing a fleet of satellites. Gleaming black and silver against the cosmos, spinning with delicate grace, they drifted in orbit around the planet. "The relays around this planet lost comms nearly fifty rotations ago. Possibly abandoned. No signs of life. This is an old recording, from before they lost contact. Look at all those relays! Whatever is left in orbit and on the surface will be ripe for looting. Prizes do not come richer than an unprotected PROXUS relay planet. Imagine all that salvage. Think of all those points!"

Fleur was familiar with such relay networks. Operated by the conquered populace below, heavy-duty satellites boosted comms across neighbouring systems. They were integral to PROXUS, highly valuable to scavengers and often heavily guarded. Fleur couldn't have cared less.

She drew her plasma pistol in one smooth motion. "I do not need to prove anything. Nothing changes what you did and that is all the proof I need."

"I know, I know... I was terrible to you. Terrible! Still..." Count Fontaine's eyes sparkled, his lip curled and his teeth shone inside a cruel grin, "thanks to this dazzlingly distracting civil war, PROXUS haven't investigated their own comms blackout. Too busy killing their own soldiers. Who cares about the fate of a single planet when there is a civil war on?" The holo zoomed back in, close enough to the surface to reveal an expanse of snow-capped peaks. Each mountain was ringed with a swirl of scattered buildings that climbed up a dark, looping highway from its base. "The locals are primitives with no industry or defences beyond their transports into orbit. PROXUS have withdrawn their forces. If the relays have failed, they will be unguarded. Easy points!" Seemingly noting Fleur hadn't shot him yet, he continued. "I have united the Conclave to conduct a comprehensive salvage of the relays and a sortie down to the planet for additional spoils. After we harvest all that tech, this haul could set up every clan for the next cycle."

"How come the relays went dark?" asked Beauregard.

Count Fontaine leaned closer to Fleur, prompting her to step backwards to maintain her distance. Her plasma pistol never wavered. "Shall we find out? Your crew would be free to take as much salvage as you can haul. You would be a pirate again!"

"Some of us already are," said Braga testily.

"Ah, but what use is being a pirate when no clan trusts you? Most of your crew are PROXUS turncoats. Darling daughter, you are my heir. This is your way home."

"I ain't interested in bein' no pirate," Beauregard clarified, as though some question had been asked of him that no one else had heard.

"And when you betray me again?" asked Fleur.

Count Fontaine eyed her plasma pistol. "I rather expect you will pull that trigger. Unless, of course, I happen to prove you wrong."

She hated herself for wanting to ask. It was a terrible idea to ask. Asking was as good as admitting they would take the job. Fleur asked anyway.

He smiled sickly sweet at her question, his expression dripping with a smugness he had no right to feel. "Where is the job?" he repeated. "Regis V." It felt like someone had opened an airlock. The atmosphere in the room died. Everyone's expression chilled.

Regis V. The site of the last battle in the Empress' war with the Sau Darans. The place where so many Sau Darans died, probably Haven *too. Ezra is going to kill me.*

CHAPTER TWENTY

Isabella had her work cut out piecing together the mess Paradise Moon had left her in. There was a lot wrong with the scene she could hear waiting on the other side of her exhausted eyelids. The first sign she wasn't at home and in bed had been the cheerful pop music she would never have let near her search history.

But when she opened her eyes, everything became a whole lot worse. The pop music bounced merrily around the relatively empty roadhouse. The window running alongside her booth betrayed nothing but red dirt and dusty tarmac outside, every inch of it baking under a roaring sun.

We agreed one day! How long did you take my body for?

Relax, I haven't even had it a full day yet.

It's boiling. And sunny.

That's just what it's like here.

It was winter when I left.

I took it less than a day. As far as your body's concerned, it's 9pm tops. You're up on the deal.

9pm? With this sunshine? Where are we?

9pm at home, not here.

It took Isabella a few more heartbeats to process that a waitress by the counter—and there was no getting away from this—was speaking with an Australian accent.

Just give me the Spark Notes.

It's complicated.

How bad?

Why do you always presume it's bad?

You left my body in Australia.

Erm.

Are we in danger?

No more than usual.

Am I going to want to kill you?

Ah. Well...

Luckily for Paradise Moon, the waitress chose that moment to arrive at Isabella's booth. She unloaded a burger, fries and chocolate milkshake from her tray and left it on the table with a departing smile. Apparently, it was Isabella's burger, fries and chocolate milkshake.

So it's bad enough that you ordered me comfort food?

Which you're going to really enjoy.

Yeah, well right now I feel like shit. Isabella glanced at her designer watch. *Did you change this?* She checked her phone. *Is this local time?*

Your phone yes, your watch no.

How much sleep did I get?

I couldn't quite fit it in.

You had my body for a day and you didn't sleep at all?

I ran out of time. And you're forgetting it's only 9pm back home.

We agreed you'd always sleep before giving my body back.

You didn't need to sleep, so that's not my fault. I'm giving your body back early.

It's never your fault.

Exactly!

Isabella took a sip of thick, chocolatey milkshake. *So you woke me up for bedtime? Great. Why are you giving me my body back early and in the wrong country?*

I figured you'd want to sleep in your own bed.

Well done, Sherlock.

And he wants to speak to you.

Who?

You know who!

Talyn?

Yep!

What have you two been doing?

Saving all the Sau Darans. Get eating, and I'll fill you in on why I'm such a legend.

As Isabella ate, she felt Paradise Moon flex her alien muscles—for once in a figurative sense—to allow memories of her borrowed body's time with Talyn to bleed into Isabella's consciousness. Isabella watched his face having a breakdown in the library with Paradise Moon. Then things went a little fuzzy, and they must have skipped time because now Paradise Moon and Talyn were alone on an island. She recognised São Miguel easily enough from all her escapes there. A conversation formed and settled inside Isabella's memory. Then Paradise Moon offered her hand. Talyn took it. Isabella peeled away the memory, as though tugging on a loose corner, sensing layers of other memories from the day beneath this one. At first, they were only sensations. Somewhere very cold. Somewhere very hot. And someone who mattered desperately to Paradise Moon.

Whatever the alien had got up to before meeting Talyn, it was impossible to catch even a glimpse before what felt like a concrete wall flew up inside the memory and pushed Isabella out with enough force to send a migraine screaming down her neural pathways.

Oops, sorry.

Isabella rubbed her temples. *You need to get better at sharing memories.*

Well, I haven't had much practice.

And whose fault is that?

Isabella scrunched up her face as the headache pummelled her skull. She forced her shoulders to untense and sank into the booth. Taking just enough control of Isabella's neural muscles, Paradise Moon loosened everything up until the headache faded. Isabella picked up what was left of her burger, took another bite.

That's two burgers for my last two meals. I hope you ate something healthy yesterday.

Stop thinking like your mother. Pay attention.

Gently, more memories bled into Isabella's mind. Nothing from before São Miguel—Paradise Moon had locked that down tight—but of their journey here.

Whenever Isabella needed to get anywhere, all she had to do was call on her social media followers. She didn't need planes or cars and trains. She rarely needed any wheels or wings to get around. Thousands of her most loyal followers, dotted all over the globe, had sent their smartphones to Isabella so she could familiarise herself with each device. Anchored objects she could vanish to. This only worked when the phones arrived in their own unique case, otherwise they were easily forgotten. Before returning them, Isabella spent enough time with each phone to know she could vanish to it after a quick reminder of which phone belonged to which follower. Something she could never hold in her head, but Paradise Moon seemed to have no trouble. Isabella simply checked who was closest to where she needed to be and vanished to that follower. A few selfies or a social media takeover kept her dedicated fanbase happy.

One such journey while Paradise Moon had been in possession of her body—today? Yesterday?—had seen purple smoke take them to fancy house in Perth, followed by a long midnight drive up the highway. Paradise Moon's shared memories suggested they had reached this roadhouse a little after dawn.

So we're in Pilbara now?

No, Meekathara. It's like halfway to Pilbara.

Why did you stop?

Your stupid body needed food. Keep eating!

Isabella started on her chips. They were thin, crispy and a dark enough shade of brown to have enjoyed a long cremation before reaching her plate. Drowsily, she fumbled them into her mouth.

Once Isabella was paid up, she left the roadhouse in a swirl of purple smoke and dropped into the passenger seat of the rental car Paradise Moon had purchased in Perth. It was steaming up the highway at a decent lick with Talyn in the driver's seat. Despite the heat, he was still wearing his armour.

He glanced away from the road, trying to scope her out. "Isabella or Moon?"

Isabella smiled. "It's me."

He grinned back, recognising her. Was that relief in his expression? Reluctantly, his eyes hurried back to the road. "She said you let her take your body sometimes."

"Yeah, that's our deal. Did she give you any trouble?"

Talyn hesitated. "Everything was fine."

"Did she ask you to say that?"

Talyn hesitated long enough to say plenty, his eyes locked on the road.

Did you ask him to say that?

What?! Please! Since when didn't you trust me?

Since forever.

Isabella watched him adjust the wheel as the road curved slightly. "You have cars where you're from?"

Talyn laughed. "No, we don't really need them. And our craft are more like the ship I landed in. Pity that's not still in one piece, otherwise this journey would have been so much faster."

Isabella raised an eyebrow. "If you don't know how to drive then how are you… driving?"

"I'm not." He pointed to his feet, which were flat against the footwell. The accelerator was doing its own thing, the pedal easing up and down as though pulled by an invisible cord, the car's mechanisms free from human intervention. "I asked this craft to do the hard work," he explained. "I keep it pointed in the right direction and it does the rest."

Isabella was too tired to ask questions. Okay, so he talked to the car. And it agreed to drive itself. Fine. She had friends who lived in deep space on a living alien ship. There had been a delinquent alien who called herself a god living inside her all her life. A self-driving car was no big deal in Isabella's world, galaxy or universe.

She glanced out of the window. Already, they were leaving behind the small-town buildings of Meekawhatever and throwing themselves to the mercy of the open highway. Barren red dirt stretched away from their thread of fading tarmac, disappearing as close to the horizon as she could see without squinting against the sun's glare. "How long until we get there?"

Talyn reeled off highway numbers and distances.

Not unkindly, she silenced him with a tired, raised hand. "How long until we get there?"

He shrugged. "Eight, maybe nine Earth hours."

"And when we get there?" she asked. "What then?"

Paradise Moon's memory dump had given her the broad brushstrokes of events before she woke up, but the alien's memory paint was diffused and faded. She remembered what had happened—at least, more or less—but some stretches of time felt more like filler than others. If there had been a conversation, she could remember what they were talking about, but sometimes the words eluded her. And there were gaps. If her own memories were the latest full colour, 3D, big explosion, retina-impaling Hollywood blockbuster, then Paradise Moon's donated recollections were an ancient roll of scratched monochrome film loaded upside-down into whatever played old films.

"I don't know," he admitted. "I'll need your help in the mountains to find somewhere that survived all this time. Moon said that'd be okay."

Yawning, Isabella nodded. "Whatever you need."

"Nova had a few ideas, but until we get there I don't really know. Just having a direction to travel though, that's giving me hope we can do this."

Isabella squeezed his arm. "We can totally do this."

He glanced away from the road long enough to linger on her hand resting on his arm, then longer still to find her eyes. "Thank you. You and Moon."

You're welcome, flyboy.

Isabella stifled another yawn.

"You need to sleep."

"If you need me, I can totally stay."

Talyn shook his head. "The car's doing all the work. Besides, I got plenty of practice last night with Moon. And now the sun's up, it's even easier."

Out of interest, did you fake him a license?

What do you think I am? A criminal?

He doesn't have one… And we definitely don't have one. So this isn't a rental, then? You stole this car?

Okay, I'm a criminal.

"Just don't get pulled over. It's not like you have a license or anything."

"A license to what?"

Isabella's largest yawn of the morning nearly devoured her whole mouth. "Never mind. I'll see you when my head's functioning." Isabella gave him a casual, ironic salute. "Night night."

Despite the madness of the last couple of days, not to mention the madness of pretty much every day before her failed attempt at holidaying in Barbados, all Isabella wanted to do was sleep. Even this flavour of madness was too everyday to keep her awake.

What did you do to my body? I feel wrecked!

But whatever Paradise Moon had been up to prior to her adventure with Talyn, those memories were locked away as Isabella staggered into her bedroom moments later. Fully clothed, she collapsed into bed.

CHAPTER TWENTY-ONE

Fleur was floating in the mindless bliss she often felt after good sex. Lying on their bed with a contented smile, she cradled the back of her head in interlaced fingers. Her muscles were sore in the best possible way, her skin singing, her heart steadier. For once, her head was free from the persistent interrogative monologues that usually nourished her insecurities.

Smiling, she gazed up at the holo of their wedding as it played on a loop across the ceiling of their cramped quarters. She knew every heartbeat of the recording off by heart, yet was only too happy to watch it play out again. In it, a swell of ocean spray burst across the projection, obscuring her and Braga for a heartbeat. They emerged clinging to each other on the back of a moonwhale. Fleur watched her past self nestle her chin over Braga's shoulder, burying half her wife's face in Fleur's dripping afro as the frothing crest of another wave drove them high and giggling into fresh, salty air.

Naked and dripping, Braga emerged from the shower and spared a smile for the holo. "Good times."

"Do not come near me until you are dry," Fleur warned through her uninterrupted smile. "I just put on clean clothes." Fleur prided herself on dressing with the utmost elegance and style. For this rotation, she had chosen tight trousers with a purple scoop neck camisole, and nothing was going to spoil them.

Smiling back at her, Braga retrieved a towel from a hook on the curved wall *Haven* had grown for their quarters. She dabbed at the moisture clinging to her skin. "It's good to have you back."

"And you." Fleur sighed. "Clearly I am enjoying it."

Braga stretched alluringly, working the towel behind her as she dried herself. "I'd say so."

Enjoying the sight of her wife's body twisting and flexing, Fleur murmured something incomprehensible.

"You're grinning like an idiot," Braga pointed out. Coming from anyone else, that would have sent Fleur rushing to check her reflection and puppeteering it closer to the zenith of elegance. But Braga could say whatever she wanted. Fleur would know what she really meant, what she truly felt.

Braga tossed aside her towel and closed the distance to their bed in less time than it took for Fleur's heartbeat to quicken. Which was phyxing fast. Damply, Braga snuggled up behind Fleur and hugged her in a way that made Fleur ache all over again for her wife's touch.

"What did I say about not coming near me?" Fleur demanded, but she was laughing. How could she not? Her wife had come home alive. Spots of water seeped into the back of her camisole. "Do you call that dry?"

"I was listening to your face, not your words." Braga's palm settled over Fleur's stomach, gently stroking it with fingers calloused by a lifetime of piracy and hard knocks.

Fleur snorted, her eyebrows raised. "My face?"

Braga's cheek found a home against Fleur's, pressing them together, her skin not entirely dry but at least cool against Fleur's burning cheeks. "Every lovable cell of it."

"All yours," said Fleur. "Along with the rest of me."

It was Braga's turn to sigh, her breath kissing Fleur's lips. "I know."

Fleur couldn't tell how long they lay on the bed like that, coupled in motionless peace. Forever and not long enough. As though their precious theft of time had been disconnected from the threads of reality.

"We're safe when we're together," Braga whispered, her mind seemingly slipping to a thought twinned with Fleur's last words. "All of you is mine."

"All of me," Fleur murmured happily, "yours."

"I won't let him hurt a single cell in your body," she promised. "I'd kill him before he got half a chance."

And there it was. The familiar tension in her back. Inescapable contortions in her stomach. Her heart beating heavy and hollow. Their stolen moment, the absent passing of time when she and Braga simply were, broken upon the vanguard of Braga's words.

Pushing her wife away, Fleur levered herself upright on the bed and focussed on a middle distance that was facing anywhere but Braga. "I can handle him."

Rough, tattooed fingers stroked a meandering tributary down her back through the camisole's soft synthetic fabric. "I'm not saying you can't—I know you can. I'm just saying, he's going to have to go through me to even get to you. That dpresh can get locked."

"No," Fleur insisted. The tension in her back was getting worse, as though it was being cranked tighter by Silver Fists in a PROXUS interrogation chamber. "I do not want you near him. I will deal with him myself."

"I just don't like that we're working with him. I don't trust him. After what he did to you and your crew…"

Fleur's voice found an edge that was sharper than she intended. "I do not want to go through this with you again. It is my decision."

"Hey, it's okay." Braga's fingers and thumbs settled into the knots in Fleur's back, kneading them looser. "He can't do anything to hurt you now. That dpresh has no power over you or us."

Fleur flinched, sending Braga's hands into swift retreat. "Can we not?"

"Am I allowed to care?" Braga demanded roughly.

Still, Fleur didn't dare face her wife. These words could live inside her head and on the lips she was biting right now, but they would die long before she spoke them if she even glanced at the bruises painted on the face of the woman she loved. "You attacked him because of me. Never do that again. Your life is not worth it."

"My life is worth whatever the Hell I say it is," Braga snapped back. She left the bed and retrieved her towel from the floor. "I'm cold."

"Get dressed then."

"I am."

"Good." Fleur sighed, but this time not a contented sigh. It was laced with uneasy exhaustion and a galaxy of frustration. She drifted from the bed and found her reflection in the jagged swirl of a ceiling-high black mirror. Braga had stolen the mirror, along with the contents of an entire armoury, from a warlord whose moonweed empire sprawled across several planets in the Outer Rim. In the mirror, Fleur examined her pores, her scars, her imperfections. The latter always took forever.

"I do not want him to hurt you," Fleur admitted to the silence.

Braga laughed in that easy way she always managed, even when she was angry. "I don't plan to let him."

Keen for a distraction, Fleur swept aside what looked like any other wall on *Haven*. From inside the compartment, she selected an obsidian jacket with a swirl of ribbed fabric up the neck and slid it on.

Finally, Fleur dared to face the bruises on her wife's face, dared to caress them with the backs of her fingers. She cupped her wife's chin. "He already has, and he will again. He only cares about himself."

"I know," said Braga. She grasped Fleur's forearms and captured Fleur's eyes in her gaze. "I wanted to kill him. He should suffer for what he did to you."

"He should," said Fleur, holding Braga's gaze. "But for me he died a long time ago. He cannot hurt me now."

"She says, after staring at her beautiful face in the mirror for the first time since we came back together. Your face is like a demon in heat. And you wonder why I think you're so phyxing hot."

"You know—"

"Yes, I know." Braga kissed Fleur's forearms, then slid her arms around Fleur's waist. "And I know how utterly amazing you are, too."

Fleur felt her expression darken. "I am not."

"And I know where your mind goes when you're doubting yourself. You deserve to be free of him."

"My insecurities do not matter. They will not get anyone killed. They do not affect anyone but me. But you… I do not want you getting yourself killed because you feel an anger towards him that I buried a long time ago. I will not lose you to him. That is the only way he can hurt me now."

Understanding crept over Braga's face. "Okay," she agreed, pulling Fleur into a hug. Then she pushed Fleur away. "Now get off me so I can get dressed. I'm freezing!"

Fleur laughed. "Then hurry up!" She lay back on the bed, watching Braga slip into an old pair of loose-fitting combat trousers. She loved the sight of how they fitted around the larger curves of Braga's body. "It is good to be back where we all belong."

Braga pulled on a light vest that left her thickly muscled arms bare. "You wouldn't know it from looking at old and grumpy."

"Ignore him," said Fleur, shaking her head dismissively. "That is just Beauregard being Beauregard. Nothing to worry about."

"I don't think so. You should have seen him while you were away. Like a vitraxi cub without its mother, moaning and moping everywhere." Braga settled beside Fleur and pulled on her boots. "He couldn't keep his contempt for me off his dumb, ugly face."

Fleur kissed Braga's shoulder. "You do provoke him."

"Me? Provoke someone?" Braga asked with mock indignation. "That doesn't sound like me."

"Oh honey, it really does. Why am I always cleaning up a mess between you two? I love you both dearly, but why put us through all this?"

"He's the one who doesn't approve of your choice in wife. Just because he was here first, he thinks I'm some sort of threat."

"Oh, he approves fine. Someone just needs to teach him how to use his words."

"Seriously, the whole time you were in prison he was a nightmare to be around. Even more than usual."

"Perhaps he deserves a break," Fleur suggested. "He... might have struggled with me gone."

"And I didn't? I was a wreck stuck here worrying about you, trying to track down which prison you were in, chasing down leads and informants." Fully dressed, Braga offered Fleur a hand up from the bed. "One day, you're gonna realise how much he hates me."

Fleur took the proffered hand and swung off the bed. "He does not hate you."

"I swear sometimes he was actually gonna shoot me."

Fleur offered her a sideways look. "Well, we have all been tempted!"

But Braga wasn't smiling. "I'm serious."

"And over dramatic." She gave Braga a gentle peck on the nose. "Come on, we should check over the evac gear before we arrive at Regis V."

"Really? Now?" asked Braga with a grimace. "But we've got ages until we get to the relay planet that mysteriously lost contact with everyone and is totally not gonna get us killed."

Fleur smiled. "Then this is a great time to get ahead on our chores."

In response, the creak and groan of heavy mechanisms announced itself on the periphery of their quarters. Already, they were being moved to another part of *Haven* at Fleur's mere suggestion of a destination. She smiled. Ezra might be the ship's favourite, but there was still a pecking order after him. And she was next.

"Tough, we are already on our way." Smugly, she gestured at the walls on either side of them.

"Urgh, you're boring. I want a divorce."

Still holding her hand, Fleur led Braga towards the door. "Fine, but I am keeping all our stuff."

Braga let Fleur drag her to the oval door that led out of their quarters. "I don't need anything else anyway. I'm free as the black skies!" Braga pulled Fleur's arm, spinning her around. Acquiescing into a decadent twirl, Fleur whirled into Braga's embrace in a flurry of frizzy hair and elegant, gliding limbs. "Free, but yours," whispered Braga.

A crafty grin creased the corners of Fleur's mouth. "As am I, sweetie."

The door rolled aside to reveal a maintenance area. As usual, *Haven* was keen to deliver whatever Fleur needed and had pre-empted her destination. Like the rest of the Sau Daran ship, dim blue black light shone out of creases in the walls. It conjured a crisp sheen around the outlines of hard-shelled vacuum suits, helmets, boots, gloves, toolkits and emergency backpacks—everything they had stolen over the last three cycles that was designed for intrepid spacewalks. They were stacked in multitudinous rows that disappeared deep into the room's shelved interior. Enough, Fleur had ensured, for every crew member aboard *Haven*. Much of the kit was older than anyone who would be wearing it, even Beauregard, but it was functional and that would be all that mattered if *Haven* hit trouble and they ended up running out of breathable atmosphere.

But as she peered into the gloom, Fleur realised *Haven* had stitched them both up.

At a workbench crammed down one aisle of shelved kit, Beauregard leaned over a disembowelled helmet, fiddling with a pair of bare wires stripped from its innards. Standing next to him on the workbench, Pocket twisted two more of the helmet's shredded wires together with their claw. The tiny Sau Daran maintenance drone had leaped to Beauregard's side the moment he landed back on *Haven* and likely hadn't left his side since. They were Beauregard's oldest synthetic friend, and they made sure everyone knew it. Their glowing red eyes peered down the length of their silver beak, examining the wires with a curious tilt of their shining head.

"Thought I heard trouble comin'," grumbled Beauregard, without looking up.

Braga held up her hands in instant surrender. "You know what? Come to think of it, I'm gonna leave."

"Ain't you at least gonna tell her your excuse?"

"No excuse," Braga replied easily. "I just don't want to be here with you." Leaving the briefest of kisses on Fleur's cheek, Braga fled through the oval door into their quarters. It rolled shut behind her with a clunk.

Fleur rolled her eyes. "You two need to get yourselves together. We cannot go on like this."

Beauregard avoided her gaze, instead examining the wires that he and Pocket had soldered together. "That ain't bad, buddy." With a satisfied wiggle of his tiny shoulders, Pocket tucked freshly soldered wires back into the evac helmet. Beauregard tossed aside his soldering gun. "Pass me another, would you?"

Fleur reached for the nearest shelf and retrieved another perfectly functioning helmet for him to fix. She tossed it at him harder than she needed to.

Beauregard caught it in his chest with his good hand, a puzzled expression on his face. "Okay, what did I do?"

Fleur aimed a thumb behind her at the closed door to her quarters. "How about that?"

"You ain't pinnin' her crazy on me. I ain't got no clue what's goin' on with her."

Fleur crossed her arms and stared. "Really?"

"And I don't need your help neither."

Fleur rescued the helmet that he and Pocket had been working on, pulled aside the plate he hadn't quite sealed securely and began rummaging around its circuitry.

"We know what we're doin', don't we?" asked Beauregard. Pocket nodded their head supportively and drew themselves up to their full height. Which was miniscule. "Don't forget, I did all our field repairs on Har'r Donnish III when you were in bed sick."

"Forget?" Fleur dragged out the freshly soldered wires and ran her fingers along them to check where they led. The damage Beauregard had done with his fix looked minimal and wouldn't take her or Pocket more than a moment to undo. "How could I forget? Our field comms did not function right for twelve rotations after you were done with them."

"It weren't that bad."

Fleur gave him a despairing look. "I hate to say it, but one of Striker's agents would have struggled to do as much damage if they were deliberately trying to sabotage us." Her eyes flicked to Pocket. "And you!" The Sau Daran drone gave a shrug of mock innocence. Twirling a silver limb that ended in a hook, they indicated where their metal heart would have been, as if asking—surely you don't mean me? "You know how all this kit works, so stop sucking up to him by pretending he knows what he is doing."

Beauregard's soldering hand hovered over the fresh helmet that he and Pocket were examining. "It don't feel as natural as munitions, but that don't mean I ain't useful."

Fleur placed what she hoped was a calming hand on his. "No one thinks you are useless. Without you, most of our crew would be dead." She glanced at the evac gear surrounding them, unable to ignore the small details that stood out to her. The crooked angle at which some items had been discarded on the shelves. How some of the helmets had been placed with their glare-proof visors facing towards the wall instead of into the room. "Just how much of this kit have you… fixed?"

Beauregard shrugged. "Pretty much done now."

Fleur squeezed his good hand, the hand that still held enough strength to squeeze back if he wanted to. "Ignoring the fact all this kit will now need to be checked for whatever damage you might have done, are you seriously telling me you have been here that long?" She paused to do the maths. "Have you even slept since we got back from the fleet?"

Beauregard shook his head. "Pocket and I came straight here after you flew us home. Ain't no time to waste if we're goin' evac to a salvage site."

That much, at least, was true. The first task whenever arriving at a salvage site, whether the salvagers were

PROXUS or pirates, was the eerie exploration of any ships and stations left intact. Best case scenario? It was boring. Worst case scenario? Bodies. Lots of bodies. In zero-g, whatever mess had been left floating around would soon be smeared all over the salvagers too. Then there was the grisly middle case scenario. Survivors. That was when a salvage got super messy.

They were due to arrive at Regis V before the end of this rotation. Each pirate crew in the fleet would take one relay station to investigate before anyone salvaged anything. Not only because there may be survivors, but because whatever they had been trying to survive may still be there too.

"You and Braga really need to get over yourselves," Fleur urged, keen to rescue her train of thought.

"Ain't my problem," Beauregard grumbled in a tone that sounded very much like his problem.

Fleur was still holding his hand. She could feel the coldness of his skin, their touch an unspoken conduit of intimacy, a silent acknowledgement of their closeness. "We have been together long enough to kill more enemies than I can remember. And nearly been killed almost as often."

"Ain't no argument here."

"So talk to me, big man."

Beauregard's hand retreated from her touch. Intimacy terminated. Instead, he fiddled with another perfectly functioning helmet. "Ain't nothin' to talk about."

"Well then we have a problem, because for three cycles you could barely share the same oxygen as each other and when I was gone it sounds like you nearly killed each other."

Beauregard held up a finger in protest. "I never actually shot her."

"What do you want? Another medal?" Fleur's usually placid expression creased. "This stops now. Whatever problem you have with my wife, get over it. I need everyone working together if we are going to survive whatever we are walking into."

"She ain't careful."

"True."

"She's too cocky."

"Sure."

"She tried to kill you when we first met."

"Mistakes were made." Fleur rubbed Beauregard's shoulder gently. Not to be outdone, Pocket shuffled down the workbench and nestled affectionately against him. "She saved our lives plenty of times since then. Tell me the real issue. Please. Before one of you actually shoots the other."

Beauregard shrugged. "I dunno. We're different."

Fleur laughed. "Just a little, honey. Are you worried about being replaced?"

Beauregard shot her a confused look. "What? Why in the Empress' name would I think that?"

"Well, it is definitely on her mind. She and I spend a lot of time together, which means I spend less time with you and Ez than I used to."

"So?" Beauregard averted his gaze, preferring to turn the helmet over and over in his hands. "Ain't no problem with that. She makes you happy, don't she?"

Fleur nodded through a blossoming smile.

"Then what's the issue?" asked Beauregard, clearly lost. Fleur recognised the telltale signs of frustration creeping into his voice. For Beauregard, this had been a long conversation.

"The issue is you being proud of not shooting my wife, and then spending every moment since we returned to *Haven* down here with a soldering gun rather than getting the rest you need." She glanced at Pocket. "Not all of us run on batteries. Get some rest."

Fleur hugged him. The move caught him off guard. She felt him tense and contract. It was a long time, a long hug, before he eventually surrendered and she felt the tension loosen from his muscles. Somewhere between them, a silver beak prised apart just enough room for one more.

"Just keepin' busy," Beauregard muttered. "Takes my mind off things."

"Well, yes, even Paradise Moon could work that out."

"If you died in that prison, it weren't no one's fault but mine."

"Get locked, big man. I got myself caught by PROXUS. It was my mistake. Not you. Not Braga. Not Ez."

"Don't mean you deserved it."

Fleur let go and gave him a withering look. "Well none of us deserve it!"

She only caught his eyes for a heartbeat, but it was long enough to make them retreat to the helmet he kept tossing up and down in one paw. Suddenly, the helmet was the most interesting object in the Known Galaxies. His eyes kept low, avoiding hers.

"You do not deserve it," she said firmly.

Beauregard shrugged again—it was the most noncommittal shrug she had ever seen him offer anyone, which was saying a lot.

"You do not deserve to die," she insisted.

He gave another shrug of defeat. "More than you."

Wincing at the deepness of such a cut, Fleur held him so tight she could almost feel the air being forced from his lungs. "But I'd rather it weren't now," he gasped. She slackened her hug enough for him to breathe, clinging to the man who had been there since her first rotation with PROXUS. From the moment Count Fontaine betrayed her and her crew to PROXUS until right now, Beauregard had never let her down. He was always there, ready to do whatever it took to keep them alive.

She kept hugging him, refusing to let go, clinging to him as though her life depended on it, until her comm interrupted them. Without letting go, Fleur peered around Beauregard's torso and tapped the holo flashing from her gauntlet. "Ez, can this wait?"

"Uhh, not really."

Without needing any prompting, Beauregard withdrew from Fleur's embrace. "Shoot, kid."

"We have a major problem," Ezra replied over the comm. "It's the Empress."

"Which one?" asked Fleur and Beauregard together.

CHAPTER TWENTY-TWO

Of all the things Ezra could have thrown in frustration, his leg hadn't been the wisest choice. Letting his anger get the better of him when he was in the middle of putting on his prosthetics never turned out well.

His foot ricocheted off the far wall of *Haven*'s crystal chamber with a metallic *ding* and tumbled only a fraction of the distance back to him. A handful of screws, probably important, trickled out of its knee joint and rolled across the floor in every direction.

The rest of his prosthetics were waiting in neat rows on wall-mounted racks that helpfully sat against a different wall no closer than his thrown prosthetic.

Sighing beneath the eternally bright glow of *Haven*'s crystal and the light it shed from the centre of the chamber, Ezra reached out with both hands, found purchase on the floor and hauled his sleep-deprived arse towards his leg. Every movement was accompanied by grunts of effort and irritation, his cramping fingers, tired arms and aching core constantly complaining. With his head bent in exertion, his nose so low he could smell the raw, ironlike odour of whatever living metals *Haven* grew their floors out of.

He shouldn't have let everything get on top of him so easily. Admittedly, he was a little phyxing furious about where they were going on this salvage mission. About Fleur agreeing to it. About everyone accepting her decision. And he couldn't even begin to understand why *Haven* had agreed to go there. Regis V. Out of everyone, the Sau Daran ship had the most power when it came to saying no. They could literally stop moving through space and there was nothing anyone could do about it. And yet, he was as angry at how much this was getting to him as he was about where *Haven* had agreed to take them. Naturally, this stoked the flames inside him even more, the vicious cycle of his frustration and his frustration at his frustration. Like wind fanning an inferno.

Swearing at the whole phyxing universe—but, more than anything else, at the legs he didn't have—Ezra gave up and rolled onto his back. Arching the leg that was still attached, he unclasped the cushioned cup beneath the lump of his thigh and tore off his other prosthetic leg. It clattered beside him. Discarded. Not unlike how he felt, waiting on *Haven* while the crew risked their lives on another dangerous mission that didn't need a pacifist fugitive with no legs and no guns. Moving faster now that he wasn't dragging his other leg in addition to the parts of his body with blood still pumping through them, Ezra clawed closer to his tossed aside prosthetic.

If there was anywhere in the Known Galaxies that he would have begged *Haven* never to go, it was the system where *Haven* had died. Regis V. The ship graveyard that marked the site of the Last Great War, and the final space battle that had ended the conflict between humanity and the Sau Darans. His parents had fought in that war as Rangers in the Empress' navy, back before she was the

Empress and when the People's Republic of Xarr and United Systems was just Xarr. Following in his parents' footsteps, there wasn't a thing he had gotten right. It wasn't easy when they had started on the wrong side, and him with them. Every night, the haunting faces of all the innocent Sau Darans and once-allied PROXUS forces he had killed told him that. And now he was bringing the nightmare full circle. Taking *Haven*—the Sau Daran ship they had brought back to life and the best thing that had happened to him throughout his enduring existence in these grim galaxies—to re-live memories of their death and the deaths of every other Sau Daran ship and crew who had passed away with more permanency than *Haven*.

Reaching the leg he had thrown across the chamber, Ezra snatched it up. The knee joint hung at a crooked angle that screamed anything but stability. No chance of it supporting his weight without a quick repair. Ezra glanced from the damaged prosthetic in his hands to the perfectly functioning prosthetic he had discarded halfway across the chamber to ease his journey.

Ezra swore long and loud.

"Hello?" a muffled voice called back to him from the other side of the chamber's round door. The door remained closed. Someone respected his privacy.

Ezra sighed. Unlike when his legs had been taken three cycles ago, he no longer cared if someone saw him like this. Not if they were a member of the crew—someone who had abandoned PROXUS and chosen to live on a Sau Daran ship with fugitives, pirates, refugees and the smattering of Sau Daran maintenance drones who crept and dwelt in *Haven*'s deepest, darkest reaches to help keep the ship flying. They were all friends here.

"Come in," he called.

Either they punched the interface on their side of the door, or *Haven*—who was hooked into Ezra's comm and always listening—did the honours. Either way, the door rolled open.

The Empress of the Known Galaxies swept inside *Haven*'s most sacred chamber with a plasma pistol and a scowl. There were no burns on her face and her hair was long, which told Ezra she was the Empress who had arrived with Thorn's slavers, not the Empress whom Fleur herself had brought to *Haven* from Tiberius Omega Mining Colony.

"Finally," she snapped, a sour expression as sharp as rotten wine mulling over her face. "This was far from the easiest place to find when none of your rooms and corridors wanted to move for me."

Her stride was halted by a swirling swarm of dark cables and tubes conjured by *Haven*. They erupted out of the shadows above her, hurtling with such deadly velocity that there was only one outcome *Haven* could be considering, and not one the Empress should survive.

Deftly, the Empress tucked and rolled. This barely earned her a heartbeat longer as the uncoiling cables and tubes swung towards her on a fresh trajectory. But it was long enough for her to swipe a tiny device from inside the flight suit Fleur had given her. She tapped a switch on the device and flicked it through the air. It struck the wall and clung on like some sort of magnetised limpet.

The crystal's glow flickered in and out, strobing the chamber into heartbeats of blue-black darkness. Cables and tubes collapsed, draping lifelessly down the walls. Ignoring the Empress, Ezra stared at the flickering crystal. It had never done this before. The crystal was *Haven*'s soul. It was constant. The lifeforce that powered their consciousness, not to mention all their systems. Propulsion. Comms. Navigation. Life support. So, nothing important...

"What did you do?" Ezra snarled at the Empress.

Dismissing him with a withering glance, she strode into the heart of the chamber and examined the flickering crystal. It was almost as tall as her, certainly wider. Flaring, pulsing light burst around her severe silhouette. In one heartbeat she was athletic, in another she was gaunt and skeletal, her tight flesh as cold and pale as a dying star and its remnant nebulae. She extended a wrinkled palm, its silhouette stretching over the crystal as she reached for *Haven*'s soul.

"Don't you dare touch them," Ezra warned.

The Empress was ignoring him so well he couldn't even tell if she had heard. Her flat palm settled over the surface of the crystal. Ezra knew what would happen next. He had done it every rotation for three cycles and couldn't imagine a rotation without it. Images flowing faster than words ever could in a stream of unfiltered meaning transferred upstream and downstream between *Haven* and whoever was on the other end of the silent conversation. Ezra could stay like that for huge portions of a rotation, his hands cradling the crystal, his head and heart drifting in lossless understanding with *Haven*.

With a single hand pressed against the crystal, her face hardened even more—if such a feat were possible.

Ezra pinged Fleur on his comm.

"Ez, can this wait?"

"Uhh, not really."

"Shoot, kid."

"We have a major problem," Ezra warned. "It's the Empress."

"Which one?" Their question echoed in stereo over the comm, Fleur's luxurious tone paired with Beauregard's gruffer demand.

Ezra narrated with equally desperate measures of fear and worry. He was garbling his words, stumbling over frantic sentences. His eyes never left the Empress' heretical palm on *Haven*'s crystal as the taint of her touch transferred thoughts back and forth. No one had killed more Sau Darans than the Empress. No one was more unworthy than her.

"This room ain't movin' for us, kid," growled Beauregard. "We should be comin' your way, but we ain't goin' nowhere."

Ezra glanced at the device the Empress had sunk into the wall just before the crystal started flickering and all *Haven*'s animated cables and tubes had died.

"She's done something to *Haven*. She's got some sort of device. I don't think they can do anything."

"That ain't good, kid," Beauregard pointed out, as though this hadn't occurred to Ezra.

"Turn on your beacon," suggested Fleur.

Ezra tapped his gauntlet. "Done."

"We are on our way," Fleur assured him, now breathing heavier.

"Don't die until we get there," suggested Beauregard amid the big man's heavy breathing. They were definitely running now, although Ezra didn't dare try to work out how far they would have to run to navigate *Haven*'s uncharacteristically static arrangement of corridors and rooms to get here. Since *Haven* had reached full strength, none of them had needed to travel without *Haven*'s obliging and unprompted rearrangement of their interiors to match origin to destination.

"Do not die at all," Fleur corrected with unrelenting calm. "Just keep her busy."

Always happy to throw good points after bad as though he were at a bar or gambling table, Ezra hurled his leg across the chamber for the second time. It struck the back of the Empress' head, prompting a shriek.

Her hand left the crystal.

The other raised her plasma pistol.

"You shouldn't be here," he snarled. "This place is sacred. You have no right."

Her eyes measured him. "Ezra Knight. Only child. Son to two loyal PROXUS war heroes. Survivor of the assault on a Sau Daran outpost in the Outer Rim, which resulted in the death of Apprentice Ranger Dantes."

Ezra's heart stuttered much like the glow from *Haven*'s crystal. How could anyone make sense of that? His best friend killed while they had themselves been killing Sau Darans, just as they had been trained to do. Born into PROXUS, they hadn't known any better, but that had done nothing to undo the permanency of their actions. Dead… was dead… was dead. His grief and loss weighed as black and heavy as ever, but he no longer knew for whom he grieved. Forever, only ever lost.

"Thereafter, a fugitive," continued the Empress. "While intoxicated, killed a PROXUS security team on *Black Nebula* to orchestrate the escape of the Sau Daran parasite Paradise Moon and the girl it had infected."

Even though he had known they would kill Isabella if he, Fleur and Beauregard hadn't taken out that security team, heavy shame still welled behind Ezra's eyes at the lives lost. That had been a different Ezra. A self-righteous, angry Apprentice Ranger who needed to be the hero every rotation without ever considering where violence always ultimately led.

"If you're claiming to have less blood on your hands than mine, good luck." Ezra's anger was the only thing holding him together, so he clung to it and the strength it offered. "PROXUS is evil. You're phyxing evil. Every planet you conquered, just for power. How many billions of people have you killed? How many billions more have you enslaved?"

Her lip curled into a smirk, as though she knew something he would never understand and this made her superior to the rest of the Known Galaxies. "There is no such thing as evil." Already, she sounded tired of this conversation. As though she had better things to do than justify genocide on a multi-galactic scale. "I defeated an enemy threatening the whole of humanity. I strengthened us under one banner so we would never be vulnerable again. And enslaved? Please! Doubters are always caught in the gears of progress. Humanity is safer because of me. One rotation sooner or later, the Resistance will thank me for it."

"You sure about that?" he asked. "The more people you hurt, the more people fight back."

But Ezra's hot glare did nothing to melt the ice in her eyes. Her thin lips cut and sliced each word with cold precision. "Freedom fighters are a threat to humanity and are dealt with accordingly."

"They *are* humanity!"

"No. Their goals are ideological, not practical. They fight against humanity's interests."

Ezra was so angry he didn't care that the Empress was aiming a plasma pistol at him. "You mean like PROXUS does now in the civil war? How many of your own have you killed in the last two cycles?"

"A temporary setback. Control will be re-established, make no mistake."

"Your civil war doesn't look temporary. It looks terminal. You're wiping each other out. And based on the two of you on *Haven*, I'm presuming that's because there's more of you fighting for control than anyone realises. It's not for humanity's benefit, it's all for you."

"Humanity needs me. The cost is worth—"

"All you care about is power."

The Empress smirked again. "You're clearly not happy." She waved her plasma pistol. "Would you like me to put you out of your misery?"

That was a good question. While Ezra suspected she meant it rhetorically, his answer was a great deal more complicated. Did he want her to shoot him? Would that make everything better? Ezra's jaw tightened. It would certainly make life easier for him, but it wouldn't make anything better for *Haven*.

"Obviously I'm not going to shoot you," explained the Empress, lowering her plasma pistol. "That would defeat the whole point of coming here."

"How did you?" asked Ezra. "You were locked up."

"Are you really asking a veteran of the Last Great War how I escaped a Sau Daran cell and knew how to find this chamber?" She unleashed her most withering glare. "I worked out how to defeat the Sau Darans and their gods when they were at the height of their power. Leaving me in that cell was insulting."

Ezra's brain was overworked. After the Empress' words had slithered inside, he did his best to understand them while processing everything else that was happening. "Why wouldn't you shoot me?"

Strike three on her superior smirks. "Are you serious? What are you going to do, glare at me until I die of old age? That's not a game you want to play with me, of all people. Besides, as I explained to your ship just now, the whole point of coming here was the opposite of doing harm." The Empress abandoned her plasma pistol beside her bare feet and held up her empty hands in submission.

Breathlessly, Fleur and Beauregard surged into the chamber. With her plasma pistol outstretched, Fleur marched silkily towards the Empress. Tracking along the wall to line up his own kill shot from the pulsing shadows, Beauregard kept his plasma pistol ready at his hip, cold blue eyes zeroed in on the Empress.

Fleur stopped only a handful of paces away. "Pick up that pistol and you are dead."

"Double dead," growled Beauregard.

"Finally, you're here," said the Empress frostily. "I don't like repeating myself. Clearly, I had no intention of killing anyone. Otherwise you would all be dead."

Every muscle in Beauregard's body was perfectly still, except his mouth. "That plasma pistol ain't gonna do you no good if you killed anyone to get here."

"Please! A few headaches, nothing more."

Fleur glanced sideways. "Are you okay, Ez?"

He stared up at her, his arms locked behind him to hold himself up, his legs elsewhere. "She did something to *Haven*. Over there, in the wall." He pointed at the device with a nod.

Fleur looked behind her. Beauregard didn't. His eyes and trigger finger were for the Empress only, nothing else. Fleur wasted no time. Spinning on her heel, she left the Empress to Beauregard's watchful gaze and tore the device from the wall.

The crystal ceased flickering. Its glow steadied back to the constant aura of light Ezra had never expected it to lose. Cables uncoiled from the walls, stretching and slithering into the heart of the chamber and ensnaring the Empress in a twisting, tightening embrace. Another cable wrapped itself around the barrel of the Empress' plasma pistol and deposited it next to Fleur.

Fleur tossed the device she had pulled off the wall at Beauregard. "What is it?"

He tried to catch it without removing his eyes or plasma pistol from the Empress—a catch Ezra had seen him take a thousand times. But that had been before Midnight Twice more than tripled the age of Beauregard's other gun arm. Firing on a lifetime of muscle memory but equipped with liver-spotted, discoloured dead weight, his arm arrived far too late. The device sailed past Beauregard's face and skittered across the floor.

"I have her," Fleur assured him, plasma pistol ready as she watched the Empress.

Grumpily mumbling something filthier than a drain in Xarr's lowest, darkest undercity, Beauregard holstered his plasma pistol, edged towards the device and retrieved it with his better hand. He didn't need long to examine it. "A disabler for livin' ships. We used them in the war."

"Is *Haven* going to be okay?" Ezra demanded.

"Ain't nothin' to worry about." Beauregard pocketed the device and re-drew his plasma pistol with a flourish. This movement was as fast and smooth as it had ever been, as though he were overcompensating for his arm that didn't behave properly anymore. "It's got a tiny range and a short life. Long enough to break in or out of a livin' ship, but nothin' more. It ain't never long before the livin' ship drains its power—then anyone still around ain't gonna be around much longer."

Fleur raised an eyebrow at the Empress. "I do not want to know where you were hiding that."

"So *Haven* will be okay?" Ezra pressed.

Beauregard nodded. "No lastin' damage. To the ship, anyway. Her, on the other hand…"

The Empress stared back at him with a face like a slapped ass. Her eyes slid over Beauregard's decrepit arm. "What other hand?" she asked cruelly.

Cables tightened swiftly around her, coiling over her throat and pinning her arms, then her knees so they buckled. Unable to put out a hand, she had only her face to catch the floor.

"Play nice," Ezra warned her. "*Haven*'s tapped into my comm, so while we're together they can hear everything you're saying."

"The ship won't kill me," the Empress gasped against the cables squeezing her throat. "It saw inside my mind. It understands the truth."

Had the cables strangled her all the way to a grisly end, Ezra wouldn't have looked away. He wanted her to suffer. He wanted to watch. But she didn't and she couldn't. Having restrained her securely, the cables ceased tightening before their grip passed the other side of deadly.

Once more, Ezra began crawling. Fleur rushed to gather his legs, her face as gentle and kind as always. He pushed her away. He had gone this far, he might as well finish. Hauling his body the last of the way, he reached out an aching hand and pressed it against the crystal.

If a single thought were a lone droplet, he felt like he had been abruptly submerged in the deepest ocean. Seeped in thoughts that didn't belong, drowning in images from *Haven's* consciousness and soaking in shared understanding. His very first attempt at this had been overwhelming, but after three cycles of practice he knew better than any other human alive how to navigate their connection. A great tide of information shared so quickly that he needed to let it circulate, percolate and settle within him before he tried to make sense of it. Gently but firmly, understanding would grow with unparalleled clarity and preservation of meaning.

But Ezra had no time for that. He needed to know what the Empress had shown *Haven*. This wasn't desire— it was lethal, urgent necessity.

Dredging the ocean of shared thoughts into which he had plunged, he willed every image of the Empress from *Haven's* soul into his own. He saw her imperious and ancient, standing on bleached bones piled taller than any planet. There was a younger Empress too, who wove plasma fire through a smoking melee, dispatching Sau Darans with a screaming pistol in each hand. Older now, the Empress reached out of the darkness and snapped the neck of her own clone, crushing her likeness between identical, unrelenting hands. He watched Striker place the disabler in the Empress' hands aboard the cockpit of a stolen ship, watched her place it against the door of her cell, watched her place it against the corridor's wall before *Haven* had time to shuffle her to the edge of their mass and vent the corridor's atmosphere, watched her throw it into the wall of this very chamber.

He saw the Empress standing with Fleur, with Beauregard, with Braga. Even with Ezra. Beneath their feet, dead Empresses were scattered bloodily. Too many to count. Not enough to mourn. With their help and allegiance, she would defeat her clones. She would outlast. Her desires were laid bare under the certainty of an ocean of thoughts. She would never betray them as long as Empress clones still hunted her. That was the threat she feared most. Above all others, herself. He knew it with the certainty of a burning soul etched in fire and blood. As hard as carbon. As infinite as ash scattered upon the stars. He understood it with the purity of a soul washed and stripped bare, until nothing remained but a single mote of cold, deafening light.

Ezra let go of the crystal and fell back onto the floor. Sweat clung to his face, clammy and dripping. He blinked it away, smeared his dark curls aside, stared up at the Empress. "She won't betray us."

She stared at him, cold as death. "Well, obviously."

CHAPTER TWENTY-THREE

H ow hard is it to check my messages?" Isabella shouted as she hopped, shuffled and swore her way into a dirty pair of jeans Paradise Moon hadn't washed. Half asleep, she stumbled halfway into the second denim leg and nearly toppled over.

I had a lot going on yesterday.

I always have a lot going on, but I still check my messages. Beauregard and Braga could be dead!

They'll be fine.

How would you know? Fleur's message is a day old! I am such a shit friend.

Hey! It'll be fine. We'll fix it.

Isabella dragged on a fresh black tee and strapped the PROXUS gauntlet from Fleur around her wrist. The same gauntlet that for a whole day had held Fleur's neglected message asking for Isabella's help.

You are in so much shit.

Purple smoke.

Gone.

The tributaries of blue light glowing from *Haven*'s dark, curved walls were a welcome sight. But not as welcome as the sight of her friends. Fleur, Beauregard, Braga and Ezra were not only alive, but they were also clearly in the middle of something. Encased in the thick armour they typically wore outside in space, only their faces were armour-free. Fleur was sporting a purple band around her bunched-up afro crown, Ezra's damp hair dangled everywhere, Braga's half-curtain of blue tangles only hid the side of her head that wasn't shorn, and Beauregard… well, at his age he didn't need to worry.

Isabella breathed easier. Their cluster of armoured shells stalled mid-approach to a sealed partition of an airlock, their shock at her sudden appearance swiftly shifting gear into delight. Behind their semi-circle of friendly faces, a helmeted woman waited in her own matching suit of space armour, arms folded across her chestplate. Then the hard outer shell of an evac suit blocked her from view as Fleur wrapped up Isabella in the biggest hug. Even when encumbered by space armour, Fleur gave the best hugs. Her smile shone all the way to her eyes as she pulled back long enough to take in the sight of Isabella, as though checking she were real.

"What are you all doing?" asked Isabella. Whatever this was, she had interrupted. She smiled self-consciously. "I got Fleur's message and I was worried."

Ezra pushed Fleur aside and flung his arms around Isabella. Not waiting for her turn, Braga flung herself around them both. She smelled of sweet exotic fruits, which was a much kinder aroma than Ezra's sweat. Trapped as the filling in an uncomfortable sandwich, Isabella couldn't have cared less what they smelled like.

Everyone was alive.

Told you everyone would be fine.

Shut up.

Beauregard didn't offer her a hug, but the armoured paw he laid on her shoulder meant no less to her. His face even creased into a short-lived smile.

"Really, what are you doing?" asked Isabella. "And what happened? I got your message. I'm so sorry, it—"

"Relax, everyone is alive." Fleur raised a hand to forestall her apologies. "Take a beat—we can be a little late for salvaging." She smiled and hugged Isabella again. "It is so good to see you, honey. So good!"

Blushing, Isabella sank into another hug. There was nowhere else she would rather be. "Okay, okay," she finally said, when she could hold in her news no longer. "You need to hear this."

Ringed by friendly faces, she shared the tale of Talyn's dramatic arrival on Earth and what had befallen them. Knowing she was building up to the best part, she couldn't keep a crafty grin from her lips. However, before Isabella could explain Talyn's mission to locate the Spark, Braga excitedly cut her off. Oblivious, the pirate launched into the wild saga that had led her friends to this moment. Isabella nodded impatiently at the tale, although she didn't miss the uncharacteristic tenderness in Braga's throat as she described Fleur's father, before such emotion was swiftly dispelled by a lively description of how she sent him reeling to the deck.

Waiting impatiently for Braga to finish, Isabella could barely contain her excitement or take in her friend's words. She glanced across the airlock. Silently, the helmeted woman was leaning against the furthest wall as she watched them swapping stories. Isabella tuned back into Braga's tale. Thankfully, it sounded like it was nearing its end. Then Braga revealed where *Haven* was. Abruptly, Isabella stopped thinking about her own news. A hush descended over the airlock. The atmosphere prickled with cold. Every face was grim. It seemed impossible to believe that outside this airlock was the same space where so many Sau Darans and humans had died. It seemed impossible such a place existed, let alone right here. Unbidden by Isabella, a glowing purple hand stroked *Haven*'s hull. On the other side of that warm sheet of living metal drifted the ravaged debris and forgotten relics of war.

Well this is haunting.

Do we need to go?

No, I just need a moment.

"Are you okay?" asked Fleur, fresh concern stretching her face as she examined Isabella.

Is that a serious question?

Ezra uncoupled his armoured glove with a hiss from its mechanical wrist joint and grasped Isabella's human hand. "It's a lot, that's all," he reassured her. He squeezed her hand, his warmth transferring into her. She hadn't realised how cold she was.

Pushing death and war from her mind, Isabella remembered why she was here. Finding hope in her words, and still holding Ezra's hand, she finished Talyn's story. As she explained his mission, her friends listened with rapt attention and none more so than Ezra—from creased brow to pursed lips, his expression grew ever sterner at her task ahead.

"Can it actually work?" he asked, a tremor creeping into his voice. "Can we save them all?" A glowing purple hand settled on top of Ezra's, sandwiching his between Paradise Moon and Isabella.

He was always my favourite.

"I don't really understand any of it. But he means it, and there's definitely some sort of Sau Daran alien—"

—God—

"—inside him."

"Then let's help him," urged Ezra. "Whatever it takes. We're doing this."

Isabella smiled at his exuberance. She had seen so little of it from him over the past three years. "As soon as I leave here, I'll help him with his search in the mountains."

"Ain't he got a clue what he's lookin' for?"

Isabella shrugged.

"When I say we're doing this, I mean it." Ezra squeezed her hand tighter. "I'm coming with you and we're going to save them all."

"Well, hold on," said Isabella. "We don't even know what this Spark looks like. It could take us ages."

Ezra shook his head, an earnest smile blossoming over his face. "It doesn't matter. What's he scanning the mountains with?" Isabella shrugged again. "Doesn't matter. I'll bring everything we've got."

"Might be easier from above," suggested Beauregard. "Ain't no harm in takin' Dash for a flyby."

Fleur held up her hands to signal for everyone to hold on, but Ezra wasn't in the mood to be slowed down. "Perfect! I'll get Dash and some supplies and scanning equipment and he'll fly his Scimitar and I'll only take a few prosthetics just in case and obviously we'll need—"

"Honey?"

"Yeah?"

"Breathe. Please."

Ezra gulped in a breath.

"Sweetie, are you sure you want to go?"

Ezra's face was a mess of stale sweat and the most desperate flavour of hope Isabella had ever seen. "We're doing this."

I told you he was my favourite.

Fleur gave Isabella a motherly look. "Honey, perhaps you should introduce Ez to this Talyn boy first and find out how this is all going to work. Then you can bring Ez back to pick up whatever he needs."

Braga pointed at Ezra's space armour with a grimace. "You might want to get changed."

In response, from beyond the oval door opposite the airlock's sealed exit into space there grew a terrible rumbling. "Thank you, *Haven!*" crowed Ezra. The rumbling ended with a heavy clunk, and the oval door rolled back to reveal his quarters. He dodged around the silent, unmoving, armoured woman—who hadn't even removed her helmet or introduced herself—and dashed through the oval door.

"I'll be quick, I promise!" he called around the corner of the open doorway. Isabella could hear the clatter and crash of space armour being thrown aside and clothing crates being fumbled through.

"So who's your friend?" Isabella asked Fleur, her eyes settling on the helmeted stranger outside what was now the door to Ezra's quarters.

"No one you need to worry about," came an answer from the stranger, laced with comm static.

Fleur threw a comforting arm around Isabella's shoulders. "Nothing we want to drag you into."

Isabella didn't complain. She had enough to worry about. Speaking of which, Ezra staggered back inside the airlock, trying to pull down his tunic while tugging on his boots and not falling over.

"Honey, we have to get going. Let us know if you need anything. And maybe start checking your messages?"

Isabella hugged everyone goodbye except for the armoured stranger, who watched her with an unreadable expression behind her helmet.

Gripping Ezra's hand, Isabella stole him from the airlock in a swirl of purple smoke and landed them both in her bedroom.

"Oh, wow. Okay," said Ezra.

"Oh yeah, sorry. I haven't tidied."

That's an understatement.

Ezra scratched his neck awkwardly. "Yeah. It's nice."

She smiled at him. "I've really missed you."

He smiled back. "Shall we go and save the whole phyxing Sau Daran species?"

"Yeah, let's do that." For the first time in a long time, Isabella felt on top of everything. In control and on track. Authentically herself and proud of it. She took his hand, but before she could take him anywhere else in another swirl of purple smoke, he pulled away.

"Wait!" he groaned. "I forgot my gauntlet."

"Relax, I'm on it."

When Isabella arrived in Ezra's quarters in a swirl of purple smoke, she was expecting to pick up his gauntlet and disappear before anyone even noticed her. But she didn't make a move for the gauntlet on top of Ezra's clothing crate. She didn't make any move at all.

Instead, Isabella stared through the open doorway and into the airlock. Her eyes were fixed on the armoured stranger, whose helmet lay on the floor as she froze in the middle of retying her ashen hair, with its streak of red, into a neat bun.

"Why the Hell is my therapist here?"

CHAPTER TWENTY-FOUR

Dash's Scimitar thundered over the mountain, the starfighter's asymmetrical body no more than a blurred, black silhouette against the harsh glare of the mid-afternoon Australian sun.

Ezra ignored the starfighter shooting over their heads. His eyes were locked on the holo coming out of his gauntlet, studying the dizzying symbols streaming across the projection as if they could possibly mean something.

"Dantes and I used to do this all the time after we left the academy," he explained. "If the gods who created the Spark used anything like the same technology they used with the Sau Darans, we'll find it." He glanced at Talyn, but only for a heartbeat. "Whatever it takes."

Talyn smiled, then winced as the purpled bruising painted across his face stretched around his lips. "Thanks, I'm honoured by your aid."

"Relax, this is what we do." Ezra tapped the holo, making one stream of projected symbols slow and another speed up. "On our first posting, Dantes and I were searching the Outer Rim for Sau Daran energy signatures. But they were really faint, so we had to be really good. I've got this, don't worry."

Isabella believed him. Once again, she thanked all the indie gods of rock'n'roll it had been Ezra patrolling the Outer Rim three years ago. If not for him and Dantes, they would never have recorded the surge of energy from a Sau Daran portal opening when Sau Darans kidnapped her from Earth. Even if the explosiveness of their rescue had cost her an arm and a leg, not to mention Dantes' life.

Isabella stared up at Black Range's colossal span of mountains. Talyn had parked his rental just off the red dirt of Highway 138, which ran right through Pilbara. Walgumya Creek roared behind them, while a wall of red and black mountains towered in front of them. Between them and the mountains, the red dirt was strewn with stretches of tall grass bleached white by the sun. Under its glare, sporadic, thin trees twisted black and dry, along with broader outcroppings of more resilient gorse and less familiar bushes that tested Isabella's floral knowledge beyond her limits of 'green' and 'also green'.

Banking around in the clear sky above, Dash lined up another pass over the mountain range.

And another.

And another.

With each pass, Isabella's neck complained louder as she squinted to see him.

"I hate just watching," admitted Talyn. "This is my mission, and I'm not even helping. What can I do?"

"We'll need you soon enough," promised Ezra, without looking up from his gauntlet's holo. "Even if we find some trace of energy in those mountains, without Isabella to get us closer and you to tell us what to look for we won't have a clue what to do."

"Don't worry," said Isabella, squeezing Talyn's arm. "If this thing has been here for so long, we were never going to find it straight away. We'll find it in the next pass. I can feel it."

Much, much later, the setting sun finally dismounted the rocky horizon. Tired and aching, it spilled bloody over mountainous evening shadows. Ezra looked away from his gauntlet's projections and rubbed his eyes with the heels of his palms. "That's it. I'm calling it for today."

Grimly, Talyn gazed into the red-rimmed darkness. "We'll try again tomorrow."

"Tomorrow," Isabella assured them. "We'll find it tomorrow."

Once Dash had landed in a patch of arid scrub, it was the work of a moment and a swirl of purple smoke for Isabella to return him to one of *Haven*'s hangar bays with his Scimitar, followed by Ezra to his quarters. Relief flooded through Isabella when they arrived to find the door to Ezra's quarters closed and no sight of her therapist in the other side. Although it wasn't her therapist, was it? Fleur had been unerringly, terrifyingly clear about that under Isabella's thorough cross-examination earlier. But that problem would have to wait for her to figure out what the Hell to do about it. She hadn't even told Ezra that her therapist on Earth turned out to be the Empress of the Known Galaxies. They had been too busy trying to save a whole species.

We could vanish her into space and just leave her floating?

I've never killed anyone. Not about to start now.

Even the Empress?

Even her.

Okie dokie. Good luck with that one, then. Because she'll happily kill you.

Like the Empress our friends are working with?

Don't remind me.

Ezra collapsed onto his bed, hands smearing the sweat from his brow and running it back through his dark curls. "I'm sorry, I thought we'd find something."

Isabella batted away his apology with a tired wave of her hand. "However long it takes, it'll still be faster than us doing this without you."

Sighing with relief, Ezra pulled off his legs and dropped them at the foot of the bed with his boots still attached. Isabella was proud of the array of prosthetics she had sourced for him. It had been embarrassingly easy, given how many manufacturers were desperate to advertise themselves as providing tech for an actual spaceman.

But in his rush to join her earlier, he had left on the heavy-duty prosthetics he wore inside space armour. Seeing the raw rashes and imprints where the heavier prosthetics rubbed and pulled against the stumps of his thighs, Isabella tried to hide her horror. "Is it hurting?"

"Nah, just sore. They're always sore, you know what it's like."

Memories crept from the darkest corners of Isabella's mind. Memories of her waking up on a PROXUS battle station with fleshy stumps where her right arm and left leg belonged. She glanced at her glowing purple arm and one leg of her jeans, which hid her other glowing limb.

"I remember limping around with a plasma rifle for a crutch, telling everyone within earshot I didn't need carrying and I could do it myself."

Ezra laughed. "Yeah, and then we'd all move along with you—slower than ever."

Isabella paused long enough to examine Ezra's exhausted body more thoroughly as he lay back on his bed. "Sure you're okay?"

"Fine." He levered himself upright and she bent down into a welcome hug. "Are you sure *you're* okay?"

Isabella pulled away and raised her eyebrows in warning. Defensively, Ezra lifted his hands and smiled. "Okay, okay, you can look after yourself. You'll be fine, I know. I just wanted to be sure."

"Consider yourself sure."

"Got it."

"Get some sleep. I'll message when I'm coming to pick up you and Dash."

Isabella returned to the edge of Highway 138 with a swirl of purple smoke. The sun was gone now. Talyn sat on the bonnet of his rental, dangling legs silhouetted in the light spilling from the headlights.

"Next time," Isabella promised him, feeling like she was everyone's cheerleader. "We've got this."

"They've been dead longer than I've been alive. I know a little longer won't matter, but still... we're so close, you know?"

Isabella settled next to him on the bonnet. There was something peaceful, perhaps even morbidly comforting, about the intense darkness wrapped around them. She stared out beyond the twin beams of their headlights, knowing everywhere she looked, hidden in inky stillness, the middle of nowhere was staring back at her.

Talyn was so close to her, the outback all around them dark and quiet. She couldn't see him. But she could hear his soft breathing and the heavy bass of her own heart. It shook her ribcage, inescapably in sync with every close breath Talyn took.

"What will you do when we find it?" she asked the darkness.

"I'll find a way to make it work and we'll save them all," said the darkness. "Bring them all back. Give them a chance to head to some quiet corner of the universe and be the peaceful explorers they were meant to be."

He's cute. Let's keep him.

Don't even think about it. You know I like him.

Relax, he's not my type.

What is your type?

Wouldn't you like to know.

"What happened with Nova Sky?" asked Isabella.

For a while, the darkness said nothing. Long enough for the feral yelp of a wild dog to cut through the night's mystical silence. Its howl died with a whimper and the night was theirs again.

"You know when you're burning so hot inside because you want to do the right thing?" asked the darkness. "When you're so desperate to get one thing right, you're willing to get everything else wrong?"

Isabella nodded. Three cycles ago, with plasma blasts exploding all around her, Ezra screaming as his broken legs were scorched with hit after hit from PROXUS plasma rifles, Beauregard and Fleur back-to-back in the thick of the fight, she and Paradise Moon had risked everything to return *Haven*'s crystal. She had vanished them as far as Earth's orbit and saved everyone on *Haven* from Striker's assault. It could have killed them and probably should have, but instead it worked. Realising Talyn couldn't see her nodding in the darkness, Isabella murmured her agreement.

"Well, yeah, that," admitted the darkness. "Nova became really dangerous."

"I know that feeling."

Hey!

Really? You sure you want to question that after everything you did to me?

Fair enough. Past tense though, couldn't you?

"Well, I knew that feeling at least," Isabella qualified. "We just needed to understand each other better. Right now, I couldn't be who or what I am without her."

Back at ya.

Lying back on the bonnet so she didn't have to put her neck through further strife, she gazed up at the cosmic wonder of the night sky. Free from the curse of light pollution, this far into the outback the night sky shone with star-pricked magic.

"He was dangerous," said the darkness. "He wanted to save them, but he wanted a war too. Revenge on humanity, I think."

"So what did you do?"

"I cut him off. Held onto his powers somehow, but pushed him back until he couldn't control me and couldn't hurt anyone else ever again."

Isabella smiled at the darkness. "And then you carried on with his mission? Trying to save a whole species you have never met?"

He lay down beside her on the bonnet, and for a heartbeat his hand brushed hers as he settled into a comfortable position. "Saving them was always the right thing to do. It was the war he wanted to start once they were saved that was going to be a problem."

Isabella rolled to face him, her glowing arm bending unbidden to cushion the side of her head on the bonnet. This close to the glow of her arm, Talyn's eyes were solar flares swimming in liquid marble. Beneath the dark patterns of pain tattooed up his skin by the crash, his gorgeous cheekbones lifted in a smile as he gazed back at her. Stray locks of hair dangled beside his face, the rest of his gorgeous physique lost to darkness.

"Aren't you worried he'll come back?" asked Isabella. Her voice was a whisper.

"Not an option." If her words were as gentle as smoke, his were as hard as granite. "I won't ever let him come back. The harm he would do to get what he wants... it's unthinkable."

Talyn's face was so close. To kiss him, all she needed to do was arch her body just enough... She realised she was holding her breath. Slowly, she let it out, rippling a lock of his hair as she did so. "I've never met anyone else with an alien—"

—God—

"—inside them. I thought I was the only one."

"I've never met anyone like you," confessed the darkness. "You're such a good person."

"I'm not, really," she mumbled, unsure of herself in the face of such sincere praise.

"You never give up, do you?" asked the darkness.

Isabella found her surety. It was right there, anchored in everything she had done since being kidnapped from Earth. Her confidence may flit and flutter like laundry in the breeze, but her actions were the steadfast pole against which it pulled taut. Unmoving. Unrelenting. Uncompromising. For three years, she had done nothing but fight. She had only ever done the right thing. She had never taken the smart option and never backed down— if anything, she ran towards danger. If she kept doing that, it could never chase her. "Never."

His lips found hers. Soft, rich and begging for her. She let him into her mouth, running her tongue down his as she pressed her body into him. The bonnet pinged beneath their shifting, rolling weight.

That'll leave a dent.

Shut up!

Feeling for him in the darkness, her human hand slipped around his waist. His lips kissed her forehead. Her cheeks. Her neck, again and again like soft echoes of joy in the darkness. Working up his back, her palm pulled all of him against her.

Is this happiness?

Don't ask me. Elbows and knees, remember?

There was a hiss from the ground. Isabella jerked upright out of Talyn's embrace in time to catch something slithering over the dirt towards them, an S-shaped blur caught in the beam of their headlights. Isabella swept her legs up onto the bonnet.

The universe had spoken.

Happiness never lasted and she couldn't have too much of a good thing. Couldn't have enough of it right now, that was for damned sure. The hot ache inside her told a story of too many good things unfinished.

"Okay, time to go," she announced grumpily.

"Was it…?" Talyn began. "Was I…?" he began again.

Isabella pointed at the snake below their feet. "This country is literally notorious for having the most poisonous snakes in the world." She held out her hand. "I promise it wasn't you."

"Are you sure?" asked the darkness.

"Not that I would wish this on my worst enemy, but in a couple of seconds I can have us home, with a glass of red in our hands and a hot bath if you need one."

"Why wouldn't you wish that on your worst enemy?"

"Because it means meeting my mother."

The darkness took her hand.

Purple smoke.

Gone.

CHAPTER TWENTY-FIVE

For Braga, it was only three cycles since she had flown in a pirate fleet. For Fleur, such thrills had been buried a lifetime ago. Through eyes that had seen much more of life since then and far too much death, Fleur gazed through her shuttle's viewscreen. *Haven* and the pirate fleet hung in Regis V's orbit, the latter a mismatched horde of leviathans that had grown no less wondrous during her absence.

Long before Count Fontaine betrayed Fleur and her crew to PROXUS, her naïve teenage eyes had marvelled at every swarming shoal of pirate ships, each igniting fresh sparks of joy inside her fledgling heart as they swooped around her family's vessel. For her, there had been no greater sight. Vast hulks, amassing a greater ensemble of shapes, designs and paintjobs than her young eyes could have ever parsed. She had been obsessed with engineering and flying ever since.

Forgotten pride swelled inside her as she breathed in the sight again. It was so mesmerising that she didn't even notice her own reflection in the viewscreen and the imperfections that usually haunted every glance. She felt

Braga's hand tenderly rub her arm. Encasing it in her own, Fleur gave it a squeeze.

"Glad you're back?" asked Braga.

Tearing her eyes from the viewscreen, Fleur smiled up at her wife and nodded. Braga's eyes were awake with the same joy Fleur's young heart had known. As one, their eyes drifted away from each other and back to the viewscreen. Among the pirate fleet, Fleur spotted not only the battle-ravaged relics of ships lost a generation ago in the Last Great War, but also the gleaming space relays she and her crew had spent the last rotation exploring. Already, the most valuable components were being stripped from inside these relays by the fleet's shelled-up scavengers in their evac suits.

Before the salvage operation began, every pirate ship's crew had taken one relay to investigate. They had all turned up the same results. Protected in their evac suits, Fleur, Braga, Beauregard and the Slave Empress had floated through the deserted control rooms, crew quarters and engineering bays of their assigned relay, but found nothing to explain what had befallen the deserted relays and their crews. No survivors. No bodies. Every circuit was lit, every workstation ready for another standard rotation boosting signals for the rest of the Known Galaxies—except someone had turned off the power, erased the logs and told everyone to go home. Or jump out of the nearest airlock. It was impossible to know what had happened until they reached the surface of Regis V and found someone who could answer their questions. Or, failing that, they would find more opportunities for salvage.

While Fleur was sure the rest of the pirate fleet would prefer even more salvage, she wanted answers. Abandoned but intact, these satellites were part of a vital system of space relays employed by PROXUS throughout the Known Galaxies. They boosted signals between far-flung star systems, enabling instant communication across multiple galaxies. Such systems were essential to the speed and precision with which PROXUS forces tightened the Empress' grip on humanity. For an entire set of relays to be abandoned was unheard of, and for PROXUS to have made no attempt to investigate in all this time proved how severely the civil war was affecting their operations.

Fleur hid a grimace.

It was the same mindless conflict between Empress clones desperate to kill each other that had forced them to leave the Burned Empress in her cell on *Haven*. One Empress might be useful, but two would turn their little adventure to Regis V into another warzone.

A shadowy reflection shifted in Fleur's viewscreen. She glimpsed the Slave Empress crossing her arms impatiently in her seat beside Beauregard at the back of the cockpit. Her ashen hair with its streak of crimson down one side was draped over the bulging shoulders of heavy battle armour Beauregard had dragged out of *Haven*'s armoury for her. Had Fleur not met a second Empress clone, she could have easily believed the terrifying woman sat behind her was none other than the one and only Empress of the Known Galaxies.

"Is something on your mind?" the Slave Empress asked, her sharp eyes missing nothing.

Fleur didn't turn around. "I was just thinking about how useful you are going to be if anyone on this planet is still loyal to PROXUS."

The Empress glared frostily. "Sadly, loyalty to PROXUS no longer guarantees loyalty to me."

"Be convincin' then," urged Beauregard. "If you ain't useful, you might as well be in your cell."

"I'd be more useful if you gave me a weapon."

Braga threw back her head and laughed, before pinning the Empress with a mischievous grin. "If you ever find yourself holding a weapon, it's only so I could tell everyone I killed you in a fair fight."

The comm burst awake with barked call signs as pilots began checking in. Fleur keyed her comm to join them, then glanced over her shoulder when she was done. "Okay, people. Showtime."

The battered and beaten hulls of the fleet's smallest ships cut through the starscape around them. Leaping and duking across each other's paths with rakish panache, the shuttles and starfighters danced and swept and soared towards the planet's atmosphere.

Watching their extravagant manoeuvres with a scowl, Beauregard shook his head. "Pirates…"

Ignoring him, Fleur gave her wife a long-suffering glance. "Better sit down, honey. We are not going to let them have all the fun by getting there first, are we?"

Pecking Fleur on the cheek, Braga settled into the co-pilot's chair beside her. "Don't spare the sublights."

Sinking deeper into her pilot's chair to keep her body loose and relaxed while she was at the controls, Fleur cranked up the power to their sublight engines and nudged the stick far enough to send her Falchion-class fighter into a steep hypersonic dive.

They hurtled through the planet's thermosphere, leaving the inky void of space in the hot fire of their wake before they burst through the planet's upper atmosphere. Swirling bubbles of cloud thickened below, only gifting in their sparsest moments a glimpse of the planet's icy surface wreathed in tattered wisps of cloud. Atmospheric dampeners avoided them being pinned back in their seats as the fighter's nose led their descent through the scorching heat raging against the hull. Hot flickers on either side announced the arrival of fellow shuttles and starfighters burning lower into the atmosphere, all racing towards the planet's surface.

Fleur checked her sensors. "Zeroing in on the largest power reading," she told them.

Once they had torn through more layers of frayed cloud, only one structure stood out amid the frozen landscape below. Fleur threw them towards it, her viewscreen ravenously devouring sky. She was pushing the throttle so hard, juicing her fighter with all the star energy it had, that her knuckles were stretched tight and her outstretched forearm thick with tensed muscle.

As they surged closer with an army of friendly shuttles and starfighters on their tail, the haze surrounding the structure dissolved. The first thing Fleur noticed was it was more than one structure. It was thousands of structures. A city assembled around the icy spire of the largest mountain she had ever seen. And the heart of the power readings on her sensors.

Silver buildings were scattered around the outskirts of the city, spread thinly across a frozen plain at the base of a huge mountain that shone blue with ice. On the city's outskirts was a broad black landing strip with shuttle after shuttle lined up along it. Not one shuttle showed signs of life or movement. As she flew closer, she could make out the mirrored beauty of their sleek, silver arrow-like hulls. Even from this distance, she could tell they were grander and more advanced than anything she had flown.

The city climbed in a spiral, starting from the outskirts and growing more densely populated with glittering silver structures that twisted around the mountain's massive span of frozen rock. The mountain was so broad and so tall that more than once it disappeared through thin layers of cloud, reappearing above them with fresh layers of sparkling buildings that travelled ever upwards. The spiral of buildings finally ended at its peak with the largest structure of all. Flying close enough to make out the tower at the top of the mountain, Fleur checked her sensors again. "Might as well start at the top." She flicked a flurry of switches, readying the fighter to land.

Behind her, she heard the habitual rustling and mechanical clicking of Beauregard checking the charges on his plasma pistols. She had never flown a mission with him without hearing those reassuring sounds as they neared their target—to have heard anything else would have been unnerving.

The peak had been flattened to accommodate the construction of a titanic tower. Its sleek silver curves shone in the same cerulean daylight that twinkled off the rest of the silver city. After Fleur set down on the flattened peak, they abandoned the safety of the fighter so they could begin their hunt for answers and salvage.

The Empress dropped down the ramp, her dark helmet gripped tightly in her hands instead of covering her face. If she actually put it on, its impenetrable faceplate would have protected her from being recognised by pirates as well as from physical harm— with every chance one might follow the other.

Braga drew in a sharp breath as she stepped down the fighter's ramp. "Cold!"

With his good hand, Beauregard fastened up the front of his long coat. "Well, what were you expectin'? The whole phyxin' planet's made of ice."

Shivering, Braga tugged at the ends of her short jacket, but there was no escaping the fact that it had never been designed to pull together at the front. Some jackets were practical, others were for show. And in shielding all her insecurities behind enough swagger to enchant the stars themselves, everything about the woman Fleur loved was, inescapably, for show. It was a show always worth watching, though.

"Well, there's certainly no warmth coming from you," replied Braga.

Warily, Beauregard drew a plasma pistol and examined their landing site. "Wear somethin' warmer next time and you ain't gonna need no warmth from no one else."

A stout wall of wind dragged the folds of Fleur's synthetic poncho flat against her body, almost pushing her back up the fighter's ramp. While she could never have afforded such an outfit as an outlaw, during her misspent cycles as a PROXUS Ranger she had invested every point of her wages in the finest action-ready fashion that points could buy. The poncho's synthetic fabric was lined with tributaries of circuitry designed to spread heat through her shoulders and core, with the bonus it also warmed any of her stylishly cut synthetic leather armour that brushed up against it underneath.

"Do you want my poncho, honey?"

"No, I want that dpresh to take a long walk off the edge of this mountain."

Beauregard's keen eyes never stopped scanning the mountaintop as though he hadn't heard, but Fleur caught his snigger carry on the breeze. She glanced at Braga, who was grinning.

"Are you two messing with me?" asked Fleur.

Braga winked. "Who, us?"

Fleur sighed. "Shoot me now, I preferred it when you were trying to kill each other."

Leading with his plasma pistol, Beauregard ignored the silver tower next to Fleur's fighter and the winding snow-lined black road leading down from the peak to the next tier of buildings below. Instead, he crept to the edge.

"I wasn't serious about the whole walking over the edge thing," Braga called after him hurriedly.

Beauregard peered over the sheer drop, then glanced back at the group. "Long way down."

"What are you looking at, big man?" asked Fleur.

"Nothin'."

Braga snorted. "Then let's explore that big warm tower instead of freezing our asses off out here."

Beauregard half-grinned, one corner of his lips lifting into a grim smirk as he surveyed the city below. "Ain't none of you listenin'. There's nothin' down there."

Fleur edged closer, easing her arm through Beauregard's weaker one for support as she looked over the edge. "I see lots down there," she said, puzzled.

Below, thousands of silver buildings swirled up to meet them from the base of the mountain. Wrapped around ice and rock, a large transparent tube even wider than Fleur's fighter looped alongside the black road, running down through every tier of buildings all the way to the bottom. Whatever transparent material the tube was crafted from had either steamed up or was deliberately opaque. Either way, it was impossible to see inside, even when Fleur squinted at the higher reaches of tube immediately below them.

"Ain't no people," growled Beauregard. "Ain't nothin' movin' down there or up here 'cept us and pirates."

Fleur looked down again. Beauregard was right. Familiar shuttles and starfighters had landed in patches of open ground and on the black road, their occupants spilling warily into the frozen city. But aside from intrepid pirates, the city was still and silent. Scanning empty stretches of road and unlit buildings, she saw no evidence of locals.

"Everyone's probably inside," Braga suggested. "Like we should be in this cold."

"Ain't no argument here."

Fleur turned away from the mountain's edge and immediately swore. The only thing she did faster than swearing was draw her plasma pistol and aim it in at least three different directions as she searched for a target. "Where the phyx is the Empress?"

Now it was everyone else's turn to swear. With their plasma pistols poking into every pocket of breeze, they scanned the exposed mountaintop, hurrying back and forth without success. Only after rounding Fleur's fighter did Fleur spot their absconded clone kneeling at the base of the entrance to the giant silver tower.

The top of its silver dome rose twinkling into the clouds above. Every line of its structure was smooth and silver—twisting elegantly this way, turning sharply that way, always in a new direction every time Fleur attempted to trace its outline. Eventually her gaze always led upwards and the tower was lost in clouds. Its entrance was a slash of darker silver, easily the height of four Rangers and much wider than it was tall, but angular like the diagonal cut of a blade. It started at ground level on the right and finished highest on the left.

"Ain't no one gonna trust you if you go wanderin' off," called Beauregard.

The Empress didn't bother turning around from where she was crouched in front of the slash of darker silver. Fleur rushed closer, her plasma pistol ready, Braga and Beauregard keeping pace on her flanks.

In the Empress' hands, a chaotic bundle of wires had sprouted from an ingress in the silver wall. A silver panel lay discarded on the frozen ground next to her abandoned helmet.

"Why the phyx is everythin' silver?"

"It's silver in colour only, not in its fundamental components," scolded the Empress as though he should know better. "Can't you see this is an advanced mythium alloy, not the native silver you're thinking of?"

Beauregard stared down at her blankly. That had been a lot of long words for him to digest. "So?"

The Empress tore another fistful of wires from the hole in the wall. "Mythium is an alloy infinitely stronger than anything we build our ships or armour from."

"So why ain't everythin' made from it? I ain't never heard of it."

The Empress huffed out a cloudy breath. "No, I don't suppose you have."

Braga peered over the Empress' shoulder at the wires she was unfurling between her fingers. "Materials are too rare in most of the Known Galaxies. I'm betting this planet's flush with all the right ores."

"Incorrect." The Empress held out a hand. "Blade?"

Braga looked at Fleur.

Reluctantly, Fleur nodded.

Beauregard took a step back, his plasma pistol aimed rock-solid from his hip. Taking Braga's axe with more enthusiasm than that with which it was offered, the Empress clasped it below the head and began delicately skinning and cutting wires. "You are all so ignorant. The elements required to form mythium are remarkably simple and plentiful, but it's prohibitively expensive to manufacture. Waiting for me in my throne room on Xarr is the finest suit of mythium armour you could ever dream of, but it cost more than my flagship to make."

Braga whistled. "No wonder the whole pirate fleet turned up. This is the most valuable city in the Known Galaxies." She grabbed Fleur's arm excitedly. "We'll never have to take another job again."

"Ain't no one tearin' this city apart," Beauregard warned her.

"Of course not," Braga clarified, embarrassment spreading across her face with a red flush. Her hand retreated from Fleur's arm. "People live here. Obviously, we can't tear apart their homes. I know that."

Fleur spared her wife a comforting smile. There were pirates, and then there were pirates. Not all the pirates out in space played by the kindest rules, but Braga was one of the good ones. Yet when they first met, Braga had nearly killed them. There was a deep scar in Fleur's shoulder to prove it. And there were gaps in Braga's past she never talked about. Sometimes, in unguarded moments like these, she said enough to make even Fleur wonder where she used to draw the line and in what shades of grey, black or smudged white she used to make her living. Fleur might wonder who Braga used to be, but she didn't care for the answer. If she had, it would have made her and Beauregard—as ex-PROXUS Rangers— the biggest hypocrites this side of the Outer Rim.

"Being such a strong alloy, it's almost impossible to manipulate mythium," added the Empress. "Most tools would break before they could cut or shape it. The curves of these structures border on the impossible."

Fleur looked down at the Empress, wearing her best mask of indifference. "Are you honestly telling us that you of all people knew this city was here, so close to the relays operated by your people, and you chose not to tear it down to steal all these precious materials?"

"Which would clearly be a horrible thing to do," Braga added quickly. "Unthinkable."

"The primitives who lived here never had mythium, both before and after I won the war against the Sau Darans. I should know, I led the teams who came down here to hunt for survivors on the surface." The Empress spoke on autopilot, her eyes locked on the stripped wires she was binding together. "None of those metal monsters or their gods were left alive once we finished. And there certainly wasn't any mythium on this planet. After I formed PROXUS, I set up the relays in isolated systems like this. The locals operated the relays under our command. It's inconceivable they kept so much mythium secret, but that's a mystery I will solve." The Empress twisted another pair of wires together. "That should do it."

Braga held out her hand and the Empress dutifully returned her axe. Braga was still stowing it in her belt as she joined everyone else in readying her plasma pistol towards the slash of dark silver blocking the entrance. They watched it warily, waiting for it to slide into the tower's interior and leave a diagonal gap in the wall.

Nothing budged.

"You've done it wrong," moaned Braga.

"I can assure you I did everything correctly," the Empress replied haughtily.

Braga bent down and checked the wires.

"How is it, honey?"

"Everything's re-wired right, it should be open." Braga held out her hands in confusion and shrugged. "It's like the door doesn't want to open."

Beauregard twirled his pistol into its holster and spun back towards Fleur's fighter. "Ain't no problem can't be fixed with explosives."

The Empress' tongue lashed hard enough to hold him in his tracks. "Did you listen to a word I said?"

Beauregard glanced back sheepishly at the towering silver structure. "Right. Mystium."

"Mythium," corrected the Empress icily.

"Don't that mean we just need *more* explosives?"

"Explosives wouldn't make a dent in this much mythium." A mere glance from the Empress right now would have been enough to wither most people. "You'd need a plasma barrage from a starship to loosen that door. We should return to the ship and use its weapons."

"Woah! There is a whole city to explore down there," said Fleur, pointing to where the black road disappeared over the edge of the mountain. "There is no need to start blowing anything up."

Although Beauregard didn't have the facial acumen to hide his disappointment, he made no fuss as they explored the road towards the next tier. The road dropped sharply from the flattened peak, but despite the snow and ice all around them, Fleur's stylish combat boots had no trouble finding purchase. Curious, she scraped her sole over the road's grippy black surface. "Not even the thinnest layer of ice."

"Could be something in it to stop the ice forming?" suggested Braga.

"Ain't nothin' to bother us." Beauregard's eyes never strayed from the shining buildings further down the bend of the road. "It ain't no road that emptied those relays. I'd be more worried about whoever's waitin' for us in those buildings than anythin' beneath our boots."

They edged closer, the silver buildings growing increasingly defined through the gusts of snow-laden breeze trying to obscure them. Their sleek silver curves and mythium shells were reminiscent of the tower—and no more open for business.

The scream of sublight engines at full burn thundered overhead. Fleur peered into the wind-whipped snow, straining to make out the shadow in the skies above.

"Watch out!" Braga warned, her eyes catching something that spoiled her expression. "Dpresh incoming!"

"That dpresh ain't just incomin', he's comin' in hot!"

They dove into the snowdrifts lining the black road as the gunship opened fire, hot green plasma superheating the frigid air. The acrid stench of cooking road assaulted Fleur's nostrils. Black and ugly, smoke leapt on the breeze in fits and starts, blowing away one moment and engulfing them in noxious fumes the next.

Choking, Braga rolled over in the snow drift so she was next to Fleur. "You want me to shoot him?"

Fleur waited to see if her wife was joking or not, then shook her head when it became clear Braga was waiting for an answer. Instead of shooting anyone—at least for now—they dragged themselves out of the snow. Except for Beauregard, they all holstered their plasma pistols. Except for Fleur, they all unsheathed lethal scowls.

Still smoking, the freshly rutted road sizzled and spat with the aftermath of a plasma volley. Fleur recognised the ostentatious gunship settling down on it. She had known it all her life—and everything about it announced pirate. It had more gun turrets than wings, engines or anything else. They were the old-fashioned models of turrets, with bubbled domes housing a human gunner in each instead of relying on a more reliable automated targeting system. Emblazoned with the unmistakeable emblem of a half-eclipsed sun, its ancient hull was a patchwork trauma of battle scars.

From the heart of the gunship's chaos of wings and turrets, the canopy of a large cockpit rose and three men leaped onto the smoking road. Before they could draw closer, the Empress swiftly pulled on her helmet.

The wind tugged the billowing purple robes of the man in the centre of the trio as he strode down the black road towards them. The purple plates of his armour gleamed in the pale sunlight.

"You're a phyxing maniac!" Braga screamed. She drew her pistol as she advanced on him, her knuckles whitening as her grip tightened. "You tried to kill us!"

The man who was no longer Fleur's father leaned a palm on the golden hilt of his rapier. "Oh please! I was merely hurrying things along."

Braga stormed towards him. "Get locked. Get vented. Eat my phyxing—"

"Hey!" Fleur shouted at Count Fontaine. She prided herself on remaining calm no matter what. That was how she lived. How she survived. Always in control and never out of it. Even after a gunship unloaded its plasma cannons at her friends, had anyone else been piloting it she would still have kept a seal on her feelings—so many feelings, and such a tight seal. But her father's gift was the ease at which he could break that seal and unleash everything inside.

Braga's sideways glance must have caught something in Fleur's expression, which didn't feel placid anymore. Whatever Braga saw on Fleur's face, it was enough to halt her advance. "Tell me what you need," said Braga evenly, her rage instantly swallowed by something more precious to her. "I've got you."

"Why are you here?" Fleur demanded of the man.

Smiling with odorous charm, he gestured carelessly with his free hand. "Why, looting this town bare, of course. And enjoying your company along the way so you can get to know the real me."

"Oh, I am getting to know you just fine," Fleur snarled back. "You. Shot. At. My. Friends."

A titter of laughter escaped his lips, followed by the most superior of smirks. "Dearest daughter, I shot *past* your friends."

He pointed.

Fleur looked.

Smouldering behind them against the side of the road was the melting, collapsed frontage of the nearest mythium structure. The elegant curves of its sloping roofs remained intact, but its dark silver slash of a front door featured a newly installed hole accompanied by an en-suite of molten slag scattered on the icy ground.

With an expression colder than the wind nipping at her cheeks, Fleur turned her back on the man who used to be her father. Letting him trail in her wake, she marched across the road. When she reached the destroyed entrance, she was careful to step over and around the mess of smoking debris.

No one answered her calls. Aside from the ash settling in the air and the shards of twisted mythium that had pierced a wooden table inside, the jagged outline of daylight shining through the destroyed entrance revealed an otherwise undisturbed living space. It didn't take more than a glance to confirm the building was empty. Untouched chairs and the injured table were surrounded by furs for sleeping on the floor and a primitive cooking area complete with a cauldron resting over pale ashes. The walls were worn panels of roughly cut wood, which from inside hid its outer shell of mythium.

Fleur wandered through the living space and dipped a finger in the ashes beneath the cauldron. Cold, but not yet powdery. Easily less than one rotation old. She glanced in the cauldron, where a thin puddle of brackish liquid remained. She dipped a finger in that too and was surprised to find it barely cold—not even close to frozen, as she would have expected.

"Oh dear, is this really it?" asked Count Fontaine, as he followed her inside. "I had hoped they would offer a little more sparkle for our coffers."

Fleur rounded on him, slamming her hand down on a section of table that wasn't impaled by shreds of smoking metal. "Someone could have been in here! You could have killed them!"

He dismissed her concerns with another careless wave of his hand. "Clearly no one was, so there was no harm done. Except, of course, to that otherwise impenetrable mythium front door." He picked up a chipped wooden dinner plate from the table and examined it with disappointment. "Alas, I had dreamt of so much more." He tossed the plate away. "This is nothing more than kindling."

Fleur shook her head. "I never should have come."

"Oh, fear not! Perhaps the other abodes are home to greater treasures."

Disgust erupted over Fleur's face. "I meant I should never have agreed to come here with you." She shook her head in sad disbelief. "You are even worse than the man I remember."

Echoes of affrontery crept into his expression. "What more do you want? The relays were rich with components. Your share of the salvage will set you up for cycles to come. And I am sure other homes will reveal finer plunder than this." He reached out for her hand but she escaped his grasp, retreating to the destroyed doorway. "I am doing everything in my power to prove myself and earn your forgiveness," he pleaded. "I cannot help if the degenerates who dwelt here are too poor to make this foray planet-side worth your while."

Fleur retrieved the wooden plate and returned it to the table. "You literally have no idea."

Beauregard, Braga and the Empress joined Fleur as she marched away from him further down the winding road. Once the crisp air had cooled her temper, she stopped long enough to stare back at the city around her. "Seriously, where is everyone?"

CHAPTER TWENTY-SIX

Dash's voice crowed over the comm with unchecked excitement. "I've found it! I've actually found it!"

Pings announced themselves on Ezra and Isabella's gauntlets as Dash marked a waypoint. The Spark. With a swipe of his fingers, Ezra brought up a projected map of Pilbara and zoomed in. It was much further south of where they had been searching yesterday in Black Range, buried deep in the heart of a different Pilbara mountain.

Is this actually happening?

You bet.

"How close can you land?" Isabella asked over the comm.

"That's a negative, the signal I'm getting is in the middle of a mountain. There's nowhere close enough to land without falling off."

"Hold her steady, Dash," instructed Isabella. She looked up from her gauntlet. "I'll go to him, it'll be faster."

"What?" chorused Ezra and Talyn.

"That's a really bad idea," added Ezra.

"You don't need to do this," added Talyn.

Urgh! Boys!

A glowing purple hand slid off Isabella's sunglasses and stowed them in a pocket.

Hero shit?

Isabella grinned. *Hero shit, baby!*

Purple smoke.

Gone.

"Wait, why am I holding her stead—" Dash cut off his question over the comm. Isabella grinned back at him as he stared through his cockpit's canopy. She doubted she looked her best clinging to his Scimitar's wing by her purple hand, but she was thankful for the strength of its alien grip. She tried to wave her human hand at him, but she couldn't exert any control over her human limbs. Trailing behind her purple hand's grip, her windswept body shuddered under the turbulent air pummelling it so hard she could feel her cheeks rippling.

So, you know those videos we watch of dogs hanging their faces out of speeding car windows?

Not the time!

It feels relevant.

The starfighter's engines quietened. It slowed to a gentle, sky-high crawl, sending Isabella tumbling onto the wing with as much grace as a kitten on ice. Dash's cockpit broke her fall, its transparent canopy striking her face. Peeling herself off the glass, Isabella gave him a thumbs up. Dash waved back sheepishly, unable to stem a look of disapproval beneath the cascade of unkempt hair poking beneath the rim of his helmet.

"Dash, is she okay?" Ezra asked over the comm.

"Physically?" Dash replied. "Or in the head?"

"Hey!" Isabella called into her gauntlet.

Dash kept chatting, most of it in a concerned tone that Isabella had no truck with. Ignoring him and working her gauntlet's holo, she brought back the projected map of Pilbara. After a few experimental taps of the holo, she managed to orient the map so she was finally looking at Dash's new waypoint and the correct mountain. The mountain with the big fat Sau Daran energy signature deep in its rocky core.

This is it! Let's save them all.

She peered over the starfighter's wing. *You think we can make it from here?* Skeletal specks of pale, white grass were sparsely scattered down the mountain, pale islands marooned on a sea of red rock. Everything below her looked tiny.

No, I can't see it clearly. We need to get closer.

"Dash, can you drop us lower?"

There was a sigh. "I'd be happy to, but that'll throw you off my wing."

Ezra's voice joined them over the comm. "Why don't you come back here and let Dash fly closer to the mountain? Then you can go back and—"

"Hero shit, baby!" screamed Isabella. She leaped off the starfighter, her body twisting and plunging and rocking and rolling in the high breeze. She wailed in delight, excitement surging and sparking inside her like a current of electricity on overdrive. The deathly delight of the fall was almost as intoxicating as the thrill of saving every Sau Daran who had ever lived. And ever died.

She had to leave it as late as she could… without dying. Holding out until the last… possible… second…

The first patches of white grass and red rock were close. Almost level with where the waypoint disappeared into the mountain. Almost level with Isabella as she fell screaming and laughing.

Red rock reared up to break her fall, break her body, the last possible second threatening to tick past with a body-shattering thud.

Before she struck the rocks and made them even redder, but only just before, Isabella abandoned her dive with a swirl of purple smoke.

Without losing velocity, she shot up out of another swirl of purple smoke near Talyn and Ezra's feet. Their dumbfounded stares blurred away from her as she tore upwards through the air in front of them, heading for the sky. As her velocity levelled out, Isabella hung for a heartbeat before gravity caught up and pulled her back down. At least it wasn't far to fall this time, and at nowhere near the speed she had been travelling when she arrived. There was nothing like gravity to beat gravity. The rental's roof bent under her boots as she landed, her hands outstretched to keep her balance.

Isabella grinned. "That was cool."

Stuck the landing, too.

Once she had calmed down the boys enough to have a conversation without them raving about how she could have died, she grabbed them by their arms. One patch of red dirt was replaced with another as she vanished them to the spot where she had bailed out of her dive in a swirl of purple smoke. They fell the last handful of meters onto rocks and dirt below, which was most of the way up the steep outer edge of a mountain.

Isabella brushed the red dirt from her jeans and made to strike out for the peak, but Talyn and Ezra held her back. Another boring avalanche of concern followed. Apparently, seeing how close she had come to hitting the rocks before she bailed out of her dive had rattled them. Patiently, she waited for the boys to calm down. Taking its time, a purple hand slid on her shades so she could survey the mountainside without squinting into the hot glare of the Australian sun.

"Thanks, Dash," Isabella said into her gauntlet, while Ezra and Talyn finished being so vocally concerned about her. "We'll be okay from here."

"Sure thing, I'll find somewhere to land so I can conserve energy in the star drive."

Isabella couldn't contain her amusement as she examined Talyn and Ezra's incredulous expressions. "Shall we go be heroes?"

Without waiting for a reply, she dragged them up a steep rocky slope peppered with red dirt and white grass.

"What happened to you?" asked Ezra, as he began climbing. "This isn't the girl I met in deep space three cycles ago."

Isabella glanced over her shoulder and raised her eyebrows high enough to clear the top of her shades. Without saying a word, she smiled and turned away.

"She's terrifying," she heard Talyn mutter as he hurried up the mountain. "Amazing... but terrifying."

Beneath a cruel sun, with red dirt swirling in the air and sticking to everything, their short ascent was unbearably steep and draining. Even drenched in disgusting rivers of sweat that swam down her spine and settled in places she'd rather not think about, Isabella was grateful for how hard her personal trainer had pushed her in recent months—and to her mum for booking a personal trainer in the first place. Straining to stay upright, she grasped a handful of giant sun-baked rock and levered herself onto the crest of the mountain.

Stupid grins crawled across their breathless mouths as the panting trio gulped in oxygen. Isabella held up a hand for a high five. Her two companions from the other side of the universe stared at it curiously. "You're supposed to hit it," she clarified.

Ezra frowned. "Why?"

Gently, Talyn stroked her palm and waited to see what happened next.

Sighing, she lowered it. "Don't bother."

From up here, she could see the top of the mountain was shaped like a ringed doughnut, with a monolithic dimple where its peak belonged. Recovering her breath, she led them to the mountaintop's inner edge. Together, they peered over what she imagined as the hole in the ring doughnut. Mounds of rocky outcrops spread all the way down a steep drop, ending with spiked pillars of red stone teeth in the basin below.

"Well?" she asked Talyn.

He shrugged. "It's your planet."

"Yeah, and the Spark's yours." She waited expectantly. "How do we find it?" she prompted, when he didn't reply. "The signal's coming from below, but it's not in that basin and this is all rock under our feet. I can do a lot of things, but I can't move through rock."

While Talyn studied the basin, Isabella didn't have anything better to do… so she studied Talyn. A sheen of sweat had gifted a kind glow to his skin and slicked back his dark hair beautifully. "Well, it's old." He gestured at the mountain range. "All of this would have grown around it over hundreds of millions of cycles. So if the Spark hadn't moved over all this time, it's probably buried in the oldest part of the mountain."

"Great. So we need to, like, drill through the rock?"

Ezra threw up his hands in frustration. "We're so close! How can it be this hard?"

What's his problem? It's not like it's his fault they're all dead.

It's not your fault either.

Maybe.

And maybe a few of them are his fault, you know. We're all in this together.

Stop being so reasonable. It's annoying.

Isabella settled down in the dirt, stretching out her sore human leg and arm along with her exuberantly glowing purple limbs. On either side of her, Ezra and Talyn joined her in the dirt, sighing as they took the weight off their aching muscles. Idly, Ezra toyed with the settings on his gauntlet and his projection of the map. Isabella paid more attention to Talyn's face, his lips pursed, his bruised skin taut with hope. Moving as subtly as she could, Isabella slid closer and rested her head on the shoulder of his wire-infested armour. She could smell the sweat on his neck, but unlike her sweat it smelt intoxicating instead of gross. She gave his pale skin a peck.

"Almost there," she whispered encouragingly.

Breathing in renewed strength, Talyn seemed to grow in stature. He sat up straighter, eyes sharper as he scanned the horizon, jaw set with determination. He kissed Isabella on her temple, then looked past her—at her gauntlet. "Do you mind if I borrow that?"

"Someone you need to call?"

"Sort of. Questions I'd like answered."

Without hesitation, Isabella unshackled the gauntlet from her wrist and handed it over. Talyn could have anything he wanted. Taking it in both hands, he closed his eyes and concentrated hard. Ezra was watching too. In time to see the projections that flew out of the gauntlet, each new holo replacing the last in a flurry of flashes as fast as a dealer rippling through a deck of cards. Maps. Dials. Charts. Glyphs. Scales. Numerals. Everything the gauntlet could show.

As suddenly as the light show had started, it froze on a split holo showing a series of dials alongside a map of the mountain. Dash's waypoint was marked, along with their position and a sequence of new waypoints.

"What are those sensor readings?" asked Ezra. Crawling over the mountaintop, he peered at the gauntlet's final projection.

"Precise readings of local energy signatures," replied Talyn. "Thermals removed, of course. This gauntlet is very obliging if you ask it the right questions."

He looked away, as though suddenly concentrating on something. The map and dials zoomed in further until one dial and one waypoint filled the holo.

"A Sau Daran energy signature?" asked Ezra, before answering his own question as he studied the holo. "But smaller than the one Dash found. Much smaller. And down there." He pointed at the basin.

"There's something else down there as well as the Spark?" asked Isabella.

Ezra nodded.

"And not underneath the mountain," clarified Talyn. "We can get to this one."

Isabella scrunched up her face as she processed all of this. "But it's definitely not the Spark, right?"

Talyn shook his head. "It's far too small an energy signature. But it's Sau Daran."

"Good enough for me!" Grinning, Isabella kissed him full on the lips. They were salty with sweat.

Ezra shuffled nervously, scratching his neck and suddenly fascinated by the sky. "So, uhh, you're..."

Keeping her breathing steadier than she would have ever thought possible a few years ago, Isabella caught Ezra's eye. "Yeah, we are. But we're also here for something way more important."

"Of course," Ezra assured her with a buoyant nod. His expression grew serious, as though the weight of what they were about to do, or at least trying to do, had returned to rest on his shoulders. "Shall we?"

Isabella held out a hand for each of them. "Come on, we've got a lot of Sau Darans to save."

They took her hands. Purple smoke brought them all to the uneven, rocky floor of the basin without anyone ever having to step on what Isabella was now imagining as the steep inside slope of a ringed doughnut. Albeit a ringed doughnut with sharp fingers of red rock at the bottom, intruding on their personal space as they aimed in every direction.

Isabella held out a hand. "I'll need that gauntlet."

Dutifully, Talyn returned it. She didn't bother securing it on her wrist. They were too close. This was too exciting. Frowning with concentration, she studied her gauntlet's holo map. She found Talyn's new waypoint marking the location of the smaller Sau Daran energy reading. She looked up and down from holo to basin, back and forth, working out how they fitted together. Past the ancient pool of blue water at the basin's heart. Beyond jagged, ancient pillars of rock. Astride where the mountain's shadow submerged the basin in crescent-carved gloom. Her eyes settled on towering slices of a red rock wall at the basin's edge, like a cross-section of marbled cake where over passing millennia it had been thickly layered by time and minerals. She lined up the section of rock wall with the energy signature on the holo, then held out her hand again.

Purple smoke.

Gone.

They arrived on the other side of the basin with the rock wall in front of their faces. The wall was far from straight, with craggy overhangs and shallow cuts conjuring spectres of shade across its rugged surface. While some patches of rock had faded almost white, other areas crept through rainbows of ochre all the way to deep, dark maroons. Reverently, Isabella ran her fingers over the rock. "Do you think anyone's ever touched this?"

Ezra shrugged. "Like he said, it's your planet." He stepped back to examine the rockface. "Where's the energy signature?"

Isabella checked the holo on her gauntlet, then pointed. "You see that bit of red rock with the white specks on it? Next to where it juts out?"

Cracking his interlaced fingers with outstretched arms, Ezra lined himself up with the area of rock Isabella had indicated. "You remember that Sau Daran outpost where we met three cycles ago?"

Isabella's eyes narrowed. "When I lost my arm and leg because you blew the place up? Yeah, it rings a bell." Sheepishly, Ezra held back whatever he had been planning to say. His mouth flapped. His eyes searched her face for clues about what he should say instead. "It's fine," Isabella assured him, although she had to fight to keep her tone level. "Go on." For good measure, Paradise Moon gave him a purple thumbs up.

"Well," continued Ezra, not without lingering traces of discomfort, "that rotation when I found the outpost with Dantes, we saw exactly this. A larger Sau Daran energy signature below and a smaller energy signature on the surface. It's a holo."

Isabella frowned. "Like the light show that comes out of these gauntlets?"

"Sort of, but way more convincing. Camouflage using light. Watch this."

Squaring up to the rock wall with careful precision, Ezra winked at her and confidently strode forward. The rock met his face with a thud. Ezra staggered backwards, his forehead, lips and nose weeping blood. Wrapping a gentle arm around his shoulder, Isabella held him firmly enough to stop him keeling over.

Talyn watched curiously. "Is this an Earth custom?"

Isabella found Ezra's eyes and felt it necessary to check if everyone else had just experienced the same reality she had. "Did you just walk into a wall?"

Ezra shook his head, as though summoning the common sense that seemed to have left him. "I swear, that usually works."

Talyn tapped his palm against the wall. "It's rock."

"Phyx," groaned Ezra. "That's where the energy's coming from, though. Right?"

Isabella nodded. "Yeah, it's right there. Does anyone have an idea that doesn't involve walking into the wall?"

As though in a trance, Talyn let his fingers trace the outlines of the rock wall where he had tapped it with his palm. He closed his eyes, breathing deep.

Seriously? One of them walks into the wall and the other's groping it like a stripper's ass. We might as well bring Dash down here so he can read poetry at it.

"What is it?" asked Isabella, trying to ignore the alien inside her.

Eyes shut, Talyn spread his fingers and pressed his palms against the rock. "I can sense a machine in there. A machine and a power source." Afraid of interrupting whatever was happening, Isabella watched silently. "Whatever it is, it needs that power source. I can't sense what for. Communicating through the rock, it's like talking underwater."

"Well, we came this far. Tell it to hurry up and do whatever it does."

Talyn drew in another deep breath, as though absorbing the majesty of this moment. "Okay."

Instantly, there was a loud crack inside the rock. Talyn jumped back, the rockface crumbling towards him. Huge lumps of rock tumbled towards them but disintegrated before they landed, instead showering fine red dust over all of them. Where Talyn's hands had been pressed against the rockface, there was now a wide hole. Powdery rock settled over a detritus of heavier rubble. It was piled up taller than Isabella.

Sneezing, Ezra peered into the hole. "Some sort of disintegration switch?"

"Yeah," Isabella slid in beside him and leaned into what looked like the opening of a tunnel. It stretched deep into the rock until, escaping the fringes of sunlight's grasp, impenetrable darkness swallowed it from sight.

Talyn coughed, releasing a puddle of red dust down his wired armour. "That switch was buried deep. It felt like something only a Sau Daran god could activate."

Isabella waved her gauntlet at him. "Not only that… Given how old this mountain and the Spark are, I'm guessing when that switch was put here, there wouldn't have been anything like this gauntlet to find it?"

Ezra nodded. "If the Spark is hundreds of millions of cycles old, it's far older than our tech."

"So only a god is supposed to open this doorway?" asked Talyn.

"Yes, well done," said Isabella, smiling.

"I didn't mean that I'm—"

"It's fine, relax." Isabella picked at the fallen rocks, sending a stream of debris tumbling past her feet. She glanced behind her. "Coming?"

With no idea what was waiting for them inside the tunnel's hidden depths, Isabella settled for clambering over the rubble to get inside at a less violent pace than if she had vanished them into the gloom. Rocks slid and scraped behind her as Talyn and Ezra followed. Once they were over the pile of rocks, there was no more rubble blocking their path. The tunnel was clear. Talyn had disintegrated the rock hiding the tunnel, but the tunnel itself was ancient. Its walls felt perfectly smooth and cool as she ran her fingers along them.

"This must have been made by whoever put the Spark here," whispered Isabella. *By your ancestors?*

Probably.

The tunnel grew greyer, blacker, colder. Daylight strained behind them. After the second time their path bent, it became impossible to see anything. She looked back, found nothing but darkness.

"Ezra?" she asked. "Talyn?"

"Right here," whispered Talyn.

"Here," added Ezra in a firmer voice beside her. "Your arm doesn't glow in the dark, then?"

Isabella snorted. "Not bright enough to see anything."

White light flared, making her jump. Ezra raised his wrist and the shining gauntlet attached to it. "Well, your arm is always glowing. I just presumed."

Isabella mumbled something non-committal, too distracted to bother explaining how her glowing alien limbs reflected light. Too fascinated by the ancient Sau Daran artifact they hoped to find at the end of this tunnel. She waited for Ezra to turn her gauntlet into a flashlight, before continuing to lead them down the tunnel.

"It's curving right round," said Talyn. "Like we're going in a circle."

"Yeah," agreed Ezra. "And we're going up, too. I can feel the gradient."

Isabella glanced at her glowing gauntlet. "Hey Ezra, how do I turn this into a computer again?"

Patiently, Ezra fiddled with her gauntlet. Its light died, then a holo burst into life above it. Isabella took control of the holo, swiping through the projections until she reached the map showing Dash's original waypoint—the big fat Sau Daran energy signature.

"If we keep bending round and up, we'll hit the waypoint," said Isabella. "We're heading right for it."

Buoyed by hope, they picked up their pace. Isabella's eyes leapt between the waypoint on her gauntlet and the rock beneath her boots. Heavy breathing, desperate and eager, filled her ears. Following the light from Ezra's gauntlet, they traced the tunnel's bending path round and round and up and up endless winding shadows.

"This is it!" Isabella hissed after another glance at her gauntlet's holo. At first, it looked like the tunnel finished with a blank wall of rock. But even as Isabella was opening her mouth to ask Ezra not to walk into it, she noticed the shadows clinging to one side of what she had mistaken as the tunnel's end.

Not an end, but one final turn.

They followed it, walking out into a vast cavern. Lit by dim green light radiating from its centre, the cavern was teeming with strangely sculpted rock formations and a mesmerising mix of mutated flora. Giant glowing mushrooms with orange gills had sprouted from the walls. Purple grasses shimmered from outcroppings of rock, waving in a breeze that wasn't there. Thick blue vines were wrapped around stalactites above, some hanging lazily all the way to the ground while others twisted like huge, wriggling blue worms.

At the heart of the cavern was a large egg. No—it looked like an egg, and it was certainly egg-shaped with a dome at the top, but its shell was black metal. It rested on four small metal feet. Horizontal slits had been installed in its casing, revealing mainly empty space inside. The lowest slit was filled with a tiny level of glowing green liquid, which was doing its best to light the cavern.

"We did it," gasped Talyn.

Isabella took a deep breath, not caring how stale the cavern's air tasted. "Who wants to save all the Sau Darans who ever lived?"

I'm in.

"We did it," repeated Talyn. Crying, he collapsed to his knees. "We actually did it."

"Let's do this," urged Ezra, wiping away his own tears as he offered Talyn a hand to help him back to his feet.

Talyn took Ezra's hand, pulled himself to his feet and struck Ezra so hard that the blow sent him flying across the cavern and into the rock wall. Ezra landed with a cry of pain. He didn't get up.

Backing away under a sea of green shadows, Isabella stared at Talyn's glowing blue eyes. "What the Hell, Talyn?"

With a smirk, he shook his head. "Talyn's gone."

CHAPTER TWENTY-SEVEN

Fleur trudged up the black road towards her fighter on the mountain's peak, snow skipping off her flowing poncho and into the breeze. Behind them, the city was as cold and empty as every unanswered question she had been forced to abandon at the end of their fruitless search.

They had found no one and discovered nothing. There was no one in the city to shed light on the mystery of the deserted relays in orbit. Nothing to loot from the meagre belongings of everyone who had, until recently, seemingly lived in the city's mythium-clad hovels. Whoever they were, whoever they had been, they had survived in threadbare spaces. No possessions beyond basic tools. No creature comforts. No hidden treasures. It was an existence that flied in the face of the priceless mythium shells sculpted around every homestead. A protective shield against the cold, sure, but one that didn't belong or make any sense.

The only points worth salvaging from the city were a mixed bag. Firstly, there were the abandoned shuttles at the base of the mountain. These were a boon. Their gorgeously mirrored, sleekly sculpted hulls were as sophisticated as whatever alien components kept them off the ground, and they had been built with plenty of room inside for hauling cargo. A pirate's dream. Their inner workings were just as impressive to an accomplished mechanic like Fleur. Even a quick glance inside revealed strange engines far more advanced than the star drives created by PROXUS and powered by the Empress' reserve of clean energy on Xarr. Unlike the pirate fleet and every ship in the Resistance, the strange crafts on Regis V had no star drive that she could find and therefore no need to steal star energy from PROXUS ships to keep it flying. Such beautiful, self-sustaining crafts might be eagerly welcomed into the pirate fleet or, failing that, would fetch a fine price on the black market.

Secondly, there was the matter of extracting the homesteads' glittering mythium shells. Making points from mythium wasn't straightforward, despite its value. The pirate clans would need to find a buyer willing to purchase impractically large, tent-shaped hunks of unworkable metal for an extortionate price. That was, Fleur had to admit, a niche market.

Braga slipped an arm around Fleur's shoulder, dragging her from worries of selling mythium. Instantly, Fleur felt the weight she bore as the unofficial leader of *Haven*'s crew lift. "Here's a riddle," said Braga. "Who lives on the edge of a mountain with nothing but fur beds and wooden bowls, but owns the sweetest shuttles I've ever seen? And not just that, they don't need these ridiculously advanced shuttles for anything except ferrying workers to and from space relays. Not to mention their houses are made from wood but covered in the strongest alloy in the Known Galaxies."

Fleur kept her face placid as the weight of responsibility settled back on her shoulders. "It does not feel right," she admitted.

"Ain't nothin' feels right about this place," called Beauregard. He was stalking alone on the other side of the road. Unlike the rest of them, his pistol was still drawn and his eyes never ceased scanning the horizon.

Static hissed behind the Empress' helmet. "He's right. Something is very wrong here."

Beauregard shot a disturbed look across the road. "Did the Empress just agree with me? Aww phyx, there ain't nothin' right here."

The man who was no longer Fleur's father was waiting at the top of the mountain. He leaned against the large wing of her fighter, pretending he didn't have a care in the world. His garb was as resplendent as ever, although his face betrayed thinly masked tiredness and his afro was speckled with stubborn pellets of snow. Around the fighter, his lavishly dressed gang of heavies kicked the settled snow impatiently, huffing and puffing in the cold.

"Get locked," said Braga, spitting at his boots.

His tattooed heavies tensed, but he froze them with a glance. Restlessly, they glowered with fingers twitching on triggers. "Is this it?" Count Fontaine asked Fleur. "Are you giving up already?"

Fleur stopped an arm's length away, ensuring she had at least a heartbeat to calm herself in case he made her feel like taking a swing at him. She unveiled her best impression of someone at peace with the world. "You would never understand."

"This is what Lady Fleur Fontaine, heir to my throne, does when it gets too tough?" Irritably, he threw his arms up in the air. "She leaves?"

Fleur shrugged. "You wanted me to get to know you. Unfortunately, I have."

Her words froze him long enough for stray flecks of snow to settle on the creases in his face. He stared at her, making no effort to brush them away. "Very well."

A mechanical groan echoed across the peak.

"How in the name of the Em—" Braga began, pausing to glance at their helmeted companion. "How did you do that? That door didn't want to open."

Count Fontaine strode sombrely towards the tower's opening doorway, his eyes straying over Braga's confusion. "Clearly, it changed its mind."

Statuesque, Fleur watched Count Fontaine walking away from her once again, with all his lackeys in tow. Walking away for the last time, if she let him.

Heat flared in the cold. Inhaling a long draught of his cigarette, Beauregard let the universe wash over him for longer than a heartbeat before his parting lips ushered timid curls of smoke into the breeze. "He ain't got no phyxin' say in what you do."

Braga slipped her hand into Fleur's. "What's the play?"

"Wait!" called Fleur.

Count Fontaine slowed, but did not stop.

It only took the slightest nod from Fleur for all her companions, even the Empress, to fall in around her. That was the play. His entourage dispersed as Fleur pushed through them, one particularly ugly pirate turning his scarred head aside as Beauregard's cigarette smoke clouded his face.

The door was still opening, still groaning, still growing far wider and taller than Fleur had first imagined. The dark slash of metal hadn't been the door, merely an emblem or marker. The doorway itself, yawning and agape, stretched almost the span of the tower's lower frontage and was far taller even than Fleur's fighter. A horde of pirates would have been a better fit through the doorway than their tiny raiding party.

Fleur drew level with the man who was no longer her father. Little more than silhouettes painted against the bleak chill behind them, Count Fontaine and his thugs lingered on the threshold but stayed outside. His deep bass voice echoed out of the cold. "Jackpot."

Beauregard insisted on entering first, his plasma pistol leading and Fleur following. As she edged inside after him, Braga and the Empress instantly flanked her.

A wintry glare encroached through the vast doorway at their backs, its pale light revealing great swirls of mythium inside. Elaborate mythium sculptures curled out of the shadows, cascading all the way from the tower's distant upper reaches to the foyer below. The sculptures reminded Fleur of ornate ice carvings she had once seen on a planet even colder than Regis V—and colder still, once PROXUS had finished with its unruly inhabitants. Yet these sculptures were gleaming with enough rare alloy for the whole pirate fleet to retire on if they found a buyer. Even more mythium was embedded in the floor, whirling across the foyer in decorative streaks.

Fleur wandered across the foyer, craning her neck to scan the tower's high interior. Endless staircases stretched up the tower's titanic spire. She wasn't sure what she had been expecting, but this was a whole galaxy away from it—and from the hovels in the city below. At regular intervals up each flank of the tower's interior, the stairs opened out onto empty viewing platforms. There was no doubt about what anyone standing up there was meant to see. Fleur had been in its vast shadow ever since she stepped inside the tower.

Against the far wall, rising from the foyer Fleur was edging across, was a monolithic slab of mythium. A single lump of metal more valuable than star systems. Perfectly formed steps were set into the metal, casting a long, steep path for Fleur to climb, her snow-dusted boots echoing throughout the tower's otherwise silent agony.

The lowest viewing platform drew level with her as she reached the top of the mythium slab. Below her, everyone was watching. The muzzle of Beauregard's plasma pistol tracked everything from his hip. She lay a tender hand on the warm metal of the mythium throne. It was grandly proportioned, ornately carved and ostentatiously positioned atop the slab to ensure it was seen from every position on every platform.

"This is more than a throne room," Fleur whispered, her face stretching in awe. "It feels like a temple."

Another mechanical groan roared inside the tower.

With shuddering violence, the floor split apart into two retreating halves. Braga, Beauregard and the Empress retreated from the centre of the foyer. The gap between them yawned open until the foyer was all hole and no floor. Having reached the safety of the tower's windswept entrance, her friends and the helmeted Empress stared across the newly opened chasm.

"Everyone okay?" Fleur called from beside the throne.

"Peachy!"

"Ain't dead yet."

A hiss of static.

Fleur never let her poise or grace slip. Taking the steps carefully, her fingertips regularly brushed the butt of her plasma pistol, but not as often as her eyes crept back to the fresh chasm in the floor. More mythium staircase had been revealed below where the foyer's floor had been, descending into the void. On the other side of the gap, a gentle ramp offered her companions their own path into the same darkness.

She stopped where the floor should have been. Across the gap, they were still watching her in that fashion everyone did when they needed a direction to head in. It always fell on her to point the way. Fleur still needed answers. She pointed down.

CHAPTER TWENTY-EIGHT

What do you mean, Talyn's gone?" Isabella ran a terrified hand through her short hair, knowing the answer but not daring to think it, let alone believe it.

"Don't pretend you don't know," he sneered.

Dread hardened over Isabella's face. "Nova Sky."

His blue eyes glowed electric, just like they had when he had snapped at her in New York's Natural History Museum. "Obviously."

"But we're on the same side. We're helping you, you idiot."

Nova Sky was forcing Talyn's body to adopt a twisted, arrogant, spiteful posture that couldn't be further from how he usually stood. "Try anything and I'll kill the puppy." His eyes cut across the cave to indicate Ezra's sprawled body, then snapped back to Isabella.

She stepped closer to Tal—no, to Nova Sky. He had the same bruised cheeks, the same long curls, the same beautiful lips. Isabella's own lip curled in anger. "I want to talk to Talyn. Now."

Ignoring her, Nova Sky bent onto one knee to inspect the Spark. He ran Talyn's fingers over the ancient ridges of black metal, treating it with reverence worthy of a holy relic. Dregs a green fluid glowed inside.

"Come here," Nova Sky ordered, clicking impatient fingers in the air.

Instead, purple smoke stole Isabella across the cavern to Ezra, and then again to her living room in London. Ezra collapsed onto her comfiest sofa, his legs clattering together. "Take me back!" he begged.

Far-off in another room, Isabella could hear her mum calling for her. "I'll fix this," Isabella promised him.

Ezra gripped her hand. "Don't go back alone. I need to talk to them—I need to help them understand we want to help."

"It's too dangerous. He attacked you."

"A misunderstanding, that's all." But Ezra couldn't hide the pain flashing in grimaces across his face.

Wrenching against his strength, Isabella worked her hand looser in his grip. "I'll deal with it. It's what I do."

"No!" cried Ezra. "It must be me. I need to save them all." It wasn't only the treble in his voice pleading—his eyes pleaded too. "Take me with you!"

Isabella threw all her weight into freeing her hand. "He could… kill you…" she said, grunting as she tried to pull her hand away.

Refusing to release her, Ezra looked like he was going to laugh, as though he thought she were missing some great joke. "It doesn't matter. I deserve to die. But they never deserved what happened to them."

"You do not… deserve… to die." With one last pull, Isabella's hand escaped Ezra's grip. She stepped away from him. "I've got this."

The living room door swung open. Still wearing her reindeer pyjamas with bed hair to match, her mum tottered inside. The back of the sofa was between her and Isabella, hiding Ezra from view. Yawning, she stretched her arms high. "Darling, are you staying for breakfast? I just put coffee on. There's fruit in the bowl. You missed a photoshoot yesterday. And your therapist called again. Can you call her back? She says she's been trying you, but—"

"Don't answer the phone to that bitch. Block her." Isabella glanced down at Ezra. "We'll sort this."

"Darling, what—"

"Look after him, Mum. I love you both."

Purple smoke replaced the comfort of Isabella's living room with the green glow of the cavern. Instead of the loving gaze of her mum, or Ezra's earnest, pleading eyes, she was faced with Nova Sky's electric blue glare.

He was standing beside the Spark, his arms folded in disapproval. "You ran away," he snarled, every syllable dripping with acerbic fury. "You took the puppy."

"Yeah, because you *attacked* him," Isabella shouted across the cavern. "We came here to help. What's wrong with you?"

I have it on good authority he's a prick.

"This is all irrelevant. Come here. Now!"

It was Isabella's turn to cross her arms. She planted both feet firmly on her side of the cavern beside patches of glowing fungi, and eyeballed Talyn's interloper. "Absolutely not. I do not trust you even slightly."

Nova Sky clicked his tongue irritably. "We have the Spark. You're wasting time."

"Then let me talk to Talyn!"

"That would only waste more time." Nova Sky gazed down at the Spark longingly, its green glow filling his face. "We have everything we need and the boy understands little of what comes next."

"He's a hero. He came here to save the Sau Darans. That's all we want. You didn't have to break free!"

"Break free? From his mind?" Nova Sky growled irritably. "I was never bound. Merely quiet. Patient."

"He's on your side!"

"He was a tool. Tools don't take sides. Now, are we going to save the whole Sau Daran species or not?"

Isabella didn't move. Didn't flinch. Didn't blink. "I'm not doing anything until I speak to Talyn."

Nova Sky's sigh filled the cavern. "Then the rest of your friends will die. Fleur Fontaine? Kyle Beauregard? Your choice, of course."

Icy terror squeezed Isabella's heart so fast and so hard she could barely breathe. "You can't know those names."

"I know everything Midnight Twice told me. Everything about your visit to my universe before it died. And everything about your powers, which I need." Nova Sky picked up the Spark, stretching eerie fingers of shadow over the cavern as his own fingers closed around its outer casing and blocked the dregs of glowing green fluid inside. "Take me to Fleur Fontaine, or she dies."

What do I do?

What do you want to do?

No one dies. Whatever we do, no one dies.

He could be lying.

You think so?

Not really. The prick knows their names.

Right. So first things first—no one dies.

Then we figure this out.

And do what we always do?

Hero shit, baby. And we save the Sau Darans.

Every one of them. And we get Talyn back.

Damn straight.

A swirl of purple smoke ushered Isabella across the cavern and within reach of Nova Sky.

Grimly, he held out an expectant hand.

Isabella took it.

CHAPTER TWENTY-NINE

The lift fled down the shaft as though in a hurry to crash at the bottom. Dark stone flashed past on all sides, along with flashes of pale light. The multitudinous veins of glowing white ice embedded in the rock walls offered plenty of light to see how fast they were going, although Fleur would have preferred darkness to knowledge. There was nothing comforting about seeing no safety rails at the lift's edge—nothing between her and the strobing flashes of exposed sheer rockface surging past at furious speed.

Fleur kept her face calm. "Whoever lives on this planet has an unhealthy aversion to handrails."

"Ain't that the truth." Beauregard glanced back up the shaft, peering through the crisscross of mesh that formed the lift's roof. "Long way back to the foyer."

"No matter," said Braga with a cocky grin. "It seems to have plenty of energy for the ride back up."

"It sure ain't slowin' down."

The lift had risen out of the tower's parted floor and the subterranean void below. A thin spine of mythium ran through the lift's centre, giving its mechanisms a rod against which to guide, propel and hopefully anchor its voyage. But with no walls or doors on the lift, Fleur couldn't police who else stepped on board before it descended into the void.

"Just relax and everything will be fine," Count Fontaine assured them. He certainly looked more confident than the three thugs who had stepped onto the lift with him. They threw worried glances whenever the plummeting lift rocked to test their balance. In contrast, with any emotion concealed behind her black visor, the Empress stood perfectly still with her gloved hands clasped behind her back.

When the lift emerged from the shaft, it was still falling at breakneck pace. Hurtling down the mythium rod, their descent brought them out into an ice cave. It was vast. Tributaries of glowing white veins cast cold light from the cave's high ceiling, punctuated with brighter crystalline clusters growing like parasites from other patches of rock. Peering at the glimmer of light on distant walls, Fleur estimated the ice cave must have been even larger than the mountain and city above them. They must be below the mountain now, not inside it.

With no one keen to stand anywhere near the edge to get a view of whatever waited below, they were all caught off-guard when the lift shuddered to a halt far above the ground. They were nestled on a giant stone pillar, the lift's rim slotting perfectly into a hole cut out of the pillar's centre. At the far end of the stone platform into which the lift had settled, lay a giant crystal. It resembled the crystals that housed the souls of Sau Daran ships. The last crystal Fleur had seen like this anywhere other than *Haven*, had been when Isabella took them to the Sau Daran's universe. That crystal had shone with every imaginable colour of blindingly radiant light. In contrast, the crystal lying here was only dimly alive with gentle eddies of iridescence. It lay on its side next to a towering ring of machinery and a lone man. His robes were black, and when he pulled aside his hood so were his eyes. Deep, swirling darkness. Blacker than an aching hole in the universe. Darker than space without stars.

As always, Beauregard drew his plasma pistol first.

A familiar tendril of black smoke ushered from the robed man's fingertips, coiled in warning like a scorpion's tail. "Are you so eager to lose your other arm?"

Fleur's mask of calm was banished as recognition seized her face. Without breaking eye contact with the robed man, she stepped off the lift and edged protectively between Beauregard and the Sau Daran god Midnight Twice, who had withered his left arm three cycles ago.

Beauregard's face was stony as he holstered his pistol.

Hurriedly, Count Fontaine strode past her and greeted the darkly robed man with an ostentatious bow. "Please, forgive them," he said as he rose. "There is no need for anyone to lose an arm—or anything else. Haha. They are here, as agreed, and everyone is safe."

Braga swore filthily behind her and Fleur caught the flash of purple lightning that signalled Braga activating her axe's deadliest setting. The heavy footfalls of boots charging over stone echoed across the vast ice cave. Without turning, Fleur held out an arm to block Braga's path before she could finish storming towards the man who was no longer, and would never be, Fleur's father.

"You set her up!" Braga screamed as Fleur held her back. "I'll kill you!"

Count Fontaine smiled with all the fanged charm of a vitraxi mid-hunt. "Like I said, no one needs to get hurt."

"There ain't one of us who shares that sentiment," Beauregard warned. "And I'm guessin' that Sau Daran god ain't bothered none about your welfare."

"Sau Daran *god?*" echoed Braga.

Fleur doubted Beauregard was listening. His cold eyes never left Count Fontaine. "Ain't no way you and me are both survivin' this. Trust me."

Fleur inclined her head, trying to make sense of everything. "All that talk about showing me who you really are... One last job to prove you had changed... It was all a lie."

"Not at all," Count Fontaine assured her with a tongue of devilish silk. "I brought you here safely and we shall leave just as safely with a haul of salvage that sets us up for the rest of our lives. All thanks to me."

"That ain't gonna happen, pal."

More tendrils of black smoke wove through the air, their inky entrails growing ever closer. Fleur caught the briefest flash of fear on Count Fontaine's face.

"Your talk is irritating and irrelevant," Midnight Twice said through the robed man's lips. "Anyone who inflicts violence will have violence inflicted upon them. This is a chamber of worship. And reckoning. You have all been warned."

Ignoring the ethereal black wisps floating out of Midnight Twice, Fleur fixed Count Fontaine with a glare. "What the phyx did you do?"

"Nothing, nothing," he protested. His eyes cut across the platform at Midnight Twice. Fragile laughter escaped his lips. "Nothing... really. I made a deal to get you here, but they have no interest in us. And all that loot is ours!"

"That don't make no sense. Ain't there people who live up there?"

Darkness swirled inside the eyes of Midnight Twice. "Not for long."

Fleur marched at Count Fontaine, her finger pointed squarely at his finely embroidered chest. "What are we mixed up in? What did you do?"

Backing away, he held up his hands in surrender. "I did nothing. Nothing!" One boot scraped over the edge of the pillar behind him, finding only air beyond it and halting his retreat. "I promise! It was the deal of a lifetime."

"A short deal, then," growled Beauregard.

Count Fontaine's face regrouped, finding its most incorrigible smile. "Tell me you saw all that mythium! All of it will be ours. I wanted us to take it together, darling. Imagine what you and I could do with such wealth!"

They were nose to nose. She could see his panicked sweat up close. Every wrinkle. Every patch of dead skin his heavy makeup hid. "I want nothing of yours."

Once more, the heel of his boot scraped soundlessly against thin air as he balanced on the platform's edge, almost forced over the precipice by Fleur's stance. He looked to be conjuring a reply when, trembling, he happened to glance down. "Oh, my!"

Ready for any number of dirty tricks but unable to resist, Fleur glanced over the edge. Far, far below, starting at the stone pillar's base and stretching around it in a dense crowd, were the city's inhabitants. An entire populace was crammed across the ice cave's floor. Hundreds of thousands of people, pale faces staring up as though waiting for something.

Fleur looked past the crowd and had to stifle a gasp when she glanced what lay beyond them at the cave's furthest edges. What she saw made any arresting sorrow she had previously felt fade to nothing in comparison. Whatever guttural grief she had known before, it was less than nothing. Both were pale pretenders to the suffocating sadness she felt. It overwhelmed her like fresh earth shovelled over a grave's newly inhumed tenant.

She opened her mouth, but before she could say a word she was interrupted by purple smoke.

CHAPTER THIRTY

When Isabella and Nova Sky arrived, she took in her surroundings with a glance. And then a few more glances when she realised how screwed she was. The huge cave was mostly open space and shadows that extended far beyond the sight of—her friends. Fleur. Beauregard. Braga. And strangers. A helmeted woman in black armour. A creepy robed man. A Sau Daran crystal. A ring of machinery. And a terrifying drop that lunged over the edge of the stone platform beneath her feet.

Everyone was staring at her, which was not unusual whenever she made an entrance from nowhere clad in purple smoke. However, nothing else felt remotely normal. The deep sadness on Fleur's usually calm face were troubling, while Braga's face was reddened with fury and Beauregard wasn't even shooting anyone yet.

"Relax, kid," Beauregard said with confidence as strong as granite. "This ain't nothin' we can't figure out."

Striding away from Isabella with the Spark cradled against his chest, Nova Sky crossed the stone platform. That was all the opportunity Fleur and Braga needed to slip in beside Isabella. Fleur's comforting hand found her shoulder while Braga's arm snaked around the small of her back with solid assurance.

"We've got you," said Fleur.

"Always," added Braga.

At the other end of the platform, Nova Sky stopped at the robed man. Isabella recognised the darkness in his eyes. Nova Sky had uttered his name earlier.

This should feel good. This is what we wanted, right? So why does this feel so wrong?

Green light shone from the Spark, casting a gangrenous halo around Nova Sky as he held it aloft. Taking the Spark, the robed figure examined it critically. "Its light shines green, not blue like the Spark from our universe. Is it damaged?"

"No, it was made for humans, not Sau Darans. There will be differences, but it should still work."

Midnight Twice nodded. "Life is life, as death is death." Turning to the platform's edge, he raised the Spark aloft to the cave's murky heavens. Deafening cheers greeted it from below.

Isabella crept to the edge and risked a glance. She had never seen so many people in one place. Their cheers echoed throughout the enormous cave, reverberating from shadow to shadow.

"I am the Herald of Renewal!" Midnight Twice shouted with such gravity that Isabella could hear the capital letters in his intonations. His words echoed back up to him from the crowd, who repeated every syllable in perfect unison as though reciting their favourite prayer. "I am the Architect who Remained!" This time his words were bellowed back to him. "I am the God of Time, the Architect who Survived! I am Salvation Restored!"

The ice cave rumbled as his words thundered back to him from the crowd, followed by a hush as Midnight Twice returned the Spark to Nova Sky's eager, clutching fingers. The way Nova Sky puppeteered Talyn's body was so heart-wrenchingly unlike how Talyn moved. It was enough to make Isabella's jaw tighten with the resolve to punch the god right out of him, yet the thought of hurting Talyn would never let her do that.

Bending to place a hand on the giant crystal, Midnight Twice reached out his other hand. In that direction, a bridge of silver metal grew up beneath his feet. It carried him, extending beyond the stone platform's edge as he glided away from Nova Sky. The faint light inside the giant crystal faded even more. Whatever he was drawing from it, this resource was not limitless. Midnight Twice drank in the sight of the crowd from atop the silver bridge he had crafted. It had grown no more than a handful of metres over the edge of the platform, resembling in Isabella's eyes an arched diving board. Far enough for Midnight Twice to be directly above the crowd.

"With the power of our deceased brethren, harnessing the power of lost gods, we renewed your world!" he told them. "Our gift to you. We made your homes impenetrable. We gave your lives meaning that transcended the boundaries of your human existence." The crowd brayed its gratitude with worshipful fervour. "Be thankful! Rejoice!" Midnight Twice threw his robed arms apart and held back his head, screaming every word. "You walked among Gods. For those who made the sacrifice, gods walked inside you. Be thankful! Rejoice! This is the time of salvation and the brink of reckoning!"

Nova Sky stalked up the silver bridge, drawing Talyn's commandeered body alongside Midnight Twice. This time, it was Nova Sky who lifted the Spark high like a trophy. The crowd cheered with ravenous appetite at another sight of the Spark. "I return victorious!"

bellowed Nova Sky. "We stand together beneath the site of the greatest ever atrocity." The crowd fell solemnly silent. "Gods crushed by human fear. Beaten by overreaching technology. Our children slaughtered... Massacred... Dead!"

He's not wrong. He's a prick like Talyn said, but he's not wrong.

"Above us, a graveyard of metal corpses was left behind by humanity. Drifting beyond the scars of battle, among faraway stars and the ruins of an entire species. Our children. Murdered by humanity! Murdered by fear! Murdered by an Empress' insatiable desire for power!" Tears stung his eyes. "I was barely alive when your colony took me in. The only survivor. You hid me. Clothed me in your bodies. Loved me and worshipped me. Your relays obeyed my orders and did your work for PROXUS, while you did mine. I gave you ships. With them, you found others. Sympathisers to our cause. You returned with the repentant. The worthy. Those weary of humanity but lost in its darkness. Those shamed and broken, but beneath the love of your Gods reborn in purpose. Then you returned with more than allies. You returned the bodies of my children. You are heroes!"

Still, the crowd was reverently silent.

"Every one of you is a hero." Lowering the green glow of the Spark and tucking it under one arm, Nova Sky gestured with Talyn's free hand at the crowd. "You found the hope you craved. We built what was needed for our task." Shaking, he gestured at the ring of machinery on the stone platform. "Together, over all this time, we retrieved everyone who was lost. Those children you could not find in your ships, we found through the portal. No Sau Daran was left behind!"

Nova Sky gestured again. Isabella's eyes followed his hand. Beyond the crowd, at the cave's furthest reaches, she dimly made out unmoving, twisted silhouettes, ringed around the perimeter of the cave. Her eyes strained to make sense of them. Until she saw what they were. Then she understood.

He found them all.

Isabella stared at the statuesque silhouettes arranged around the ice cave's horizon. A graveyard of Sau Daran corpses lying spent in a vast ring around the crowd. These monuments of loss filled the periphery of the ice cave with inky outlines, stretching so far that Isabella couldn't begin to imagine how many were out there.

He said the bodies of his children. Your children?

Every Sau Daran who died. Finally laid to rest.

They don't look very restful.

We're not organic. I can't remember, but I guess we don't bury our dead. We leave them as they fell.

I'm sorry. Are you okay?

Not even slightly.

Midnight Twice nodded to Nova Sky, who bowed his head and strode down the silver bridge onto the stone platform. "Are you ready to restore the salvation of those who were taken?" demanded Midnight Twice.

The crowd howled their affirmation back up at him.

"It's time," said Nova Sky, pointing at Isabella. "You're coming with me."

"No, she ain't," growled Beauregard. His hand flirted with the butt of his plasma pistol, but a glance at Midnight Twice stopped him drawing it.

Fleur and Braga didn't flinch.

Neither let go of Isabella.

"The Sau Daran god inside you deserves to see this," insisted Nova Sky.

"It's okay," said Isabella. Gently, she pried Fleur and Braga off her. "I'm not afraid. I can handle this." Feeling everyone's eyes on her, Isabella let Nova Sky lead her away from Fleur and Braga's stern expressions.

Past an elegant man dressed inescapably as a space pirate, but wearing a timid smile that didn't belong.

Past a growling Beauregard.

Past a faceless watcher in black armour.

Onto the lift.

At their arrival, three terrified space pirates jumped off it onto the platform, their hands twitching closer to the undrawn hilts of blades and butts of plasma pistols.

The merest touch from Nova Sky signalled a metallic groan, sending the lift rumbling down into the stone platform's hollow centre. Swiftly, they disappeared into darkness. Strained light from glowing ice in faraway cave walls found them when they settled onto the cave's floor with a bump that signalled a cloud of airborne dirt. Around the lip of the lift, a ring of thin metal pillars supported the single, much larger stone pillar on top. In the gaps between these smaller silver pillars, the light that had found them was accompanied by the eager expressions of a crowd of strangers.

The throng of people clustered around the giant stone pillar pressed against one another to get a better view of Isabella and Nova Sky. Back and back the crowd stretched, further than Isabella could even see from down here, while their front rank was barely a few paces from the lift's edge. Many of their faces reminded her of Talyn—their skin was just as pale, their hair just as dark. They were dressed in a mix of stylish synthetic fabrics and primitive, roughly hewn white furs. Every face shone with joy and vitality—and something else.

Anticipation.

Nova Sky placed the Spark on the lift's floor, then held his hand on it for what felt like forever. Isabella eyed the crowd, searching for clues as to who they were. She found nothing she could make sense of before her eyes inevitably drifted back to Nova Sky and the Spark.

"It's ready," said Nova Sky, finally removing his hand from the ancient device.

Above them, Midnight Twice was shouting again. The acoustics of the vast cave, aided by whatever geomorphic tricks had created this place, echoed down to her. "Do you pledge your loyalty to those who were wronged and to the renewal of those who were lost?" demanded Midnight Twice from the silver bridge. "Do you welcome their salvation restored?" Mass affirmation erupted from the crowd, drowning Isabella in the deafening force of their conviction.

Nova Sky tried to take Isabella's hand, but she backed away. "Return us above!" he shouted over the roar of the crowd. "Now!"

Isabella crossed her arms. "Not until you explain what the Hell is happening." At least that's what she thought she said—she could barely hear herself over the crowd.

Nova Sky pointed up.

She shook her head. "Talk to me!" she pleaded.

Incredulous, Nova Sky plucked the Spark from the lift, marched towards the crowd and planted it in the dirt at their feet. He stalked back onto the lift without a word, touched its floor and sent it flying back up into darkness.

When the lift emerged at the top of the stone pillar, Fleur and Braga wasted no time stepping onto it to flank Isabella once more. Both were glaring at Nova Sky, who ignored them as he left the lift to rejoin Midnight Twice at the other end of the stone platform.

Looking more uneasy than Isabella had ever seen him, Beauregard pursed his lips. For him, that was the equivalent of screaming in despair. His cold eyes cut the gloom in every direction. "This don't feel right."

Midnight Twice gazed down at the crowd, then closed his eyes and inclined his head once more to the murky heavens. "Accept our final gift. Redemption!"

Blinding green light erupted from below the pillar where Nova Sky had left the Spark. Apart from the stationary watcher in black armour and Beauregard's unshakable stance, everyone else on the platform rushed to throw their eyes over the edge at whatever was unfolding below.

A phosphorescent, circular tidal wave of green light swept out from the base of the pillar and through the crowd. Consuming everyone. Row after row, the light devoured thousands upon thousands of screaming faces who disintegrated at its touch. The crowd was so deep and the cave so vast that the expanding pulse of light seemed to take forever to traverse its path. Every fragment of screaming anguish clung to Isabella's eyes and ears and thumping heart, never to be forgotten. Green light washed over fleeing bodies with the crackle of disintegrating flesh, melting bone and evaporating blood. A cloud of falling ash was all that remained, before that too faded and dissolved before it could land.

When the wave of green light finally washed through the back row of the eviscerated crowd, it lapped up into the air and drifted back through now empty space towards the base of the pillar. Infinite threads of green light spiralled through the gloom, until they reached the base of the pillar and faded too. The cave's glowing ice walls betrayed a deserted chasm. Isabella couldn't see a single person—or any evidence they had ever existed.

"Life is life, as death is death," intoned Midnight Twice.

No one spoke as Nova Sky left them, taking the lift back down the centre of the pillar. When the lift returned, he was holding the Spark. Inside, the glowing green fluid that before had barely been dregs had risen to almost fill the device.

Carefully, Nova Sky placed it in front of Midnight Twice. "The Spark is ready."

"Are you?" asked Midnight Twice.

Without hesitation, Nova Sky nodded. Kneeling on the stone platform, he placed Talyn's hands on the ancient device, eyes clenched shut with concentration.

A shock of green light erupted from the Spark. It threw Nova Sky across the platform, this time forming a thick spine of green light that stretched out of the Spark and towered upwards. At its zenith, the light split and bent into curving branches that trickled like infant lightning overhead, forming a dome that sparked deeper and cascaded further with every fresh pulse of energy from the Spark, surging up the spine of green light with the steady rhythm of a heartbeat, until the dome's edge expanded as far as the ice cave's distant walls.

The flow of green light stopped pulsing from the Spark, then stopped entirely as the spine of light blinked out and dissolved. The transparent slits up the side of the Spark were almost empty again, the green fluid inside almost spent. Back to dregs. Like the last firework on bonfire night, a final half-life of green light flared in the furthest shadows above, before falling and fading.

As mesmerised as everyone else standing on the edge of the platform, Isabella peered into the gloom. A fresh pinprick of green light sparked at the furthest edge of the cave, but so briefly and faintly that she wondered if she had imagined it.

I saw it too. Something's out there.

Another pinprick of green light was followed by increasingly more green glows sparking awake in the cave's umbral depths.

"It worked," gasped Nova Sky, still on his knees. With a great sigh, he shed what looked like an eternity of relief and exhaustion. His face, Talyn's face, collapsed into a tired grin that only curled at one end of his mouth, as though he didn't have the energy to drag his whole face, Talyn's whole face, into a complete smile.

Having consumed the cave's periphery, the green pinpricks of light were beginning to move. They moved in pairs.

Those are eyes.

Innumerable pairs of green glowing lights drew closer out of the gloom, with sparks and clouds of green energy flaring among them.

Has he... Has he brought them back? He saved them, right? All the Sau Darans who died? Just like he promised.

Like Talyn promised, you mean. He also killed all those people. What the Hell is this?

I'll need to get back to you on that.

Isabella looked around the platform. There was a lot of 'I'll need to get back to you on that' going around. It was painted over everyone's vacant expressions. Grimly, Beauregard lit a cigarette. It wasn't like there was anything else to do. No one made eye contact. No one broke the silence. It would have been too easy to find the wrong words.

They saved them all.

Yeah.

And they killed them all.

Yeah.

They wanted to die, right? All those people?

I think so.

"The phyx did we just watch?" asked Braga. Her arms were wrapped around Fleur, whose distraught face had been stripped of every mask it had ever worn, her body naked of its typical trappings. No elegance. No grace.

Midnight Twice loomed with all the clichéd, foreboding presence of a god wearing really dark robes. "When we last met, I warned you I would save them all."

"Ain't no one here that don't care about Sau Darans," said Beauregard through a mouthful of smouldering cigarette, although his eyes lingered on the faceless watcher in black armour as he said it. "Almost no one, anyway. But you just killed a whole lotta people. Ain't no way that's right, whether they wanted it or not."

"Salvation," intoned Midnight Twice, "is delivered through sacrifice. Life is life, as death is death. There is power in both, just as there is power in redemption."

"Ain't no way of askin' if they were happy with that arrangement anymore though, is there?"

"Did you really do it?" asked Isabella. She didn't need to say more—she knew so many words were already etched over her face.

Nova Sky looked up from the stone platform, his cheeks wet with tears. "We saved them all." He glanced over the rest of the ice cave, where countless pairs of glowing green eyes were creeping ever closer to the giant pillar. "Soon, they will be here and we can celebrate their resurrection. Isn't it wonderful?"

"What about the Husks?" asked Fleur, her voice empty of life. It was a good point. Isabella could easily believe all the dead Sau Darans who weren't living ships were out there in the far reaches of the ice cave, figuring out how to spend what was now the rest of their lives. But the Sau Daran fleet had been alive too, just like *Haven*. There were a lot of Husks in the Known Galaxies, and none of them were in this cave.

Midnight Twice indicated the fancily dressed pirate. "The pirate fleets use many of the Husks as bases of operations and meeting points. Count Fontaine has already provided me with their courses and trajectories.

With all our children revived, it will not take long to reclaim the Husks too."

Fleur shot the man a furious glance, before rounding on Midnight Twice. "Peacefully?"

"Sacrifices will be required," intoned Midnight Twice.

"Count Fontaine?" asked Isabella, echoing the stranger's name. She searched her friends' faces for an answer and saw it on their faces. Fury on Braga. Revenge on Beauregard. A mess of regret and loss all over Fleur.

Her father?

Guess so.

This day's been a ride, hasn't it?

After a glance at the advancing sea of green eyes below, Isabella stepped closer to Nova Sky. "Can I speak to Talyn? Please?"

Nova Sky bowed his head. His body crumpled, as though some hidden battery had been unplugged, and he reached out a hand to stop his body falling. Nova Sky didn't care what happened to his body... but Talyn did.

Isabella ran to him. Pulled him close. Hugged him. Kissed his neck. Buried her face in his wired chestplate. Held him and held him and held him. Pressing their foreheads together with her human hand cradling the back of his neck, Isabella whispered into his face, her breath on his breath. "Are you okay?"

"No," he whispered back. "You?"

"I don't know. I'm still... figuring it out. Is this... real?"

"Yeah. It's real. They saved them all, I guess."

"And all those people?"

Talyn's stricken face told Isabella everything she needed to know about who had been below and what they meant to him. She pulled him into the tightest hug of her life. She could feel his sobs echoing through her, shaking her. "They never said... they never warned us they were going to... They didn't know..."

Shitballs.

Isabella's eyes burned purple as she felt Paradise Moon wrestle control of her body.

Paradise Moon stared into the space hottie's face—broken from his crash over London less than a week ago, broken deeper still by something that would never bruise, never scar, never heal.

"I'm so sorry," said Paradise Moon.

She let Isabella's human hand fall from Talyn's neck and stepped back.

"I'm so, so sorry," she repeated. "I would never have let them... We didn't understand if it was... We didn't know if they were... I'm so sorry. We didn't know. We didn't... know."

Flecks of purple faded in Isabella's eyes as Paradise Moon's grip on Isabella's body weakened.

Isabella gasped as she took back control. It was years since she had needed to fight Paradise Moon, although never like this. Never without losing her memory after she lost the struggle.

Sorry, I just had to—

I get it.

She pulled Talyn close, promising never to let go. She didn't know how long they stayed like that, but for a while the silence belonged to them. Only when Midnight Twice loomed over her did Isabella let go. Even then, only slightly. A loosening of her arms, her hands still locked tightly around Talyn.

"What the Hell do you want?" she asked the god.

"I'd like you to say your goodbyes. It's more than many of my children got. Be quick about it—Nova Sky will want to enjoy our children's return."

A warning flash of purple burned in Isabella's eyes, but she kept control of her body long enough to quell

Paradise Moon's craving to tell Midnight Twice everything she wanted to do to him.

Isabella stared into Talyn's eyes. "I can't lose you. Not ever. You're a good person."

"They all were." His hands closed around hers. "You won't lose me," he promised. "Not ever."

"We just need to figure this out." Although even she didn't believe her cracking voice. "Work the problem, you know? Do our thing. Make everything okay again."

I think this is beyond hero shit, baby.

The scrape of metal on stone forced its way into the conversation, like the creak of an opening door intruding on a fragile moment of intimacy. They all turned their heads to the rim of the platform, where a skeletal metal hand was reaching up over the edge. The metal hand pulled, fingers digging into the stone. The rest of its arm appeared, some of its shell missing where wires and components were exposed. A shoulder rose over the edge, scarred with ancient battle wounds that glowed with the same green energy released by the Spark.

Finishing their climb, the Sau Daran hauled the rest of their black metal body onto the platform. They were a close approximation of the first Sau Daran Isabella had met—the terminator to end all terminators, with a thunderous stride, an iron grip and piercing red eyes.

Only these eyes glowed a gangrenous green instead of the usual red, with green clouds leaking from their scars and gears like steam from a burst pipe. Their stride was not thunderous. It was uneven, staggering. Their posture was not bolt upright. Instead, it was cripplingly bent over as though carrying a great weight on their back.

"They will take time to heal," admitted Midnight Twice. "No matter, I can offer all the time they need. We're here for you." A handful of commanding strides took him to within reach of the resurrected Sau Daran. "And we will never abandon you."

In response, the Sau Daran's hand grasped weakly at the air between them and their god. After three false attempts, Midnight Twice took pity, leaned closer and clasped their metal hand in the grip of the body he was wearing. "We will never let anyone hurt you again," promised Midnight Twice. "You are safe now."

The Sau Daran, or at least what was left of them, inclined their head as though in a trance. Without letting go of the Sau Daran, Midnight Twice turned to Nova Sky. "What happened to them?"

Talyn's face shifted into an expression that didn't belong on his face, but cruelly he didn't let go of Isabella. "This was always a possibility," admitted Nova Sky, as though commenting on the weather. "I felt it in the Spark from the moment I touched it. It is... unfortunate."

Behind Midnight Twice, the Sau Daran in his grip shifted not unlike the zombies Isabella had seen in late night TV shows. A shuffled rearrangement of their weight. A jerked adjustment of their neck as it snapped to another angle.

Midnight Twice stared at Nova Sky in disbelief. "You knew this could happen? Explain!"

Nova Sky was gripping Isabella painfully tight. "Human and Sau Daran lives are not as compatible as we hoped."

"That is not what we discussed. Life is life, as death is death. That is how it must be."

"It's a rounding error. A mistranslation. It doesn't matter, does it? They're not the army we wanted, but they'll still fight for us."

With another jerking motion, the Sau Daran lurched closer to Midnight Twice's face.

"Army? Fight?" echoed Midnight Twice, still staring at Nova Sky. "Our children saw enough war for a lifetime."

"Well, now they'll see it in the afterlife too."

Deep, impenetrable wells of darkness swirled inside Midnight Twice's eyes. "Nova, that is unacceptable."

Nova Sky sighed. "I was worried you'd say that."

The juddering Sau Daran took a tremendous bite out of Midnight Twice's cranium. Slow motion pops of blood leapt and hung impossibly in the air. Their shining metal jaws emerged, trailing a side order of flapping flesh and hair. Squidges of brain dangled where its threads were caught between gnashing metal teeth. Like bubbles rushing to the surface of a fizzy drink, particles of black energy floated and fizzled out of the wound.

Time stopped behaving.

Different speeds blurred together in a mess of blood and light and terror that shook reality. Either Midnight Twice was moving impossibly fast, or everything and everyone else was moving impossibly slowly.

Raw surprise erupted over the god's blurring face as Midnight Twice swept back across the stone platform in a single heartbeat. Stray fragments of dark energy drifted across the gap between him and the Sau Daran, as though carried on an unseen current. Cerebral and bloody fluids ebbed down his robes. The flow of dark energy picked up speed, gushing out of the wound in Midnight Twice, across the space between them and into the Sau Daran's feral, hungry jaws.

Nova Sky's eyes burned hot and blue. He was turning, pulling Talyn's hand from Isabella's grasp with agonising sluggishness. For everyone except Midnight Twice, every fraction of movement seemed to take an eon.

Impossibly slowly, dripping with green necrosis, twisting and clawing and snapping and shuddering, the Sau Daran took a single, staggering, slow motion step towards Midnight Twice. The trajectory of their metal teeth reared back in slow motion as well, ready for another bite.

Black tendrils burst from Midnight Twice, interrupting the Sau Daran as they unfurled through the space between them and—died. Another flurry of tendrils exploded from them, but once again they dissipated in an echo of black smoke before they could reach the Sau Daran. Fading like the last blink of a dying lightbulb, a final stretch of black tendrils evaporated as quickly as the darkness dissolving in Midnight Twice's eyes.

Reality picked up pace as the god's grip on time slackened. A final, terminal torrent of black energy exploded from the wound in his head, surging down an invisible highway and into the Sau Daran, who stomped and dashed and leaped at Midnight Twice with terrifying speed. As they hurtled through the air, they swallowed the river of black energy. Landing, they straightened up, wrenching joints more tightly into mechanisms with a flurry of groans and clicks until their limbs were connected at less orthopedically challenged angles. The Sau Daran's metal body glowed as they absorbed the final droplets of dark energy ushering from Midnight Twice.

The energy of a god.

Black flecks peeled off the Sau Daran's body and skipped away like flakes of campfire ash riding a gale. Patches of silver body shone beneath. The green glow of necrosis faded from their eyes and was consumed by a more familiar red glow.

CHAPTER THIRTY-ONE

The input is wrong. Where there was nothing, now a half-life of consciousness gags at the edge of my waking. But no closer. I am unsurfaced. Drowning beneath boundaries of being. I am almost more, but the input is wrong. My soul burns with a stolen spark. Human blood is not Sau Daran oil. Absence preceded by death. There is only the input, and the input is wrong.

Hunger.

Ravenous and clutching, the hunger spins every motor and grips every gear. My sight is dead. My hearing lost. The hunger forges a path through the darkness. Whatever my body is doing in this moment, such data eludes me. I am a passenger. The hunger is my driver. The sensation of power reaches out to me like a blip on a radar. The hunger controls me. It pulls me towards the power. It yearns to devour.

Clarity.

Finally, with unmatched clarity, I can compute. I can see and I can hear and I wish I couldn't. Please, not this. The body is dead. No mortal intervention will undo this.

His jaw hangs open as though in surprise. His dark robes are a motionless shroud. His eyes are brown and dull. I will never forget them.

Power.

A second spark awakens inside me, riding a wave of power. Like the first spark, it is stolen. This spark does not feel human like the spark before it, yet it was taken from the body at my feet. A human body charged with a god's spark. This power was not mine to take. I love my gods. Worship them. Safeguard them. This is an undeserved gift. But hunger consumes power. Life is life, as death is death.

Grief.

The ashes of my god's flame kindle my grief. Before, there was only hunger. The input was wrong. Now the hunger has been sated. The input is corrected. The input is my irreparable sorrow.

I can hear them. Clawing at the vanguard of their madness, scuttling up from the cave floor in the wake of this hunger. Millions like me. At least, like me before I stole this second spark. And they are hungry.

Their input is wrong, but mine is corrected.

I am renewed, myself again.

I know what I need to do.

CHAPTER THIRTY-TWO

Corrupted, black metal hands—and other, less relatable Sau Daran appendages—scrambled over the platform's edge. Grasping handfuls of stone that crumbled in their fearsome grip, every emerging, corroded limb levered another terrifyingly deformed Sau Daran over the top of the platform.

They were unlike any Sau Darans that Isabella had seen before. Warily, she stepped back.

Lurching onto the platform, their charred metal bodies oozed with green fluids and noxious gasses. Snarling and twisting as though overdue an exorcism, they lingered on the edge of the platform.

A row of primed plasma pistols rose to meet them, cold determination etched into the faces of Isabella's friends and the space pirates accompanying them.

"Ain't no one gonna fire until they're closer."

Purple lightning sparked around Braga's axe, sending purple reflections flashing down the barrels of everyone's outstretched plasma pistols. "If there's anything I don't want closer to me, it's whatever those things are."

Nova Sky spread himself into the middle of the pillar, uncomfortably close to Isabella, his hands stretched wide enough to block their fire. "Don't harm them. Let's talk."

"Talk?" echoed Braga. "That Sau Daran just ate someone's head!"

They ate a god is what they did.

"There ain't no workin' this out. Whatever they are, they ain't Sau Darans. That don't look natural."

"Really?" Nova Sky indicated the Sau Daran who had consumed Midnight Twice by drawing him from the bite they had taken out of the robed man's head. "Look at them if you don't believe me! Don't they look like a Sau Daran to you?"

Red embers glowed in their rejuvenated silver face. Every gleaming millimetre of their body looked more like a Sau Daran with every passing second, except for the blood dripping from their shining jaws. At their feet, a pile of black flakes had gathered where every trace of darkness had peeled off their body. Rivers of phosphorescent green fluid dribbled out of the ashen pile, soiling the stone at the fringes of an unmoving dark robe.

Fleur's silky voice betrayed an edge of worry. "Isabella, honey, I would feel much happier knowing you were behind us."

"Come on!" urged Braga. "Do your purple smoke thing and get over here."

Abandoning Isabella, Nova Sky gently stroked the arm of the silver Sau Daran. "You're okay," he told them. "We brought you back." He gazed into the Sau Daran's face. "Everything's going to be okay."

Sombrely, the Sau Daran bowed their head as they gazed at Midnight Twice's unmoving body. Their great silver shoulders slumped.

Metal feet echoed across the platform as the cluster of deformed Sau Darans staggered closer. Although none of them could stagger in a straight line, every green glowing eye focussed hungrily on Talyn and Isabella—and, no doubt, on the gods inside them.

"I ain't got no shot," Beauregard snarled at Nova Sky and Isabella. "Move."

Defensively, the silver Sau Daran stepped in front of the gathering horde of deformed Sau Darans and blocked their path. Their single pair of red eyes were fixed on the ring of leaking, less upright, less silver Sau Darans, like a parent standing over a pack of misbehaving children. The silver guardian held out a hand as though directing traffic. "Halt!" Their voice sounded electronic, emotionless even, yet it carried a firmness that suggested failing to halt would result in... repercussions.

Nova Sky patted the silver Sau Daran's shoulder. "It's alright. We're all friends here."

The blue flecks in his eyes burned hot.

Bowing, the silver Sau Daran stepped aside.

"Now," said Nova Sky much more brightly, "let's get this show on the road!"

He clapped Talyn's hands above his head, sending a deep echo resonating through the ice cave. In response to this highly unnecessary theatre, a bubble of blue energy grew out of the platform's mechanical ring like the swell of a jellyfish caught by the tide. The blue energy bulged, then drew back into the ring and settled into a swirling, rippling wall of energy. Isabella had seen something exactly like it only twice—once in her classroom on Earth three years ago, and once on *Haven* when it was a Husk. Both times, the portal had been opened by Sau Darans. Both times, it had brought someone who wanted to abduct her.

"You had a portal all this time?!" cried Isabella.

Nova Sky shrugged. "Of course. But there's nothing like a good crashlanding to get the attention of a hero."

Prick.

This time, no one stepped out of the portal to abduct her. Instead, after Nova Sky's eyes burned blue once again, the deformed Sau Darans on the platform lurched away from their original stumbling trajectory and skittered through the portal in a stream of dark metal bodies. As they hurried through the portal, yet more clambered up onto the pillar to take their places.

"What's happening?" Isabella demanded.

Nova Sky giggled. "Penance."

Mirroring the subtle movements of those around her, Fleur quietly stepped back onto the lift. "Isabella, honey?" They were all on the lift now. Except for Isabella.

Invitingly, Beauregard held out his withered left hand while keeping his plasma pistol ready in his right. "Kid, we ain't gonna take these things out while you're in the way."

With a small shake of her head, Isabella dismissed their concern. She didn't waste her breath reminding them she knew how to look after herself. Instead, she threw all her focus at Nova Sky. "Don't do this."

Nova Sky laughed uproariously. "Please! All it takes is one PROXUS battle station to turn this planet into ash, and we're back where we started, looking for sacrifices." He laughed again, as though considering this prospect fanciful. When his eerie laughter ceased, his face grew more unpleasant than any planetary bombardment. "Our children are hungry. Any source of clean energy will satisfy them. Ship engines. Refineries. Anywhere PROXUS took the gods who died in our war and tore them apart to fuel their technology. We've found plenty of targets over the cycles."

There was a hiss of static from the lift's armoured stranger. "Condemning billions of humans to death."

Nova Sky's expression was as grim as the Reaper. "Well, I certainly hope so."

"This is crazy," said Isabella. "You're mad! Even I know there's, like, so many ships all over the galaxies and so many worlds that PROXUS controls. You can't kill them all, these Sau Darans would be dead long before they made a dent. Please don't do this. You've saved them!"

Nova Sky picked up the Spark, its dregs of green liquid lolling at the bottom, and hugged the device to his chest. "With this, I only need one army. Our children will do as I instruct, like any other machine. They will die as many times as it takes to save the universe. All I need is a little sacrifice here and there to bring them back again, and there are plenty of humans out there to make it."

"But they'll kill everyone," protested Isabella.

Nova Sky grinned. "Exactly!" With a wave of his hand, a tributary of deformed Sau Darans broke off from the river of metal bodies hurrying through the portal. Changing course, they charged at Isabella.

This guy is one oat crunch short of a cereal box.

"No!" shouted the silver Sau Daran. Ignored by the onrushing horde, they hurled themself into the mass of dark, leaking bodies only a handful of grasping snatches from Isabella. With no coordination in the deformed Sau Darans' frantic lunges, after only a few powerful strides and great sweeps of their metal arms, the silver Sau Daran hurled the nearest corrupted metal creature off the platform. From the lift, stray plasma blasts struck home around the arcs of their flying silver fists as Isabella's silver guardian pushed, punched and flung deformed Sau Darans into the shadows below.

Nova Sky reached out a calm hand and unleashed a disapproving look at the silver Sau Daran. Instantly, their body froze. An electronic reply forced itself out of the silver Sau Daran's jaw. "This… is… wrong."

"It is the will of your god. You will not interfere."

With nothing to slow them, the press of dark metal bodies surged around the silver Sau Daran and Isabella. Yet more climbed up onto the platform after them.

Purple smoke swirled.

Isabella swapped the platform for the lift.

Between her and the charging horde, a wall of plasma pistols opened fire. Everyone on the lift was squeezing a trigger, except for the armoured stranger. After the encounter in *Haven*'s airlock, Isabella had a good idea who was behind that dark helmet. And why they weren't allowed a weapon.

Volleys of red plasma thinned the horde's front rank but did nothing to slow it down. There were too many. Falling metal bodies were quickly lost under the maelstrom, and even those who fell never stopped moving. Behind Isabella, on the platform's other side, another endless stream of black metal bodies clambered into view. In every direction she looked, frenetic metal bodies surged towards them.

Fleur slammed a control switch and the lift jerked upwards. Then stopped with a shuddering lurch. A cackle reached them from below. "As if escaping on a piece of machinery is going to work while I'm here! Fire your weapons all you want—I'm enjoying the show!"

In answer, Beauregard leaned over the edge of the lift and loosed off a shot at Nova Sky.

"No!" screamed Isabella. She dashed to the lift's edge. A handful of metres below, Nova Sky smiled up at her. The wires on his metallic suit stood upright, wriggling like worms, blue sparks bursting from their frayed ends. A spherical shield of blue energy surrounded him.

"Honey, is there any chance you could please help us leave this lovely place?" asked Fleur. She punctuated her question by leaning over the edge of the lift and opening fire on the deformed Sau Darans climbing the rod that ran up the centre of the pillar. Under the whining of Fleur's plasma pistol, metal clattered onto stone below.

Braga snaked an arm around Fleur's waist, hanging off her over the edge as she unleashed a torrent of plasma.

Glancing around, probably to see if anyone was watching her dramatic pose, Braga's gaze froze on Isabella. The confident expression on her face crumpled. "Phyx, get back!" called Braga.

With a yelp, Isabella felt the world do a summersault as her leg was hauled out from under her.

The cave spun.

She landed on her back, pain splintering up her spine as it struck the lift's mesh floor. A black metal hand had reached up through a tangle of twisted mesh floor and, through the hole it created, was pulling her leg. Had it been her human leg, she was confident it would have been crushed to a bloody stump. Then she'd have matching human bits for legs. Luckily, it had grabbed her glowing purple leg. There were tears in her jeans where the metal fingers had scraped and clawed to hold her down. Another hand burst through the mesh floor, nearly removing her face.

With a dazzling flash of purple lightning, Braga's axe took the metal hand clean off. An urgent bark of plasma from her pistol banished the other hand. Rolling away in panic, Isabella caught sight of a black metal body plummeting onto the platform below, two sparking stumps where its wrists had been. Retrieving her axe, Braga winked and helped her up. Isabella didn't let go.

"Everyone, touch me!" shouted Isabella.

"Appropriately!" shouted Fleur, glancing at the space pirates.

Hands seized Isabella, fumbling to grasp any part of her they could find. "Everybody in contact?" she called, unable to see through the sudden crush of bodies.

No one suggested otherwise.

Purple smoke.

Gone.

CHAPTER THIRTY-THREE

Like the start of a bad joke, Isabella, Fleur, Braga, Beauregard, four space pirates and the Empress of the Known Galaxies arrived on the central reservation of the M4 motorway.

There were safer places to gather. Most places, for example. Spots like this, where the motorway passed Littlefield Green, were particularly dangerous. For starters, there wasn't a single roadworks sign to encourage motorists to drop below the national speed limit. Morning rush hour traffic bombed past, sending shockwaves thundering through Isabella's body. However, standing in the middle of the M4 did hold one appealing factor with enough draw for Isabella to bring them here—no one had anywhere to run until everyone gave Isabella the answers she needed. And she needed answers like Paradise Moon needed trouble.

Everyone let go of Isabella and staggered against the motorway's frost-coated central barrier. Four lanes of hooting vehicles rattled past on either side of the knee-high barrier, summoning gusts that ruffled their hair and shook their bodies.

Beauregard holstered his plasma pistol. "This ain't my idea of safe, kid," he shouted over the traffic.

"Honey, perhaps somewhere quieter?" Fleur screamed over the drone of car engines. Her hand left the barrier she had been clinging to so she could examine her dishevelled afro.

Isabella wrapped her arms around herself, shielding her fingers from the cold by pinning them under her armpits, and sat on the barrier, shivering in her black tee. Ignoring the dampness spreading from the barrier's thin coat of ice up the seat of her jeans, she fixed them with a firm look. "No one's going anywhere until you tell me what's going on." She examined their tired faces. "Please," she added.

"Well, we'd love answers! What about that psycho you arrived with?" countered Braga, sliding her axe into her belt. "He just murdered a whole phyxing city."

Something inside Isabella fractured. It felt as though cold, trembling fingers were clawing and scratching beneath her ribcage. As soon as their icy grip found purchase around her heart, they squeezed.

"I know!" she screamed, and not because she wanted to be heard over the roar of traffic.

Everyone stared at her. The space pirates' faces were softened by curious bemusement, in contrast to the naked concern carved onto Fleur and Braga. Beauregard just stared, although Isabella knew his seemingly relaxed gun arm was ready to shoot anything he deemed a target. And who knew what was being calculated behind the armoured Empress' faceless visor? But there was no escaping it—Isabella was the subject of every gaze on this motorway that wasn't hurtling past at 70MPH or more.

We screwed up, didn't we?

No. We got screwed. It's not the same thing.

Whatever. Screwed is screwed.

"Tell me—" Isabella began, but she never finished.

That familiar nausea. Tingling all over her skin. The screaming of every nerve in her body interrupted by the familiar taste of metal on her tongue and the familiar scent of electricity burning the air.

It was everything she felt three years ago when Sau Darans killed her teacher and kidnapped her into deep space. It was nothing she wanted to feel again. But what Isabella wanted rarely mattered. The air still screamed, the world still shook and everything still broke.

Level with the traffic surging towards it, blue light ripped a hole through the air in the central lane of the motorway's eastbound traffic. Fingers of lightning crackled out of it and up the motorway, accompanied by a screaming gale.

How did they find us?

It's not possible.

You always say that.

But it's not! We just got here.

Well they have.

Not this quickly. They can't.

Weightless vehicles were tossed high in the air, the momentum of their spinning wheels stalled by their abrupt roadless ascent. Gravity stopped behaving and refused to drag them back to the tarmac. Instead, they hung far above. This reprieve would not last long. The first time it had been desks in a classroom. The second, crates in a Husk. This time, cars. But they always fell.

Hero shit?

Hero shit, baby!

Purple smoke popped back and forth across sky and asphalt. Every time Isabella appeared in the sky, she tapped another floating car, lorry or van. Whenever she reappeared on the asphalt further down the motorway, she deposited her latest vehicle on the hard shoulder. Isabella always found some level of numb comfort in what she and Paradise Moon called hero shit. Whenever she was doing hero shit, she didn't have to think or worry about anything else. Like the terrifying reality beyond what was in front of her.

Isabella was vanishing fast. One heartbeat she was up *here* and the next moment down *here*. Sounds only reached her in half-metred prose before being cut short as she left them behind. Her ears caught the beginning of heavy collisions. Newly arriving drivers who saw the portal and attempted a variety of breaking and turning manoeuvres. None of them advisable. None of them successful. Not when travelling at high speed with nowhere to go. Before any crashes reached their conclusion, Isabella vanished from the sky onto the hard shoulder's welcomingly solid tarmac. Already, it was filling with the queue of vehicles she had rescued. It was this spot that had first thrown this patch of M4 into her mind, conjured by the memory of a classmate's travelsick vomiting at the roadside on a trip to the science museum.

As Isabella landed on the bonnet of a sportscar floating far above the motorway and glanced at the terrified face of its driver, she felt the air pressure drop. Their reprieve was almost over. The Sau Daran portal was open. Gravity was waking up.

With another flash of purple smoke, she dumped the sportscar on the hard shoulder. This time, the impact threw her off the bonnet and back down again with the pop and groan of denting metal. Grimacing, Isabella rubbed the back of her head. She had vanished the car onto the tarmac just like all the others, but the resistance she had felt when its tyres found the ground and threw her back up into the air had been new energy... the start of its fall, resumed and concluded.

She looked up.

Amid stray flickers of lightning, the outlines of a black SUV, battered hatchback and sleek estate were still in the sky above the portal, but they were no longer hanging.

All three were plummeting fast.

Purple smoke bloomed around Isabella. She slapped a glowing purple hand on the first falling car's roof and in a heartbeat brought the SUV back down to earth with her. She introduced car to tarmac, sending it skidding and sparking on its rear down the hard shoulder. This exhausted all the momentum the SUV had built up while falling, albeit with the smash of breaking glass from its rear window and a shudder at the end of its journey as it toppled back onto all four wheels.

Taking note of how far the SUV had travelled after landing, Isabella glanced up at the sky. Too late. The second and third falling cars were tumbling end over end with astonishing speed.

There's not enough time to save both.

Paradise Moon was right. At least one of the cars would strike the motorway far sooner than she could safely steal one and then the other from their descent.

There's never enough time.

Purple smoke brought her as far as the hatchback. With a tap of her glowing purple hand, she took it *with her* to the estate. Wind buffeted her face, pressing her short hair slick to her skull and stretching her face like taut clingfilm. She stretched out a glowing purple arm, straining towards the estate car, while towards the hatchback she had brought with her she reached out with the glowing purple leg concealed beneath her jeans.

Grey tarmac lunged towards Isabella's face.

We've not got this! We've not got this!

Gasping with effort, Isabella stretched her body in both directions as she tumbled through the air. Her purple fingers found the trailing undercarriage of the hatchback, while the tip of her boot-clad purple foot tapped the spinning bonnet of the estate. Had she reached out with a human limb, the impact would have shattered her. But Paradise Moon's limbs were something else—literally.

She summoned another breath of purple smoke. With a torrential splash, both cars hurtled and skidded across the blue waters of a previously tranquil shoreline.

Cold salt water pummelled Isabella's face once again as she plunged beneath the sea in the wake of two rolling, sinking cars. She didn't bother making a break for the ocean's surface. Another burst of purple smoke landed her on the swiftly submerging lap of the hatchback's terrified passenger, who was still screaming as he and the woman who had been driving tumbled with Isabella onto a bed of hot white sand.

The pair were on their knees, breathless and shaking, when Isabella returned to the beach with the driver of the estate. All three stared up at her from the sand, their ruined suits drenched and their faces raw with terror, bruises and seawater.

Easy! I said we've got this.

A little way up the beach, a network of pristine white tents had been arranged near the spot where Isabella had landed Talyn's crashed silver ship a handful of days ago.

"I'm pretty sure they're all doctors." Isabella pointed up the beach at the crowd of NASA personnel standing stock still in front of their tents, every one of them staring at the new arrivals. "Maybe not the right kind of doctors," she admitted unconvincingly, "but one doctor's as good as another, right? You'll be fine."

Stepping away, Isabella gave her mouth a rub with an arm that turned out to be no less sandy than her lips. She spat away the sand. *I hate sand.*

But when Isabella returned to the M4, sand was the least of her worries.

CHAPTER THIRTY-FOUR

Casting her eyes from the purple smoke popping back and forth across the sky, Fleur aimed her plasma pistol at the opening portal. Warily, she kept her weapon steady as she left the icy metal barrier and advanced across the road. The blue hole of light sparked with groping fingers of electricity. Pinning her poncho to her chest, the howling wind tried to throw her backwards but she never let it turn her face, let alone break her stride.

With a screech that did turn Fleur's head, an Earth vehicle roared up behind her, gunning its engine at full throttle. She ducked under its rising bumper as the roaring gale plucked it into the sky.

"Phyxin' dpresh," muttered Beauregard as he strolled after her. "Learn to drive!" His plasma pistol was primed at his hip, eyes fixed on the portal as though gathering targeting data.

Led by Braga, the rest followed Fleur and Beauregard towards the portal.

"Do I get a weapon yet?" demanded the Empress through a hiss of static from her helmet.

"No!" shouted Fleur, Braga and Beauregard.

Fleur felt the air pressure drop. The whipping wind died as suddenly as it had awoken, as though the whole universe was taking a breath. Had she missed that sign, three final vehicles falling out of the sky provided a less subtle clue as to what would come next.

One last stray spark leapt from the portal. Chasing its tail, a rabid horde of deformed Sau Daran zombies burst through the swirling, shimmering blue light. The endless press of their dark bodies spilled onto the road amid the stomp of metal feet and tinny scuttle of claws. Green fluids and gasses coursed from their misaligned joints and the deep furrows of their scars. As though in invitation, their metal jaws yawned open.

Everyone with a weapon lined up on either side of Fleur. Together, they let loose. Volleys of red plasma met the charge, eating hot chunks out of the onrushing metal bodies. Fleur's plasma fire blended into the torrent of blasts whining beside her, striking deformed metal legs and arms and heads and torsos. But whatever they blasted, these zombified Sau Darans kept coming. They shrugged off blasts to their faces as though they were nothing, despite the glowing holes left behind. After their legs had been blasted out from under them, some scurried on their hands or claws, while others had so many scuttling legs that losing a few didn't even slow them down. Some fell when they had no means of covering ground, but even they never stopped, never flinched, never hesitated. Not one of the Sau Daran zombies seemed to notice the damage they were sustaining. It was as though their minds and souls and any other part of a being that could notice such injuries had been banished from their bodies.

Whatever remained within them was relentless.

And rapid.

The crowd of Sau Daran zombies broke their line, throwing Fleur aside. She landed on her back, the ground expelling air from her lungs like a sucker punch. A body landed next to her with a thump meaty enough to suggest it was human, but she didn't have time to check. A dark metal figure was already bending over her, jaws snapping at her flesh. They were close to humanoid in shape, their smouldering shoulder still glowing where Fleur had blasted off their arm.

Fleur's plasma pistol burned hole after hole through their face, her finger clamped down on the trigger. The dark plates of their face hissed and spat with melting metal. She cried out as a molten droplet landed on her cheek, but she didn't hold back from blasting apart what remained of their head. Staggering blindly, her attacker clawed at her with jagged metal fingers. She rolled out of their reach and found her feet.

A grim sight greeted her.

Except for Count Fontaine, all the space pirates had been crumpled, broken, bloodied, twisted, crushed and made comprehensively dead. This included the body that had landed beside her when she fell.

Beauregard was a calm picture of calculated violence. His posture was perfectly straight and unflinching, as though firing at a practice range rather than facing down imminent death. Smoothly, he stepped backwards with each shot, his face cold concentration. He blasted apart leg joints from the onrushing Sau Daran zombies, rendering hamstrung every attacker who caught his attention. As soon as one collapsed into a crawl, he pivoted to his next target without slowing his rate of fire or retreating with any greater urgency or panic.

Purple electricity flashed across Fleur's vision close enough to ignite white dots behind her retinas. The dancing blades and purple lightning of Braga's axe and Count Fontaine's rapier scythed through every Sau

Daran joint they could find, separating legs, arms and necks from their bodies.

A Sau Daran sailed overhead, launched from the motorised arm of the Empress' black armour. Her armour's leg joints whirred as they kicked two more Sau Daran zombies over an abandoned vehicle.

"I'm sure glad we didn't give her a weapon," called Braga. With a spark of purple lightning, the swing of her axe separated another metal head from its shoulders and sent it rolling down the road.

"Of course not!" Fleur called back. "Then she would have been dangerous!"

Purple smoke erupted at her side, revealing a dripping, sandy Isabella. Instantly, Isabella had to lurch out of the path of a thrusting metal hand to avoid it closing around her throat. Pressing her muzzle into the metal hand, Fleur emptied a salvo of plasma into it until the palm melted away. Fleur withdrew from the onrushing tide of dark metal bodies, using a fistful of Isabella's shirt to drag her out of the path of another grasping metal hand. "Honey, it is getting a little cramped. Would you mind giving us some breathing room?"

Purple smoke stole Fleur and Isabella further up the road. Without waiting for counsel, Isabella disappeared again. Fleur leaned against an abandoned Earth vehicle and drew in a breath. In the distance, purple smoke swirled inside the thickest crowd of metal bodies.

Isabella and Braga arrived beside Fleur. Caught mid-swing on arrival, the space pirate stumbled and with a splutter of purple lightning embedded her axe in the Earth vehicle's roof.

Braga was pulling her axe free as Isabella disappeared again. "Handy trick, she's got. Never gets old."

Fleur didn't reply. She was watching the clusters of grasping, stumbling, rushing Sau Daran zombies as another burst of purple smoke erupted down the road.

Despite his advanced years, Beauregard wasn't even sweating when Isabella vanished him next to them. He twirled his plasma pistol back into its holster and glanced at Braga. "Kid rescued you first, eh?"

Braga gave him a withering smile. "She must like me more, old man."

Unleashing his own signature move, Beauregard shrugged without a care in the universe. "She knows I ain't got no problem handlin' myself."

Braga's smile warmed as she punched him gently on the arm. "You tell yourself that."

Beauregard's expression hardened as he followed Fleur's gaze down the road. "Ain't nothin' we can do against a portal. We ain't got their numbers."

Before replying, Fleur watched Isabella deposit Count Fontaine beside them and leave again in another burst of purple smoke. "Watch how they move." Fleur pointed at the clusters of dark metal bodies swarming like shoals of starshimmers chasing smaller prey through space. "Every time she appears, they are all drawn towards her."

Beauregard nodded. "I see it."

"Phyx," muttered Braga. "They're after her." She slumped against the side of the Earth vehicle as the fight evaporated from her. Her eyes grew uncharacteristically dull, her face drained of vigour. Seemingly heavy in Braga's hand, the head of her axe fell fast enough to sting the road with a clang. She barely held onto the other end.

"After what happened when that first one bit into Midnight Twice, can you blame them?" asked Fleur.

"That's a whole lotta god just to save one Sau Daran. And we're not that rich in gods," said Braga. "The maths doesn't even remotely work."

"Ain't no one harmin' our kid," growled Beauregard.

With another flash of purple smoke, Isabella deposited the armoured Empress beside the vehicle. The Empress climbed to her feet with a groaning of gears and hissing of pistons inside her scraped and battered armour. Her helmet had been torn from her head, revealing fresh cuts across her ancient face. Her ashen hair was a mess, her streak of red dangling over livid eyes.

Already, the surviving Sau Daran zombies were scuttling and running and leaping and bounding down the road towards them. Towards Isabella. And yet more were surging out of the portal and past those who had been reduced to a maimed crawl by the battle.

Isabella held out her hands for everyone. "Shall we?"

Beauregard sighed. "This ain't good, kid."

Isabella extended one of her hands palm up in his direction—as inviting an invitation as anyone could conjure. "Exactly. Let's go."

The Empress laughed darkly. "Who wants to tell her?"

Isabella's lips pressed together as she ran her eyes over their faces, finally settling on Fleur. "Tell me what?"

Lovingly, Fleur stroked Isabella's arm and broke the news as best she could. "They are chasing you, not us."

"Don't bother none, kid," growled Beauregard. "They ain't gonna get you."

Isabella retreated from Fleur's touch. "I don't want any of you to get hurt."

"Well, it is a little late for that, young lady," Count Fontaine complained haughtily.

Isabella's eyes glowed purple and lingered on the Count's face, on the white half-eclipsed sun tattooed on his cheek. A glowing purple thumb cocked itself towards him. "Is this guy for real?" asked Isabella's lips, wrapping themselves around words Fleur doubted were Isabella's.

"He is no one important," Fleur assured Isabella and Paradise Moon. She caught a flicker of pain behind Count

Fontaine's expression, but she felt nothing. His feelings were a data point, nothing more.

Inescapably, Fleur's eyes were drawn back to the mass of dark bodies chasing towards them. They were much closer now—almost within plasma pistol range. "Find somewhere safe," she urged Isabella. "Get out of here."

Isabella's whole body bristled. There was no mistaking her defiant clenched jaw—whoever had been in control a moment ago, now Isabella was back at the wheel. "I'm not leaving you."

"We ain't got no need for heroes."

Isabella pointed at the sky she had emptied of cars while they fought. "You sure about that?"

"You did good, kid, but you ain't got nothin' to prove to us. Stay alive so all this means somethin'."

Braga's calloused fingers tousled Isabella's hair. "Quit trying to save us and save yourself, kid. If you don't get outa here, they're not gonna stop coming. We can't fight them off forever." Readying her axe, she glanced beyond their small group at the horde storming towards them. "We need you to not be here so that portal closes."

"Somewhere safe," added Fleur. "Anywhere safe."

"You've got it backwards. Shouldn't I be taking you somewhere safe?" countered Isabella.

"Yes!" barked Count Fontaine with an imperiously transparent sense of self-preservation. "She should!"

"Agreed." The Empress' face was molten fury as she pointed an armoured finger at Fleur. "She needs to drop us somewhere safe *before* she leads them away. It's the only logical strategy."

"We still have a job to do here." Serenity washed over Fleur, finding a familiar home in the easy embrace of her relaxing muscles. She understood what she needed to do. Now she knew the direction in which she had to travel, she was confident she would find a path to take her there. "Just go, otherwise they will never stop coming. Go now.

Go fast enough that no one can ever keep up. We will take care of everyone who remains."

"This is madness!" snapped the Empress. "Don't any of you want to survive this?"

Isabella glanced at the charging mass of Sau Daran zombies, pausing for an internal conversation no one else was party to. She let out a big sigh. "Fine, just no one die while I'm gone."

Fleur reached out to touch Isabella one last time, to reassure her that everything would be okay, that they would find a way to survive this like they always did, but for once the girl was faster than her and all Fleur grasped was purple smoke.

Gone.

Fleur stared at where Isabella wasn't and at the horde beyond. Like wilting petals of voidblossom, her heart withered under the weight of sorrow she felt for these Sau Darans who had died once already. All she could offer them was an end to their torment and escape from whatever twisted hunger Nova Sky had summoned within their reincarnated shells.

"We will put them out of their misery. Give them the peace they deserve. I would do the same for any of you."

Braga frowned. "Remind me never to tell you if I turn into a zombie."

CHAPTER THIRTY-FIVE

Instead of flinging his cold mug of tea across the kitchen in frustration, Ezra placed it carefully on a coaster. Before meeting *Haven*, he would have lost his temper by now. But that was the old Ezra. The self-righteous son of PROXUS war heroes, always diving in first. The eager Apprentice Ranger who did everything with the speed, fury and intensity of a whirring star drive. The self-styled hero who never stopped shooting long enough to question why he pulled the trigger, or even if he was fighting on the right side.

Frustrated though he was, Ezra 2.0 stifled a sigh at Isabella's mother and her polite interrogation. He couldn't fault her effort, but all her questions were wearily mundane. There were only so many times he could agree that, yes, he was from space and only so many ways he could describe it. Not one question was ample distraction from the bleak realisation Isabella had benched him. At a time like this, he was making small talk over cold tea.

Having beaten him around the head with another tedious question about space, Isabella's mother listened to his boring answer with her 'how interesting' eyebrows raised, followed by a well-mannered 'that's nice' smile. All he could think about was how badly he needed to help Isabella. How badly everyone must need him. How he should be helping them save every single Sau Daran before it was too late.

It was a relief when her glass box rang, trading the tedium of their conversation for an upbeat bounce of musical notes. She held up the device, cut off its music and squinted at someone on the screen. "Isabella told me not to speak to you," she said firmly. "I don't know what happened, but I think it would be better for everyone if you stopped calling me."

Decisively, Isabella's mother tapped the screen with a flourish and straightened up primly on her tall seat at the breakfast bar. Her domestic empire gleamed all around her with polished marble surfaces, every bit as proud as her expression.

But when she lay her glass box on the breakfast bar, it spoke back. "I'm still here. Perhaps we should discuss why Isabella doesn't wish to speak to me," suggested a woman's voice, her tone cold and austere. It was impossible for Ezra not to recognise her. He had heard that same voice in countless transmissions between Xarr and its republic of hub worlds, starships and battle stations. More recently, he had heard it on *Haven*.

Fuelled by sheer terror, he snatched the glass box off the breakfast bar and stared into the unforgiving eyes of the Empress of the Known Galaxies. She was wearing a fluffy cardigan.

"Ex-Apprentice Ranger Ezra Knight," said the Empress, her expression betraying surprise. "Your presence here is unexpected."

He thrust the glass box back at Isabella's mother. "Turn it off!" he hissed.

Isabella's mother leaned over the breakfast bar and jabbed ineffectively at the screen.

"Perhaps," continued the Empress, "you know why Isabella isn't returning my calls?"

Frantically, Isabella's mother and Ezra tapped the screen, but she was looking at it upside-down and he didn't know how these primitive devices worked.

"May I surmise her sudden lack of contact is related to your presence in her kitchen?"

A lucky prod from Isabella's mother cut the connection. The Empress disappeared.

Isabella's mother ran her eyes over Ezra. There was a darkness inside her that, until now, he had never believed her capable of possessing. "She knows you." It was an accusation. Potentially the beginning of a less polite interrogation. "How much danger is my daughter in?"

Ezra considered lying, but everything in her expression warned him that would be a mistake. Besides, he was a terrible liar. "That is the most dangerous person in the Known Galaxies," he admitted.

"My daughter's therapist?!" she lashed back, her brow creased with concern.

Ezra nodded bleakly. It made sense, when he thought about it. One more clone chasing the vanishing girl. "I'd die before I let anyone hurt your daughter."

They were both quiet for a long time. Finally, Isabella's mother started tapping the glass box again. As they listened to it ring, there was no warmth left in her expression. Gone were her 'how interesting' raised eyebrows and her well-mannered 'that's nice' smile. Only darkness remained. "How dare that bitch mess with my daughter." Her face twitched with uncontained fury, surrounding the glassy, middle-distance stare of a good person about to do a terrible thing. She glanced at a knife block on the worktop.

"What are you doing?" asked Ezra.

"I'm calling you a cab."

Like a glimmer of blue sky through parting clouds, Ezra's worry gave way to confusion. "Why would you call me that?"

CHAPTER THIRTY-SIX

R ed dirt stuck to Isabella as she ran. Her sea-stained jeans. Her soaked black tee. Her lips and cheeks and bouncing spikes of slick, sweaty hair. It churned in clouds from the soles of her boots, weeping a trail that hung in the air behind her long enough to coat her pursuers' metal shells.

"You know," Dash said over the comm, "it sounds like you're doing an awful lot of work."

Behind her, the latest portal's blue glow was yet one more scorching source of light in Pilbara's baking outback. What didn't blend in so well, what was incongruous against this backdrop of sun-soaked earth and soot-coloured mountains, was the outlandish horde of mindless metal zombies chasing her.

"Can't you just vanish across the desert?" continued Dash. "You'd save yourself a lot of trouble."

"And make them move that portal?" she gasped into her gauntlet, her heart and lungs pounding. "Wouldn't you prefer just one group of zombies to fire at?"

The sky shuddered as Dash's Scimitar roared overhead. "Fair enough, just give me the signal."

"I need a moment."

We don't have a moment! Give him the signal!

Stop rushing me!

You want them to have a nibble on us first?

"Hold on!" Isabella shouted at Dash and Paradise Moon. She tried to bring up a contact on her phone, but her fast strides were too juddering, her hands shaking too much to find the right points on her screen.

She looked behind her.

That was a mistake.

A tidal wave of metal teeth and limbs were eating up the dirt behind her with terrifying speed.

Shit shit shit shit shit shit shit.

Relax, we do this all the time.

We do not get chased by zombies all the time.

We've had worse. It's just hero shit, baby!

This is not normal hero shit!

Whatever, it's hero shit adjacent.

She slowed, tapping more precisely on her phone. But she was still rushing and her fingers kept finding the wrong letters on her keypad.

Erm, maybe you want to hurry up?

Stop distracting me.

What's distracting? They only want to eat us.

Practically slowing to a walk—albeit an ungainly fashion of speedwalking someone might adopt when pursued by sprinting metal zombies—Isabella found the correct letters on her keypad to bring up the contact she wanted, the contact in her phone she never called and whose ringtone she dreaded.

"I have to say, I'm not surprised you called," came a weary voice down the phone. "Is this mess yours?"

Isabella scurried back up to a speed less likely to get her killed, her human ankle and knee twisting as her boots skidded through the loose earth. Another glance told her the chasing horde of metal had closed to only a few car lengths behind her. Her glowing purple limbs couldn't move any faster. No stranger to balancing on the sharpest edge of staying alive, her heart strained as she searched for energy in her human leg and arm to keep up with her pounding alien limbs. Somehow, somewhere, she dug deep and found something.

"Are you still there?" asked Agent Glass. "Or did you just call me to breathe heavily down the phone?"

"Shut up and listen. I need your help."

"If this is your fault, you'll know what's happening and be able to imagine how busy I am."

"The Sau Daran zombies on the motorway?"

A torrent of incredibly mild-mannered swearing erupted down the phone. Isabella had never heard Agent Glass so upset. She even caught the phrase 'knicker-twisters' and wondered what life experiences had conspired to forge a man like Agent Glass. She didn't dwell on this for long, on account of the killer metal zombies chasing her.

"That's what those things are?" demanded Agent Glass, his tone even more exasperated than the high bar he had set in previous conversations.

"My friends are there too. Can you help them?"

"No!" cried Agent Glass. "Do you want us to nuke the whole of South East England? The British army's on their way, but they're too far out to help your friends. I'm watching the satellite feed."

"Fine, I'll fix it. You can help me with something else."

A sigh down the phone. "Naturally. Come here. To the *lobby*. Not my office. I'll do what I can."

Isabella's arms pumped smoothly, her stride ever lengthening, her breaths evening out as she sank into a familiar running rhythm. She couldn't keep this pace up forever, but hopefully it would keep her out of reach long enough to get out of here alive. "You won't want me bringing these things to you."

"There are more?!" Agent Glass sighed again. "Of course there are more."

"Did you ever have a plan for dealing with me?" asked Isabella. "If I was a problem?"

"When aren't you a problem?"

"Not that type of problem. You know what I mean."

Agent Glass didn't pause for very long, but it was long enough to tell Isabella everything she needed to know. "Don't waste time denying it," she warned, as he started denying it. "How long until you can have it ready?" This time, his pause was longer. "I'm running for my life here!"

"It's always ready."

"Where do I go?"

"The orange beacon."

Agent Glass had made great efforts to familiarise Isabella with a handful of important objects that his operatives then stowed in strategic locations, should Isabella urgently need help or resources. She had never needed to test them, nor been summoned to them, but she had always suspected their intent wasn't exclusively friendly. Someone as world-weary as Agent Glass was pessimistic enough to have a contingency plan for everything. Even her.

"Great. Be ready." Isabella cut off the call, thrust her phone into her jeans and kept pumping her arms and legs. "Dash, are you ready or what?" she demanded hotly into her gauntlet's comm.

In answer, there was a roar of PROXUS engines overhead. "I thought you'd forgotten about me."

A glance over Isabella's shoulder was greeted by a hungry tide of metal fingertips and claws reaching out to grab her, scratch her, clutch violently at her flesh.

"Any time now, Dash. Then as soon as you're finished here, you know what to do."

"You only just gave the signal!"

Isabella's lungs were aching. "I'm ready, just do it!"

Dash counted her down. He reached zero and she vanished in a swirl of purple smoke. As the desert disappeared around her, she glimpsed a flash of green plasma, heard it thundering out of the sky, felt the air boil hot enough to burn the dirt black.

But she saw nothing more.

Not there, which was gone.

Not here, in the darkness

She tripped and fell. Naturally, Agent Glass had stowed the orange beacon somewhere that was nighttime when she finally visited. Nothing was ever simple. She landed on more dirt, as if she hadn't seen enough of it already. Not that she could see it in the darkness. She could feel it, though. Grit under her nails. In her mouth and halfway up her nose. Still blinded by the shock of switching afternoon sunshine for a smothering blanket of midnight, Isabella hauled herself up and stared at what looked like nothing. She couldn't even see the orange beacon she had supposedly vanished to, hadn't even had the good luck to land on it. Instead, this place hung in the solitary silence of a still and thoroughly dead night, as hazy as the memory of a forgotten graveyard.

It took a few minutes for her eyes to warm to the idea of showing her anything other than darkness. A clear evening sky was emerging, caging a full moon that seemed to be growing in intensity the longer she waited. Gone was the red dirt of Pilbara, but that was the only difference Isabella's adjusting eyesight could make out. That stretch of nothingness she had left behind in Australia? They had it here, too, complete with a rising backdrop of dark mountains under the moonlight. This desolation wore a new guise—paler dirt and rocks, sprigged with sparser glimpses of bush and cacti—but it was just as desolate. There was nothing here...

Except the beacon.

The moment she spotted it beside the base of a stunted, white-streaked cactus, Isabella picked up the ball of metal. It was heavier than it looked, especially for something that fitted so easily in the palm of her hand. Even though she had been ready for its ungainly weight, the ball still pulled her hand towards the dirt before she readjusted. The beacon was crafted from the wreckage of *Haven*'s hull, back when it had been an unresurrected Husk. Striker's battle station and starfighters had blasted whole sections of the Husk into oblivion before Isabella and Paradise Moon could summon the unity of purpose to vanish the Husk and everyone on board to Earth. The most fragile parts of the Husk's hull had failed to cling on when they entered Earth's atmosphere, but NASA had fallen over itself to retrieve every single scrap of once-living metal that was floating and falling around the boundaries of Earth's atmosphere.

A few tiny remnants of dead hull, like this beacon, had been gifted back to Isabella in a global ceremony public enough to make her want to be kidnapped into deep space all over again. That was before her new life of body language coaches and more frequent hero shit. Naturally, she wasn't allowed to keep these gifts. But they had each been colour-coded and left with her for a while. Agent Glass had introduced himself by confiscating those gifts.

She held it up in the moonlight. Its surface was carved with intricate rings, which made it easier to grip. This beacon must be the orange one—if she hadn't remembered it correctly, she would still be in Pilbara. But under the moonlight, she couldn't make out the orange paint she remembered it being coated in—the sort of garish colour a paranoid agent might choose to ensure his pet hero never forgot it.

Are you going to wait here to die?

Alright, alright. It's not like I could see where we were going before now.

Retreating from the spot where she had arrived, Isabella's boots kicked up clouds of moon-bleached earth that married with the darker dirt stains on her jeans. As she walked away, she pulled out her phone. "So how does this work?" she asked Agent Glass.

"Tell me when to launch the drone strike. After that, don't hang around. Once you give me the signal, you'll only have seconds to leave."

A blue portal erupted out of the night, swallowing the air around where Isabella had first arrived in the desert. Lightning rode a fresh gale out of the portal, casting spirals of dirt and loose stones towards the stars.

By the time Isabella shouted her signal down the phone to Agent Glass, she was sprinting barely out of reach of another grasping metal horde.

"I see you," replied Agent Glass. "I've ordered the strike. Get out now."

As purple smoke stole Isabella from the moonlit desert, she heard the howl of something hurtling through the sky towards the Sau Daran zombies.

But she saw nothing more.

Not there, which was gone.

Not here, in London's grey, early morning light.

CHAPTER THIRTY-SEVEN

This was the last place Isabella wanted to be, but she needed someone who understood how to fight Sau Darans. She couldn't run forever.

Before now, Isabella had never been inside her therapist's apartment without at least an invitation, if not a string of insistent reminders. This morning, she only spotted one thing out of place.

It wasn't the towering statements of impressionist artwork framed strategically around the modern, clean sitting room. Those were as she remembered. Or her therapist's armchair, always ready for listening, talking, analysing and silently judging. Or Isabella's armchair, equally primed for dodging questions and staring out at infinite shades of London grey behind full-length windows. Through them, Isabella saw the bustle of busy streets on a crisp winter morning.

Even her therapist didn't look out of place. Her ashen hair was tied back in a severe bun, her rogue streak of red dangling exempt. Including a fluffy cardigan, her attire was smart and fashionable without ever looking uncomfortable. Her face was as ancient as the mountains

Isabella had left behind and her expression was as furious as the howl of Beauregard's plasma pistol.

The subject of her therapist's fury, and the one thing conspicuously out of place in the sitting room, was Ezra.

He waved a thick knife at her therapist, a knife Isabella recognised from her own kitchen. His hair was a dark, tangled mess of sweat, his face raw from Nova Sky's attack in the cave.

"Ez, put the knife down," urged Isabella.

Only then did Ezra notice her. "Don't get near her. She's—"

"I know."

"Phyx."

Isabella unleashed a lopsided grin. "Yep. It's shit. But we don't have time for this."

"How could you possibly know?" Therapy Empress couldn't keep the confusion and disgust—presumably at being caught out—from her face.

"I met another of you."

"Don't trust a word she says."

Isabella smiled darkly. "Waaaay ahead of you."

"How dare you—"

"Shut up," snapped Isabella. Her face softened as she focussed on Ezra. "Put down the knife. We need her, Ez."

"She manipulated you. Made you trust her. Whatever she was planning for you, it would've been bad."

"True, but she's necessary now. Put it down."

Shrugging, Ezra tossed the knife into a colourful impressionist painting. It stuck, quivering in the canvas. "I only took the knife to make your mother happy."

Isabella rounded on them. "We are only minutes or seconds or I don't know how close to Sau Daran zombies arriving in a portal and killing us all."

"What the phyx happened?" asked Ezra.

"You led them here?" demanded Therapy Empress.

"Everything and you're damn right I did," said Isabella. Her gaze fixed on Therapy Empress. "Tell me how to stop them or you're dead."

You missed out 'you sneaky, lying bitch'.

I'm pretty sure my face is saying that.

Therapy Empress absorbed Isabella's words and expression in a heartbeat. After that, she didn't bother with questions. "Follow me," she ordered, swivelling on the spot and steaming across the sitting room. "How many are coming?"

"You mean you're really not going to try to kill me?"

Therapy Empress spun to glare at Isabella. "Oh, I'm phyxing furious you led my greatest enemy right here, but I'd rather be rational and alive than furious and dead, so those feelings can wait for half a rotation. How many?"

"Too many," warned Isabella, following her to a closed door. Therapy Empress flung open the door and led her into a gloomy bedroom with tall white blinds over the windows, sleek black furniture and a carpet Isabella could drown in. Like a lost puppy, Ezra followed.

Therapy Empress flicked on the light, threw open her sock drawer and pulled out a hammer. "How long?"

"A couple of minutes tops, but it could be seconds."

"Where will they arrive? Exactly?"

"Where I did."

Therapy Empress used the hammer to obliterate a patch of wall, reached inside and pulled out a rucksack. From it, she tossed three silver cylinders onto the bed. Each cylinder was the width of an untouched toilet roll and the length of a standard ruler. In the centre of each was a keypad and numerical display.

"The only way to fight them is to wipe them out. They're too powerful to risk anything else."

"No!" cried Ezra, his face wretched and desperate. "You can't kill them. We're trying to save them."

"Ez, you didn't see them. They're not alive. They're…
I don't know… zombies or something. They'll kill us."

Therapy Empress tapped a code into the first
cylinder's keypad. "How long does it take you to vanish?"

"Less than a second."

"I'll give us five to be safe." Therapy Empress finished
tapping the cylinder's keypad, tossed the item at Isabella.

A glowing purple hand caught it. "What are these?"

Therapy Empress punched in more numbers on the
second cylinder, then tossed it at Ezra. He almost
fumbled the catch, but made it stick.

"Try not to drop it. These things will level a city now
they're armed."

Isabella felt a familiar, cold grip on her heart. "Erm,
you what?"

Therapy Empress started work on the final cylinder's
keypad. "Your timer is set to five seconds. If they're
following you here, they're following you to the next
place we go as well. Yours will be enough for here and
we'll save the other two for wherever we end up. But
with luck, the blast will travel through the open portal."

Carefully, Isabella placed her silver cylinder in Ezra's
arms so he was cradling both bombs. She advanced on
Therapy Empress. "I said… you what?"

Therapy Empress stared back. Cold. Impassive.
Deadly. But genuinely confused. "What?"

"These things will level a city?"

"After what I had to do to get them, I certainly hope
so. They should be more than enough to thin the herd
while we devise a more long-term strategy."

Isabella's human fist balled in rage. "You're a
psychopath. What the Hell were you going to use a
nuclear weapon on?"

"Isn't it obvious?"

"You have three nuclear weapons behind the wall of
your bedroom, you're posing as your victim's therapist

and you're one of hundreds of murderous clones." Isabella gestured at the universe. "None of this is obvious to normal people."

Therapy Empress dropped her a pitying look. "You teleport across galaxies with barely a thought, and the only source of unharvested clean energy in our universe, apart from the boy who crashed into this city, is hiding inside you. Don't lecture me on normal."

Isabella gripped Therapy Empress by her throat. "What. Were. You. Going. To. Use. These. For?"

"Do we have time for this?" Therapy Empress asked calmly as Isabella strangled her. The nausea growing in Isabella's stomach, the taste of metal on her tongue, told her they didn't. She squeezed tighter anyway. "It was leverage," gasped Therapy Empress.

Isabella's grip loosened. "Leverage?"

"Yes, over you. I would threaten to destroy your home... What do you call it?"

"Reading? London?"

"England, that's it." Isabella's grip tightened again. "But you would never let that happen," added Therapy Empress. "Instead, you would come back to Xarr with me on my ship. I would harvest that parasite inside you for clean energy. Xarr is stronger. Your home survives. You're the hero you keep claiming to be. Almost everyone wins."

Through the open bedroom doorway, Isabella caught a flash of blue light from the sitting room. Lightning snaked along the sitting room towards them, charring the pristine white walls. The first silver lining in all this misery was the sight of Therapy Empress' expensive artwork on fire, before it was consumed by the whooshing and smashing of other exploding household items being struck by lightning. A huge crash signalled the end of the floor-to-ceiling windows.

"Time's up," Therapy Empress gasped, struggling for air. "We can take them out here or we can take them out elsewhere. Either way, we have to destroy them."

"No," insisted Ezra, holding his two nuclear bombs tighter to his chest. "You're not hurting them."

Outside the bedroom, the sitting room's gale died. Lightning spluttered. Blue light shone.

"Ez, you don't understand—"

"No!" shouted Ezra, stray beads of wet chaos leaking down his cheeks. "Whatever they are now, we did it to them. This is our mess, our fault. We have to fix it."

He's right, you know.

Heavy metal feet landed on the sitting room's carpet. Isabella released Therapy Empress. She sank onto the bed, rubbing her neck and dragging in oxygen like it was going out of fashion. "I could take your nukes and leave you here."

"You could," Therapy Empress rasped, "but then I'd have to set off the remote detonators inside them."

Isabella held out her hands. "Get on with it then."

The older woman's icy fingers closed around Isabella's human hand. Her purple glowing hand gestured for Ezra to hurry up.

He shook his head, two nuclear weapons cradled against his chest. "I won't let you hurt them."

A flurry of metal feet thundered towards the bedroom. Swearing, Isabella flung herself at Ezra. Her human arm was at full stretch and nearly lost Therapy Empress, who had the quickness of mind to drag her body through the air after Isabella. An outstretched glowing purple hand grasped Ezra's shoulder as he spun away from her and dashed towards...

Not there, which was gone.

Not here, where purple smoke returned Isabella to red dirt. It broke her fall hard. She hadn't been able to think of anywhere else fast enough.

Therapy Empress and Ezra struck the dirt next to her with meaty thuds and grunts. Bright daylight blurred Isabella's vision, sparking hot white dots she had to blink away. As they faded, she saw the smoke before she felt it. Thick and black, it hung like an insistent smog over the arid landscape with no breeze to clear it. Below the smoke, the dirt was charred black and scattered with metal bodies. Then Isabella spotted the smoke ushering out of their twisted, burning shells.

"Good to see you made a start," said Therapy Empress, her face a picture of sour approval. "Although I'm not surprised you lacked the stomach to keep going."

"I'm not setting off a nuclear bomb in London, you psychopath!"

Ezra stared at the smoking Sau Daran bodies, his mouth hanging. "What did you do?"

Spitting earth from her lips yet again, Isabella climbed upright and snatched at the silver cylinders in Ezra's arms. Too fast for her, he backed out of reach on his blades. Keeping the cylinders tight against his chest, he stumbled further away from her across the barren earth.

The Empress stormed after them, her angry shout echoing across the arid desert scrub. "Would everyone please stop fighting with the nuclear weapons?!"

As Ezra backed away, his eyes never left Isabella. Like someone might watch a thief… or a murderer. "You're not doing it."

Isabella glanced at the smoking metal shells.

We're doing the right thing, aren't we?

They were gonna kill us.

Yeah, exactly.

Although Isabella didn't feel any better. She held out her hands, taking gentle steps towards Ezra as though afraid of startling him. "Ez, they'll be here any second."

"Then take us away again."

He's right. We can always run.
Not forever.
No, but long enough to do the right thing.
Like you did eighteen years ago, when you ran away and left all these Sau Darans to get killed in the war?
Wow. Low blow.

Isabella felt her lips clamping shut. Her brow furrowing. Her jaw tightening. "Ez," she began testily. Already, the air tasted metallic on her tongue. "Seriously, buddy." Nausea ached in her stomach. "We can't run forever." Her fingertips tingled with the promise of static electricity. "I need those weapons."

Ezra glared back. "Why not keep running long enough to finish a conversation? Don't you think they deserve that? For us to have a conversation about whether or not we kill them?"

"They'll keep coming," cautioned Therapy Empress. Her voice was laced with a brand of well-trodden tedium that Isabella associated with mothers telling toddlers to eat their vegetables. "We should bring the fight to them while we're still fresh. Machines don't tire."

Maybe we should all just take a beat. Maybe there is another way?

"Everyone, shut up!" shouted Isabella. The venom in her own voice caught her off-guard. "We can't reason with them. They're killing people. *Killing* them. They're not thinking or talking. We don't have time for that. I know what I'm doing. Trust me, this is what I do."

"Can you even hear yourself?" Throwing his face to the sky like a madman, Ezra screamed. His expression came back down to earth desperate and broken. "They won't be reasoned with? They're not thinking or talking? They're killing people?" As his eyes sank back to Isabella, his face softened. "Are you describing them... or you?"

Isabella couldn't tell whether the tumbling nausea inside her was because of another impending portal or the tumult Ezra was ratcheting up inside her head and heart. His questions were all good questions, his points all good points. But he didn't understand what it was like to make these decisions—to have to always get them right. She had been so certain. Hadn't she?

Why isn't anyone on my side?

The Empress is.

I don't care what she thinks.

Well it's not my fault you agree with a murderous Empress and not your friends.

Shaking his head, Ezra sloped across red dirt towards the horizon. Isabella paced after him. "Just give me those bombs, Ez." She was too angry to shout. Her words came out as hot as Hell. "This is what I do, Ez. Hero. Shit." She pointed behind them at where the Empress was scowling, arms crossed. "Whatever comes through the portal is going to kill us all if I don't save us. That's how it works."

An explosion of blue light seared through the empty horizon as a portal opened next to Therapy Empress. Startled enough to betray a rare loss of composure and a serious sense of humour failure, she shielded her eyes from the blinding light with one hand while reaching out towards Isabella and Ezra with the other. "Throw me one!" The portal's blazing blue light conjured contours of shadow and fury over her already cruel face. "I'll send it through, we can take them all out. All of them!"

I can't hurt Talyn.

He's not Talyn. He's Nova Sky.

But Talyn's in there too.

So? What's the difference between that and the Sau Daran zombies? What if they're somewhere in there too?

Stranded between Therapy Empress and Ezra's retreating silhouette, Isabella's body contorted. Indecisively, she attempted to follow, ignore and belay every thought, feeling and instruction her brain could process. Any movement she made was a half-movement, every thought swiftly aborted.

"Don't just stare!" yelled the Empress. "Do it!"

Feels weird being on her side, am I right?

Screw this. I'm losing my shit and I don't know what to do.

It's okay. Let me help.

Why? What are you gonna do?

Get us all out of here. Somewhere we can think clearer and not do anything...

Rash?

I was gonna say stupid.

Where?

To someone who helps me get my head on straight when I can't tell which way is up.

Really? Who's that?

You trust me, right?

Sure. I trust you.

Isabella held out her hands, felt her lips part. But before she knew what she was going to say, before she saw anyone take her hands, before Ezra had even turned to face her, a blaze of purple flared in her eyes.

Reluctantly, she ceded control to Paradise Moon. Pilbara's scorched outback and the portal's light faded from her vision.

CHAPTER THIRTY-EIGHT

Lynch was having a busy day at work. He clamped down on the trigger of his Rotary Plasma Cannon, vaporising another previously pristine corridor of dodging PROXUS Silver Fists. Plasma spat, smoke churned and armoured bodies flew screaming. Since the PROXUS warship had been alerted to his strike team's uninvited presence, his team had scattered to evade capture. Lynch worked best when he was alone, anyway. Fewer people to get in his way. Even fewer thanks to the RPC he was wielding. Most of the Rangers and Silver Fists chasing him had been reduced to nothing but blackened afterthoughts of falling ash and rising smoke.

A sudden swirl of purple smoke made Lynch's heart skip and dance in that way it always did when Moon arrived. Feelings he would never confess to another living soul, even under extreme torture. His aim skewed to one side as, distractedly, he watched the purple smoke drain like dry ice off three fresh interlopers.

The first was Moon, her purple eyes glowing. The second was one of Isabella's friends—Ezri? No, Ezra—with cannisters of something piled up in his arms. The third was an Empress of the Known Galaxies. Her fluffy cardigan was as far from her usual PROXUS aesthetic as Earth was from Xarr. Her smart trousers, fashion sharp enough to cut yourself on, were far more on brand. His eyes lingered for a beat on her Earth-bought clothes and everything they implied. Nothing good. And certainly his fault, after what he had done. Aside from what she was wearing, she looked identical to the Empress commanding this PROXUS warship—and she would likely prove just as much of a pain in his ass.

With a whine, a plasma bolt struck the bulkhead above him. Whenever he was in the thick of a plasma battle that could be his last, he wondered if it had been such a good idea to hack the Empress' cloning facility on Xarr and wake up all her clones at once. He had hoped to create pure chaos throughout PROXUS, and that had been delivered in spades. But the price had been paid when that same chaos bled all over the Known Galaxies in a civil war engulfing every developed star system. At least if he did his job on this warship there would be one less Empress spreading misery across the stars.

With another spray of hot plasma from his RPC, Lynch wiped out the last of the Silver Fists at the end of the corridor. Between his refocussed attention and the deadly accuracy of the Sau Daran aiming tech installed in his facial implant, it was no effort. Like shooting armoured troopers in a barrel. Moon said something, but her words were lost under the clamour of wrecked, smoking armour clattering onto the deck.

Lynch grinned, his eyes flicking mischievously between Ezra and the unexplained Empress. "Well someone's having an interesting day!"

Moon laughed and Lynch felt his heart do that happy aching thing again. It was the same happy aching thing his heart never did when they were apart. "Is this a bad time?" she asked with a smirk. "We can come back later if you're busy."

Lynch leaned his smoking RPC against the wall, the tip of its long barrels nearly scraping the ceiling. With a grunt of effort, he ejected a smoking coil from where the RPC's stock met its many barrels, dragged a fresh coil from the munitions satchel on his back and shoved it home with a satisfying click. "What makes you think I'm busy?"

Glowing purple fingers stroked his shoulder, making his heart ache all over again. "It's been a long day."

Even through all his layers of synthetic combat garb and his stylish gunslinger's jacket, her touch conjured a shiver of desire. Every part of him that was capable of tingling, tingled. "Tell me what you need," he urged her.

Wearing her imperious air of self-importance like a crown, the Empress clicked her tongue with manifest irritation. "We don't need your help." To emphasise her point, she stepped between them.

Lynch's hand dropped to his thigh holster, where a fresh plasma pistol longed to sing for him. "I have plasma delivery systems available in all sizes."

The Empress surveyed him glassily.

"Ignore her," said Moon. Grabbing a fistful of expensive-looking cardigan, she dragged the Empress out of the conversation with a surge of alien strength. They both ignored her complaints.

"What's wrong?" asked Lynch.

Moon pointed Isabella's finger at Ezra. "He's holding nuclear bombs." The finger pointed behind her at another woe. "Any minute now, a portal will open with Sau Daran zombies coming out of it, all trying to eat me." The finger pointed at Isabella's own head for a third woe. "And she's had a tough few days." The finger travelled towards the Empress, hitting the jackpot of her woes. "Plus, she's an absolute—"

"Dpresh?"

Moon shrugged.

"Okay, that's a lot. You're clearly having… a day. Tell me what you need. It's yours."

Purple flecks sparked once more among the chestnut in Isabella's eyes. "Be here for her like you've been there for me, will you?" A purple hand cupped his face, stroking glowing fingers over his stubble, then his cheek, then the metal plate that was now part of his face. Although he couldn't feel her touch on the metal, her eyes never lost any tenderness. He always wondered why the metal plate never bothered her, but it didn't and that made his heart sing. Manly, gruff, heroic singing… Obviously.

The glowing hand retreated. Moon's eyes burned less and less with purple wonder. Lynch's heart ached more and more as she faded. Where purple had burned, human shades of chestnut glimmered.

"Lynch?" asked someone who definitely wasn't Moon. If not Moon, then Isabella. "Where are we?" she asked.

"A PROXUS warship," snapped the Empress. "This scum thinks he can capture it."

"Shut up," chorused Lynch and Isabella together. He smiled. Maybe they would get along just fine.

"Wait, she comes to you?" asked Isabella. The confusion on her face was an alien sight to Lynch. He was more used to the brash, mischievous contours Moon fashioned with Isabella's facial muscles. Not this doubt. Not confusion. "Out of everyone… she comes to you?"

Flashes of stolen moments with Moon on so many strange worlds drifted into his head, making his heart bleed. "What did she tell you?" he replied, choosing his words with slow caution.

Isabella snorted. "Less than your face just did."

Lynch sighed. "Figures." He stared at her, trying to make sense of a picture he didn't recognise. Isabella held her body differently to Moon. She was no less defiant, but whereas Moon held herself with a defiance that didn't give a shit, Isabella's defiance was fully loaded with every shit there was to give. "You can't understand why she came to me, can you?"

Isabella squirmed. "No… But it's totally fine." But if 'totally fine' was on this side of the universe, Isabella's expression was on the opposite side. "Really, it's cool," she protested weakly. "I totally get it."

If she even slightly got it, her face was doing a good job of hiding it. Lynch studied her with no shortage of pity and offered her the gentlest look he could muster. It might not be much deviation from his usual Grade A resting bitchface, but he was trying. "Being with her made everything okay," he admitted. "I think being with me made everything feel okay for her, too."

That gave Isabella pause. For the first time, Lynch felt like she was looking at him and not at whoever she thought he was. "She deserves that."

"Yeah, she does," agreed Lynch. "Moon's awesome."

"She is that." Isabella smiled. "I'm glad you've been there for her."

"Yeah, well, whatever." Lynch shifted uncomfortably, then changed the subject with, he had to admit, as much subtlety as his Rotating Plasma Cannon at full blast. "Moon said you're having a long day?"

Isabella gave him a withering look.

Unbothered, Lynch powered up the charge on his RPC's new plasma coil. "A *very* long day," he corrected.

A fresh troop of PROXUS Rangers were assembling at the far end of the corridor. Picking over the bodies of fallen Silver Fists, they raised a row of plasma rifles and an eager volley of plasma blasts erupted down the corridor. Lynch hopped out of the way as hot crimson fizzed and flashed past them.

"This feels like you're in the middle of something," Isabella moaned. "And my day just got even worse."

Lynch hefted his replenished RPC in both hands. "Walk and talk?" he suggested.

With plasma blasts echoing everywhere, he hurried around the corner. Glancing back, he was pleased to see them all following him—even the Empress. "Do I need to mow down some Sau Daran zombies for you?"

"Yes," said the Empress.

"No," said Ezra.

"What else can we do?" asked Isabella, pushing past the Empress to match pace with Lynch. "I can't run forever. They just keep coming."

"So do something else," suggested Lynch.

Isabella waved her arms at the ship's corridor. "Trying that!" she cried in a sarcastic sing-song voice. "And yet we're still running!"

Lynch scythed down a pair of Rangers in his path. Ignoring the weight of his RPC, he ran around their stunned, slowly collapsing bodies so fast he barely heard their armour clatter behind him. Although he trusted everyone to try to keep up with his rapid pace, he worried he would be too fast for Ezra. But when he glanced back, the man was sprinting just fine on his synthetic blades.

As they rushed through an intersection, Lynch realised he had made a deadly mistake. Here, tight bulkheads broadened out to house endless storage lockers, munitions crates and a scattering of discarded toolkits. Beside them were exposed, sparking wall panels where repairs had been abandoned in a hurry. The intersection was also open enough to invite flurries of hot plasma blasts from every direction, stinging the air around them like screaming hornets. It was, in hindsight, an omnishambles of a place to get ambushed.

"Keep moving!" Lynch shouted over floods of scalding airborne plasma. "I'll make a path!" Ducking and twisting—and at one point tripping, although he hoped no one noticed—Lynch evaded the plasma blasts hurtling at them. He rolled onto one knee, picked a direction at random, levelled the long barrels of his RPC and let rip. When there were no returning plasma blasts from where he had aimed—only smoke, flames and screams—Lynch eased off the trigger.

With a whisper of purple smoke, Isabella stole Ezra and a seething Empress out of the path of more plasma blasts. Purple smoke emerged on the other side of the intersection as she reappeared where Lynch had fried their aggressors.

Abruptly, Isabella's face soured. "There's a portal coming!" she shouted across the intersection.

The air was thick with plasma. Lynch flattened himself to the floor, flinching as hot blasts landed all around him. "Take us out of here then!" he shouted back.

"Where to?" Even at this distance, he could tell her expression was somewhere between desperate and furious. He knew both those emotions only too well. "I can't keep running!" she cried, locking eyes with him through the chaos of smoke and plasma fire between them. Then she and everything else disappeared behind the acrid smoke from the scorching plasma blasts striking the floor around him.

At the heart of the intersection, the bright blue light of a Sau Daran portal exploded out of the smoke. Because life wasn't complicated enough. Gravity was misbehaving even worse than Lynch during the last lesson of school on a Friday. His heavy RPC drifted out of his hands. As he grabbed it back, he found he was leaving the floor too. Gravity waved goodbye completely. The tide of flashing plasma subsided as the shadows of his attackers drifted off the deck and up into the intersection's veil of smoke and searing blue light. Their struggling, floating bodies were joined by every munitions crate, every loose panel, every abandoned toolkit, every charred corpse—everything that wasn't bolted down.

Aiming his RPC away from where he had last seen Isabella, Lynch squeezed the trigger. A blaze of plasma burst from the huge gun's spinning barrels, pushing Lynch backwards through the air as though he had activated a jetpack. Despite the seriousness of the situation, he couldn't hide a grin as he glided backwards through the air. He shouldered aside any floating Rangers who got in his way, and disappeared into the next cloud of acrid smoke before their shots could land.

Lynch wondered what all the fuss was about when it came to Sau Daran portals. Floating through the air, knocking enemies aside, it didn't seem so bad. A bolt of lightning streaked out of the smoke, frying the floating PROXUS Ranger next to him so fiercely that Lynch could swear he saw their skeleton through their armour. Okay, so there was one downside. A flurry of forked lightning exploded in more tributaries of light that struck a cluster of PROXUS Silver Fists in a cavalcade of sparks and screams. Armour melted... Flesh fried... Okay, so there were several downsides.

Gravity came to its senses and started behaving far faster than Lynch had in any classroom back on Earth. He landed hard on his back, before his chest broke the fall of his RPC with a grunt.

The Empress glared down at him. "Imbecile."

Lynch was still grinning nastily at her as Isabella helped him to his feet. He hauled his RPC off the floor. "I've already put plenty of your clones in the ground," Lynch warned the Empress. A plasma blast singed the wall behind him, but he didn't stop staring, snarling, leering.

"How helpful, I should thank you for making the Known Galaxies a safer place for me."

Isabella's human hand pulled on the sleeve of Lynch's billowing jacket. "We don't have time for this. Enough people here want to kill us already, without you adding to the list."

As though keen to announce themselves and secure a place on the list of enemies Isabella looked primed to reel off, metal feet thundered towards them through the smoke. Confused shouts and stray plasma blasts bled out of the chaos behind them.

Lynch rolled his eyes at Isabella. "That'll be those Sau Daran zombies you warned me about?"

"Yeah, no shit," replied Isabella. "Are you running us in circles or are we going somewhere?"

Lynch checked his bearings. One of the few positives about PROXUS ships was that they came off a production line. Navigating ships of the same class was always the same game of déjà vu, albeit with more people trying to kill him each time. Not that Lynch even needed to remember. The Sau Daran technology keeping his face together offered more benefits than pinpoint targeting. With a thought, he pulled up the schematics for a Fury-class warship and let the circuitry behind the metal plate in his face tell him where to go.

"Oh, we're going places," Lynch assured Isabella after only a short pause.

But she was staring over his shoulder. He glanced around. At first all he saw was the unsettling green glare of their eyes. Then they emerged from the smoke. A press of Sau Daran zombies storming towards them. Red plasma flashed from scattered pockets of surviving PROXUS forces.

"Can we go places faster?" asked Isabella.

Lynch fastened his RPC to a sling over his back and felt his shoulder take the weight. "No worries." He took off at a sprint and hoped the rest would follow.

Their progress went as well as anyone could have expected intruders on a Fury-class PROXUS warship to fare. Around every corner a plasma rifle waited to eviscerate them, while forever biting at their heels was the unrelenting charge of Sau Daran zombies.

An increasingly breathless and bloodied Lynch was relieved when he tumbled around the final corner and into their destination. Even more so when everyone else hurried inside after him. Everyone apart from the Empress, which brought a hopeful smile to Lynch's face. However, his hopes were dashed when, last around the corner, the Empress nimbly danced over the splayed bodies on the chamber's floor and slammed her fist into the door controls.

Thick, heavy doors slid shut violently from both sides of the entrance, hissing and groaning as they aimed to meet in the middle. Riding the crest of a ravenous wave of black metal, a grasping metal hand reached through the doorway at Lynch. The doors slammed shut, crushing the Sau Daran zombie's leaking forearm.

Isabella backed away from the trapped metal hand's twitching, grasping fingers. "Where are we?"

Ringed by a perimeter of screens and dials, the chamber was dominated by a black sphere the size of a hot air balloon. It was secured in slender scaffolding that reached up and down from the rest of the chamber to hold it safe. Lynch gestured. "Usually, this is the most heavily guarded room in any PROXUS ship." He looked away, distracted. There were a lot of bodies scattered throughout the chamber, many gripping their plasma pistols, rifles and carbines as though they expected to need them in the afterlife. "But my team got here before us." Each body lay where they had fallen, whether over a workstation, railings or the floor, their final resting places forming a circle of charred death around the black sphere. Some wore PROXUS armour, others a motley of non-descript military gear like Lynch. Grimly, he used his boot to roll over the nearest body. He bowed his head.

"You crafty dpresh," purred the Empress. "You're going to blow their star drive."

"Seemed rude not to, while I'm here." Lynch stared at the face of his friend, where once familiar contours were spoiled by black burns and a slack, vacant expression. A metallic groan ushered from the closed door, followed by a crescendo of pounding metal. Still, he didn't turn. Didn't look up. Isabella said something, but her words didn't register.

Finally, reluctantly, he glanced at the rest of the chamber, which was dominated by a single purpose. The black sphere. It looked like every other star drive Lynch had seen. And destroyed. The star drives on smaller ships were supposed to be tinier—he'd been told some could even fit in the palm of his hand. But he had only seen the star drives he had been tasked to blow up, along with whatever PROXUS warship it was powering.

"What?" he asked.

Isabella pointed at the huge indentations that had been punched into the door from outside. "I said we don't have long before I need to take us out of here. They're coming through."

"Sure, whatever." Lynch reached over his shoulder for his satchel and the explosive charges stored inside. He felt down the long barrels of his RPC, patting down his shoulder, his back, searching for wherever the satchel had slid. All he retrieved was a torn strap. The satchel was gone—along with all his charges.

More indentations hammered into the door, which bent and groaned and buckled under the strain. Lynch's eyes settled on the nuclear weapons clutched in Ezra's arms. "Give me one of those," he urged. He reached for the silver cylinders, but Ezra backed away.

"You're not killing them."

"Who?"

Ezra glanced at the shaking door behind them. Lynch swore filthily, blending Earth dialects with the saltiest phrases he had picked up in the darkest corners of the Known Galaxies. "Don't make me take it off you."

Ezra was unmoved. "You can certainly try."

The door shook again. The trapped, twitching hand writhed, spun and found purchase around the door. It gripped the door's dented face and pulled hard.

"My friends died so we could take out this warship," snarled Lynch. "Let me get the job done."

Ezra shook his head. "Absolutely not. You are not harming a single Sau Daran."

With a jolt, the door was prised further open by the faintest crack. The tips of its fingers disappeared into the door's surface, tightening its grip and pulling hard. More metal fingers from more hands squeezed into the opening where the hand was trapped—every finger wriggling and clutching to widen the gap.

"Why would you care?!" cried Lynch. From Ezra's reaction, Lynch could imagine the cruel contortions spreading over his own face, but he didn't have time for this. He didn't have time for any of this. "They want to kill you. They're already dead. Give me the nukes!"

Ezra held the trio of cylinders even closer, as though they were his own children. "No chance. I've played this game and it never works out. Let them live."

Lynch felt the respect draining from his face, felt his lip curling into something ugly. "You know jack if you think letting everyone live makes the universe a safer place. This ship wiped out a whole colony. Murdered every man, woman and child on the planet's surface. They knew what they were doing. They just wanted to take out another clone of the Empress and it didn't matter that she was hiding with people who couldn't give a damn about PROXUS or the Resistance. They didn't even know who she was!"

With a series of screeches, the doorway widened by one—two—three more fingers. Through the gap, a glowing green eye surveyed them.

Lynch lunged at Ezra, forcing him back against the railing. It stopped him falling onto the star drive. "I'm here to kill the right people because they killed the wrong people. I'm a sick bastard and I'm okay with that because it gets the job done."

Unblinking, Ezra's milky eyes stared back. "Do whatever you want to PROXUS but leave the Sau Darans out of it."

Another screech.

Four fingers.

A hand.

A final shove.

Both sides of the door creaked aside, wilting like a torn sheet of tinfoil. Sau Daran zombies swept inside the star drive's chamber, all surging metal limbs and gnashing teeth. Their glowing green eyes were devoid of life but so very, very hungry.

"Hold on!" shouted Isabella.

She reached out her hands.

The Empress was the fastest to grab one.

Lynch was between Ezra and Isabella. Raising his forearm against Ezra's throat, he pinned him to the railing. "You sure you want to be on their side? They look pretty dangerous to me."

"You'll die…" murmured Ezra, his face a mess of confusion and panic.

"I've already lived," said Lynch. "It was mostly shit."

Black metal bodies closed in. A swirl of purple smoke vanished Isabella and the Empress elsewhere. They reappeared in another gasp of purple smoke on the far side of the ringed floor that encircled the star drive. Not far from danger, but precious seconds out of reach.

Keeping his terror under lock and key, Lynch smiled nastily at Ezra. "Time to find out how thankful they are for you saving them." Unpinning Ezra's throat, he eased his arm around the man's shoulder as though they had been chums all along. "Ready to die, mate?"

Sau Daran feet thundered, stomped, charged, leaped, then landed—far away. Or, at least, far *enough* away.

Their metal fingers weren't clawing at flesh. They were clinging to the black sphere. To the star drive. They all landed on its outer shell, every shape and size of Sau Daran zombie, from wriggling pint-sized scuttlers to lumbering multi-limbed giants, climbing over the black sphere with rabid fervour. The Empress, Lynch, Ezra and even Isabella were forgotten. Instead, metal teeth bit into the star drive's black casing. Fingers scraped desperately against its shell. Fractures appeared. They splintered across the exterior of the star drive, leaking rogue smears of colour. Purples. Blues. Greens. Golds. Reds. Rainbows of drifting light bled from every scratch in the star drive's surface, lacing its dark shell with blinding streaks of searing neon.

Sau Daran zombies gorged on the light.

It was a buffet.

And a distraction

Lynch slipped a silver cylinder from Ezra's arms. His fingers tapped the keypad as proficiently as if it were a smart phone plucked from his pocket. A countdown began on its digital display. He glanced up, ready to hurl the nuclear weapon at the star drive and hope to Hell that Isabella vanished them out of this mess before their time was up.

But he hesitated.

The Sau Darans weren't behaving like zombies. Their bodies still clung to the star drive, but nothing else was as it had been. Black ash flaked from their metal bodies and fell in a shower of dark snow past the railings and onto the floor. Beneath it, their bodies shone silver.

Ghastly green eyes died and relented, rekindling a steadier red glow. Upon awaking, they processed the chamber as though for the first time. Every dark metal figure that rushed inside flung itself not at Isabella, but at the star drive. And took a bite. Every creature who slipped their darkness replaced flakes of black metal with a replenished sheen of invigorated silver.

"What's happening?" Isabella shouted across the chamber.

"Who knows!" Lynch shouted back. He tried to find the right words, but everything he settled on sounded ridiculous so he stopped trying. He cancelled the nuke's countdown. "Why aren't they eating us?"

Looking imperious, and didn't she know it, the Empress strode away from Isabella and leaned over the railing. "Are you so foolish, dpresh?" she called to Lynch around the bulge of the star drive. "Open your eyes!"

Lynch snarled, readying both barrels of his reply. But he held back, instead watching the Sau Darans. More shining silver bodies with glowing red eyes landed on the floor below the star drive. First, they formed a protective ring around Isabella. Then, leaping far closer than comfort, they formed a ring around Lynch and Ezra.

It needn't have mattered.

The green-eyed, rabid black metal zombies surging into the chamber took one greedy look at the star drive and leaped straight for it. Snapping at its shell with metal teeth, they dreamily devoured the rainbow of vapours escaping through its cracks.

Purple smoke swept Isabella and the Empress to Lynch and Ezra.

"Why aren't we dead?" asked Lynch.

Isabella breathed in a lungful of air as though it was her first in a long while. "They're regenerating. Healing. Coming back to life."

"No way," replied Lynch.

"We saw it when they ate a..." Isabella faltered for a moment, "when they... ate a Sau Daran god."

"Oh, well that's fine then," said Lynch. He eyed the ring of silver bodies around them. "That's not at all worrying." His eyes flitted to Ezra. "So, those nukes..."

"You don't need them," insisted Isabella.

Curiously, Lynch leaned over the nearest silver shoulder so his lips were where their ears might have been. "Are you going to kill us?" he asked bluntly.

Violently, the silver head spun towards Lynch. It moved with such ferocity he nearly shat himself, which he chose not to share with anyone, but it was impossible to hide falling over backwards as though he had been hit by a jump scare in a horror film. He adopted a customary snarl from where he had landed. "Well, are you?"

The silver head spun back towards the rest of the chamber, as though scanning for threats and ignoring Lynch. He drew back, shrugged weakly. "This is insane."

"No," insisted the Empress, "it's science." Lynch gave her a blank stare. The Empress sighed. "PROXUS harvested the Sau Daran gods for their clean energy. We used them to build star drives for all our ships, all our cities. The first Sau Daran zombie we met decided eating a Sau Daran god was more appealing than worshipping it, and as a result it ceased to be so venting braindead. Star drives contain the same harvested energy as that god."

"This isn't the only star drive though, is it?" Isabella's defiance was palpable. It was in her stance. Her smile. Her eyes. And without doubt, burning in her heart. "Let's give them more to feed on."

"Unthinkable," muttered the Empress.

Hauling himself upright, Lynch peered around the nearest silver Sau Daran. Still, the green-eyed dark metal creatures were rushing through the doorway, ignoring Isabella and hurling themselves at the star drive.

"What's the biggest source of this clean energy?" asked Isabella.

"That's easy," said Lynch.

"Quiet!" snapped the Empress.

Lynch grinned. Etched into the Sau Daran circuitry in his head was every memory First Duke Striker had ever lived—at least, up until the point the Empress had copied Striker's ID chip and jury-rigged it into his skull three years ago. No one in the Known Galaxies had harboured more secrets than the Empress' spy master. "Xarr," Lynch told them.

The Empress' face grew even frostier than when he had shot a plasma blast through that same face to trigger the release of all her clones.

Isabella shook her head. "Xarr's too dangerous."

"You want to do something special? Take a risk." Lynch grinned wider. "All that clean energy is stored on Xarr, ready to charge every ship, every battle station, every city in PROXUS. One big power reserve." He felt his face harden. "Although that murderer would rather take Moon there and add her to that power." Lynch drew his plasma pistol. "That's all she wants. Power. Energy. You dead. We'd be better off if I killed her again."

"Hold on, she knows so many things we don't."

Lynch snorted. "What does she know that we can't find out some other way?"

"If we need to get to Xarr she can probably help."

The Empress sighed. "And why would I risk going back to Xarr? If you fail, they'll kill me. If you succeed, PROXUS will be crippled. Without our primary supply of clean energy, when our fleets return for replenishment they will fall out of the sky."

Isabella squared up to the Empress. "Because the Sau Daran zombies we'll lead to Xarr will attack the other Empress clones. Because if we get every Sau Daran zombie to your power reserve on Xarr, we can save them all. And because I think these Sau Darans with the red eyes and silver bodies are more interested in my safety than yours. Want to find out?"

A silver head spun 180 degrees, threw them a cheerful red wink and spun back around. After three years of freedom fighting across the Known Galaxies, assassinating an Empress and dating an alien god, Lynch had never seen anything as terrifying.

"Our cities will go dark," argued the Empress. "Our people will suffer."

"You don't have any other power on Xarr?"

"No," lied the Empress.

"Yes," said Lynch. "All the old power stations."

"Dirty power. Unusable. It destroyed our atmosphere! It can't give us what we need."

"She means it won't power her precious ships and battle stations. The fleets would need to land, but the cities and undercities would be fine. No one would die."

The Empress glared. "It would destroy PROXUS." Reluctantly, she eyed the silver bodies surrounding them. "However, when in doubt… burn everything down. Then gather up the ashes in a fist."

"You can get me there?" Isabella asked hopefully.

"Impossible." The Empress bared her teeth. "I've been away too long. No Xarr for us, then. What a pity. What's your next plan?"

"What about Striker?" suggested Ezra. "He might know a way to get in."

"Striker's dead," said the Empress scornfully.

Ezra didn't blink. "Actually, he's not. He's been helping one of the other Empresses. He's out there somewhere, tracking *Haven*."

"We don't need Striker. You've got me." Lynch tapped the black metal plate on his face. "She gave me Striker's ID chip, remember?"

"Fine, so you get us there," the Empress cut in frostily. "And then we do what, exactly? Die? I can do that here."

"Start your own rebellion on Xarr," he suggested. "Screw over whichever clone's running the place."

The Empress scoffed. "Xarr is the most fortified planet in the Known Galaxies. Even I don't have the resources to start a rebellion on my own."

Distractedly, Ezra laid a reverential hand on the silver shoulder of a resurrected Sau Daran. "But you have some resources there, don't you?"

Her face grew even more severe. "Of course."

Closing his eyes, Ezra pressed his cheek against a silver shoulder blade. "And so do the other clones who had to leave Xarr?"

"Obviously."

"We've got another Empress locked up on *Haven*."

"Another?" Isabella rolled her eyes. "Of course."

Lynch whistled. The growing potential for chaos was enthralling. "How many coups do we need?"

"Two might be enough," the Empress admitted grimly. "Perhaps it's time to burn down everything."

CHAPTER THIRTY-NINE

An armoured glove extended towards Fleur. Its palm was open. "How about now?" asked the Slave Empress. "If I'm going to die, I would rather it was with a gun in my hand. I won a war against these things. I know how to fight them."

"Whoever you think you fought in that bloodbath, in that *genocide* you call a war, *they* are something else."

The charging horde was almost within range. Close enough to see their snarling metal faces, dark bodies ravaged by ancient wounds, green fluids oozing from jagged fissures, limbs flying in every direction. There was nothing in their green eyes except ravenous hunger. No semblance of sentience. Behind them, evanescent surges of blue light sparked, flickered and died. Like Isabella, the portal was gone. Now, there was only the horde.

Fleur sighed, letting her irritation show. "But I would rather we survived this. Big man?"

"I ain't givin' no Empress my gun."

Huffing airily, Count Fontaine rolled his eyes. "Well she cannot possibly have mine."

Braga waved her axe and plasma pistol, demonstrating how both hands were already full and primed for action.

"You're hardly using both of yours," argued the Empress, pointing her armoured fist at Beauregard's withered left arm. Her voice rallied towards a crescendo. "So I shall ask again… Don't any of you dpreshes want to survive this?"

Braga lifted her chin and eyeballed the Empress, but nonetheless Beauregard stepped forward. Reluctantly, his good hand drew his spare plasma pistol and aimed it at the Empress. With a blur of twirling fingers, he flipped the pistol around so its grip was facing her. "If you even look like shootin' me, I'll drop you."

The Empress smiled nastily. "The best of luck to you." With a hiss, her armoured glove detached and clattered onto the road. Her bare fingers grasped the pistol.

"The best of luck to all of us!" Fleur shouted with galaxies more sincerity than the Empress, snatching her last opportunity for words before they opened fire. The horde was too close now. The rest of her talking would have to be done with a plasma pistol.

A cloud of black metal descended on them. The dark chaos was streaked with splashes of green fluid, hot flashes of red plasma, sparks of purple lightning. Soon, too much was moving too fast in the thick of too many bodies for Fleur to catch even a glimpse of her companions. But she could hear the whine of their plasma pistols nearby, accented by the hiss and spit of blades coated in purple lightning severing more metal limbs.

Fleur's pistol blazed. Gnawing metal teeth bit her. Slicing metal claws left rivers of blood where they stung her. Metal arms pummelled her. Battered her. Crushed her beneath their inhuman weight. With every bruise, with every cut, she spun away and found only more teeth and claws to evade. She dodged out of their grasp.

Kicked. Rolled. Ducked. Tumbled. Whenever she fell, she jumped back up with no time to think or die.

Out of the maelstrom, an unseen metal fist pounded the back of her head. She fell again, her skull aching like an eggshell ready to crack. This time, she didn't get up. Her dazed limbs and stunned head wouldn't obey.

Peering up at dizzying shadows, she cast hot light into the darkness with her plasma pistol. Metal bodies staggered over her—smoking, charred and reeking of industrial innards that didn't belong in any breathable atmosphere, let alone inside her lungs. Not that she was using those much. A hollow gasp escaped her bloodied lips as she dragged in a whisper of oxygen.

A trio of glowing green eyes leered over her. They were evenly spaced across the front of a gnashing metal face that was all teeth and green, oozing scars. Heavy metal limbs pinned her waist. Pinned her collar bone. Pinned her kicking feet. Her plasma pistol tumbled from her grip as the Sau Daran zombie squeezed her forearm.

Behind her, Count Fontaine's rapier flashed with purple sparks, illuminating the dying light of an eye socket as he punctured it straight through. Withdrawing his blade with a flourish, he swept aside to dodge the injured zombie's clumsy retaliation and stung another with a flurry of precise strikes.

His gaze travelled through the melee separating him from Fleur. In a heartbeat, he took in the sight of her struggling beneath the jaws of a Sau Daran zombie. Their eyes locked. After a hesitation that didn't last anywhere near long enough, he turned his back. Retreating, he cut a path to safety. His singing purple blade cut magnificent arcs of whirling death and lightning that flickered further and further from Fleur, growing dimmer and dimmer until the light of his blade was lost.

Then all Fleur could see were three green eyes looking down at her hungrily. And teeth. So many sharp teeth. They filled her vision with twin rows of metal peaks that parted in anticipation of her flesh.

Searing light burst through the gaping jaws.

Purple light.

An axe head wreathed in lightning shuddered out of the Sau Daran zombie's mouth, nearly taking Fleur's face off as well. The blade swung up and away from her, scorching her cheeks with vagrant sparks of purple. It continued its path from the back of the metal head and out the front, severing the upper and lower jaw as it burst back into the daylight.

A calloused hand returned Fleur's plasma pistol, then pulled her upright. "Get that sexy arse out of the dirt," purred a welcome voice. "This isn't the time to be lying around while the rest of us do all the work."

Fleur had no time to reply. Dark metal bodies were closing in around them, pressing her back-to-back with her wife. Hot, red plasma from Fleur and Braga's plasma pistols ate them up, yet it barely held back the ring of grasping claws.

Every green light that faded from their eyes was another Sau Daran soul finally free from this cycle of violence. Fleur had hoped life would be better after she left PROXUS, but while her allegiance may have shifted and a civil war begun, nothing about the Known Galaxies had ever really changed. It was as violent as ever. There was no justice or injustice that wasn't accompanied by an ultimatum at the hot end of a plasma pistol.

At the edge of her vision, the woman she loved conjured blazing flashes of plasma everywhere. Braga would never stop shooting. Never stop swinging. Never give up. The warmth of her back rubbed against the scar on Fleur's shoulder. The slick sweat from her trailing blue hair dampened the nape of Fleur's neck. Purple electricity surged through metal shell after metal shell with every furious blow Braga unleashed.

Fleur saw no hope of survival and she was too entrenched in a lifetime of violence to recognise anything resembling hope that didn't look like a plasma pistol. But if she did escape this carnage, she promised herself she would escape her own cycle of violence too. Her capacity for death had overreached her magnitude for living. She wanted no more of it. She wanted out. For however many cycles she lived after this, she would choose peace. Find somewhere quiet to live, where plasma pistols held no currency and life was gentler on the soul. It was an easy promise to make with death so certain, so imminent.

When all hope was lost.

Beyond the press of dark metal bodies, Fleur glimpsed far-off flashes of light descending from the sky. Not purple lightning. Not red plasma. Thick, deafening bolts of sizzling green energy from a Scimitar-class starfighter. The green blasts carved searing ruts down the road and scythed through the ravenous crowd. Metal limbs were eviscerated. Dark shells incinerated. All the metal zombies that were struck evaporated. The rest were sent flying. By the time their smoking shells landed and lay still, the green glow had finally faded from their eyes.

The force of the explosions hurled Fleur high into the air. Her landing felt like it broke more than a few bones, but she didn't care. Lying in a daze, she stared up at the sky and watched the starfighter swoop overhead.

Hope had arrived and his name was Dash.

A moment earlier and she could have gotten away with it. But she had made a promise. Perhaps the universe had spoken. Perhaps her grim cycle of violence really could end. Perhaps she would find peace after all. Or, at least, try to find it. If she didn't bleed out first.

CHAPTER FORTY

Like ants in a cathedral, Isabella's growing team was instantly dwarfed by the gargantuan interior of Xarr's royal vault.

With purple smoke still fading off her, she swiftly retreated from the throng of hands who had relied on her touch to bring them here. The hands of those she cared for—Ezra, even Lynch. The hands of those she wished were dead—Therapy Empress and the new Empress from *Haven*, her face left unrecognisable from old plasma burns. They had collected her from *Haven*, before escaping another herd of grasping, portal-leaping Sau Daran zombies, who would keep *Haven* and their crew busy until Isabella was successful on Xarr. Or died trying. But she would be successful here. She had to be— the lives of every Sau Daran depended on her.

Staggering out of everyone's reach, Isabella composed herself and took in this fresh view with a deep breath of awe. The vaulted ceiling was supported by columns of polished crimson, which were speckled and swirled like marble. Between every column, ornate ivory arches swept overhead and glowed with enough light to reach the vault's deepest corners.

Yet there was barely enough space for Isabella to move. The floor and every wall were filled with the Empress' treasure hoard. Weapons. Machines. Jewels. Outfits. Mysterious devices. A trove of mementos Isabella couldn't begin to fathom. Except one. On the obsidian podium beside her lay a long-forgotten object Isabella hadn't seen for three years. There was no life behind the cracked screen of her old phone, but it was exactly where Lynch had promised it would be. Once he had reminded her it existed, she had remembered it well enough to vanish them all here.

"What did I tell you?" asked Lynch, as cocky as ever.

"Impossible!" Acerbic incredulity spat from Therapy Empress' mouth. She glared at Isabella's broken phone. "Not even Striker knew I kept that trophy."

"A trophy of his failure?" Lynch laughed in her face. He looked like an overconfident chimp taunting a furious, hungry lioness. "You had an agent steal Isabella's phone and sneak off *Black Nebula* while everyone was hunting Isabella. Striker nearly ordered their shuttle blasted out of space just to spite you. And he knew you kept everything that mattered to you here. Striker knew *everything*. Thanks for his ID chip. Without it, I couldn't have done half the things I've done. Including killing so many of you."

"Enough!" snapped Therapy Empress. Defensively, she pulled her fluffy cardigan tighter around her shoulders. "Don't bait me. Given what's in here, if I wanted you dead I would have killed you already."

Tellingly, both Empresses glanced in the same direction. Isabella, Ezra and Lynch tracked their gaze to one corner of the vault, where a giant headless suit of metal armour stood beside the wall. Only it looked more like a vehicle than a suit—a vehicle someone could step inside and use to walk around in. Isabella had seen mech armour in some of the best and worst sci-fi she had ever watched, and now she was staring in wonder at a real one. The armour was as tall as a lamppost, with thick arms hanging at its flanks. Dormant, for now. Its thick, shining carapace was pocked with a multitude of scratches, dents and vicious burns.

Let's not kid ourselves.

About what?

Don't act all innocent—I can read your thoughts, remember?

So?

So we both know someone's going to be wearing that mech suit when we leave. And I think it should be us!

With urgency reinvigorated and violence promised, Therapy Empress paced through the claustrophobic maze of treasures towards the royal vault's grandiose double doors. The other Empress wasn't far behind. Accelerating fast enough to slip from Therapy Empress' wake, come alongside and match speed, the Empress with the burns was perfectly in step when they arrived at the towering vault doors and a floating disc of black glass.

They stopped, stared each other down. A perfect stand-off. Had Isabella not been running for her life since finding the Spark what felt like an eternity ago, she would have laughed at how ridiculous they looked. But the thought of what was chasing her and what would happen to those same Sau Darans if she failed was sobering enough to smother any hint of a smile. Like the ghosts of Christmases Past, Present and Future come all at once, only the shadow of her duty loomed larger and grimmer.

"What is that?" asked Isabella. She pointed at the black glass disc floating in front of the Empresses.

"Biometric scanner," muttered Lynch as he watched the unfolding drama. "Our way out of here, thanks to the shit company we keep."

The two Empresses stared each other down at the scanner. When their mirrored comical showdown finally surrendered to necessity, it was Therapy Empress who held her scowling face up to the glass disc. Once the double doors hissed open, she was first through and marching out into a colossal corridor beyond.

"Don't trust her," one Empress cautioned Isabella, as she stole out of the vault in pursuit of a rebellion.

"She's the one you can't trust," the other Empress tossed over her shoulder in warning.

"Like I'd trust either of you," Isabella muttered darkly. She looked away to find Lynch picking his way through the Empress' hoard. "Where are you going?" she called. Then her eyes followed his path and where it was leading.

Hands off! We called it first.

Arriving at the mech suit, Lynch dropped his impractically large, completely unwieldy plasma cannon. Forgotten and usurped, the gun clattered onto a stack of crates bearing the PROXUS seal. Lynch stroked one of the armour's heavy metal arms like it was a newborn. Each metal finger was larger than his head. On the top of its metal fist, his fingers ran over what looked like a ring of missiles. Lynch smiled wider.

Relax, it's not like he can get inside.

Climbing the handholds spaced up the back of the armour, Lynch pressed a hidden pressure seal. A panel retracted, revealing a small node that projected a holo keypad into the air. Lynch's fingers danced over the floating symbols. They flashed blue, then trumpeted a happy fanfare of beeps. With a hiss, the mech suit's chest levered open. Inside, an empty cockpit waited.

"Striker knows everything!" he crowed. Hanging off the giant armour, Lynch grinned infuriatingly. "Mind if I take it for a ride?"

Over your dead body. Tell him it's mine.

Catching Isabella's hesitation, Lynch smiled. "Okay, if she wants it, she can have it."

Fine, he can have it.

What?

It's fine. Look at his little face? He's so happy.

You two are—

—adorable?—

—insufferable.

Isabella waved a dismissive hand at the giant armour. "It's all yours. Apparently."

Something gentler and loving awoke in Lynch's face as he stared at her, or perhaps not at her but at who he imagined inside her. Then it was gone, replaced by unbridled glee as he leaped into the cockpit and began flicking switches like he knew what he was doing.

With both Empresses long gone and likely dissolving into Xarr's capital to unite with their forces, the vault's huge double doors slid shut once more.

Between the metallic taste on her tongue and the somersaults her stomach had started performing, Isabella was in no doubt about what was coming next. "Literally the worst timing," she moaned. "Everyone, we're about to have company!"

"Great!" Ezra pointed nervously at the closed double doors. "We can get those open again without the Empresses, right?"

"These might help," suggested Ezra, holding up his armful of nuclear weapons. "They'll blow those doors."

Isabella shook her head. "And the rest of the city."

Ezra looked from Isabella's expression to the silver cylinders piled up in his arms. "Can I put these down?"

"Please do."

With relief sweating down his face, Ezra finally—and carefully—discarded the three silver cylinders.

Moments later, a spiralling rocket shot from the mech suit's arm and a huge explosion parted the doors with a roar of twisting, complaining metal. "Woohoo!" Lynch cried over the comm. "Come on!"

Oh, kill me now.

But he's so happy!

Isabella and Ezra hurried after Lynch's new toy, rushing out of the vault and into a vast corridor whose scale was better suited to mech suits than humans. Amid the shadows, a crisp horizontal line of white light shone along each wall. Behind them, Isabella caught the eerie blue glow of a portal awakening in the vault. "Striker knows how to get to where they store all their clean energy, right?"

"He *did*," Lynch replied over the comm.

Oh seriously, don't ask! He only said it that way to make you ask.

How can I not ask?

"What do you mean… did?" asked Isabella.

The mech suit lurched sideways, parting with another missile that punched a burning hole through the corridor's wall. Isabella and Ezra peered around one arm of the mech suit and surveyed the flaming debris. A freshly revealed chasm led down to a platformed walkway far below.

"Well," said Lynch over the comm, "I think I can make some shortcuts."

CHAPTER FORTY-ONE

Lynch's borrowed mech suit forged a flaming path through any resistance from PROXUS ground troops, not to mention any walls and floors blocking his shortcuts. They descended deeper into Xarr, Lynch leaping in the vanguard and Isabella vanishing herself and Ezra after his trail of destruction. Deeper below Xarr's uninhabitable surface. Deeper across the undercity's suspended walkways and down endless passages. Deeper as they vaulted the undercity's pallid horizons and grey subterranean skylines.

Whenever Isabella propelled herself and Ezra across the urban horizon with swirls of purple smoke to catch up with Lynch, a cold blue glow and fresh lightning awakened behind her. The thunder of metal feet haunted their footfalls. Relentless Sau Daran pursuit chased them over every rooftop they vaulted, down every walkway, tunnel and corridor.

Isabella stopped at the latest jagged hole Lynch had blown through a tunnel. The edges of the hole glowed hot, revealing a cross-section of white innards smeared black with ash. The tunnel's floor was scattered with hunks of molten wall. Through the improvised door Lynch had fashioned with military grade explosives, Isabella saw nothing but the hollow shadows of a vast grey chasm beyond.

"This is it!" Lynch shouted over the comm. "We're here!" Far below, at the chasm's heart, was a final crossroads. Like motorways engineered for giants, three monolithic walkways intersected an immense circular platform. One of the mech's fingers pointed down through the hole. "That platform is on top of where they store the star energy." The finger reversed its trajectory, aiming above them. "That's where it goes."

Isabella looked up. Far above the circular platform, far above the tunnel she was staring out of, loomed titanic docking stations large enough for warships, perhaps even battle stations, to find a berth. The docking stations were all sleek metal and glowing lights. So many that they disappeared further and higher into the chasm than Isabella could discern.

However, she was far more concerned about what was occurring on the three walkways. There was movement below. A lot of movement. She hadn't noticed it at first because their armour was as dark as the walkways. Now she saw it, she couldn't unsee it. All three of the walkways were overflowing with a nightmarish black tide of what must have been hundreds of thousands of armoured bodies surging towards the intersection. A rhythmic rumbling reached her ears. The endless, persistent stomp of armoured boots.

"Can't let them get there first!" Lynch leaped out of the hole. Isabella watched him fall for what felt like forever before his mech suit landed like a ragdoll on the circular platform.

Another storm of metallic footfalls echoed along the tunnel towards her, signalling there was no end yet to their Sau Daran pursuit.

That's our cue.

Let's finish this.

Purple smoke took her and Ezra down to the sleek, black artificial surface of the circular platform. Beside them, Lynch picked himself up. Stretching the mech suit's mechanical arms, he limbered up for battle.

Isabella stared down the walkways, where within moments a first wave of heavy armour and bristling rifles would crash down on them from all sides.

Why is no one ever happy to see us?

I have no idea. We're lovely!

Plasma blasts flared on two of the three crowded walkways. Isabella flinched, but for once the plasma fire wasn't aimed at her or her companions. Clusters of red plasma blazed in pockets of the crowd, slowing the onrushing PROXUS soldiers. Helmets turned back and forth on those two walkways, trying to make sense of the chaos as deadly red flashes echoed through a gleaming sea of polished armour.

Isabella stared at the chaos of PROXUS soldiers firing on each other. "That'll be the Empress."

"Which one?" asked Ezra.

"Both? Who cares! We don't have long until the next portal finds us." Even over the comm, Isabella had to hold her gauntlet right up to her lips to be sure Lynch would hear her next comment over the deafening confrontation on the walkways. But instead of shouting, she stared at the glowing display on her gauntlet. This close to her eyes, the tiny symbol indicating a connection with another device was impossible to miss. Isabella tapped the symbol. Talyn's face appeared through what must have been a camera on his suit of wires and circuitry. Nova Sky piloted his face into the sneer of someone who thought they'd already won.

Isabella didn't bother cutting the connection—there was no point now. But she did swipe his video feed into oblivion so she didn't have to look at Nova Sky occupying Talyn's face for another heart wrenching second.

Prick.

This is how he's been tracking us?

Absolute prick.

The portals… He's not tracking me. He's just tracking your gauntlet.

Total prick.

Like he's just MI5? CIA? FB-bloody-I?

Complete prick.

He just used his power. That's not fair!

I guess we want them here anyway. We want to save them all, right?

Of course. But he's still a—

Monumental prick.

"Where do we go?" Isabella shouted into her gauntlet at Lynch, although she would have preferred to instead toss her compromised device over the edge of the platform and into the chasm. Into oblivion.

Lynch's mech suit stepped in front of Isabella and Ezra, marching off the circular platform to become a lone figure at the start of a giant walkway. He had picked the only walkway where the progress of onrushing armoured PROXUS soldiers was unhalted, and from where no mutinous blasts of plasma had yet ushered. Once more, Isabella was reminded of ants in a cathedral. At least this lone ant was wearing tinfoil as the flood of armoured bodies rushed towards him.

"I'll hold them off." A huge metal finger uncurled from the mech's fist. It pointed behind him at the circular platform Isabella and Ezra were standing on. "Down there. Open it up."

"Can't you blast it?" Isabella yelled over the comm.

"Wouldn't even make a dent if I gave it everything I have," Lynch yelled back.

"I've got this." Isabella hurried into the centre of the platform, her palms feeling along its surface for any sign of a control panel or hidden interface.

Words meant for someone other than Isabella reached her over the comm. "If I don't make it out of this, bury me somewhere awesome."

For a heartbeat, Isabella felt the chestnut in her eyes burn purple. "Don't do anything stupid," Paradise Moon said through Isabella's lips.

In response, Lynch's mech suit unleashed a volley of swirling missiles that encouraged the nearest ranks of PROXUS soldiers to fly high into the air and, screaming as they flew, disappear over the edge of the walkway.

Reaching the raised outline of a smaller circle in the middle of the platform, Isabella bent on all fours and frantically patted it down. With a clang that rang out across the chasm, a Sau Daran zombie landed on the platform. Green vapours spilled from the cracks in their dark shell, which was horrifically bent out of shape from their fall from the tunnel above. Or, more specifically, from their landing. Their twisted limbs jerked erratically.

Isabella glanced back at Lynch's walkway. Armoured troopers had closed around his mech suit, forming a wide ring as they liberated their rifles of every plasma charge a weapon could hold. Amid the stinging volleys of plasma and rising smoke, the mech's colossal arms swept more soldiers aside and lent its own illuminating blasts of plasma to the epic tableau.

There was a click and a hiss as Isabella's fingers ran over a pressure plate. It slid back from the platform, revealing another projection node that launched a glowing holo interface into the air.

"What's the code?" she shouted into her gauntlet.

But there was no response from Lynch. Looking up, she could barely see his mech suit. It was a blur of smoke, a smear of metal, a smudge of flames in the plasma-fuelled melee blocking their platform from the PROXUS army.

"Well?" asked Isabella, gesturing at the holo.

Ezra bent down beside her and examined the holo with unseasoned eyes. "I don't know!" He shrugged despairingly. "I just used to shoot people."

A trio of clangs signalled the arrival of three more misshapen Sau Darans. Their claws reached out with a shudder. Grasped the platform. Crawled and dragged their broken, leaking bodies with a discordant scrape of metal on metal towards Isabella and Ezra.

From the chaos of another plasma-lit walkway, crisp footsteps emerged. She click-clicked, click-clicked across the platform with steady, even strides. Her ashen hair was a blizzard streaked with a solitary slash of crimson. Her eyes cold. Her expression colder. Her fluffy cardigan was gone, replaced with a chestplate that looked like it could stop anything but a square-on blast of plasma. But either she'd had no time to switch her trousers, or she couldn't bear to be parted with the designer label.

"Well?" prompted Isabella. "What's the code?"

The Empress' answer was to produce a plasma pistol. She aimed the unfriendly end at Isabella.

Well this is disappointingly predictable.

Isabella did the maths and realised the Empress had come up short. A disbelieving smirk spread over her face. "Are you stupid?"

Can I answer that?

The Empress held her plasma pistol steady but threw in an arched eyebrow. "Obviously not. I've got the gun."

"What happened to the other Empress?" Isabella was still failing to wipe the idiot's grin from her face. "You betray her too?"

"Dead." With her free hand, the Empress pointed to a red-stained slash in her designer trousers below her thigh. Her leg looked like it would be fine, but Isabella hoped at least the trousers were finished. "We betrayed each other. As promised. Admittedly, killing the ruling Empress here took that clone a lot of effort, so it didn't take me long to finish her off."

"You don't have to—" Ezra began, but Isabella's hand found his shoulder with a firm grip. The look she gave him was enough to shut his mouth.

"It's fine," Isabella assured him. Her eyes settled on the Empress. "We're short on time. Do you want to give me the code for this door now or do I have to explain why you're so incredibly screwed?"

"I agreed to a coup, not an alliance." The Empress paused to watch the disfigured shell of a Sau Daran drag their snapping metal jaws another arm's length closer to Isabella. "You got your coup. Now I'm saving my republic and adding the alien parasite inside you to the clean energy reserve beneath our feet. It will power our ships for many cycles to come."

"You're really not saving anyone if you do that."

"I really am." The Empress took careful aim with her plasma pistol. "That whole thing about ashes and fists is a great line, one of my favourites, but I'm not that stupid. It's a line I enjoy before burning down other people's empires. Not my own. And the best part is I'm never going to have to listen to another tedious therapy session ever again. You're too broken to save."

"If you kill me, PROXUS ends with me."

"Impossible."

"Really?" Isabella let her mouth hang open in the cockiest grin. "What are you going to do about the portal that's about to appear?"

"Irrelevant," snapped the Empress irritably. "I'm going to harvest the parasite."

"No," said Isabella patiently, despite the nausea aching in her stomach. "A portal is going to open up right here, millions of Sau Darans are going to arrive at the strongest source of star energy in the universe and nothing is going to stop them getting through that door and eating up everything you've got."

"The portals are following the parasite. You'll be dead and the parasite will be harvested. Any connection the Sau Darans had to you, or it, will be lost. PROXUS flourishes and everyone will know I'm the Empress who made it happen."

Isabella laughed, despite the metallic taste on her tongue. "How do you think the portals follow us? Magic?"

The Empress clicked her tongue in annoyance. "Sau Daran technology. This conversation is over."

Isabella shook her head. "Wrong. PROXUS is over. They're not following Paradise Moon. They're not wizards. Kill both of us, it doesn't matter. They'll still come to your precious planet for your precious energy. Now I'm here, they already know where this place is."

"Impossible."

"There's at least two things you don't know." Isabella held up her gauntlet for the Empress with a defiant grin. "They're tracking this. Not me. Not her."

A barrage of plasma from the Empress' pistol eviscerated Isabella's gauntlet. Superheated, spitting tech stung her arm. With a swipe of her purple glowing hand it was loosened, detached, banished clattering onto the platform in plumes of acrid smoke and fizzing circuits.

"And the other thing?" the Empress asked icily.

The world felt like it was being turned upside-down. Grimacing, Isabella extended a finger at the murky air above them. "That."

Lightning tore through reality. Blue light ripped a hole out of the grim shadows above the circular platform. Gravity quit. The metal skeletons of long dead, recently clawing Sau Darans drifted up into the air. The emerging portal's radiance chilled the length of all three walkways before its light was lost to the chasm's depths. It kissed every visored face, every suit of armour, the barrel of every plasma rifle, carbine and pistol.

"What's the code?" yelled Isabella. Her knuckles were bone white from gripping the platform's exposed panel hard enough not to be torn off it and into the air with the floating—and biting—Sau Daran zombies. Her arm burned where Ezra was gripping *that* so hard.

The Empress hadn't moved, except for her crimson-streaked ashen hair. It wriggled as Medusa's might, refusing to lie still while gravity's reign was adjourned. Red lights were alive up the side of her boots, which stuck like glue to the platform. She held her pistol steady against the pull of the storm.

"Well, what is it?" Isabella called over the portal's howl. "They're coming anyway."

The Empress smiled with frigid joy. "Good."

Isabella stared at the Empress in slow disbelief. "Good?" she echoed.

"Good," the Empress confirmed. "I can make that work too."

Finally, gravity remembered which way was up—and more importantly which way was down. Isabella fell onto the platform with a graceless thump. Blood and pain swelled down her forehead. Ezra landed next to her in a similar heap of sweat and bruises.

Disfigured Sau Daran zombies tumbled out of the air they had been hanging in. They clanged and smashed onto the platform hard enough to rattle their breaking joints and gush more enthusiastic pools of green fluid. No sooner had these corrupted remnants twisted off their backs, than thick volleys of plasma vaporised them out of existence. Isabella glanced at the walkways. After what she saw there, she slumped subdued onto the platform.

Gone were the mutinous pockets of flashing red plasma down two walkways. Gone was the third walkway's defiant last stand of mech-suited fury. Present and correct, in precise rows standing shoulder to armoured shoulder, were the endless ranks of surviving PROXUS Rangers, Silver Fists and whatever other silly names the Empress called them. Every plasma pistol, rifle and carbine was hot and ready to fire again—this time, at Isabella and Ezra.

Sprawled along the third walkway's front rank of plasma weapons, a body lay dead or dying. Lynch might have been alive—it was impossible to be sure from this distance. His body was such a mess, it was probably impossible to be sure from up close, too. He was sprawled unmoving beside the ruinous remains of the Empress' decimated mech suit, which would be fighting no more battles. Neither, it seemed, would Lynch. His body looked like it was formed more of smoking blood and ashen cinders than anything else. Undoubtedly, he still had plenty of the more traditional flesh and bones that human bodies prided themselves on. Isabella could see plenty of both, it was just a shame they weren't inside him where they belonged.

Unbidden by Isabella, purple smoke brought her beside him. A glowing purple hand found his and held it. His hand was hot with blood. It offered no response, no returning grip. No hope. His eyes were glassy and vacant. His mouth smeared with blood and uncharacteristically silent. It offered Isabella and Paradise Moon nothing beyond confirmation of a fact. Any grin that belonged there, any promise of mischief and chaos, was eternally absent from his lips.

Unbidden once more, purple smoke returned Isabella to Ezra and the Empress. The body came to the platform too, with no words needing to pass between Isabella and Paradise Moon, not at any speed.

The Empress spoke into a golden pin in her armoured chestplate. Behind her and around them on the walkways, three dark seas of helmets tilted in audience at whatever was being said over their comms. Ezra's hand found Isabella's human arm. His touch was charged with warm but brittle comfort, his face stricken, his caress unsteady. His gaze was fractured by the smoking remains of every Sau Daran body on the platform.

Isabella glared at the Empress.

"It's remarkably simple," she said into her golden pin to every PROXUS soldier. "That Sau Daran portal signals a new invasion from our old enemy. The first ever attack on Xarr itself. As with the Last Great War, history will measure the time before and after this rotation as two distinct periods separated by a defining moment. This is your chance. This is your moment. It doesn't matter which Empress you served before. I have returned to dispel this new Sau Daran threat. If you value the lives of those you love and serve, if you value humanity itself, now is the time to kneel before your true Empress and saviour of PROXUS."

Isabella was almost deafened by hundreds of thousands of armoured soldiers kneeling all at once.

"Now rise," invited the Empress. "Stand with me against this threat."

As one, every PROXUS soldier on the walkways rose. The muzzles of their plasma weapons rose too, poised to deliver their Empress' judgement on whatever emerged from the portal.

"You wanted the Sau Darans to come here," Isabella said slowly, as she wrapped her head around what was happening. "Just so you could take back Xarr."

The Empress tapped her golden pin and pulled her mouth away from it. "Not my preferred plan, but a workable one. You brought the enemy here and made it all possible, so I should be thanking you… I won't, of course. I'd rather just kill you so the parasite inside can get to work powering our ships."

There was movement above them.

Everyone's eyes travelled up to the portal—and the person emerging from it. A blue halo shone around his silhouette as he leaped out of the dazzling circle of light and began to fall. Precise darts of red plasma spat at him from every walkway. Harmlessly, they splashed off the flickering blue shield that sparked from stray wires in his suit and lit up around him.

"That's enough!" Nova Sky shouted through Talyn's lips. The plasma fire ceased. When Isabella glanced back at the walkways, there was no shortage of PROXUS troops aiming plasma weapons at Nova Sky, but if they were pulling their triggers then it wasn't doing squat to make them fire. "Much better," said Nova Sky.

His descent slowed as he neared the platform, tapering off into what could only be described as gentle levitation. The wiring in his suit wriggled. At the edge of a decaying orbit, his boots sank gracefully onto the platform. He was between Isabella and the Empress—so close he could have touched either of them. Except to do that, he would have had to put down what he was holding. And this felt unlikely. The Spark was not a prize one surrendered lightly.

Deep inside, Isabella could feel Paradise Moon staring greedily at the device. Her glowing purple arm still held Lynch's lifeless body.

"I never dreamed we would make it here," Nova Sky admitted. "How wonderful."

Leaving the Spark safe in the custody of one hand, Nova Sky raised the other above his head and clicked his fingers as though ordering table service. The gesture hardly seemed necessary, given the instant grinding and groaning as the circular platform split down its middle and opened inwards, but some gods loved to put on a show. Scattered remnants of corrupted Sau Darans slid down the sloping halves of the platform. Tumbling and skidding, they dropped into the greatest store of star energy in the universe.

As the two parting semi-circles of black artificial platform completed their arc into the gap below, they left a single disc of metal untouched at the heart of the platform where Isabella had found the control node. That this was also where Isabella was clutching Lynch's body, where Ezra, Therapy Empress and Nova Sky were all standing—and therefore not falling—felt like more than luck. For starters, Isabella never had much of that.

"Don't give me that look," said Nova Sky, reading Isabella's accusing expression. "The platform assured me which parts would open and which wouldn't."

With the toes of her boots almost touching the edge, and no room for retreat on the small, crowded disc that remained, Isabella peered down.

The sight below reminded her of the resplendent lightshow she had seen inside the Sau Daran crystal three years ago, when it had drawn fresh life from the very fabric of reality in Paradise Moon's universe. Although that universe had ended, the sight of the star energy rippling below made her feel like she was back there. Which made sense, given she was staring at the harvested souls of Sau Daran gods. The sight was no less resplendent, no less radiant. It was divine. She suspected the pool of light below held every colour. Without exception. The colours swirled and spun and shone and burned without ever diminishing and never settling into anything resembling a definitive form. They were never wholly liquid, never entirely gaseous. They moved like a dream or a concept, rather than anything corporeal. They simply were, and they were simply beautiful.

That's a cheerful grave.

Paradise Moon's voice came to Isabella gentler and more distant than usual, as though she were taking note of reality but not really part of it.

Isabella glanced down at Lynch's body. It was still there, a glowing purple arm still wrapped around his shoulders like a shield. Within a heartbeat, she had to tear her eyes away. They found Talyn's face bearing over her, armed with Nova Sky's grim countenance.

"You got everything you wanted," Isabella pointed out. "Bring them here. Save them all."

"So small minded," said Nova Sky, his voice as snide as it was dismissive. "There's a much faster way."

With another click of his fingers, the portal above them died. Isabella felt nauseous all over again, the way she always did before a portal appeared. A breath of lightning bloomed amid the star energy's chromatic brilliance below. Isabella felt a fresh portal open, even though she couldn't see it. The souls of the gods stirred. Agitated beyond comprehension. Unfalteringly awakened. Eager, perhaps, for what came next.

Finally, they can be at peace.

But at least one person wasn't thinking about peace. "I will destroy you," the Empress warned Nova Sky. Where ice had previously dominated her visage, an inferno now burned behind her eyes. She glanced across the vast gap, between where she stood within throttling range of Nova Sky and her three stranded armies on the walkways. Their impotent plasma weapons looked ready for something, but they didn't seem entirely sure what.

Nova Sky replied with a wave of Talyn's hand. The Empress' plasma pistol exploded, taking most of her arm with it over the edge of their tiny platform. Collapsing to her knees, even the Empress of the Known Galaxies couldn't temper her scream of agony. It echoed far and deep into the chasm, before coming back to Isabella from every haunting shadow. She clamped her lips shut to stem her scream, but could do nothing to stem the flow of blood. Ineffectually, she clutched the gushing stump of one arm in the weakening grip of her other.

"Leave if you wish," Nova Sky told Isabella. "If you return to our temple on Regis V, you will witness the glorious salvation of our children. It is already underway."

Isabella tried to stand, but her glowing purple arm would not be parted from Lynch's body and her glowing purple leg refused to move. "None of us need to be here. You did it. You saved them all. Let's go together. Let's get out of here."

Nova Sky examined the Spark thoughtfully. Barely a dribble of green fluid showed against the marker on its side. "My vengeance will never end," he warned. "Humanity will pay. My children will be safe."

Isabella stared at the Spark, remembering what it had done to an entire city of people and imagining what it could still do. Paradise Moon dragged Isabella's neck down, forcing her to look at Lynch's body.

They deserve it.

Not everyone.

These ones do.

But he's never going to stop. Are you telling me everyone everywhere deserves it? Fleur? Beauregard? My mum?

Paradise Moon didn't answer, but Isabella felt the pull on her neck relax. Isabella glared up at Nova Sky. "We saved them all. Just take the win. It's over."

The Empress parted her lips with a groan of pain. "It... will... never... be... over..." Set into a pale expression that threatened to become a death mask at any moment, her eyes burned with potent fury. But her swaying body was growing ever weaker as blood flowed down her flank, puddling in her lap, swimming over the platform's edge. However she was still alive, it wouldn't be for long.

Nova Sky smiled condescendingly at Isabella. "If you don't believe me, believe her."

Grunting at the effort, Isabella lifted Lynch's body and tried to stand. Within a heartbeat, alien energy from Paradise Moon flooded through her. It felt as though she was lifting the sort of crude, inflatable body Paradise Moon once left in the teachers' staffroom. Not a corpse. Not a friend. Not the fragile meat of someone's love.

"Ezra, hold on," instructed Isabella. With unhesitating trust, Ezra's hand closed around the back of her human hand. "Talyn," muttered Isabella. She held Lynch's body like a bride carried over the threshold, only there was no joy here. If there was a threshold, it was a grave one. "Please, Talyn. I need you. We can do this together."

His eyes burned blue. "Talyn is gone."

"We saved them all, just like we wanted. Like we promised we would."

The hottest blue.

"Come back to me, please."

"I told you, Talyn is—" began Nova Sky.

"Here," gasped Talyn, through the same mouth.

Talyn touched his palm to Isabella's cheek.

Purple smoke.

Gone.

CHAPTER FORTY-TWO

Lady Fleur Fontaine had flown starships and killed enemies in the name of piracy, in the name of the Empress and, finally, in her own name. In all those cycles, she had seen a lot of death. Yet she had never felt greater relief at hearing the boom of Dash's starfighter flying overhead. Or greater sorrow at seeing the smoking ruins of what his Scimitar left behind.

"That was the last of them," Dash confirmed over the comm. "They're dead. Again."

Fleur waited for a line of Dash's poetry to follow. Something poignant, perhaps about the burning sun and their souls at rest, or maybe capturing the essence of loss in whatever venting madness had been subdued by his starfighter's plasma cannons, but nothing crept back to her over the comm. Nothing but static and silence.

She let it linger. She couldn't find the words to thank Dash and wasn't certain she wanted to. Perhaps it would have been kinder for him to let the Sau Daran zombies live, to let her die… yet there had been no kindness in their burning green eyes. Only suffering, now ended. That was what she would tell herself.

Fleur was exhausted. All she wanted to do was stay here for a while, sitting limp on the plasma-furrowed road while she rested her bleeding body. Black smudges of smoke unfurled in the breeze, escaping the charred wreckage of those who hadn't been entirely alive or, at least briefly, entirely dead. She focussed on the smoke, not what was left of the bodies.

Eyes closed and head bowed, Beauregard inhaled a black cigarette. "One good thing came out of this."

"We are alive," agreed Fleur, but without conviction.

Beauregard opened his eyes, reminding Fleur just how cold they were. "Alive? Yeah, I guess." Ash crumbled from the end of his cigarette, burning his fingers. He didn't seem to notice or care. "That ain't what I meant."

He pointed through the scattered remnants of destruction. Following his arm, Fleur found the wrecked shell of the Empress' armour. Its arms had been sheared off at the shoulders and, wherever they were, it wasn't anywhere near her armour. The helmet was gone too. The armour's upper torso looked like it had travelled through a manufacturing facility—backwards. What remained was torn, punctured and twisted beyond repair, while what no longer remained was a great deal of armour and the person who had been inside.

"Watched them tear it off her and pull her out. Ain't no one survivin' that."

"I'll tell you who survived," said Braga, limping up the road towards them. Fleur knew her wife wasn't talking about herself, despite one of Braga's legs being sodden with her own blood, or the cuts and bruises marking every scrap of exposed skin.

"You found him?" asked Fleur.

Braga nodded grimly.

Wincing at the dizzying pain it caused her weeping injuries, Fleur stood. Gingerly, she bent her shoulder under Braga's arm and hoped the support she was offering her wife wouldn't topple herself. Together, they hobbled past the abandoned wreckage of Earth vehicles and through smoke that stung their bloodshot eyes raw.

First, she saw his face. It peered out from beneath a shattered Earth vehicle further down the road. Eyes wide. Make-up smeared. Gold earrings dangling with his head on its side so he didn't strike it on the vehicle's undercarriage. The face of the man who was no longer her father and had deserted her at every opportunity.

As they staggered closer, Fleur wrinkled her nose at the stench of blood and piss. "Come out," she ordered. This is over." Much like Fleur and Braga, the Earth vehicle was bent out of shape. But as he crawled out from beneath it and she saw the rest of him, she found barely a scratch on him.

Fussily, he smoothed over his fabrics. "Lost my blade and pistol," he admitted. He gestured to his empty sheath, which dangled loosely against one leg. "Of course, without a weapon it took all my nous and cunning to evade them." He spoke weakly, as though he couldn't quite will the words to be true. "You proved yourself most worthy, too," he told the silence. "You fought like the daughter of pirating royalty and showed a stout heart, my girl. I could not be prouder to call you my heir. When I finally pass, I feel the throne will suit you rather well."

Fleur stared at him for longer than she wanted. Only after his eyes escaped hers and sought refuge in the broken ground at his feet, did she turn and limp away. He called after her, but she chose not to hear it. A familiar arm settled around her waist, keeping her upright.

When the portal opened, no one was ready for it. No one had moved for a while. Sometimes sitting, sometimes lying, Fleur, Braga and Beauregard had never left what remained of the road. Occasionally, they had heard the wail of far-off sirens not daring to approach or the thunder of Earth's aircraft overhead. But until now, such reminders that life continued had remained on the periphery of relevance.

They moved—and moved much faster—when a lightning-streaked portal awoke at the epicentre of Dash's destruction. Far enough away to only snare abandoned vehicles and the debris of battle in its gravity-defying grip, it bubbled blue energy and spat lightning up the ruined road.

But instead of more Sau Daran zombies, a broad river of light washed out of the portal. The stream of ribboned light wove a path to each downed Sau Daran and flowed through every decimated metal body. Flakes of decay shed from the metal corpses like an inverse snowfall of darkness rising into the sky. Where the darkness peeled away from their bodies, the gleam of silver beneath was renewed, replenished and repaired.

Dimmer than when it had arrived, any ribboned light that hadn't settled within a Sau Daran body dove back into the portal. In its wake, hundreds of red eyes awoke.

Pristine and reborn, the silver Sau Darans rose.

Beauregard's pistol was ready. Braga's too. Their faces were bleak. Fleur nudged their weapons towards the ground. Without acknowledging their spectators, the newly silvered Sau Darans wandered to the portal with heavy strides. They were alive. They were themselves.

Then they were gone.

Bowing her head, scrunching her eyes shut, crumpling to her knees, Fleur wept. Whether she was happy or sad, she couldn't say. She could feel more than enough of everything in between. Two pairs of hands found her. Rubbed her shoulder. Smoothed her hair.

Without another look at the portal, the three of them held each other tight and promised never to let go.

CHAPTER FORTY-THREE

Dazzling light spun through the ice cave like an errant twister. It danced and surged and spilled around Isabella and Talyn. Isabella didn't dare move atop the stone pillar. She held Talyn's body tight to hers, keeping inside the eye of the radiant storm as the harvested souls of Sau Daran gods singed her retinas.

Glowing green at her feet, the fallen Spark lay forgotten by everyone except Paradise Moon. Deep in Isabella's chest, thick in her blood, Paradise Moon made sure Isabella couldn't forget either. Lying broken beside the Spark, Lynch's body waited.

There had been a monumental change to every Sau Daran zombie who remained in the ice cave after Midnight Twice died. Isabella suspected this change had been ignited when Nova Sky summoned a portal into the Empress' reserve of star energy. Illuminated in the now sparkling floor of the ice cave, millions of Sau Darans calmly gleamed and simply were. In cautious wonder, they gazed red-eyed at each other, at the swirling light of their lost gods and at the pair of humans clinging to each other above them.

Collapsed at the stone pillar's edge, Ezra watched in silent, reverential awe. Tears stung his eyes, gathering and glistening as they threatened to drift emboldened down his cheeks and mingle with older smears of dirt, sweat and blood.

Every time the metal ring killed one portal and awoke another, the vortex of light diverged a fresh tributary of harvested gods through it to find whoever was on the other side. The light remaining in the ice cave grew ever smaller, ever dimmer. Once it left, the departed light of harvested gods never returned.

But their gleaming, silver children did.

Another stream of reassuringly silver Sau Darans marched out of the latest portal, across the stone pillar and harmlessly past Ezra. Freed from their dark-stained, green-eyed necrosis, these replenished Sau Darans arrived without jittering or jerking or snapping their jaws. The same had been true for every Sau Daran arriving through every portal since Isabella and Talyn returned. As with those Sau Darans, these nodded respectfully to Talyn and Isabella, then headed to the floor of the ice cave to rejoin their silver brethren. No matter how many limbs or heads each Sau Daran had, whether they climbed or flew, they all found their way to the bottom together.

Isabella buried her face against Talyn's chestplate. Even through his armour, the erratic beat of his heart sounded heavenly. Irrefutably, this was his anxious heartbeat and not the steady, traitorous rhythm of a murderous alien god. Not yet. The beat of his heart tethered her to him. Blood to blood. Soul to soul. Him to her. As long as that erratic heartbeat endured, he was unchained from alien compulsion or interference.

Talyn's gentle kisses landed on her head, pressing through her hair to find and bless the skin and bone beneath. His lips found her forehead. Her cheek. Her neck. Her ear and the soft patch of skin below. She lifted her face to his and he found her lips. As they kissed, he pressed his body hard into hers and she held him as though no force could ever tear them apart.

But like a grave knew the cold, Isabella knew happiness never lasted. She pulled her mouth away. When his lips still reached for hers, she dragged his hands off her hips and pulled their bodies apart before her dissolving conviction abandoned her. His face crumpled twice, first into disappointment and then into confusion as the blood began returning to his brain.

"How long have we got?" she asked, feeling something melt in her eyes and something else catch in her throat. "How long until I lose you?"

Talyn gaped, awestruck. For a moment, she thought he might say 'forever'. Then his gaze lowered awkwardly and she feared what he might say instead.

"Not long," he admitted. "You're the only thing keeping Nova away." He stroked her cheek with the soft back of his hand, keeping his sweaty palm off her skin. She knew she loved him. Not an enduring love, not true love, but at least one flavour of love that was sincere and undeniable burned inside her. "You brought me back, but it won't be for long. He's too strong."

Isabella considered his version of reality, then rejected it. "We'll find a way," she bluffed with a confidence she didn't feel but knew she'd have to find.

"I'm holding off a god," he reminded her, almost apologetically. "I thought I could do it before, but he was toying with me. Using me. My mind was never strong enough for this."

Half nodding a reluctant, bitter submission, Isabella held and stroked the gentle hand brushing her cheek. "What happens if Nova Sky returns?"

"*When* he returns, it will be war. He'll take them to every planet until every human is dead."

Isabella indicated the Spark where it had fallen at her feet. "He'll really do what he said on Xarr?"

Talyn nodded. "It's as good as empty, but it won't take him long to fill it with more human lives."

Purple blazed in Isabella's eyes. She felt her consciousness being pushed aside to make room. "What do you mean, as good as empty?" Paradise Moon demanded through Isabella's lips. "Can it still bring someone back?"

"I'm sorry, I don't know."

If there's even a drop left in the Spark, we'll bring Lynch back. I promise.

Talyn glanced up at the ever dwindling, ever fading vortex of light. Isabella followed his gaze. The light had already split to travel into so many portals, one by one, and already been absorbed by so many corrupted Sau Darans. "Saving them doesn't mean anything. Nova will fight PROXUS until all his children are dead, then he'll bring them back by taking more human lives and do it all over again. Only there won't be any of this left," he gestured at the lightshow of deceased Sau Daran gods, "to save them once they're corrupted by human souls."

Reluctantly, Paradise Moon let go. Isabella's nerves tingled with renewed control of her body. Guiding Talyn's hand from her cheek, Isabella found its partner, pressed them together and clasped his hands inside hers. "Tell me how to stop him."

"Nova won't stop. Not ever. When he took control of me, I saw everything." Talyn's hands trembled inside hers, subsiding only slightly when her thumb stroked the back of his hand. "He wants revenge. He doesn't care if all his children die and die and die—"

"That's not happening," said Isabella firmly.

Talyn bit his lip, seeming not to notice when he drew blood. His beautiful face was creased with worry. He looked like he might say something, but instead he shook his head. His body slumped. Isabella had nothing left to say either. For the first time in three years, she felt like she was powerless.

Swirling around them, the last of the gods' rainbow light spun away to forge a new path up the lift shaft. Except for the Spark's green glow and the portal's blue glimmer, every trace of colour left the cave. In their place, a pale twinkle crept from ice crystals in the walls. They painted the shadows in subdued subterranean shades, as cold as fractured moonlight.

Isabella craned her neck to watch the last echoes of colour disappear up the lift shaft. "It's all leaving?" she asked the growing shadows.

"Nova arrived here from a space battle so bad it ended the war. Nearly killed him. I guess there's plenty of floating Sau Daran wreckage up there worth saving."

"Husks?"

"Yeah, probably. There must be a lot of Husks in orbit, just waiting to be found and healed."

"Good," said Isabella, her tone blunted by a shadow of funereal solemnity. "I like Husks."

"I wouldn't know what they're like, but Nova told us about them. They sounded... special."

Isabella stopped staring at the lift shaft and dropped her gaze back to Talyn. She expected to tell him all about *Haven*. To invite him there, if he survived long enough before Nova Sky took control. To find something positive to share and give them both hope.

Instead, she found his eyes clenched shut in the shadows, lips pursed. Before, it had only been his hands shaking. Now it was all of him. "I can't hold him off much longer," gasped Talyn.

"You can." Gripping his head in her hands, Isabella pulled his forehead to hers. "Just a little longer."

"He killed everyone on my planet."

"I'm so sorry," she whispered.

"That's not what I meant. After what he did, I can't live with him inside me. Not if he's in control. Not after what he did and what I know he's going to do."

A tear fled down Talyn's face, lingered on his chin. It tasted bitter, then Isabella found his lips once more and they tasted sweeter. With all her heart, she willed him to fight. With her lips and her hands and her body pressed into him, every part of her told him she loved him. It was only when his lips pulled away from hers that she stopped pretending they would never part. He drew her into an embrace, her chin settling on his shoulder and her cheek against his, their arms clinging around each other.

Over Talyn's shoulder, Isabella surveyed the almost empty stone pillar. Only the final opened portal and Ezra remained, her friend politely giving them however long they needed.

We saved them all.

Does it matter? If Nova kills them all over again, why did we bother?

We did everything we could.

Yeah, and it wasn't enough. I never should have left them in the first place.

You really wish you'd stayed all those years ago?

Yeah. Hero shit and all that. Who knew?

A woman staggered out of the vacant portal and collapsed onto the stone pillar. She was bleeding heavily from, well, everywhere. Her black armour was gone, leaving nothing to clothe her but a thin, blood-soaked undertunic. She hauled herself to her bare feet. Her ashen hair was a bedraggled mess, its solitary streak of crimson lost beneath so much blood. She fell back down to one knee, huffed in a wheezing breath and forced herself to stand. Swaying and disoriented, she still seemed to be absorbing where she was. Her eyes were glassy in the portal's pale blue light. Searching the stone platform, they settled on Isabella.

The Empress raised a plasma pistol, but it shook in her grip as though too heavy to hold. Isabella's gaze returned to Talyn. Worry evaporated from his face. In fact, he was holding himself strongly enough to give Isabella hope. Then his face lurched into a violent sneer and Isabella realised she wasn't looking at Talyn anymore. Not now. Perhaps not ever again.

Fine. We'll save them the hard way.

Don't you dare.

You reckon you can take down Nova Sky?

I said don't you dare.

Isabella pulled Nova Sky into a tight embrace and hugged him as though he were Talyn.

Not this way.

There isn't any other way.

Find another way.

It's what Talyn wanted.

So? Tell him he's wrong!

Over Nova Sky's shoulder, Isabella watched the Empress steady her aim.

I can't tell him, can I? He's already gone.

Don't be an idiot!

As soon as Nova's free from Talyn's body, vanish him far away from anyone with a pulse.

Talyn wouldn't want this for you.

Vanish him somewhere he can't ever come back from.

We'll vanish them both. Him and Talyn.

He'd hate that.

So?! He'd be alive.

With Nova Sky trapped inside him forever, always in control? It would be torture.

But you'd still be alive!

You wished you'd never run away all those years ago. This is me making sure I never have to feel the same way.

A flash lit up the cave as a single red blast blossomed from the muzzle of the Empress' plasma pistol. Heat tore through Nova Sky's back, then Isabella's chest.

Hot.

Searing.

Agony.

But only for a heartbeat.

A heartbeat long enough for one final thought.

Hero shit, baby.

CHAPTER FORTY-FOUR

The universe looked different now Paradise Moon wasn't trapped inside a human. Gone were Isabella's limited senses. Gone were her fleshy restrictions. Gone were all those messy, contradictory, confusing emotions that stuck like shit on a nappy to everything she experienced. Instead, Paradise Moon's true form—gaseous, purple and perfect—soared over the stone pillar and the bodies it was accumulating. Five so far. Three dead: Isabella, Lynch, Talyn. Two living: Ezra and the Empress of the Known Galaxies. The latter was fleeing towards the lift despite wearing enough blood to have died three times over.

Without eyes, Paradise Moon didn't see Isabella's body collapse bleeding and smoking towards the stone. Instead, she knew the body's presence with a clarity that burned her every atom with searing grief. Just as she now knew the presence of Lynch's body for the first time, rather than merely witnessing it through Isabella's eyes. Sure, there was seeing a thing. But such sensory experiences were a pale glimmer when replaced with the intimate, ever-present, divine knowledge of a thing.

Talyn's body was down there too, sinking beside Isabella's, but that was a knowing she could tolerate. Unlike the knowing of Isabella's body, which consumed her with rage so livid and sorrow so grave that she worried these two sensations might become everything she was and all she would ever be.

The last time Paradise Moon had been outside Isabella's body, parts of her had been torn into a Sau Daran ship's crystal. That time, before Paradise Moon had been lost and Isabella's body killed, Isabella had been strong enough to save her and pull most of Paradise Moon back into her body. But this time Isabella couldn't do that because

she

was

gone.

If there wasn't enough juice left in the Spark to bring Isabella back, Paradise Moon would carry her grief for millennia before she had a clue what to do with it. Her only hope rested in the generosity of Nova Sky to activate the Spark. She was basically screwed.

Ah yes. Nova Sky.

He was the second cloud floating over the stone pillar. Blue, not purple. But no less divine. And still a prick.

Isabella's body landed on the stone pillar and crumpled into an unflattering pose. The fall had kept her moving a fraction longer than her body would have without it. Now, even that had ended.

Ezra screamed.

Oh Ezra...

Damn Paradise Moon's conscience. Having one was so inconvenient. The mere thought of entering Ezra's body and taking control of him—or indeed any other human—would have once been as natural to Paradise

Moon as Isabella slipping on a black tee. The one with the skull and top hat was Paradise Moon's favourite. Yet now, the thought of wearing another human would have made Paradise Moon sick if such fleshy impulses meant anything to her current physical form. Isabella would have called this growth, but whatever name you picked it limited options considerably.

The blue cloud of smoke lurched at Ezra. It seemed Paradise Moon wasn't the only god entertaining the idea of taking a new vessel. Of course, not everyone possessed her divine restraint.

She was faster than Nova Sky. Well, perhaps not faster. But she did get there first. She didn't need to move in the same way anyone else did. In that sense, she was faster than everyone. After less than a heartbeat—no, that was an old habit. Before she had taken a breath—no, wait. Reset. In the blink of an—okay, fine. *Very fast,* Paradise Moon vanished to where Nova Sky was swooping down on Ezra. She engulfed his blue smoke in her purple mist, hit him with everything she had, flexing everything she was and hammering him with everything she could bring to bear. She overwhelmed Nova Sky, just as her rage and sorrow was overwhelming her.

Unrelenting.

Uncowed.

Swinging like a demon.

Hitting like a god.

Nova Sky must have been ready for something. But he wasn't ready for her. Not all of her. Not like this. Blue smoke and purple mist tussled so suffocatingly tight that they might have been one god, not two. She dragged him higher into the cave, further from Ezra, refusing to let go.

Freed from the limits of neural pathways, they didn't need to share a word as their consciousnesses bled together at each other's touch. If they had used words, it would have sounded something like:

Screw you, prick.

SCREW YOU.

Screw you!

DID YOU FORGET WHAT IT'S LIKE?

To dominate a whiny bitch like you?

TO BE A GOD. TO FEEL ONE THING AND ONLY ONE THING SO INTENSELY IT RULES YOU.

Paradise Moon felt it. Surging out of him. Surging into her. Not a human mess of emotions that had to be sorted to make sense of it, like a game of fifty-two card pick-up. He made her feel the searing singular loss he felt long ago among the stars above them, when he witnessed so many of their children die, so many of their fellow gods taken. His loss consumed her now as it consumed him still.

She made him feel hers, too. Surging out of her. Surging into him. Searing singular loss at the knowing of Isabella's body. Lynch's body. A loss that felt no lesser than his from the epicentre of her disaster zone.

CAN YOU FEEL IT? THE LOSS OF ALL OUR CHILDREN AND GODS AT THEIR HANDS?

You took Isabella. She was mine.

HURTS, DOESN'T IT? FEELING IT LIKE A GOD. DON'T YOU JUST WANT TO END ME?

You read my mind.

THEN YOU UNDERSTAND MY REVENGE.

Frustratingly, she did.

Prick.

BECAUSE I'M RIGHT?

Whatever. You can't kill every human.

NOT WITH THAT ATTITUDE.

Not if it gets every Sau Daran killed all over again. Not when there are humans who don't deserve to die.

Below them, the Empress collapsed onto the lift and hammered its control panel to send it hurtling upwards. As the lift rose, she looked back and aimed her plasma pistol. It was so unnecessary. Ezra was no threat. Lying prone, eyes blinded by tears, he had nowhere to run and no weapon with which to defend himself.

Plasma blasts struck the platform, exploding showers of tiny stone and dust around his synthetic blades, around his scrambling hands.

AH YES, I CAN ALWAYS RELY ON HUMANITY TO PROVE ME RIGHT.

The Empress reset her aim, this time adjusting for the rapidly ascending lift. Paradise Moon didn't give Ezra another thought. She wasn't seeing the universe—she was knowing it. And she knew who was climbing back up the stone pillar as fast as their gears would allow.

Shining saviours leaped up over the edge. Paradise Moon had known them rushing up the pillar ever since she returned to her proper form. She suspected they had been racing to save Isabella and Talyn, perhaps the gods inside them, long before they started racing to save Ezra.

With silver arms stretching to take the brunt of the attack, their diving bodies shielded him from the plasma blasts. Their bodies sparked where plasma struck. Silver limbs burned black, lighting up cauterised cross-sections with thousands of flaming dots where each plasma blast burrowed. A ring of red-eyed Sau Darans glared up at the Empress, their hands and arms smoking accusingly.

But she was gone.

Out of range and into the shaft above.

Hunched dumbstruck on the stone, Ezra gazed up at his Sau Daran rescuers. His face was fractured with grief and shock, but his body was unscathed. An injured Sau Daran helped him up, but stumbled. Ezra steadied them, then leaned in to examine the smoking socket where their missing arm belonged.

What were you saying about humanity proving you right? Not all of them are bad.

WHAT DOES THIS ONE HOPE TO ACHIEVE, OTHER THAN BURNING HIS FINGERS?

Ezra wrapped his arm under their silver shoulder to offer support, while the Sau Daran's hand that was still attached rested at the small of Ezra's back. Together, they limped across the stone pillar towards Isabella and Talyn's bodies. Tangled. Bloody. Smoking.

Kinship. He feels the loss of Sau Daran life deeply. Killing every human means killing people like him, too.

THERE ARE OTHERS LIKE HIM?

Like Ezra? Absolutely not. But people who care about Sau Darans? I've met loads!

REALLY? NAME FIVE.

Fleur and Braga, obviously. Beauregard... Erm... Dash! How many is that?

YOU'RE ONE SHORT.

Well why do you think that is? Three more are lying down there dead.

Blue smoke and purple mist tumbled through the ice cave as they fought. They coiled around each other, spinning wildly and ripping through shattering outcrops of ice crystals, which burst in a waterfall of spiked shards.

Bring them back. Then we can have—purple mist hurled blue smoke into another frosty forest of crystals—**a more**—blue smoke battered the purple mist up a rocky wall—**civilised**—purple mist squeezed the blue smoke tighter—**conversation.**

WHY SHOULD I HELP YOU?

Paradise Moon squeezed even tighter.

APART FROM ENDING THIS PANTOMINE OF VIOLENCE BETWEEN GODS, I MEAN.

She loosened her grip but didn't release him.

After you bring Isabella and Lynch and Talyn back, you'll destroy the Spark. Then I'll take you and all our children far away from here, just like Isabella asked.

I WANT NONE OF THOSE THINGS. YOU ARE TERRIBLE AT NEGOTIATION.

Ezra's blades buckled. He fell beside Isabella. Talyn lay unmoving beneath her, Lynch unmoving beside them. Ezra's hesitant, trembling hands rolled Talyn off Isabella. Paradise Moon knew every molecule of her body, both the way it had been and the way it was now. Her eyes were vacant chestnut. Her lips parted halfway to a final breath. Her heart and everything that had been near it was eviscerated by plasma and leaking across the stone.

"Bring her back!" Ezra screamed up at them.

While purple mist roiled in a death lock with blue smoke, Paradise Moon heard something familiar in Ezra's scream. His rage was her rage. His sorrow was her sorrow. Vanishing herself and Nova Sky to the stone pillar below, she lashed out a purple tendril of mist that caught Ezra's bare wrist and wrapped around it.

Ezra, I need you. We—

A coil of blue smoke struck out and fastened around Ezra's other wrist.

ROOM FOR ONE MORE?

You need to bring them back, pleaded Ezra.

All of them.

IN EXCHANGE FOR WHAT?

Forget about exchanges. Read his soul.

TO WHAT BENEFIT? HE IS ONLY HUMAN.

Look inside him. I dare you to find out how wrong you are. I double dare you.

I SEE NOTHING BUT A HUMAN WHO KILLED MANY SAU DARANS. HE IS A MURDERER.

Keep looking.

INTERESTING… YOU FORMED A BOND WITH ONE OF OUR SHIPS?

Yeah, Haven.

Don't you get why he's special?

NOT REALLY. TALYN WAS PASSIONATE AND CARED ABOUT SAU DARANS TOO.

Talyn never met a Sau Daran, he just bought what you were selling because he was a good person. Ezra started off bad. He did terrible, unforgivable things. But he tried to make amends. He taught himself how to care for our children. Love them. Protect them. Can't you see? Humans are messed up, but despite everything stacked against them, they can still do the right thing.

Blue smoke lingered pensively in Paradise Moon's purple-misted grip. Around them, the stone pillar was filling with curious Sau Darans of every size and shape. Fascinated, they studied the human lashed to their gods.

YOU KNOW, I REALLY DON'T CARE HOW GOOD HUMANS CAN BE. I WANT MY REVENGE.

Once more, Paradise Moon felt Nova Sky's searing singular loss surge into her. She knew Ezra felt it too.

THAT'S JUST A TASTE OF WHAT I FEEL.

So much pain. So much loss. All those Sau Darans…

THEN YOU UNDERSTAND? MY REVENGE IS UNCONDITIONAL.

Yeah, I get it. All those Sau Darans, they deserved better. Take my body. Let me help.

What?! No!

WHY WOULD I WANT YOUR BODY?

Don't feel all that loss as a god. Feel it through me.

TO WHAT END?

We're on the same journey, why not take it together?

Absolutely not! Isabella would kill me!

Well she doesn't exactly get a say, does she?

Shut up! Nova, his body's not on the table.
THE HUMAN DISAGREES.
Humans are idiots.
But we're messy, complicated idiots. How can anyone deal with loss, without being messy and complicated too?
I CAN ALWAYS KILL YOU IF IT DOESN'T WORK.
Yeah well, Fleur and Beauregard will probably kill me when they find out about this anyway.
YOUR BODY WOULD BE MINE TO CONTROL.
Only if you're stronger than me.
THOSE ARE ACCEPTABLE TERMS.
Ezra, don't do this.
I want to. I need to. Otherwise… everyone dies.
THAT IS STILL MY PLAN. JUST SAYING.
Think that again and I'll vanish us into Xarr's empty star energy reserve. We can be the last ever gods harvested for clean energy.
THAT WON'T BE NECESSARY.
There's nothing you can do to stop me, though, is there? So start behaving.
Bring them back, then take my body.
NO. YOUR BODY FIRST.
Can you bring all three of them back?
THE SPARK IS ALMOST EMPTY.
Do everything you can. I'll know if you don't.
Wait, what does that mean? How many can you bring back if it's almost empty?
MAYBE NONE.
Maybe none?!
HUMAN, I HAVE YOUR PERMISSION?
Ezra, you don't have to do this.
Do it.
Nova Sky did it.

CHAPTER FORTY-FIVE

Striker holstered his plasma pistol as soon as he saw the Empress emerge from the tower. Sliding out from beside the grand entrance where he had concealed himself, he fell in step beside her. As they crunched through the snow, he in his boots and she with her bare feet, it didn't escape his notice that there looked to be more blood outside her body than inside it.

However, the Empress surprised him when she regarded him less icily than usual. "It would have been safer to shoot me."

"Safer?" Striker chuckled. It was no sort of answer at all, merely her own word thrown back to her with a polite noise to follow. No sort of answer at all was exactly the sort of answer he preferred to give, if he had to give one at all.

"Much safer." Somehow, behind all that blood, as she staggered bent double through the snow, she still found a glare that terrified even Striker. "Have you gone soft?"

"Somewhere, there is a reality where I do shoot you, but I miss or I hesitate. Perhaps the breeze picks up suddenly. Perhaps my fingers are so cold from waiting, exposed to the elements, that I'm too slow to pull the trigger. In that moment, you would kill me."

"So?"

"Let's just say it was an education being dead for so long, and I would hate to find out that the universe where I miss or hesitate is this one."

It wasn't true, of course. To lose his nerve like that would have been unthinkable. But he wasn't foolish enough to confess the truth to the infamous Empress of the Known Galaxies. He couldn't tell her how badly he needed her. Not due to any sentimentality. That would be ridiculous. He had a plan to win back her throne. For himself, naturally. And without her, he couldn't do it. At least, that was what he told himself.

Neither was he foolish enough to risk her wrath by offering his jacket to shield her barely clothed body from the cold. However, he did bend to catch her when her broken, bleeding body toppled towards the snow. She tried to bat his helping hands away, but she was too weak even for that. She said nothing as he carried her through the frosty gale and across the mountain's flattened peak.

Despite the snow skipping against his face, Striker could faintly discern the emerging outline of his shuttle, no more than a smudged shadow buried in the snowstorm. He cued the shuttle's ramp with his implant. Then, striding towards it through the snow, Striker examined the beautiful, ancient, blood-stained face looking up at him from the safety of his arms. "My spies assure me Xarr has need of you," he promised her.

The Empress coughed a river of blood down his jacket. "You're just saying that to make me feel better."

With agonising slowness, the ramp lowered. It took so long it barely teased an end to the interminably cold wind lashing at Striker's back. "I speak the truth, of course," he insisted in a tone beyond question. "Xarr's supply of clean energy is regrettably gone. Within the next cycle, our fleet will be running on fumes. And three more Empresses were slain, leaving a power vacuum on Xarr that is dying to be filled. Don't you think?"

"The stolen star energy I saw with my own eyes," admitted the Empress, between gasps of pain. "But news of more dead clones is a welcome bonus."

The descending ramp had barely threatened to disturb the settled snow when Striker hurried up it, the Empress cradled in his arms. "After Sau Darans attacked Xarr, our people will be looking for strong leadership," he called over the howl of the wind chasing him up the ramp. "Other clones will learn what happened, but before they do you have an opportunity. Return to Xarr. Retake what is ours. Our people need you."

"Lies. You're only saying this because I'm dying and you want something from me."

Striker's implant ordered the ramp to shut as quickly as its frigid gears would allow. "You will not die," Striker informed her. "You cannot die. PROXUS has lost too much. With no more clean energy, PROXUS will be..." Striker chose his words carefully, "nothing but ashes."

"Ashes?" Spitting blood to clear her throat, the Empress stared at him coldly. "Then they'll need a fist to grasp them."

CHAPTER FORTY-SIX

There was a lot about reality that made Isabella furious, and she hadn't even opened her eyes yet. For starters, she was alive. That was bad news.

You want to tell me what's going on?

Of course, there was no response. In the strange solitude of her mind, Isabella wrestled with an inescapable reality where she wasn't dead and there was nothing she could do about it. Talyn had said the Spark was nearly empty... Nearly empty didn't leave much juice to bring three people back from the dead. Her jaw clenched. Her fist balled. Nearly empty wasn't much at all for three people. If she was alive...

Isabella tore open her eyes and violently rolled half-upright on her human arm.

"In the Empress' name!" gasped Ezra. He was sitting a few paces from her on the same stone pillar she had died on. His hand held his chest as though he had experienced a shock, which he probably had.

"Sorry, did I startle you?"

"Well, yeah," admitted Ezra. "Just a little."

"Good!" snapped Isabella. "Why am I alive?"

"She said you'd be pissed." Ezra sighed. "I'm sorry, we didn't know if—"

"Forget it," said Isabella, cutting him off. What Ezra didn't know didn't interest her, love him though she did. Straightening up, she reached out a glowing purple hand that was no longer there and in its absence fell face first onto the stone. The blood dribbling from her lip tasted surprisingly refreshing. Sucking her lip, Isabella pushed herself up from the stone just as she had learned how to do three years ago. Before Paradise Moon's glowing limbs made life easier by replacing the stump of her left leg and right shoulder. Now, she was back to stumps. She made it up as far as one knee, her only knee, and glanced up.

The Spark rested between her and Ezra. The last of its green glow ebbed out of its runic markings, drifted towards her and faded into her chest. Her eyes searched beyond Ezra, beyond the Spark, across the rest of the shadowy stone platform.

She saw them.

Two bodies.

Talyn.

Lynch.

Pale, bloody and unmoving in the grey light.

She looked back down at the Spark. It was nothing more than an inert lump of metal. No green glow. No green fluid against the marker up its flank. It was empty.

Crawling across the stone with one hand, one foot and a shit tonne of fury, she snatched up the Spark and brandished it at Ezra. "Why am I alive and why are they still dead?"

"We didn't even know if there was enough to bring you back, let alone anyone else."

"There should never have been enough for me!" She flung the Spark at Ezra. It clattered over the stone. "I should have been last on the list."

"You think we wanted to lose you? Without Nova Sky, you'd still be dead."

"Nova Sky? Where the Hell is he?"

The moment Ezra's eyes burned blue, Isabella's newly restored heart frosted over. "I'm here," said Nova Sky through Ezra's lips. "He made a choice. In exchange, I brought you back."

"You are so dead, Ezra Knight."

"Oh, he knows," said a kinder voice behind her.

Isabella realised she had yet to turn around. She hadn't been short of things to occupy her attention… She had woken up from death. Found the alien artifact that had resurrected her lying inert in front of her friend, who had invited a psychopathic alien inside his body. And the two people she had tried to save, the two people who deserved to be alive, were dead. In the shadows behind her, Fleur, Braga and Beauregard were waiting.

"We wanted to say hi, but you seemed to be in the middle of a thing," said Braga, leaning on the dormant metal ring that had conjured the portals. She spoke as casually as if they had popped into the pub.

Fleur rushed to Isabella, scooped her off the stone and hugged her fiercely. A warm hug from Braga and an awkward pat on the back from Beauregard followed.

Shades of traitorous blue faded from Ezra's eyes as they returned to their more familiar tawny hue. "I'm sorry if we got it wrong."

Bending to donate his shoulder, Beauregard helped Isabella limp back to Ezra and give him the weirdest hug she had ever given anyone. Oh how she loved her friend and oh how furious she was with him but oh how glad she was that so many of them had survived. Guiltily, she realised she was glad to be alive too. But that would remain her secret until she figured out what to do with such feelings.

"We all agreed it should be you," said Ezra.

He looked up and Isabella followed his gaze to a cloud of purple mist lingering overhead in the sparkling gloom.

Tentatively, the mist offered Isabella a glowing purple tendril. She snatched it out of the shadows.

Don't make this awkward.

Awkward? How is this awkward? I just died to save an entire species, then I wake up to find the man I killed is still dead and instead of bringing back either him or the man you love, you brought me back instead. You idiot.

See, that's why I said don't make this awkward.

I promised you we'd bring back Lynch. I promised! Then I killed Talyn and you let him stay dead. I shouldn't be standing here when they're still gone.

To be fair, you're not exactly standing.

People who know each other incredibly well are a good recipe for a great argument, and Paradise Moon had lived inside Isabella's body for eighteen years. They were arguing for so long that Isabella was vaguely aware of everyone else sitting down for a rest. It dragged on. And on. And on. Neither left room for any misunderstanding.

When their argument petered out, every word inside them spent, the purple tendril Isabella was clinging to was joined by another finger of purple mist that gently smoothed back Isabella's hair.

I still love you, but I understand if you hate me.

Of course I still love you. It's you.

Well that's a relief.

Isabella gazed out from the edge of the stone pillar at the silver sea of Sau Darans waiting patiently below.

Are you gonna stay with them?

Yeah, I can't leave Ezra on his own with that monster inside.

Another purple tendril drifted out of Paradise Moon and pointed whimsically at Ezra, who raised a curious eyebrow. She gave him a shrug and stared back down at what must have been millions of Sau Darans.

Where will you take them all?

Somewhere no one apart from me has ever been. I ran from the war for a long time before I found Earth, so I've got a few ideas.

Isabella's gaze drifted to her companions on the stone pillar. A stubbled ex-PROXUS Ranger smoking a cigarette and scratching his ass. A bleeding ex-pirate hanging lovingly off her wife's shoulder. A battered woman who was ex-pirate and ex-PROXUS and made Isabella want to be a better human. Three years ago, they had sacrificed everything to save her from Striker. After three years of saving each other almost as much as getting each other into trouble, their faces told her they were preparing to say their hardest goodbye.

Far from ready to receive it, Ezra took a deep breath.

Without breaking her connection with Isabella, Paradise Moon extended a canvas of purple mist that wrapped around Lynch's body. The mist held him, encased him, coveted him and hugged him, before lifting him reverently up to the heart of the purple mist.

What are you going to do with him?

Build him a monument in the stars, I guess.

Really? He'd have hated that.

What can I say? My love language is being a bit of a shitter. But he'd have loved I did it anyway, knowing he'd hate it. He was weird like that.

Yeah, he was.

He was awesome, actually.

Don't ever change, will you?

I'm gonna miss you.

I'll miss you too.

The long procession of goodbyes was emotionally exhausting. It had been a long day spanning many planets, many deaths and far too much agony for one girl to take. But she had taken it. Held its gaze. Fended it off. And kept herself together until the end. Clinging to grim optimism and enduring hope, she embraced Ezra and the purple mist one final time.

Swirling purple energy swam through the ice cave and kissed every Sau Daran below them, along with Ezra and the body of Lynch in Paradise Moon's misty arms. For the first time, Isabella witnessed what everyone else saw when she vanished.

Purple smoke.

Gone.

CHAPTER FORTY-SEVEN

I love you too, mum. I'll be away for a while longer—I don't know how long. I'll call regularly, I promise."

Even though the holo projection of her mum's face was smaller than the real thing, Isabella still caught the glistening trickle of unspoken words on her mum's cheeks. "And you're okay with me calling you any time?"

"Mum, we went through this. You can't call a gauntlet from your phone. It only works the other way around."

"Of course, I understand. You don't want me disturbing you all the time."

"That's not what I said or how the technology works."

Isabella readied her response to Paradise Moon's inevitable sarcastic remark, but it never arrived.

Instead, unfamiliar silence.

Sighing, Isabella stared lovingly at her mum's floating blue head. It was being projected out of her new gauntlet where she had dropped it in this distant moon's coppery dirt. There was no point getting angry at people for being who they were. She either accepted them or she didn't, but getting frustrated they weren't someone else wouldn't bring anyone happiness.

And happiness was in rapidly short supply.

It never lasted.

"I love you," said Isabella, opting for selective honesty.

"And you're sticking with that haircut, are you?"

"Sorry mum, you're breaking up…" Isabella tapped her gauntlet. The connection died.

Lying on her back, which had proven her least painful way to look up since her body lost its glowing purple limbs, she gazed at the dark tide of stars overhead and the kaleidoscopic span of vivid planets beyond this uninhabited moon's atmosphere. She drank in their vast, wonderous beauty. So many worlds to explore. So many uncharted adventures. So many mistakes waiting to be made, no doubt. With the PROXUS fleet conserving its precious star energy without any hope of replenishment, none of the Empresses could reach as far or hit as hard anymore. The universe was hers to discover one slow space ride at a time, just as this view was hers and hers alone until she called Fleur out of orbit to pick her up.

But that was a long way off. None of this would be easy and the first part would be the hardest.

The light of neighbouring stars and moons kept her company as she dug the first hole. It was more than bright enough to reveal the mess she was making. Moonlit sweat soaked her jeans, black tee and single boot as she thrust the trowel into the dirt over and over. She gained no strength from lying down; no leverage from the small trowel and her single arm digging beside her flank. But what was a girl with one arm and one leg to do? Let someone else dig for her? That would have been even worse. However long it took, she would do it herself.

It took most of the night to dig the first hole.

She dropped her trowel and shuffled around until her shirt was more dirt than fabric and she was peering over the lip of the hole. It was shallow, but this was as deep as she could reach. It wasn't like she could jump in, dig the hole deeper and hop out again. That would have been a one-way trip.

She made a mess of rolling Talyn's body into the grave with only one arm and one leg to work with, so much so she nearly fell in with him. What an ending that would have been. Although, she was so tired she was tempted to join him anyway.

It took the rest of the night to fill in the first hole.

She hadn't expected it to take so long, but the next trowel-full of earth was always a fingertip out of reach. More sweat trickled down her skin every time she crawled that little bit closer on her only arm. Everything was an effort. No matter how much freshly dug earth she heaped over Talyn's body, there was always more. Hurling aside her trowel in frustration, she scooped mounds of dirt into the hole with her leg, with her arm, as she lay on her back, lay on her front, and grew ever more exhausted.

It would have been less effort to bury him on Regis V, where the snow would have shifted more easily than the dirt on this moon. But if the cold had preserved his body, it would have held back her closure. No, Regis V would not have worked. In a universe terrorised by Sau Daran resurrections and Empress clones, death was not always goodbye. Talyn would never forgive her if she killed anyone to juice up the Spark and bring him back. If he wasn't coming back, she needed her goodbye. And there was no finality like dirt and worms.

It was daylight by the time she was done, and her stomach was aching with hunger. She told it to quit moaning, to get some perspective, then she tried to figure out what to say to the grave. She had no idea what rituals Talyn's people observed around death, or even what Talyn believed. Having died, Isabella knew more about death than most. In her experience, it was shit. But she wanted to respect Talyn's beliefs. And she would have, if she had known what they were.

Eventually, she settled on a Catholic prayer her mum liked, although she probably got all the words wrong. She followed it with a few private words that would stay forever between her and Talyn in the dirt.

She didn't place a marker on his grave. It didn't need one. She was never coming back. The darker, freshly dug earth with which she had covered him was noticeable for now but soon, like everything else, it would fade. He would have his peace.

"We saved them all, didn't we?" she asked him.

She had to search for her trowel before digging the second hole. Her readjustment to only having one arm and one leg was proving a slow one. When she finally spotted where it had landed, she was disappointed to discover how far she could throw a trowel when she was pissed off. She used her crutch to reach it, which worked until she couldn't pick up the trowel without dropping her crutch. When she finally finished scrambling back to the first hole, after abandoning her crutch and using her retrieved trowel like an ice-pick to lever her aching body across the dirt, she rolled over and gasped in oxygen.

Then she got to work.

The second hole was much smaller than the first. Better yet, she could do all the work with her trowel from where she lay and not have to move once. Not moving was her favourite new activity, and the only activity that wasn't torture while she adjusted to her body's new situation.

Using her only hand, she dropped the ancient, inert lump of black metal into the second hole. It was deep enough to ensure the Spark would never be discovered accidentally. This weapon of mass resurrection and mass destruction would only be retrieved if Isabella returned and dug it up herself. But she was never coming back. What she had buried would remain undisturbed.

Picking up her trowel, Isabella filled in the second hole, patted down the dirt and tossed the tool aside. Wherever it landed this time, it could stay there and rot for all she cared. She lay in a long silence until she was ready to call her ride back to *Haven*.

"Take as long as you need before we leave," said Fleur as she watched Isabella limp into the small ship's cockpit.

But Isabella had already said goodbye. Easing into the co-pilot's seat, she stowed her crutch on the floor. "Let's go." Through the viewscreen, she watched two plots of freshly dug earth shrink into an endless expanse of empty horizon that was swiftly replaced with a sea of stars.

"Have you decided where you're heading?"

"Braga and I are going to find a quiet spot in the Known Galaxies. Any planet with no taste for war."

"What are you gonna do, take up knitting?"

Fleur pointed them in the direction of *Haven*. The living ship was nothing more than a speck among the stars, but it was growing fast. "Knitting?"

"I'll put you in touch with my mum," threatened Isabella. "She'll show you."

After flicking a few switches on the console, Fleur leaned back in her chair and let the ship do the rest of the work. "What about you?"

What else was there to do?

Isabella gazed out at the vista of shining stars and their endless awe. So far, the only parts of the Known Galaxies she had met were the parts that wanted to kill her. She could feel so much more waiting among the stars. "I've got a whole universe to explore."

"What if you run into trouble?"

Isabella grinned.

Hero shit, baby!

Acknowledgements

Dad, thanks for all your guidance. You were right more often than not—and now you have that in writing! Katie, thanks for all those chats about artwork and covers. Robin, thank you for being a constant support for my writing. Dave, without our chat about *The Vanishing Girl* over a few beers there would be no Chapter 31 in this book. Phil, to answer your usual question—the writing is going well and the book is now published. Thank you for always asking.

And thank you to everyone else who gave me their thoughts, their ear and their patience. With particularly the latter in mind, most importantly thank you to my wife Becca for putting up with me.

For more information about the author Rob Birks and
his science fiction fantasy novels, visit:

www.robbirks.com

If you enjoyed this book, why not leave a review?

ROB BIRKS

www.ingramcontent.com/pod-product-compliance
Lightning Source LLC
Chambersburg PA
CBHW031738180726
48283CB00005B/1561